OXFORD WORLD'S CLASSICS

AN INDISCRETION IN THE LIFE OF AN HEIRESS
AND OTHER STORIES

THOMAS HARDY was born in Higher Bockhampton, Dorset, on 2 June 1840; his father was a builder in a small way of business, and he was educated locally and in Dorchester before being articled to an architect. After sixteen years in that profession and the publication of his earliest novel *Desperate Remedies* (1871), he determined to make his career in literature; not, however, before his work as an architect had led to his meeting, at St Juliot in Cornwall, Emma Gifford, who became his first wife in 1874.

In the 1860s Hardy had written a substantial amount of unpublished verse, but during the next twenty years almost all his creative effort went into novels and short stories. *Jude the Obscure*, the last written of his novels, came out in 1895, closing a sequence of fiction that includes *Far from the Madding Crowd* (1874), *The Return of the Native* (1878), *Two on a Tower* (1882), *The Mayor of Casterbridge* (1886), and *Tess of the d'Urbervilles* (1891).

Hardy maintained in later life that only in poetry could he truly express his ideas; and the more than nine hundred poems in his collected verse (almost all published after 1898) possess great individuality and power.

In 1910 Hardy was awarded the Order of Merit; in 1912 Emma died and two years later he married Florence Dugdale. Thomas Hardy died in January 1928; the work he left behind—the novels, the poetry, and the epic drama *The Dynasts*—forms one of the supreme achievements in English imaginative literature.

PAMELA DALZIEL is Associate Professor of English at the University of British Columbia and General Editor of the Clarendon Dickens edition. She has published numerous articles on Hardy and has edited *Thomas Hardy: The Excluded and Collaborative Stories* (1992), *Thomas Hardy's 'Studies, Specimens &c.' Notebook* (1994), and *A Pair of Blue Eyes* (1998).

OXFORD WORLD'S CLASSICS

For over 100 years Oxford World's Classics have brought
readers closer to the world's great literature. Now with over 700
titles—from the 4,000-year-old myths of Mesopotamia to the
twentieth century's greatest novels—the series makes available
lesser-known as well as celebrated writing.

The pocket-sized hardbacks of the early years contained
introductions by Virginia Woolf, T. S. Eliot, Graham Greene,
and other literary figures which enriched the experience of reading.
Today the series is recognized for its fine scholarship and
reliability in texts that span world literature, drama and poetry,
religion, philosophy and politics. Each edition includes perceptive
commentary and essential background information to meet the
changing needs of readers.

OXFORD WORLD'S CLASSICS

━━

THOMAS HARDY

An Indiscretion in the Life of an Heiress

and Other Stories

━━

Edited with an Introduction and Notes by
PAMELA DALZIEL

OXFORD
UNIVERSITY PRESS

OXFORD
UNIVERSITY PRESS

Great Clarendon Street, Oxford OX2 6DP

Oxford University Press is a department of the University of Oxford.
It furthers the University's objective of excellence in research, scholarship,
and education by publishing worldwide in

Oxford New York

Auckland Bangkok Buenos Aires Cape Town Chennai
Dar es Salaam Delhi Hong Kong Istanbul Karachi Kolkata
Kuala Lumpur Madrid Melbourne Mexico City Mumbai Nairobi
São Paulo Shanghai Singapore Taipei Tokyo Toronto

with an associated company in Berlin

Oxford is a registered trade mark of Oxford University Press
in the UK and in certain other countries

Published in the United States
by Oxford University Press Inc., New York

Introduction, Note on the Text, Select Bibliography,
Explanatory Notes © Pamela Dalziel 1994
Chronology © Simon Gatrell 1985
Text of The Unconquerable © Trustees of the Florence Dugdale Estate 1992

The moral rights of the author have been asserted
Database right Oxford University Press (maker)

First published as a World's Classics paperback 1994
Reissued as an Oxford World's Classics paperback 1998

British Library Cataloguing in Publication Data

Data available

Library of Congress Cataloging in Publication Data
Hardy, Thomas, 1840–1928.
An indiscretion in the life of an heiress and other stories /
edited with an introduction and notes by Pamela Dalziel.
p.   cm.—(Oxford world's classics)
Includes bibliographical references.
I. Dalziel, Pamela.   II. Title.   III. Series.
PR4750.16   1994   823'.8—dc20   93–45652

ISBN 0–19–283685–4

3 5 7 9 10 8 6 4 2

Printed in Great Britain by
Clays Ltd, St Ives plc

CONTENTS

GENERAL EDITOR'S PREFACE

THE first concern in The World's Classics editions of Hardy's works has been with the texts. Individual editors have compared every version of the novel or stories that Hardy might have revised, and have noted variant readings in words, punctuation, and styling in each of these substantive texts; they have thus been able to exclude much that their experience suggests that Hardy did not intend. In some cases, this is the first time that the novel has appeared in a critical edition purged of errors and oversights; where possible Hardy's manuscript punctuation is used, rather than what his compositors thought he should have written.

Some account of the editor's discoveries will be found in the Note on the Text in each volume, while the most interesting revisions their work has revealed are included as an element of the Explanatory Notes. In some cases a Clarendon Press edition of the novel provides a wealth of further material for the reader interested in the way Hardy's writing developed from manuscript to final collected edition.

SIMON GATRELL

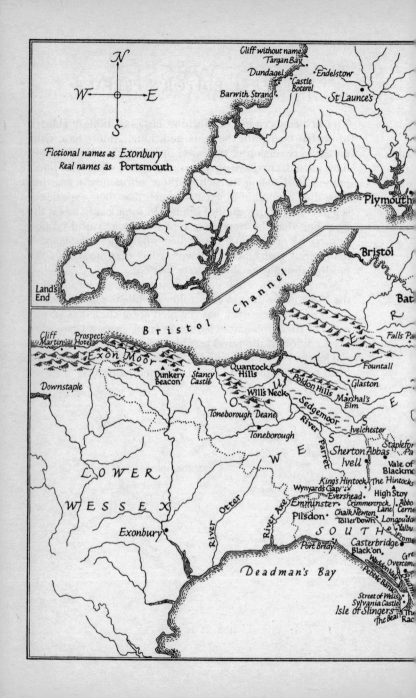

HARDY'S WESSEX
OF THE NOVELS AND POEMS

0   10   20
Miles

River Thames

Lumsdon •   • Christminster

N O R T H

The Brown House   • Alfredston

M I D -   • Cresscombe   River Thames

Marygreen   Castle Royal

Marlbury Downs   W E S S E X   Gaymead   • Aldbrickham

• Kennetbridge

W E S S E X

Inkpen Beacon

Stoke Barehills •   Quartershot

The Great Plain   Weydon Priors   • Icenway House

Stonehenge •

U P P E R

tour Head   • Wintoncester

Leddenton   Melchester   Fernel Hall

Marlott   Shaston   • Deansleigh Park

Wingreen   W E S S E X

The Chase   The Slopes

Trantridge Cross   Chaseborough

tourcastle   Knollingwood Hall   • Southampton

ulbarrow   Shottsford   Lornton   The Great   Portsmouth

• Forum   Inn   • Bramshurst

ntcombe   Yewsholt   • Warborne   Forest   Solentsea

sh   • Chene Manor

atherbury   • Welland R. Stour

• Kingsbere

N E S S E X   • Sandbourne

Egdon Heath   The Island

albothays • Anglebury

rie • Wellbridge   npool

• Nether Minton

• Corvesgate   • Knollsea

lmind Cove

ightship

The Channel

INTRODUCTION

I

As a thoroughly professional writer, entirely dependent upon his literary earnings, Thomas Hardy was always ready during his fiction-writing career—and especially in its earlier phases—to take advantage of the openings for short stories in the proliferating magazines of the day. Because of his eventual success, at once literary and commercial, he had many opportunities to review, collect, and revise all of his works, in both prose and verse, and his designedly 'definitive' and canonical Wessex Edition of 1912–31 included no less than four volumes of short stories: *Wessex Tales* (first published in 1888), *A Group of Noble Dames* (1891), *Life's Little Ironies* (1894), and *A Changed Man* (1913). The contents of the first three of these collections had been so selected and organized as to embody some degree of thematic or structural unity,[1] but *A Changed Man* was put together precisely in order to gather in a number of miscellaneous stories that had not found a place in earlier collections but had nevertheless continued in circulation—often because a pre-1891 publication date had left them without copyright protection in the United States.

Even so, a number of stories, varying from the exceptionally brief to the unusually long, remained permanently excluded from Hardy's collective volumes, and it is to these that the present volume is devoted. Its contents fall into two broad categories, the one comprised of the stories by Hardy which he left uncollected (and in one case unpublished) at the time of his death in 1928, the other of stories similarly uncollected (and in one case unpublished) that were not in any case entirely his work but the products of acknowledged or unacknowledged collaborations with younger women to whom he

---

[1] See Kristin Brady, *The Short Stories of Thomas Hardy: Tales of Past and Present* (London: Macmillan, 1982).

was emotionally attached. These latter stories will be considered as a group at the end of this introduction, but it was in any event a foregone conclusion that Hardy would not include any of them in his own collective volumes, especially since the only one publicly associated with his name—'The Spectre of the Real', the product of his chiefly romantic, partly professional relationship with Florence Henniker—was included, shortly after its first publication and with both names still attached, in a volume of Henniker's. Hardy's participation in work published by Florence Dugdale prior to their marriage in 1914 was a subject to which neither of them had any reason or wish to draw attention, and in the case of 'The Unconquerable'—by far the most interesting of their joint productions—the decision was made not to seek publication at all, perhaps on the grounds that its Hardyan features would be all too readily recognizable.

The reasons, however, why a number of Hardy's own stories remained permanently excluded from his collective volumes are various and sometimes complex. It is certainly true that some of the items now being brought together are brief and slight and that Hardy might well have passed them over on those grounds alone, but others are altogether more substantial and seem to have been marginalized by Hardy criticism and scholarship essentially because Hardy himself displaced them from his canon—much as his organization of the Wessex Edition emphasized the novels he valued most at the expense of those he valued less. In such instances the motivation for displacement can almost always be found in some special circumstance of compositional, publishing, or personal history rather than in a negative authorial assessment of the work itself.

'How I Built Myself a House', for example, the earliest of Hardy's stories—the earliest, indeed, of all his known publications—can scarcely claim either distinction or importance: it is short and lightweight, and Hardy himself referred to it in later years as a 'humorous trifle'.[2] Yet it remains of real inter-

---

[2] *The Life and Work of Thomas Hardy* (hereafter *Life*), ed. Michael Millgate (London: Macmillan, 1984), 49.

est as reflecting the experiences of Hardy's architectural career, as marking (if a little prematurely) the initiation of his literary career, and as a rare instance of his use of the first-person narrative voice. Hardy had no objection to its republication in *Chambers's Journal* sixty years after its first appearance, in 1865, in the magazine's pages, and it seems reasonable to suggest that he might well have collected it—perhaps as a prose 'sketch' rather than as a short story—had a suitable context ever offered itself.

'Destiny and a Blue Cloak', written ten years later than 'How I Built Myself a House' but at a time when Hardy had still not fully established himself, was solicited and published by the *New-York Times* in 1874. That it did not appear in the United Kingdom was evidently a deliberate choice on Hardy's part: he perhaps saw that it was not up to the standard of his best work, especially as represented by the recently published *Far from the Madding Crowd*, and he must also have been conscious both of his introduction of incidents from the career of his Dorchester friend and rival, Hooper Tolbort, and of his prospective use of some of the story's central elements of plot and characterization in his next novel, *The Hand of Ethelberta*. Though Hardy did not in this instance lose sight of the story—in the late 1920s he was able, through his wife, to identify its inferior quality and its relationship to *The Hand of Ethelberta* as the reasons for its having never been reprinted[3]—he can scarcely have considered it as a candidate for collection, and since it had never been picked up and circulated in any of the American piracies of his works he was under no pressure to include it in the miscellaneous tidying-up represented by *A Changed Man*.

Hardy seems to have written 'The Thieves Who Couldn't Help Sneezing' in response to an invitation from the editor of *Father Christmas*, the children's annual in which the story appeared in December 1877. Though sufficiently effective within such a context—the annual was in any case chiefly remarkable for its illustrations—the story was rendered

---

[3] Typescript (Purdy Collection, Beinecke Library) of replies to queries, relating mainly to the MS of *The Woodlanders*, from the collector Howard Bliss.

almost inherently uncollectable by its brevity (2,600 words) and the fact of its being addressed specifically to children.

Hardy's other children's story, 'Our Exploits at West Poley', is a much longer and more considerable piece of work—its acceptability to its intended audience demonstrated by numerous reprintings in the second half of the twentieth century—but its generic distinctiveness from his other work in the short-story form must again have militated against its finding an appropriate place in any of his collective volumes. Hardy may in any case have been deterred from collecting 'Our Exploits' because of uncertainty as to its status, possibly compounded by the lack of any version of its text. He sold the story in November 1883 to the popular Boston children's magazine *The Youth's Companion*, subsequently revised it to meet that magazine's specifications, but seems never to have learned of its long-delayed appearance, nine years later, in the pages of quite another magazine, the Boston *Household*, which claimed to be 'DEVOTED TO THE INTERESTS OF THE AMERICAN HOUSEWIFE'.

It has already been suggested that potentially detectable personal references in 'Destiny and a Blue Cloak' may have contributed to Hardy's willingness to let that story rest in obscurity, and there can be no doubt that the long-term fates of two other stories, 'The Doctor's Legend' and 'Old Mrs Chundle', were determined by their thinly disguised invocation of characters and narrative elements drawn from two prominent Dorset families. In 'The Doctor's Legend', which seems originally to have been designed for inclusion in *A Group of Noble Dames*, Hardy drew extensively upon historical and, especially, legendary accounts of the lives of Joseph Damer, 1st Earl of Dorchester, and his son, touching especially on the desecration of ancient graves said to have occurred during the former's rebuilding and landscaping of Milton Abbey during the latter half of the eighteenth century. Since Hardy knew that the Damer family and its history were still well known in Dorset and that some of the story's descriptive as well as narrative details had been taken fairly directly from the relevant section of the standard county history, John

Hutchins's *The History and Antiquities of the County of Dorset*, he seems—as with 'Destiny'—to have been well satisfied with American publication only, omitting 'The Doctor's Legend' not only from *A Group of Noble Dames* but from all of his short-story collections.

'Old Mrs Chundle', for its part, never published during Hardy's lifetime, was based upon an episode in the early career of the Revd Henry Moule, the much-admired vicar of Fordington, all of whose seven sons Hardy had known well. The sensitivities likely to be troubled were thus numerous and immediate, especially while any of those sons still lived, and Hardy's preservation of the manuscript of the story seems to confirm its status as a work deemed potentially publishable but deliberately withheld—hence automatically uncollected —on personal grounds.

Of all the pieces Hardy left uncollected at the time of his death by far the most important was the long—almost novella-length—story, 'An Indiscretion in the Life of an Heiress'. Written, apparently at considerable speed, in the spring of 1878 in response to a request from the *New Quarterly Magazine* for a story of at least 40 pages, 'Indiscretion' is of particular interest not only for its own substantial sake but because of its pervasive indebtedness to Hardy's never-published first novel, *The Poor Man and the Lady*. For the story of the writing of *Poor Man* in 1867–8 and for its characterization as 'socialistic, not to say revolutionary', Hardy himself, in the autobiographical *Life*,[4] is necessarily the principal if sometimes doubtful author-ity, but enough information is available from other sources— including 'Indiscretion' itself—to enable at least an outline of the novel to be speculatively constructed.[5] What is certainly clear is that although Hardy had already drawn upon the abandoned *Poor Man* manuscript when writing such earlier novels as *Desperate Remedies*, *A Pair of Blue Eyes*, and especially *Under the Greenwood Tree*, enough of the central plot and

[4] *Life*, 58–64.

[5] See *Thomas Hardy: The Excluded and Collaborative Stories*, ed. Pamela Dalziel (Oxford: Clarendon Press, 1992), 69–80.

action still remained unused for him to be able to adapt it successfully, and for the most part directly, to the *New Quarterly*'s specifications.

Hardy's persistence in excluding 'Indiscretion' from his collective volumes was evidently a reflection not so much of any low valuation of the story as of a long-cherished if never-realized intention to use it as the basis of a reconstruction of *The Poor Man and the Lady* itself. Questioned about the absence of 'Indiscretion' at the time when *A Changed Man* was being published, Hardy explained that he had omitted the story, 'a sort of patchwork of the remains of "The Poor Man & the Lady"', partly because it seemed a 'pale shadow' of the lost novel but chiefly because 'I thought I might find it amusing in my old age to endeavour to restore the original from the modification, aided by my memory & a fragment still in existence of "The P.M. & Lady"—merely a few pages.'[6]

II

The few critics who have granted 'Indiscretion' any sustained attention have tended to speak of it somewhat dismissively, though often acknowledging, with J. M. Barrie, that it is both 'charming' and unmistakably Hardyan.[7] The most significant recent studies, however, focus on its representation of gender and class. Patricia Ingham, for example, has pointed out that in Hardy's early works, including 'Indiscretion', the categories of woman (usually 'lady') and poor man are not always discrete and that in fact woman becomes a vehicle of metaphor for the equally marginalized poor man—as, for example, in *Two on a Tower* when Swithin St Cleeve's love for his social superior reduces him to waiting as 'helplessly as a girl' for a chance of encountering her.[8] If in 'Indiscretion' there is

[6] *The Collected Letters of Thomas Hardy* (hereafter *Collected Letters*), ed. Richard Little Purdy and Michael Millgate, 7 vols. (Oxford: Clarendon Press, 1978–88), iv. 306.

[7] 4 Nov. 1934 letter to Florence Hardy (Morris Parrish Collection, Princeton University).

[8] Patricia Ingham, *Thomas Hardy* (Hemel Hempstead: Harvester Wheatsheaf, 1989), 53–4.

no such direct identification of Egbert's subordinate position with a woman's, there is certainly a confusion and to some extent a reversal of conventional male-female roles. Egbert wishes that 'he might own [Geraldine], not exactly as a wife, but as a being superior to himself—in the sense in which a servant may be said to own a master.' The traditional emphasis on the man's possession of the woman remains, but it is she who is represented as the authority figure—and, indeed, it is Geraldine who wields power in relation to her father's scheme for enlarging the park and evicting Egbert's grandfather. Even after the marriage Egbert is depicted as the subordinate partner, 'humour[ing] her in everything' and, in spite of his desire to assume the role of protector, allowing her to confront her father alone.

The confusion of established social and sexual hierarchies is also, as Penny Boumelha remarks, the result of Geraldine's own awareness of the conflict between 'her dominant class role and the submissive, acquiescent part assigned to her by sex':[9] she does not wish Egbert to address her familiarly as 'Geraldine', but because of the intimacy of their relationship 'Madam', used 'at the warmest moments', seems conveniently 'to change its nature from that of a mere title to a soft pet sound'. Between 'the natural woman', emotionally dependent on Egbert, and the 'fine-lady portion of her existence', asserting her social superiority, there is a continual tension: Egbert himself observes that she seems to be 'ever and only moved by the superior of two antagonistic forces'. Forced to confront the probable public response should their relationship become known, Geraldine weeps outright and implores, 'Don't, don't make it so bad!', only to go on to insist with some hauteur: 'they *dare* not speak so disrespectfully of me, or of any one I choose to favour'.

Presented predominantly from Egbert's point of view—not surprisingly, perhaps, since *The Poor Man and the Lady* had been narrated 'By the Poor Man'—'Indiscretion' at a basic level invites sympathy for him and hence for the 'natural'

[9] Penny Boumelha, *Thomas Hardy and Women: Sexual Ideology and Narrative Form* (Brighton: Harvester, 1982), 35.

rather than the 'fine-lady' side of Geraldine. But at the same time the omniscient narrator, set up as a wise authority figure, is clearly one who subscribes to the belief that—to quote from the Browning epigraph to the eighth chapter—'The world and its ways have a certain worth'. The adjectives repeatedly applied to the lovers' behaviour—unreasoning, unreflecting, and reckless—suggest a culpable irrationality, a refusal to confront the inevitable consequences of their conduct. Other voices of conventional authority—from the Fairland clergyman to public opinion as expressed in the newspaper paragraph—also insist upon their rashness, and even Egbert's grandfather predicts that 'it can but end in pain'. The social barriers are presented as immovable, capable of being ignored but not of being eliminated; the lovers can hold hands under the cord during the concert, but they cannot remove it. Egbert and Geraldine increasingly come to recognize this themselves. He despairingly wonders 'in what uneasiness, yearning, and misery' their intimacy can end, Geraldine 'in a cottage as his wife, or himself in a mansion as her husband' seeming 'alike painfully incredible'. She, for her part, is from the beginning uneasy about their lack of common experience and her subsequent renunciation of the relationship scarcely comes as a surprise.

The disparateness of their spheres is repeatedly emphasized through a variety of metaphorical and visual effects. The first view of Geraldine, for example, frames her as a solitary sitter enclosed in her ancestral pew: only she and the preacher face westward; Egbert and all the villagers face eastward. During the stone-laying ceremony, again, she is flanked on one side by her father and their friends, on the other by Egbert[10] and the schoolchildren, while at her death her father, with other members of the household, remains on the left side of the bed, Egbert on the right. This hierarchical patterning also occurs in the concert scene and, still more palpably, in the depiction of Egbert as standing in 'unobserved retirement' while Geraldine, literally 'above' him,

---

[10] He is specifically identified only in the unrevised version of the text (see p. xxxvii), however.

drives along Piccadilly in a landau. In the threshing-machine scene her carriage stops 'outside the hedge' bordering the farmer's field: she must 'descend' and pass through the gate to reach Egbert and the engine, and her narrow escape from death portentously suggests the dangers of entering a sphere not her own, effectively foreshadowing the fatal consequences of her marriage.

In concluding with Geraldine's death, Hardy chose one of the two most conventional closure devices, the other of course being marriage. Given the presented context of unbridgeable class differences, a traditional romance ending with reconciliation succeeding marriage would doubtless have taxed the reader's credulity even more than the conveniently sudden death: as John Bayley remarks, 'the most sentimental reader must have got the point that such a marriage could hardly do'.[11] The epigraph to the final chapter, while most obviously a prefiguration of Geraldine's death, also suggests that had she lived happiness would still have proved ephemeral, the lines from Edmund Waller's 'Go, Lovely Rose!' in fact lamenting 'The common fate of all things rare':

> How small a part of time they share
> That are so wondrous sweet and fair!

When killing off Geraldine, however, and thus avoiding confrontation of the more radical social questions raised by the narrative, Hardy overlooks her rebellious past in order to depict her as a dying angel: 'It was a gentle death. She was as acquiescent as if she had been a saint, which was not the least striking and uncommon feature in the life of this fair and unfortunate lady.' In so doing he effectively aligned himself with such 'feminist' contemporaries as Mary Braddon, Rhoda Broughton, and Mrs Henry Wood, who portrayed female characters resisting established authority but concluded their novels—evasively, as it now seems—with the heroine's repentance, death, or admission of insanity.[12]

---

[11] John Bayley, *An Essay on Hardy* (Cambridge: Cambridge University Press, 1978), 142.

[12] See Elaine Showalter, *A Literature of Their Own: British Women Novelists from Brontë to Lessing* (Princeton: Princeton University Press, 1977), 153–81.

At the same time 'Indiscretion' does contain—like much of that 'feminist' fiction—considerable elements of social criticism. To balance the apparently conformist epigraph from Browning's 'The Statue and the Bust' there is one from Thackeray's *The Book of Snobs* ('Come forward, some great marshal, and organise equality in society') and Geraldine's first letter points up, somewhat petulantly, the implications of privileging position over integrity: 'It is cruel of life to be like this towards us when we have done no wrong.' Made to feel 'half ashamed' of loving Egbert, Geraldine comes to believe that perhaps 'it would be better to become a lady of title, with a large park and houses of [her] own, than the wife of any man of genius who was poor', and in her renunciatory letter she frankly accepts society's dictates: 'If I could accept your addresses without an entire loss of position I would do so; but, since this cannot be, we must forget each other.' The element of compulsion is implicit here, however, and made explicit in her subsequent confession ('such influences have been brought to bear upon me that at last I have hardly known what I was doing'), and it is clear that much of Geraldine's difficulty derives from her position as a woman in a patriarchal society. She insists that 'To be woven and tied in with the world by blood, acquaintance, tradition, and external habit, is to a woman to be utterly at the beck of that world's customs.' Although of age, she is still very much subordinate to her father's authority and to the filial duty and womanly self-denial society demands of her: 'I am not my own mistress—I have my father to please . . . I must please him. There is no help for this.' She even 'dares' not talk freely about the situation. That in spite of such pressures Geraldine does break away and elope with Egbert is at once an indication of how intolerable the arranged marriage was to her and an indictment of the society which was prepared to sanction the 'sacrifice'.

III

'Indiscretion' is unique among the contents of the present volume in terms of both its length and its importance, the preservation of so many elements from *The Poor Man and the Lady* rendering it absolutely central to the tracing and understanding of Hardy's development as a writer of fiction. But if the other stories seem—whether intrinsically or as a consequence of Hardy's own marginalizing neglect—to belong at the fringes rather than at the centre of his achievement, they often have a special interest precisely as representing developmental dead-ends, paths briefly explored but then, for whatever reason, abandoned. A number of them certainly incorporate varieties of technique, subject matter, and even genre that are otherwise found in the Hardy canon either sparsely or not at all.

'How I Built Myself a House', for instance, has generally been considered worthy of attention on the single ground of its status as Hardy's first published work, written in 1864 for the amusement, initially, of his colleagues in the offices of Arthur Blomfield, one of the busiest of London architects during this period of intense urbanization. Technically the story is inconsistent and even unstable, torn between an unabashedly Dickensian style—especially in such comic scenes as the climbing of the scaffold and the exchange between the architect and his clerk—and an aspiration towards Thackerayan satire. Hardy had not yet adopted the advice of his early mentor Horace Moule ('you must in the end write *your own* style, unless you w$^{\underline{d}}$ be a mere imitator'),[13] and was writing very much under the shadow of his famous Victorian predecessors. But it was perhaps awareness of that shadow, combined with his need as a beginning writer to find material of his own, that led Hardy to draw heavily upon his personal experience of architecture and architects—thus foreshadowing such works as *Desperate Remedies, A Pair of Blue Eyes,* and *A Laodicean*—and to choose as his protagonist-narrator a 'typical' middle-class client whose treatment at the hands of his wife, the architect, the foreman, the builder, and the surveyor effectively, if comically, prefigures the fate of those numerous Hardyan characters who 'feel the painful sting . . . of modern mankind, the disproportion between the desire for serenity

[13] 2 July 1863 letter (Dorset Country Museum).

and the power of obtaining it'.[14] The middle-class narrator, however, was not to be a familiar figure in Hardy's later fiction—although the 'Poor Man', as risen into the middle class, presumably fell into that category—nor did first-person narration itself recur in his prose fiction (as distinct from his verse) on more than a very few occasions: he even resorted to the third person when writing the autobiographical *Life* near the very end of his career. 'How I Built Myself a House' remains, in fact, one of Hardy's rare exercises in the sustained use of a fully dramatized and clearly non-authorial first-person narrator, and when the story is seen within the context of Hardy's career as a whole its most remarkable feature emerges as its combination of this technical false start—doubtless recognized as such following the failure of *Poor Man*—with the successful identification of a workable area of subject matter.

'Our Exploits at West Poley' might on the face of it be deemed a failure on both counts, combining as it does another (if far more sophisticated) experiment in first-person narration with a subsequently unpursued venture into the growing market for children's literature.[15] The earlier 'The Thieves Who Couldn't Help Sneezing' had been short and slight: set vaguely in the Vale of Blackmoor area of Dorset at some not very clearly defined period in the past, it seems to have been written quickly and with little sense of historical consistency. The conventionally fabular opening, the portentous allusion to the slow growth of oak trees, and the miscellaneous references to 'Sir Simon' the 'Baronet', to the battlemented mansion, and to royal visitors all seem to have served chiefly as available devices for enhancing the story's modest narrative pretensions and suggesting a time sufficiently remote, hence sufficiently mysterious, to render acceptable the occurrence of modestly exceptional events. In

[14] Thomas Hardy, review of *Poems of Rural Life in the Dorset Dialect*, by William Barnes, *New Quarterly Magazine* (Oct. 1879), 472.
[15] Hardy did, however, assist Florence Dugdale in the composition of *The Book of Baby Beasts*, *The Book of Baby Birds*, and *The Book of Baby Pets* in 1911, 1912, and 1913, respectively.

'Our Exploits' the narrative is again contained well within the limits of the humanly explicable—suggestive of fable, it none the less eschews the fabulous—but that has not prevented it from becoming, after being so long lost to view, the best known of the stories included in this volume. Reprinted in a number of editions and in several anthologies since its initial rediscovery and republication by Richard L. Purdy in 1952, it has even been made the basis of two films.

The publication history of 'Our Exploits' sufficiently testifies to its widespread acceptance as a successful work of children's literature, and it is altogether more ambitious than 'Thieves' in its combination of elements from seemingly incompatible genres—allegory and realism, pastoral romance and boys' adventure story. At the same time, it perhaps displays more obvious weaknesses, its greater length increasing the difficulty of sustaining the kind of interest demanded by most juvenile readers (it seems symptomatic that both stories contain scenes in which children imitate magicians). Ultimately, perhaps, the children's story about boys' exploits is of less interest than the adults' story, also implicitly present, about a man's recollection and representation of those adventures, especially since that representation depends upon subtle manipulation of the first-person viewpoint used throughout.

In 'A Tradition of Eighteen Hundred and Four', the only other instance in Hardy's fiction of an adult narrator recounting childhood experience in the first person, the unnamed narrator's framing comments set up Solomon Selby's story *as story*, a fireside tale told to a receptive audience on a rainy night by a frequent teller. As in Hardy's other framed narratives—notably 'A Few Crusted Characters', the *Group of Noble Dames* stories, and especially 'What the Shepherd Saw'—the very presence of a frame establishes distance and invites reader scepticism. In 'Our Exploits', on the other hand, Leonard's unframed narrative, as the only account available, has to be taken to some extent on trust, but the two invocations of the reader, themselves unusual in Hardy's fiction, do draw attention to the fact that this, too, is a tale self-consciously addressed to an audience. What is most significant here, however, is not the story-telling process itself—how a personal narrative is transformed into a local tradition, for example—but how the tale as told reveals the character of the teller.

Leonard is a retrospective narrator, reviewing the past with the advantages of hindsight and maturity, and inevitably distorting it. Like Jane Eyre or Henry Esmond, he also—consciously or otherwise—attempts to manipulate the reader's response. Frequent allusions to the 'long distance of years' point up the narrative perspective but also insist on the countervailing vividness and, by extension, reliability of Leonard's memory: 'I seem to hear the pattering of that mill-wheel when we walked by it, as well as if it were going now; and yet how many years have passed since the sound beat last upon my ears.' But inconsistencies within the text challenge any easy confidence in Leonard's narration. Some of these confusions (about the number of days that have passed, for example, or about Job's new position) may result from authorial carelessness or editorial intervention, but others are at once more subversive and seemingly intentional.

Early in the story it is Leonard who both discovers the second hole in the cave and suggests that the stream could be turned into it, and when Steve decides to put the idea into practice Leonard presents the undertaking as a joint one, speaking of the 'harm *we* had unintentionally done by *our* manœuvre' (emphasis added). As the story progresses, however, Leonard increasingly minimizes his role—hence his culpability—in tampering with the river-head. When trapped in the cave he refers to Steve as the original discoverer of the second outlet, and as the waters rise Steve is reported as exclaiming, 'This is all my fault!', adding, when Job attempts to accept his share of the blame, 'But I began it all'. Leonard, on the other hand, now ignores his own participation, simply (and piously) suggesting that they should say their prayers. Thereafter he continues to distance and hence exculpate himself, making reference only to 'the misfortune initiated by *Steve*' and '*his* explorations' (emphasis added). 'Our Exploits', in short, become Steve's exploits.

In the latter stages of the story Leonard's only independent action of any significance is the throwing of the stone which ultimately leads to the boys' rescue. In contrast to the glossing over of his participation in the mischievous exploits, this timely act is made much of, ostentatiously introduced by a classical quotation, described in detail, and subsequently reinvoked with a reduplicated emphasis on Leonard's role: 'Thus when a stone ascended from this abyss (the stone I threw) the searchers were amazed'. But if Leonard attempts through his control of the retrospective narrative to present his youthful self in what seems to his mature self the most favourable light, the very obviousness of this endeavour, combined with its inbuilt narrative inconsistencies, effectively alerts the reader to the fact—if not the precise extent—of Leonard's unreliability. What does in any case emerge from Leonard's increasingly self-righteous and occasionally pompous self-justification is a less than admirable personality, and if Richard Purdy was correct in perceiving in Leonard 'a reminiscence of Hardy himself and his boyhood',[16] then the self-portrait is not an altogether attractive one.

The possibility of an autobiographical element in 'Our Exploits' seems consistent with John Bayley's suggestion that Hardy characteristically used the short story as 'a kind of safety-valve, for things in [his mentality] which demanded direct and even crude expression',[17] and both 'Old Mrs Chundle' and 'The Doctor's Legend' could in their very different ways be considered as just such author-indulgent exercises. Hardy's purpose in 'Old Mrs Chundle' seems to have been, quite simply, to realize on paper the possibilities, at once poignant and comic, of an anecdote about a man who had been important to him (the Revd Henry Moule) received—it would appear—from a man who had been dear to him (Henry Joseph Moule, Henry Moule's eldest son). His

---

[16] Richard Little Purdy, ed., *Our Exploits at West Poley* [limited edn.] (London: Geoffrey Cumberlege, Oxford University Press, 1952), p. xii.

[17] John Bayley, *The Short Story: Henry James to Elizabeth Bowen* (Brighton: Harvester, 1988), 123.

failure to publish the story presumably derived from a sense
that the Henry Moule figure appeared in a less than sympathetic light, but he may also have been aware that his treatment of the unnamed curate—like his depiction of the Revd
James Clare, another Henry Moule figure, in *Tess of the
d'Urbervilles*—revealed complexities and possible contradic-
tions in his own attitudes towards religion and the pastoral
office.

The story's early paragraphs are at once humorous and
heavily ironic at the expense of the curate's fastidiousness,
zealousness, and naïvety. Young and inexperienced, he
preaches from the head rather than the heart, as taught—so
the standard Evangelical three-point, text-centred sermon
clearly suggests—rather than as lived, preaching morality and
loving-kindness even though he feels anything but brotherly
love for Mrs Chundle and shows little moral concern in his
subsequent neglect of her. The sermon is, however, the structural centre of the story, initiating a series of reversals that
culminate in the curate's remorseful recognition not only
of the consequences of his neglect but, above all, of Mrs
Chundle's benevolent misinterpretation of his conduct. As he
kneels to make his anguished confession, he presents an
image of anonymous, dehumanized pain—'a black shape on
the hot white of the sunned trackway'—that bears little resemblance to the earlier 'reverend gentleman' with his 'finest
cambric handkerchief' and 'eloquent' verbal flow. Since Mrs
Chundle dies without discovering her error, the story's concluding ironies are sharp rather than bitter, and its final
words—'he rose, brushed the knees of his trousers, and
walked on'—allow the hopeful implication that the curate
will now go onward and forward, like Henry Moule himself,
a wiser if sadder man. It seems a more sympathetic reading
of the clerical role—and a closer approximation to moral
fable—than Hardy usually permitted himself, and these considerations may also have weighed against its publication.

The applicability of Bayley's generalization to 'The Doctor's Legend' is of a rather different kind, especially given the
story's unrealized relationship to *A Group of Noble Dames*, exco-
riated by T. S. Eliot as a work of self-expression in which the

self expressed seemed not to be 'a particularly wholesome or edifying matter of communication'.[18] That Hardy had a penchant for the macabre is demonstrated not only by his published work—most notably stories such as 'The Withered Arm' and 'Barbara of the House of Grebe'—but also by various personal comments. To the writer Arthur Symons, for example, he acknowledged both his fascination with the '*weird*' and his 'weakness' for reading such 'popular fiction—or, not to use the horrid word popular, fiction absorbing to the man in his slippers over the fire late at night'.[19] Moreover, in a letter defending 'Barbara of the House of Grebe' against the *Pall Mall Gazette* reviewer's description of it as 'a hideous, a hateful fantasy', he insisted: 'But supposing "Barbara of the House of Grebe" to be indeed a grisly narrative. A good horror has its place in art. Shall we, for instance, condemn "Alonzo the Brave"? For my part I would not give up a single worm of his skull.'[20]

Later in the same self-justificatory and only superficially jocular letter Hardy declared that in 'Barbara of the House of Grebe' he had protected the sensibilities of his readers by the way in which the action was 'thrown back into a second plane or middle distance, being described by a character to characters, and not point-blank by author to reader'. To which the reviewer (in a letter published in the same issue of the *Gazette*) was able to make the smart and not unreasonable reply that 'If Mr. Hardy suggests a hateful picture to the imagination, it is none the less hateful because the machinery he uses happens to be more or less old-fashioned and inartistic.' And yet the superimposed framework in both *A Group of Noble Dames* and 'The Doctor's Legend' does create both narrative and historical distance and achieve a corresponding reduction of horrific impact by reminding the reader that these are what Hardy called 'traditionary' tales being told for narrative effect to a specific (if only lightly dramatized) audience. The frame

---

[18] T. S. Eliot, *After Strange Gods: A Primer of Modern Heresy* (London: Faber and Faber, 1934), 54, 57–8.

[19] 20 Oct. 1905, *Collected Letters*, iii. 184.

[20] 'The Merry Wives of Wessex', *Pall Mall Gazette* (10 July 1891), 2.

in 'The Doctor's Legend' was clearly intrinsic to the story's method: rendered in a sense dispensable by the exclusion of the story from the *Group of Noble Dames* collection, it could easily have been removed, but instead it was emphasized by the very choice of title and the addition to the manuscript of such comments as 'I give the superstition for what it is worth'. Hardy was thus able to indulge in dubious Gothic fantasies and imaginative recreations of history while at least ostensibly absolved of responsibility for questions of credibility, morality, or simple good taste.

The doctor's sceptical remarks certainly help to establish an impression of his own reliability as narrator, and he asserts judgemental objectivity by variously declaring, 'On this point I express no opinion' and 'I leave others to judge'. But his neutrality is in fact specious, his social attitudes early emerging from his description of the central character as 'our illustrious self-seeker', a 'worthy gentleman [who] was of so elevated and refined a nature that he never gave a penny to women who uttered bad words in their trouble and rage, or who wore dirty aprons in view of his front door'. Even so, by explicitly refusing to pass judgement the doctor does differ from the narrators in *A Group of Noble Dames*: where the *Noble Dames* stories characteristically conclude, as Kristin Brady observes, with the narrator's or his auditors' convention-bound misreading of its moral,[21] 'The Doctor's Legend' simply ends with a short account from an omniscient point of view of the way in which the doctor's own thoughtfulness at the conclusion of his tale is shared by his listeners, 'as they sat with their eyes fixed upon the fire'. It might well be said that, in the absence of the sexual subject matter so central to *A Group of Noble Dames*, 'The Doctor's Legend' is less susceptible to narrow-minded moralistic misinterpretation, and it is certainly true that the overt moral allegory emphasizing the inevitability of judgement and the ultimate downfall of the wicked would be difficult to misconstrue. But in so far as the story can be read as a moral fable its central 'message' seems clearly, like the narrative itself, to be 'thrown back into a second

---

[21] Brady, 54.

plane or middle distance'. The doctor seems closer to Hardy himself than do the narrators of *A Group of Noble Dames*, and the most interesting aspect of 'The Doctor's Legend' as a whole is perhaps the degree to which Hardy's quotation of a text from Isaiah—powerfully denunciatory, richly imaged, and appropriately grisly ('the worm is spread under thee, and the worms cover thee')—enabled him to place in the Easter number of a religious paper a story essentially of savage violence and revenge, disturbingly macabre and fundamentally directed towards the condemnation of social vanities and aristocratic tyrannies.

Elements of disturbance and subversion are also strikingly present in 'Destiny and a Blue Cloak' in spite of—or perhaps precisely because of—the many visible evidences of its hasty and even casual composition. The Hardyan plot elements in 'Destiny' are obvious enough—the mistaken identity, the secret engagement, the departure in search of economic betterment, the stealthy exchange of letters, the fatefully delayed return, and, climactically, the ruthlessly ironic mistiming—and it is not surprising that the story has been remembered chiefly as an example of the kind of contrived and sensational plot to which Hardy tended to resort when creatively exhausted or financially pressured. But the story also demands to be read as a poignant statement—rare at this early stage of Hardy's career—on the social marginalization of women.

That Agatha Pollin is neither a passive nor an ultra-virtuous victim is likely to recommend her to most twentieth-century readers and it seems clear that even to her Victorian audience she was intended to be a sympathetic figure. Most of the action is presented from her point of view—though in conventional patriarchal language—and no attempt is made to vindicate the social norms which can be seen as compelling much of her 'unwomanly' behaviour. It is not Agatha's fault that Oswald Wingate mistakes her for someone else, and since the number of eligible young men is so severely limited she can scarcely be condemned for disingenuously exploiting circumstances not of her creation. Oswald's initial confusion over Agatha's identity is in fact typical of the tendency of the adult male characters to regard her as something other than the individual she is. Although Oswald subsequently insists that he loves her for herself ('you are yourself anyhow. It is you I like, and nobody else in the world—not the name'), he initially approaches her solely because of her supposed reputation for beauty, believing her to be a completely different woman. Others similarly see her only in and on their own terms. For Lovill she is 'innocent', a 'child' (appropriately addressed in baby-talk), and a 'goddess', as well as a decoration ('What a pretty maid!'), an object ('What a nice young thing!'), an animal ('A pretty creature, . . . the little mouse!'), and always a potential possession. Agatha's uncle, referring to her as a child and even as Lovill's plaything ('He'll . . . dress ye up like a doll'), blatantly uses her as an asset to be bargained with: 'if you will marry Farmer Lovill, he offers to clear off the debt, and there will no longer be any delay about my own marriage; in short, away I can go. I mean to, and there's an end on't.'

The degree of Agatha's dehumanization is remarkable, even for the protagonist of a story probably written between *Far from the Madding Crowd* and *The Hand of Ethelberta*, with their own vivid depictions of the woman as, respectively, a desired (and continually watched) object and a marketable commodity. But whereas Bathsheba and, especially, Ethelberta to some extent recognize and even exploit conventional male responses, Agatha is almost exclusively victimized by them. In no other Hardy work is the paucity of options for women more bleakly presented than in 'Destiny': given her uncle's refusal to accept further financial responsibility for her, Agatha has little choice but to marry, and even if her escape attempt had been successful it would have been extraordinarily difficult to support herself in London by means her society would have deemed 'respectable'. Even her rival, Frances, who does manipulate for her own advantage the conventional responses of the miller and the parson, emerges as a victim of patriarchal society: her options are similarly circumscribed and she, too, becomes 'the wife of a man [she cares] not an atom about'.

IV

Hardy's profound if not always fully articulated concern for the social, economic, and sexual exploitation of women within contemporary society was not to re-emerge with comparable directness until the publication of *Tess of the d'Urbervilles* in 1891. After that novel—certainly after the presentation of the rather special case of Sue Bridehead in *Jude the Obscure* (1895)—that concern again became somewhat muted in Hardy's own work even while it continued to receive indirect expression through his collaboration with such women as Florence Henniker, Agnes Grove (who did not, however, write fiction),[22] and Florence Dugdale.

Hardy had met Henniker, daughter of Richard Monckton Milnes and now wife of a distinguished soldier, in May 1893, and had been immediately and powerfully attracted to her. The intensity of his feelings, glimpsed in surviving letters and openly celebrated in some of his most moving poems,[23] led him to adopt any stratagem—from lessons in architecture to literary collaboration—which might help to establish an intimate and potentially romantic friendship. Henniker, for her part, had no interest in any such liaison but she was happy enough, as a published but not particularly celebrated writer, to be on familiar terms with 'the author of *Tess*' and to embark with him in July 1893 on a collaborative story originally called 'Desire' and eventually published as 'The Spectre of the Real'. Although the compositional history of the story is exceedingly complicated,[24] it seems clear from surviving pre-publication materials that the plot was Hardy's[25] but the actual writing Henniker's, except in so far as Hardy

[22] See Hardy's letters to Grove in *Collected Letters*, ii.
[23] e.g., 'At an Inn', 'A Broken Appointment', 'The Division', 'In Death Divided', 'The Month's Calendar', and 'A Thunderstorm in Town'.
[24] See *Excluded and Collaborative Stories*, 262–81.
[25] There are a number of familiar Hardyan plot elements, including the 'poor man and the lady' courtship, the post-nuptial disillusionment and agreement to separate, the unexpected return of the husband on the eve of his wife's remarriage, and the convenient death by drowning.

extensively revised her manuscript and wrote a new conclusion.

Both Henniker and Hardy were familiar with the so-called 'New Fiction' of the 1890s, notorious for its openly sexual character and variously condemned for pessimism, morbidity, and decadence, and 'Spectre', very much of its moment in its choice of a specifically sexual subject matter, can usefully be situated within the terms of the New Fiction debate. Explicit reference is made to numerous ideas of 'the new school',[26] as when Jim declares that his views have become 'considerably emancipated' and tells Rosalys:

> We must philosophically look on the marriage as an awkward fact in our lives, which won't prevent our loving elsewhere when we feel inclined. In my opinion this early error will carry one advantage with it—that we shall be unable to extinguish any love we may each feel for another person by a sordid matrimonial knot—unless, indeed, after seven years of obliviousness to one another's existence.

The mouthpiece of this new morality, however, is consistently presented as a negative figure. The more sympathetic Rosalys, on the other hand, is shocked by this argument, and her decision to marry Parkhurst seven years after Jim's disappearance is presented as an act not of social defiance but of feminine naïvety. She desires conventional marriage, first with Jim and then with Parkhurst, and is attracted to the latter by his possession of 'rigid notions of duty and honour'. If 'Spectre' none the less seems distinctly modern—and distinctly Hardyan—in its emphasis on the woman feeling 'caged and trapped' in her marriage and on the 'slackening of a man's passion for a woman when she becomes his property', it becomes considerably less so once the reader realizes that the entrapment is presented as a consequence, not of marriage *per se*, but specifically of a marriage entered into for the wrong—that is to say, sexual—reasons, and that it is only within such a context that male possession and dominance are negatively perceived.

The predominance of Henniker's hand in the actual writing out of the story—the textual realization of the plot out-

---

[26] Subsequently revised to 'your fast sets'.

line—is amply suggested by the way in which Rosalys's tendency to define herself in terms of male opinion, specifically Parkhurst's, is depicted without any kind of criticism or even ironic awareness, and by her obvious distance from the New Woman type as defined by Hardy with reference to Sue Bridehead in his 1912 preface to *Jude the Obscure*: 'the slight, pale "bachelor" girl—the intellectualized, emancipated bundle of nerves'. Rosalys's name may combine the symbolic rose and lily, but there is nothing lily-like, little sign of excessive sensibility, in the rapidity of her recovery from the double or perhaps triple trauma of Jim's return, sexual importunity, and death: she marries Parkhurst, at all events, just a few hours later. As the rose dominates her name, so the sexual dominates her personality, and the consistent narratorial response to this sexuality as representing 'the lower and weaker side of her nature' is so crudely judgemental as to be clearly non-Hardyan.

But even if much of the writing is not Hardy's, he did put his name to the finished product, and 'Spectre' is perhaps best seen within the context of a multi-level dialogue between Hardy and Henniker. The narrator's position is a reflection of Henniker's: it also corresponds to the position she was currently asserting in her personal relationship with her collaborator. Hardy, knowing her views, and seeking above all her approval, evidently recognized that this was not the place to continue his exploration of developments associated with the New Fiction. During the revision process, however, he did assert himself to the point of emphasizing Rosalys's sexual attraction, adding, for example, the details of her 'ready mouth' and 'quick breath', stressing Jim's assurance of sexual power by inserting into the final scenes his commanding 'Come—damn you, dear—put up your mouth[27] as you used to!', and confirming Rosalys's continued inability to resist Jim's advances, either in or, so to speak, out of season. Significantly, when Henniker was revising 'Spectre' for inclusion in her 1896 volume *In Scarlet and Grey*, she not only deleted these Hardyan passages but made other alterations tending in

[27] Subsequently revised to 'face'.

the same direction, almost all of them bowdlerizations necessitated by Hardy's additions.[28] She clearly had reservations
about the story even in its expurgated form, insisting in a
letter to a reviewer that 'Though of course Mr H's share has
great cleverness, it is not really a *sympathetic*, or pleasant
story.'[29]

More than a decade later Hardy entered into a similar,
if altogether less passionate, relationship with Florence
Dugdale, who subsequently became his second wife. Dugdale,
thirty-eight years Hardy's junior, was a schoolteacher and
aspiring writer who, at the time of her meeting with Hardy in
1905, had already published several pamphlet-length stories
for the Society for Promoting Christian Knowledge and was
about to publish a volume of stories for Collins. Several other
books appeared shortly thereafter—all children's stories of
thoroughly conventional kinds, didactic morality tales or sen-
timentalized sketches involving small creatures. Hardy's encouragement and assistance, always privately given, led to a
broadening of Dugdale's literary horizons and the publication of several stories for adults. Most of these have a distinctly
Hardyan cast—the simplistic moral fables give way to tales of
life's little, or somewhat larger, ironies[30]—and Hardy's collaboration in their composition appears to have been similar
in kind, though perhaps not in extent, to his participation in
the writing of 'Spectre', Hardy providing the plot outlines,
Dugdale writing the stories out, and Hardy revising them in
typescript or proof, or both.

The proofs of 'Blue Jimmy: The Horse Stealer' (published
over Dugdale's name in 1911), for example, carry extensive
revisions in Hardy's hand, and it has been suggested that the
story was in fact entirely written by him.[31] Different though

[28] See n. to p. 205.

[29] 23 July 1896, to Coulson Kernahan (Berg Collection, New York Public
Library).

[30] See, e.g., 'The Apotheosis of the Minx', *Cornhill* (May 1908), 642–53, and
'The Scholar's Wife', *Pall Mall Gazette* (Jan. 1909), 78–82. These stories have
not, however, been included in the present volume because no external
evidence of Hardy's involvement in their composition exists.

[31] Robert Gittings, *The Older Hardy* (London: Heinemann, 1978), 180.

the story is from Dugdale's previous work in both its episodic structure and its wholly unsentimental narrative, it seems more probable that Hardy supplied Dugdale with the basic outlines of the local tradition on which the story is based and directed her to the contemporary accounts of the horse-thief's trials in the *Dorset County Chronicle* and the *Taunton Courier*—paragraphs on which she drew with a literalness fully justifying Hardy's subsequently recommending the piece to the *Cornhill* not as a story but as a 'record'.[32]

Hardy, then, can probably be said to have 'provided' the plot of 'Blue Jimmy', but not in the same sense that he provided the plot for 'Spectre' or, in all probability, for the most Hardyan of the stories signed by Dugdale, 'The Unconquerable'. 'The Unconquerable' was never published and survives only in a typescript which Hardy has heavily revised. Once again the collaboration appears to have followed the now familiar pattern, Hardy supplying the plot, Dugdale writing it up, and Hardy introducing substantial revisions. As a tale of mistimings and missed opportunities concluding with an ironic twist, 'The Unconquerable' is a far darker and more sceptical narrative than any of Dugdale's earlier stories or any of the crudely patriotic and 'inspirational' journalism she published—surely to her husband's intense embarrassment—during the period of the First World War.[33] Moreover, the similarities with respect to Hardy's story 'Fellow-Townsmen' are obvious: Fadelle arrives at Gertrude's home a few hours after her engagement to Wingate, just as Barnet discovers his wife's death a few minutes before Lucy's marriage to Downe; the widowed Gertrude reconsiders her refusal of Fadelle but fails to act in sufficient time, just as Lucy, having decided to allow herself 'to be induced to reconsider' Barnet, waits 'years and years' for a return that never occurs; and so

[32] See *Collected Letters*, iv. 114.

[33] See, e.g., ' "Greater Love Hath No Man . . .": The Story of a Village Ne'er-Do-Weel', *Sunday Pictorial* (13 June 1915), 7, and 'War's Awakening: How Duty's Call Came to a Bachelor Girl' (22 Aug. 1915), 7. The former was published over 'Mrs. Thomas Hardy', the latter (significantly) over 'Florence E. Dugdale'.

xxxvi   *Introduction*

forth. The two stories also share structural similarities—most
notably, the swings of fortune which appear to favour alter-
nately first one friend and then the other but come to rest in
the realization that all these apparent triumphs are finally
specious.

What is most interesting about 'The Unconquerable', however, is its exploration of a man's ability to wield power after
death, even to the point of determining his own posthumous
image. The subject matter seems particularly significant when
considered in relation to the knowledge that Dugdale became Hardy's wife and then his widow and in that latter role
found herself publishing his ghost-written official biography
over her own name—and enduring those trials and tribula-
tions of literary executorship so vividly narrated in Michael
Millgate's *Testamentary Acts*.[34] If the non-publication of 'The
Unconquerable' seems hard to explain—the story is clearly
superior not only to all of Dugdale's stories but even to many
of Hardy's—one might plausibly speculate that the plot came
to seem embarrassingly close to the bone.

[34] Michael Millgate, *Testamentary Acts: Browning, Tennyson, James, Hardy*
(Oxford: Clarendon Press, 1992), 156–68.

NOTE ON THE TEXTS

The texts of the stories in this volume are those established
for the Clarendon Press edition, *Thomas Hardy: The Excluded
and Collaborative Stories* (1992). Copy-text for four of the ten
stories is the sole authoritative edition printed during Hardy's
lifetime: 'How I Built Myself a House' in *Chambers's Journal*, 18
March 1865;[1] 'Destiny and a Blue Cloak' in the *New-York
Times*, 4 October 1874; 'The Thieves Who Couldn't Help
Sneezing' in *Father Christmas* [December] 1877; and 'Our
Exploits at West Poley' in the *Household*, November 1892–
April 1893. For 'Old Mrs Chundle' and 'The Unconquerable'
the copy-text is again the sole surviving textual witness: for the
former, the holograph manuscript in the Dorset County Mu-
seum; for the latter, Florence Dugdale's typescript with Har-
dy's revisions, also in the Dorset County Museum. Copy-text
for 'The Doctor's Legend' is the manuscript (in the Berg
Collection of the New York Public Library) written out by
Emma Hardy and revised by Hardy, and for 'Blue Jimmy: The
Horse Stealer' the proofs of the *Cornhill* printing (in the
Frederick B. Adams collection) corrected by Hardy, the only
other surviving witness in each instance being the periodical
printing itself, authorized but clearly not incorporating further authorial revision: the *Independent*, 26 March 1891, and
the *Cornhill*, February 1911.

For 'An Indiscretion in the Life of an Heiress' the copy-
text is the July 1878 *New Quarterly Magazine* printing. The
only other authoritative edition is the 29 June–27 July
1878 *Harper's Weekly* printing, presumably set from the uncorrected *New Quarterly* proofs. The *Harper's Weekly* text thus
represents an earlier, unrevised, and, as far as Hardy was
concerned, essentially unfinished version of 'Indiscretion',
though it remains of particular interest as being one stage
closer to the manuscript, hence to Hardy's lost first novel,

---

[1] The 6 Dec. 1924 *Chambers's Journal* printing was also authorized by Hardy,
but it does not introduce a single variant.

The Poor Man and the Lady, from which 'Indiscretion' was derived.

'The Spectre of the Real' survives in three authoritative pre-publication texts (all in the Frederick B. Adams collection): the ribbon copy of the first typescript, showing holograph corrections by both Henniker and Hardy; a carbon copy, showing holograph revisions by Hardy only, of the second typescript, which was professionally prepared from the first typescript as revised; and a set of the *To-Day* proofs, also showing holograph revisions by Hardy. As the witness closest to the lost manuscript, the first typescript as revised—first by Henniker and then by Hardy—has been taken as copy-text, and virtually all the subsequent revisions made by Hardy on the later typescript and magazine proofs are incorporated.[2] The non-authoritative variants introduced in the *To-Day* printing (17 November 1894) and in the six Bacheller syndicate printings[3] (derived from the uncorrected *To-Day* proofs) have not been incorporated into the edited text, nor have the variants introduced by Henniker when revising—primarily bowdlerizing—'Spectre' for her collective volume, *In Scarlet and Grey* (1896).

Emendation of the copy-texts of all the other stories, with the exception of 'Our Exploits', consists almost entirely of the correction of obvious errors and the removal of demonstrably non-Hardyan usage (e.g. US spellings and single quotation marks). In the case of 'Our Exploits', where Hardy not only did not see proof but presumably did not even know of the story's publication, more extensive emendation has been necessary, including the removal of superfluous commas which obscure meaning and the emendation of compositorial misreadings (e.g. 'pills' for 'frills' in the phrase 'frills, lace, coats of mail').

---

[2] Hardy's second-typescript and proof revisions have not been incorporated when they were made in response to non-authoritative readings (i.e. variants introduced by the typist or the compositors).

[3] *Philadelphia Press*, 15–21 Nov. 1894; *Kansas City Star*, 17–22 Nov. 1894; *Minneapolis Tribune*, 19–23 Nov. 1894; New York *Press*, 19–23 Nov. 1894; *Nebraska State Journal*, 20–4 Nov. 1894; San Francisco *Examiner*, 2 and 9 Dec. 1894.

The more significant textual variants are recorded in the Explanatory Notes to this edition; a complete listing of variants and emendations for each of the stories can be found in *The Excluded and Collaborative Stories.*

SELECT BIBLIOGRAPHY

The most authoritative biography of Hardy, Michael Millgate's *Thomas Hardy: A Biography* (Oxford: Oxford University Press, 1982), comments on most of the stories included in the present volume. Several of the stories also figure in Robert Gittings's *Young Thomas Hardy* (London: Heinemann, 1975) and *The Older Hardy* (London: Heinemann, 1978), and in his and Jo Manton's *The Second Mrs Hardy* (London: Heinemann, 1979). Relevant surviving correspondence can be found in *The Collected Letters of Thomas Hardy*, ed. Richard Little Purdy and Michael Millgate, 7 vols. (Oxford: Clarendon Press, 1978–88). *Thomas Hardy: The Excluded and Collaborative Stories*, ed. Pamela Dalziel (Oxford: Clarendon Press, 1992), provides detailed accounts of each story's composition and (where relevant) publication history, as well as listings of all textual variants in surviving manuscripts, typescripts, proofs, and authorially authorized editions.

The stories have received very little substantial criticism. Kristin Brady does, however, touch upon all of the non-collaborative stories in the final chapter of *The Short Stories of Thomas Hardy: Tales of Past and Present* (London: Macmillan, 1982). Brief but significant comment on 'An Indiscretion in the Life of an Heiress' can also be found in Penny Boumelha, *Thomas Hardy and Women: Sexual Ideology and Narrative Form* (Brighton: Harvester, 1982); Patricia Ingham, *Thomas Hardy* (Hemel Hempstead: Harvester Wheatsheaf, 1989); and David Lodge, 'Thomas Hardy as Cinematic Novelist', in *Thomas Hardy After Fifty Years*, ed. Lance St John Butler (London: Macmillan, 1977).

A CHRONOLOGY OF THOMAS HARDY

1840   2 June: Thomas Hardy born, first child of Thomas and Jemima (Hand) Hardy, five and a half months after their marriage. His father was a builder in a small but slowly developing way of business, thus setting the family apart socially from the 'work-folk' whom they closely resembled in financial circumstances.

1848   Entered the newly opened Stinsford National School.

1849   Sent to Dorchester British School kept by Isaac Last.

1853   Last established an independent 'commercial academy', and Hardy became a pupil there. His education was practical and effective, including Latin, some French, theoretical and applied mathematics, and commercial studies.

1856   11 July: articled to Dorchester architect John Hicks. Soon after this he became friendly with Horace Moule, an important influence on his life.

1860   Summer: Hardy's articles, having been extended for a year, completed. Employed by Hicks as an assistant.

1862   17 April: Without a position, travelled to London, but soon employed by Arthur Blomfield as a 'Gothic draughtsman'. November: Elected to the Architectural Association; began to find his feet in London.

1863   Won architectural prizes; began to consider some form of writing as a means of support.

1863–7   Possibly became engaged to Eliza Nicholls.

1865   March: 'How I Built Myself a House' published in *Chambers's Journal*. Began to write poetry.

1866   Hardy's commitment to the Church and his religious belief seem to have declined though he probably experienced no dramatic loss of faith.

1867   Returned to Dorset. Began his never-published first novel.

1868   Sent MS of *The Poor Man and the Lady* to four publishers, where it was read by Morley and Meredith, amongst others, but finally rejected.

1869   Worked in Weymouth for the Architect Crickmay; began writing *Desperate Remedies*.

1870   In order to take 'a plan and particulars' of the church, Hardy journeyed to St Juliot, near Boscastle in North

Cornwall; there he met Emma Lavinia Gifford, who became his wife four years later.

1871   *Desperate Remedies* published after Hardy had advanced £75.

1872   *Under the Greenwood Tree* published; the copyright sold to Tinsley for £30. Hardy moved temporarily to London to work in the offices of T. Roger Smith. Contracted to provide serial for *Tinsleys' Magazine* for £200 (to include first edition rights). *A Pair of Blue Eyes* began to appear in September. Hardy decided to relinquish architecture and concentrate on writing. Leslie Stephen requested a serial for the *Cornhill Magazine*.

1873   *A Pair of Blue Eyes* published in three volumes; Horace Moule, his close adviser and friend, committed suicide in Cambridge.

1874   *Far From the Madding Crowd* begun as a serial in *Cornhill* under Leslie Stephen's editorship and published later in the year in two volumes. Hardy married Emma Gifford on 17 September; they honeymooned in Paris and returned to live in London.

1875   *Cornhill* serialized *The Hand of Ethelberta*. The Hardys moved from London to Swanage in Dorset.

1876   Further moves to Yeovil and Sturminster Newton, where Hardy began writing *The Return of the Native*.

1878   Return to London (Tooting). *The Return of the Native* serialized in *Belgravia* and published in three volumes, to which Hardy affixed a map of the novel's environment. Made researches in the British Museum for the background of *The Trumpet-Major*.

1879   With 'The Distracted Young Preacher', began regularly to publish short stories.

1880   *Good Words* serialized *The Trumpet-Major*, which was also published in three volumes with covers designed by Hardy. In October he became seriously ill and believed himself close to death; the cause of his illness uncertain, but led to five months' total inactivity.

1881   *A Laodicean*, mostly written from his bed, published as a serial in *Harper's New Monthly Magazine* (the first in the new European edition), and in three volumes. The Hardys returned to Dorset, living at Wimborne Minster.

1882   Controversy with Pinero over Hardy's adaptation of *Far From the Madding Crowd* and Pinero's use of the same material. Hardy's third novel in three years, *Two on a Tower*, serialized in the *Atlantic Monthly* and issued in three volumes.

1883 The final move of his life—from Wimborne to Dorchester, though into temporary accommodation while his own house was being built.

1884 Made a Justice of the Peace and began to receive invitations from aristocracy. Began writing *The Mayor of Casterbridge*.

1885 Max Gate, designed by Hardy and built by his brother Henry, completed; on the outskirts of Dorchester, it remained his home for the rest of his life.

1886 *The Mayor of Casterbridge* serialized in the *Graphic* and brought out in two volumes; in the same year *The Woodlanders* began its run in *Macmillan's Magazine*. William Barnes, the Dorset poet and friend of Hardy, died.

1887 *The Woodlanders* issued in three volumes. The Hardys visited France and Italy. Began work on *Tess of the d'Urbervilles*.

1888 Hardy's first collection of short stories, *Wessex Tales*, published in two volumes. Also published the first of three significant essays on the theory of fiction, *The Profitable Reading of Fiction*.

1889 The novel that was to become *Tess* rejected by Tillotson's Fiction Bureau, which had commissioned it; subsequent further rejections fuelled the bitterness behind a second essay, *Candour in English Fiction*, published in January of the following year.

1890 *A Group of Noble Dames* appeared in the *Graphic*.

1891 *Tess of the d'Urbervilles* serialized in the *Graphic* and published in three volumes; *A Group of Noble Dames* brought out in one volume. The third important essay, *The Science of Fiction*, appeared. A Copyright Bill passed through the United States Congress in time for *Tess* to benefit from its provisions, a factor of considerable financial significance in Hardy's career.

1892 Father died 20 July. *The Pursuit of the Well-Beloved* serialized in the *Illustrated London News*.

1893 Met Florence Henniker, object of the intensest of his romantic attachments to artistic women. Wrote *The Spectre of the Real* in collaboration with her. Began writing *Jude the Obscure*.

1894   Third collection of short stories, *Life's Little Ironies*, published in one volume.

1895   First collected edition of Hardy's work begun; published by Osgood, McIlvaine, it included the first edition of *Jude the Obscure*, previously serialized in *Harper's New Monthly Magazine*. Some reviews of *Jude* quite savage, a contributory factor in Hardy's writing no further novels. Hardy dramatized *Tess*.

1896   The first group of major poems with identifiable dates written since the 1860s; they included the three *In Tenebris* poems and *Wessex Heights*.

1897   *The Well-Beloved*, substantially revised from the 1892 serialization, published as part of the Osgood, McIlvaine edition. Visited Switzerland.

1898   Hardy's first collection of verse published, *Wessex Poems*; comprising mainly poems written in the 1860s and 1890s; and illustrated by himself.

1899   Boer War began, to which Hardy responded in verse. The gradual physical separation between Hardy and Emma intensified, following the mental separation that set in after the publication of *Jude the Obscure*.

1901   *Poems of the Past and the Present* published.

1902   Changed publishers for the last time, to Macmillan.

1904   First part of *The Dynasts* appeared. 3 April: Hardy's mother died, leaving a tremendous gap in his life.

1905   Met Florence Dugdale. Received LL.D. from Aberdeen University.

1906   *The Dynasts* completed with the publication of the third part; it embodied Hardy's most complete statement of his philosophical outlook. Also published his *Select Poems of William Barnes*, undertaken as a memorial to his great predecessor. The first Dorchester dramatization of a Hardy novel, *The Trumpet-Major*. Meredith and Swinburne died, leaving Hardy as the greatest living English writer.

1909   Relationship with Florence Dugdale deepened. *Time's Laughingstocks*, Hardy's third volume of poems, published.

1910   Awarded the Order of Merit, having previously refused a knighthood. Received the freedom of Dorchester.

1912   Second collected edition of Hardy's works begun, the Wessex Edition. Received the gold medal of the Royal Society of Literature. 27 November: Emma Hardy died; as a direct result Hardy began writing the poems of 1912–13.

1913   Visited Cornwall in search of his and Emma's youth. Awarded Litt.D. at Cambridge and became an Honorary Fellow of Magdalene College—a partial fulfilment of an early aspiration. His final collection of short stories published, *A Changed Man*.

1914   10 February: married Florence Dugdale. *Satires of Circumstance* published. First World War began; Hardy's attitude to the future of humanity coloured by it in a profound way.

1915   At the age of 75 Hardy began to become reclusive. Frank George, his chosen heir, killed at Gallipoli. Hardy's sister Mary died 24 November.

1916   *Selected Poems of Thomas Hardy* published.

1917   Hardy's fifth collection of verse published, *Moments of Vision*. He and Florence began work on what was eventually to become *The Life of Thomas Hardy*.

1919–20 The de luxe edition of Hardy's work issued, the Mellstock Edition.

1922   *Late Lyrics and Earlier*, with its important Preface, published.

1923   Florence Henniker died. The Prince of Wales visited Max Gate. Friendship with T. E. Lawrence developed. *The Queen of Cornwall* published.

1924   Hardy's adaptation of *Tess* acted in Dorchester with the last of his romantic attachments, Gertrude Bugler, in the title role.

1925   *Tess* acted in London, but not by Miss Bugler. *Human Shows, Far Phantasies, Songs, and Trifles*, Hardy's seventh volume of verse, published.

1928   11 January: Hardy died. His final book of poems, *Winter Words*, published posthumously.

An Indiscretion in the Life of an Heiress
and Other Stories

HOW I BUILT MYSELF A HOUSE

My wife Sophia, myself, and the beginning of a happy line, formerly lived in the suburbs of London, in the sort of house called a Highly-Desirable Semi-detached Villa. But in reality our residence was the very opposite of what we wished it to be. We had no room for our friends when they visited us, and we were obliged to keep our coals out of doors in a heap against the back-wall. If we managed to squeeze a few acquaintances round our table to dinner, there was very great difficulty in serving it; and on such occasions the maid, for want of side-board room, would take to putting the dishes in the staircase, or on stools and chairs in the passage, so that if anybody else came after we had sat down, he usually went away again, disgusted at seeing the remains of what we had already got through standing in these places, and perhaps the celery waiting in a corner hard by. It was therefore only natural that on wet days, chimney-sweepings, and those cleaning times when chairs may be seen with their legs upwards, a tub blocking a doorway, and yourself walking about edgeways among the things, we called the villa hard names, and that we resolved to escape from it as soon as it would be politic, in a monetary sense, to carry out a notion which had long been in our minds.

This notion was to build a house of our own a little further out of town than where we had hitherto lived. The new residence was to be right and proper in every respect. It was to be of some mysterious size and proportion, which would make us both peculiarly happy ever afterwards—that had always been a settled thing. It was neither to cost too much nor too little, but just enough to fitly inaugurate the new happiness. Its situation was to be in a healthy spot, on a stratum of dry gravel, about ninety feet above the springs. There were to be trees to the north, and a pretty view to the south. It was also to be easily accessible by rail.

Eighteen months ago, a third baby being our latest blessing, we began to put the above-mentioned ideas into practice.

As the house itself, rather than its position, is what I wish particularly to speak of, I will not dwell upon the innumerable difficulties that were to be overcome before a suitable spot could be found. Maps marked out in little pink and green oblongs clinging to a winding road, became as familiar to my eyes as my own hand. I learned, too, all about the coloured plans of Land to be Let for Building Purposes, which are exhibited at railway stations and in agents' windows—that sketches of cabbages in rows, or artistically irregular, meant large trees that would afford a cooling shade when they had been planted and had grown up—that patches of blue showed fishponds and fountains; and that a wide straight road to the edge of the map was the way to the station, a corner of which was occasionally shown, as if it would come within a convenient distance, disguise the fact as the owners might.

After a considerable time had been spent in these studies, I began to see that some of our intentions in the matter of site must be given up. The trees to the north went first. After a short struggle, they were followed by the ninety feet above the springs. Sophia, with all wifely tenacity, stuck to the pretty view long after I was beaten about the gravel subsoil. In the end, we decided upon a place imagined to be rather convenient, and rather healthy, but possessing no other advantage worth mentioning. I took it on a lease for the established period, ninety-nine years.

We next thought about an architect. A friend of mine, who sometimes sends a paper on art and science to the magazines, strongly recommended a Mr Penny, a gentleman whom he considered to have architectural talent of every kind, but if he was a trifle more skilful in any one branch of his profession than in another, it was in designing excellent houses for families of moderate means. I at once proposed to Sophia that we should think over some arrangement of rooms which would be likely to suit us, and then call upon the architect, that he might put our plan into proper shape.

I made my sketch, and my wife made hers. Her drawing and dining rooms were very large, nearly twice the size of mine, though her doors and windows showed sound judgment. We soon found that there was no such thing as fitting our ideas together, do what we would. When we had come to no conclusion at all, we called at Mr Penny's office. I began telling him my business, upon which he took a sheet of foolscap, and made numerous imposing notes, with large brackets and dashes to them. Sitting there with him in his office, surrounded by rolls of paper, circles, squares, triangles, compasses, and many other of the inventions which have been sought out by men from time to time, and perceiving that all these were the realities which had been faintly shadowed forth to me by Euclid some years before, it is no wonder that I became a puppet in his hands. He settled everything in a miraculous way. We were told the only possible size we could have the rooms, the only way we should be allowed to go upstairs, and the exact quantity of wine we might order at once, so as to fit the wine-cellar he had in his head. His professional opinions, propelled by his facts, seemed to float into my mind whether I wished to receive them or not. I thought at the time that Sophia, from her silence, was in the same helpless state; but she has since told me it was quite otherwise, and that she was only a little tired.

I had been very anxious all along that the stipulated cost, eighteen hundred pounds, should not be exceeded, and I impressed this again upon Mr Penny.

"I will give you an approximate estimate for the sort of thing we are thinking of," he said. "Linem." (This was the clerk.)

"Did you speak, sir?"

"Forty-nine by fifty-four by twenty-eight, twice fourteen by thirty-one by eleven, and several small items which we will call one hundred and sixty."

"Eighty-two thousand four hundred—"

"But eighteen hundred at the very outside," I began, "is what—"

"Feet, my dear sir—feet, cubic feet," said Mr Penny. "Put it down at sixpence a foot, Linem, remainders not an object."

"Two thousand two hundred pounds." This was too much.

"Well, try it at something less, leaving out all below hundreds, Linem."

"About eighteen hundred and seventy pounds."

"Very satisfactory, in my opinion," said Mr Penny turning to me. "What do you think?"

"You are so particular, John," interrupted my wife. "I am sure it is exceedingly moderate: elegance and extreme cheapness never do go together."

(It may be here remarked that Sophia never calls me "my dear" before strangers. She considers that, like the ancient practice in besieged cities of throwing loaves over the walls, it really denotes a want rather than an abundance of them within.)

I did not trouble the architect any further, and we rose to leave.

"Be sure you make a nice conservatory, Mr Penny," said my wife; "something that has character about it. If it could only be in the Chinese style, with beautiful ornaments at the corners, like Mrs Smith's, only better," she continued, turning to me with a glance in which a broken tenth commandment might have been seen.

"Some sketches shall be forwarded, which I think will suit you," answered Mr Penny pleasantly, looking as if he had possessed for some years a complete guide to the minds of all people who intended to build.

It is needless to go through the whole history of the plan-making. A builder had been chosen, and the house marked out, when we went down to the place one morning to see how the foundations looked.

It is a strange fact, that a person's new house drawn in outline on the ground where it is to stand, looks ridiculously and inconveniently small. The notion it gives one is, that any portion of one's after-life spent within such boundaries must of necessity be rendered wretched on account of bruises daily received by running against the partitions, doorposts, and fireplaces. In my case, the lines showing sitting-rooms seemed to denote cells; the kitchen looked as if it might develop into a large box; whilst the study appeared to consist chiefly of a fireplace and a door. We were told that houses always looked so; but Sophia's disgust at the sight of such a diminutive drawing-room was not to be lessened by any scientific reasoning. Six feet longer—four feet then—three it must be, she argued; and the room was accordingly lengthened. I felt rather relieved when at last I got her off the ground, and on the road home.

The building gradually crept upwards, and put forth chimneys. We were standing beside it one day, looking at the men at work on the top, when the builder's foreman came towards us.

"Being your own house, sir, and as we are finishing the last chimney, you would perhaps like to go up," he said.

"I am sure I should much, if I were a man," was my wife's observation to me. "The landscape must appear so lovely from that height."

This remark placed me in something of a dilemma, for it must be confessed that I am not given to climbing. The sight of cliffs, roofs, scaffoldings, and elevated places in general, which have no sides to keep people from slipping off, always causes me to feel how infinitely preferable a position at the bottom is to a position at the top of them. But as my house was by no means lofty, and it was but for once, I said I would go up.

My knees felt a good deal in the way as I ascended the ladder; but that was not so disagreeable as the thrill which passed through me as I followed my guide along two narrow planks, one bending beneath each foot. However, having once started, I kept on, and next climbed another ladder, thin and weak-looking, and not tied at the top. I could not help thinking, as I viewed the horizon between the steps, what a shocking thing it would be if any part should break; and to get rid of the thought, I adopted the device of mentally criticising the leading articles in that morning's *Times;* but as the plan did not answer, I tried to fancy that, though strangely enough it seemed otherwise, I was only four feet from the ground. This was a failure too; and just as I had commenced upon an idea that great quantities of feather-beds were spread below, I reached the top scaffold.

"Rather high," I said to the foreman, trying, but failing to appear unconcerned.

"Well, no," he answered; "nothing to what it is sometimes (I'll just trouble you not to step upon the end of that plank there, as it will turn over); though you may as well fall from here as from the top of the Monument for the matter of life being quite extinct when they pick you up," he continued, looking around at the weather and the crops, as it were.

Then a workman, with a load of bricks, stamped along the boards, and overturned them at my feet, causing me to shake up and down like the little servant-men behind private cabs. I asked, in trepidation, if the bricks were not dangerously heavy, thinking of a newspaper paragraph headed "Frightful Accident from an Overloaded Scaffold."

"Just what I was going to say. Dan has certainly too many there," answered the man. "But it won't break down if we walk without springing, and don't sneeze, though the mortar-boy's hooping-cough was strong enough in my poor brother Jim's case," he continued abstractedly, as if he himself possessed several necks, and could afford to break one or two.

My wife was picking daisies a little distance off, apparently in a state of complete indifference as to whether I was on the scaffold, at the foot of it, or in St George's Hospital; so I roused myself for a descent, and tried the small ladder. I cannot accurately say how I did get down; but during that performance, my body seemed perforated by holes, through which breezes blew in all directions. As I got nearer the earth, they went away. It may be supposed that my wife's notion of the height differed considerably from my own, and she inquired particularly for the landscape, which I had quite forgotten; but the discovery of that fact did not cause me to break a resolution not to trouble my chimneys again.

Beyond a continual anxiety and frequent journeyings along the sides of a triangle, of which the old house, the new house, and the architect's office were the corners, nothing worth mentioning happened till the building was nearly finished. Sophia's ardour in the business, which at the beginning was so intense, had nearly burned itself out, so I was left pretty much to myself in getting over the later difficulties. Amongst them was the question of a porch. I had often been annoyed whilst waiting outside a door on a wet day at being exposed to the wind and rain, and it was my favourite notion that I would have a model porch whenever I should build a house. Thus it was very vexing to recollect, just as the workmen were finishing off, that I had never mentioned the subject to Mr Penny, and that he had not suggested anything about one to me.

"A porch or no porch is entirely a matter of personal feeling and taste," was his remark, in answer to a complaint from me; "so, of course, I did not put one without its being mentioned. But it happens that in this case it would be an improvement—a feature, in fact. There is this objection, that the roof will close up the window of the little place on the landing; but we may get ventilation by making an opening higher up, if you don't mind a trifling darkness, or rather gloom."

My first thought was that this might tend to reduce myself and family to a state of chronic melancholy; but remembering there were reflectors advertised to throw sunlight into any nook almost, I agreed to the inconvenience, for the sake of the porch, though I found afterwards that the gloom was for all time, the patent reflector, naturally enough, sending its spot of light against the opposite wall, where it was not wanted, and leaving none about the landing, where it was.

In getting a house built for a specified sum by contract with a builder, there is a certain pit-fall into which unwary people are sure to step—this accident is technically termed "getting into extras." It is evident that the only way to get out again without making a town-talk about yourself, is to pay the builder a large sum of money over and above the contract amount—the value of course of the extras. In the present case, I knew very well that the perceptible additions would have to be paid for. Common sense, and Mr Penny himself perhaps, should have told me a little more distinctly that I must pay if I said "yes" to questions whether I preferred one window a trifle larger than it was originally intended, another a trifle smaller, second thoughts as to where a doorway should be, and so on. Then came a host of things "not included"—a sink in the scullery, a rain-water tank and a pump, a trap-door into the roof, a scraper, a weather-cock and four letters, ventilators in the nursery, same in the kitchen, all of which worked vigorously enough, but the wrong way; patent remarkable bell-pulls; a royal letters extraordinary kitchen-range, which it would cost exactly threepence three-farthings to keep a fire in for twelve hours, and yet cook any joint in any way, warm up what was left yesterday, boil the vegetables, and do the ironing. But not keeping a strict account of all these expenses, and thinking myself safe in Mr Penny's hands from any enormous increase, I was astounded to find that the additions altogether came to some hundreds of pounds. I could almost go through the worry of building another house, to show how carefully I would avoid getting into extras again.

Then they have to be wound up. A surveyor is called in from somewhere, and, by a fiction, his heart's desire is supposed to be that you shall not be overcharged one halfpenny by the builder for the additions. The builder names a certain sum as the value of a portion—say double its worth, the surveyor then names a sum, about half its true value. They then fight it out by word of mouth, and gradually bringing their valuations nearer and nearer together, at last meet in the middle. All my accounts underwent this operation.

A Families-removing van carried our furniture and effects to the new building without giving us much trouble; but a number of vexing little incidents occurred on our settling down, which I should have felt more deeply had not a sort of Martinmas summer of Sophia's interest in the affair now set in, and lightened them considerably. Smoke was one of our nuisances. On lighting the study-fire, every particle of smoke came curling into the room. In our trouble, we sent for the architect, who immediately asked if we had tried the plan of opening the register to cure it. We had not, but we did so, and the smoke ascended at once. The last thing I remember was Sophia jumping up one night and frightening me out of my senses with the exclamation: "O that builder! Not a single bar of any sort is there to the nursery-windows. John, some day those poor little children will tumble out in their innocence—how should they know better?—and be dashed to pieces. Why *did* you put the nursery on the second floor?" And you may be sure that some bars were put up the very next morning.

DESTINY AND A BLUE CLOAK

I

"Good morning, Miss Lovill!" said the young man, in the free manner usual with him toward pretty and inexperienced country girls.

Agatha Pollin—the maiden addressed—instantly perceived how the mistake had arisen. Miss Lovill was the owner of a blue autumn wrapper, exceptionally gay for a village; and Agatha, in a spirit of emulation rather than originality, had purchased a similarly enviable article for herself, which she wore to-day for the first time. It may be mentioned that the two young women had ridden together from their homes to Maiden-Newton on this foggy September morning, Agatha prolonging her journey thence to Weymouth by train, and leaving her acquaintance at the former place. The remark was made to her on Weymouth esplanade.

Agatha was now about to reply very naturally, "I am not Miss Lovill," and she went so far as to turn up her face to him for the purpose, when he added, "I've been hoping to meet you. I have heard of your—well, I must say it—beauty, long ago, though I only came to Beaminster yesterday."

Agatha bowed—her contradiction hung back—and they walked slowly along the esplanade together without speaking another word after the above point-blank remark of his. It was evident that her new friend could never have seen either herself or Miss Lovill except from a distance.

And Agatha trembled as well as bowed. This Miss Lovill—Frances Lovill—was of great and long renown as the beauty of Cloton village, near Beaminster. She was five and twenty and fully developed, while Agatha was only the niece of the miller of the same place, just nineteen, and of no repute as yet for comeliness, though she undoubtedly could boast of much. Now, were the speaker, Oswald Winwood, to be told that he had not lighted upon the true Helen, he would instantly apologize for his mistake and leave her side, a contingency of no great matter but for one curious emotional circumstance—Agatha had already lost her heart to him. Only in secret had she acquired this interest in Winwood—by hearing much report of his talent and by watching him several times from a window; but she loved none the less in that she had discovered that Miss Lovill's desire to meet and talk with the same intellectual luminary was in a fair way of approaching the intensity of her own. We are never unbiased appraisers, even in love, and rivalry usually operates as a stimulant to esteem even while it is acting as an obstacle to opportunity. So it had been with Agatha in her talk to Miss Lovill that morning concerning Oswald Winwood.

The Weymouth season was almost at an end, and but few loungers were to be seen on the parades, particularly at this early hour. Agatha looked over the iridescent sea, from which the veil of mist was slowly rising, at the white cliffs on the left, now just beginning to gleam in a weak sunlight, at the one solitary yacht in the midst, and still delayed her explanation. Her companion went on:

"The mist is vanishing, look, and I think it will be fine, after all. Shall you stay in Weymouth the whole day?"

"No. I am going to Portland by the twelve o'clock steamboat. But I return here again at six to go home by the seven o'clock train."

"I go to Maiden Newton by the same train, and then to Beaminster by the carrier."

"So do I."

"Not, I suppose, to walk from Beaminster to Cloton at that time in the evening?"

"I shall be met by somebody—but it is only a mile, you know."

That is how it all began; the continuation it is not necessary to detail at length. Both being somewhat young and impulsive, social forms were not scrupulously attended to. She discovered him to be on board the steamer as it ploughed the emerald waves of Weymouth Bay, although he had wished her a formal good-bye at the pier. He had altered his mind, he said, and thought that he would come to Portland, too. They returned by the same boat, walked the velvet sands till the train started, and entered a carriage together.

All this time, in the midst of her happiness, Agatha's conscience was sombre with guiltiness at not having yet told him of his mistake. It was true that he had not more than once or twice called her by Miss Lovill's name since the first greeting in the morning; but he certainly was still under the impression that she was Frances Lovill. Yet she perceived that though he had been led to her by another's name, it was her own proper person that he was so rapidly getting to love, and Agatha's feminine insight suggested blissfully to her that the face belonging to the name would after this encounter have no power to drag him away from the face of the day's romance.

They reached Maiden-Newton at dusk, and went to the inn door, where stood the old-fashioned hooded van which was to take them to Beaminster. It was on the point of starting, and when they had mounted in front the old man at once drove up the long hill leading out of the village.

"This has been a charming experience to me, Miss Lovill," Oswald said, as they sat side by side. "Accidental meetings have a way of making themselves pleasant when contrived ones quite fail to do it."

It was absolutely necessary to confess this time, though all her bliss were at once destroyed.

"I am not really Miss Lovill!" she faltered.

"What! not the young lady—and are you really not Frances Lovill?" he exclaimed, in surprise.

"O forgive me, Mr Winwood! I have wanted so to tell you of your mistake; indeed I have, all day—but I couldn't—and it is so wicked and wrong of me! I am only poor Agatha Pollin, at the mill."

"But why couldn't you tell me?"

"Because I was afraid that if I did you would go away from me and not care for me any more, and I l-l-love you so dearly!"

The carrier being on foot beside the horse, the van being so dark, and Oswald's feelings being rather warm, he could not for his life avoid kissing her there and then.

"Well," he said, "it doesn't matter; you are yourself anyhow. It is you I like, and nobody else in the world—not the name. But, you know, I was really looking for Miss Lovill this morning. I saw the back of her head yesterday, and I have often heard how very good-looking she is. Ah! suppose you had been she. I wonder—"

He did not complete the sentence. The driver mounted again, touched the horse with the whip, and they jogged on.

"You forgive me?" she said.

"Entirely—absolutely—the reason justified everything. How strange that you should have been caring deeply for me, and I ignorant of it all the time!"

They descended into Beaminster and alighted, Oswald handing her down. They had not moved from the spot when another female figure also alighted, dropped her fare into the carrier's hand, and glided away.

"Who is that?" said Oswald to the carrier. "Why, I thought we were the only passengers!"

"What?" said the carrier, who was rather stupid.

"Who is that woman?"

"Miss Lovill, of Cloton. She altered her mind about staying at Beaminster, and is come home again."

" Oh!" said Agatha, almost sinking to the earth. "She has heard it all. What shall I do, what shall I do?"

"Never mind it a bit," said Oswald.

II

The mill stood beside the village high-road, from which it was separated by the stream, the latter forming also the boundary of the mill garden, orchard, and paddock on that side. A visitor crossed a little wood bridge embedded in oozy, aquatic growths, and found himself in a space where usually stood a waggon laden with sacks, surrounded by a number of bright-feathered fowls.

It was now, however, just dusk, but the mill was not closed, a stripe of light stretching as usual from the open door across the front, across the river, across the road, into the hedge beyond. On the bridge, which was aside from the line of light, a young man and girl stood talking together. Soon they moved a little way apart, and then it was apparent that their right hands were joined. In receding one from the other they began to swing their arms gently backward and forward between them.

"Come a little way up the lane, Agatha, since it is the last time," he said. "I don't like parting here. You know your uncle does not object."

"He doesn't object because he knows nothing to object to," she whispered. And they both then contemplated the fine, stalwart figure of the said uncle, who could be seen moving about inside the mill, illuminated by the candle, and circumscribed by a faint halo of flour, and hindered by the whirr of the mill from hearing anything so gentle as lovers' talk.

Oswald had not relinquished her hand, and, submitting herself to a bondage she appeared to love better than freedom, Agatha followed him across the bridge, and they went down the lane engaged in the low, sad talk common to all such cases, interspersed with remarks peculiar to their own.

"It is nothing so fearful to contemplate," he said. "Many live there for years in a state of rude health, and return home in the same happy condition. So shall I."

"I hope you will."

"But aren't you glad I am going? It is better to do well in India than badly here. Say you are glad, dearest; it will fortify me when I am gone."

"I am glad," she murmured faintly. "I mean I am glad in my mind. I don't think that in my heart I am glad."

"Thanks to Macaulay, of honoured memory, I have as good a chance as the best of them!" he said, with ardour. "What a great thing competitive examination is; it will put good men in good places, and make inferior men move lower down; all bureaucratic jobbery will be swept away."

"What's bureaucratic, Oswald?"

"Oh! that's what they call it, you know. It is—well, I don't exactly know what it is. I know this, that it is the name of what I hate, and that it isn't competitive examination."

"At any rate it is a very bad thing," she said, conclusively.

"Very bad, indeed; you may take my word for that."

Then the parting scene began, in the dark, under the heavy-headed trees which shut out sky and stars. "And since I shall be in London till the Spring," he remarked, "the parting doesn't seem so bad—so all at once. Perhaps you may come to London before the Spring, Agatha."

"I may; but I don't think I shall."

"We must hope on all the same. Then there will be the examination, and then I shall know my fate."

"I hope you'll fail!—there, I've said it; I couldn't help it, Oswald!" she exclaimed, bursting out crying. "You would come home again then!"

"How can you be so disheartening and wicked, Agatha! I—I didn't expect—"

"No, no; I don't wish it; I wish you to be best, top, very very best!" she said. "I didn't mean the other; indeed, dear Oswald, I didn't. And will you be sure to come to me when you are rich? Sure to come?"

"If I'm on this earth I'll come home and marry you."

And then followed the good-bye.

III

In the Spring came the examination. One morning a newspaper directed by Oswald was placed in her hands, and she opened it to find it was a copy of the *Times*. In the middle of the sheet, in the most conspicuous place, in the excellent neighbourhood of the leading articles, was a list of names, and the first on the list was Oswald Winwood. Attached to his name, as showing where he was educated, was the simple title of some obscure little academy, while underneath came public school and college men in shoals. Such a case occurs sometimes, and it occurred then.

How Agatha clapped her hands! for her selfish wish to have him in England at any price, even that of failure, had been but a paroxysm of the wretched parting, and was now quite extinct. Circumstances combined to hinder another meeting between them before his departure, and, accordingly, making up her mind to the inevitable in a way which would have done honour to an older head, she fixed her mental vision on that sunlit future—far away, yet always nearing—and contemplated its probabilities with a firm hope.

At length he had arrived in India, and now Agatha had only to work and wait; and the former made the latter more easy. In her spare hours she would wander about the river brinks and into the coppices, and there weave thoughts of him by processes that young women understand so well. She kept a diary, and in this, since there were few events to chronicle in her daily life, she sketched the changes of the landscape, noted the arrival and departure of birds of passage, the times of storms and foul weather—all which information, being mixed up with her life and taking colour from it, she sent as scraps in her letters to him, deriving most of her enjoyment in contemplating his.

Oswald, on his part, corresponded very regularly. Knowing the days of the Indian mail, she would go at such times to meet the post-man in early morning, and to her unvarying inquiry, "A letter for me?" it was seldom, indeed, that there came a disappointing answer. Thus the season passed, and Oswald told her he should be a judge some day, with many other details, which, in her mind, were viewed chiefly in their bearing on the grand consummation—that he was to come home and marry her.

Meanwhile, as the girl grew older and more womanly, the woman whose name she had once stolen for a day grew more of an old maid, and showed symptoms of fading. One day Agatha's uncle, who, though still a handsome man in the prime of life, was a widower with four children, to whom she acted the part of eldest sister, told Agatha that Frances Lovill was about to become his second wife.

"Well!" said Agatha, and thought, "What an end for a beauty!"

And yet it was all reasonable enough, notwithstanding that Miss Lovill might have looked a little higher. Agatha knew that this step would produce great alterations in the small household of Cloton Mill, and the idea of having as aunt and ruler the woman to whom she was in some sense indebted for a lover, affected Agatha with a slight thrill of dread. Yet nothing had ever been spoken between the two women to show

that Frances had heard, much less resented, the explanation
in the van on that night of the return from Weymouth.

IV

On a certain day old farmer Lovill called. He was of the
same family as Frances, though their relationship was distant.
A considerable business in corn had been done from time to
time between miller and farmer, but the latter had seldom
called at Pollin's house. He was a bachelor, or he would
probably never have appeared in this history, and he was
mostly full of a boyish merriment rare in one of his years. To-
day his business with the miller had been so imperative as to
bring him in person, and it was evident from their talk in the
mill that the matter was payment. Perhaps ten minutes had
been spent in serious converse when the old farmer turned
away from the door, and, without saying good-morning,
went toward the bridge. This was unusual for a man of his
temperament.

He was an old man—really and fairly old—sixty-five years of
age at least. He was not exactly feeble, but he found a stick
useful when walking in a high wind. His eyes were not yet
bleared, but in their corners was occasionally a moisture like
majolica glaze—entirely absent in youth. His face was not
shrivelled, but there were unmistakable puckers in some
places. And hence the old gentleman, unmarried, substantial,
and cheery as he was, was not doted on by the young girls of
Cloton as he had been by their mothers in former time. Each
year his breast impended a little further over his toes, and his
chin a little further over his breast, and in proportion as he
turned down his nose to earth did pretty females turn up
theirs at him. They might have liked him as a friend had he
not shown the abnormal wish to be regarded as a lover. To
Agatha Pollin this aged youth was positively distasteful.

It happened that at the hour of Mr Lovill's visit Agatha was
bending over the pool at the mill head, sousing some white
fabric in the water. She was quite unconscious of the farmer's
presence near her, and continued dipping and rinsing in the
idlest phase possible to industry, until she remained quite

still, holding the article under the water, and looking at her own reflection within it. The river, though gliding slowly, was yet so smooth that to the old man on the bridge she existed in duplicate—the pouting mouth, the little nose, the frizzed hair, the bit of blue ribbon, as they existed over the surface, being but a degree more distinct than the same features beneath.

"What a pretty maid!" said the old man to himself. He walked up the margin of the stream, and stood beside her.

"Oh!" said Agatha, starting with surprise. In her flurry she relinquished the article she had been rinsing, which slowly turned over and sank deeper, and made toward the hatch of the mill-wheel.

"There—it will get into the wheel, and be torn to pieces!" she exclaimed.

"I'll fish it out with my stick, my dear," said Farmer Lovill, and kneeling cautiously down he began hooking and crooking with all his might. "What thing is it—of much value?"

"Yes; it is my best one!" she said involuntarily.

"It—what is the it?"

"Only something—a piece of linen." Just then the farmer hooked the endangered article, and dragging it out, held it high on his walking-stick—dripping, but safe.

"Why, it is a chemise!" he said.

The girl looked red, and instead of taking it from the end of the stick, turned away.

"Hee-hee!" laughed the ancient man. "Well, my dear, there's nothing to be ashamed of that I can see in owning to such a necessary and innocent article of clothing. There, I'll put it on the grass for you, and you shall take it when I am gone."

Then Farmer Lovill retired, lifting his fingers privately, to express amazement on a small scale, and murmuring, "What a nice young thing! Well, to be sure. Yes, a nice child—young woman rather; indeed, a marriageable woman, come to that; of course she is."

The doting old person thought of the young one all this day in a way that the young one did not think of him. He thought so much about her, that in the evening, instead of going to bed, he hobbled privately out by the back door into the moonlight, crossed a field or two, and stood in the lane, looking at the mill—not more in the hope of getting a glimpse of the attractive girl inside than for the pleasure of realizing that she was there.

A light moved within, came nearer, and ascended. The staircase window was large, and he saw his goddess going up with a candle in her hand. This was indeed worth coming for. He feared he was seen by her as well, yet hoped otherwise in the interests of his passion, for she came and drew down the window blind, completely shutting out his gaze. The light vanished from this part, and reappeared in a window a little further on.

The lover drew nearer; this, then, was her bedroom. He rested vigorously upon his stick, and straightening his back nearly to a perpendicular, turned up his amorous face.

She came to the window, paused, then opened it.

"Bess its deary-eary heart! it is going to speak to me!" said the old man, moistening his lips, resting still more desperately upon his stick, and straightening himself yet an inch taller. "She saw me then!"

Agatha, however, made no sign; she was bent on a far different purpose. In a box on her window-sill was a row of mignonette, which had been sadly neglected since her lover's departure, and she began to water it, as if inspired by a sudden recollection of its condition. She poured from her water-jug slowly along the plants, and then, to her astonishment, discerned her elderly friend below.

"A rude old thing!" she murmured.

Directing the spout of the jug over the edge of the box, and looking in another direction that it might appear to be an accident, she allowed the stream to spatter down upon her admirer's face, neck, and shoulders, causing him to beat a quick retreat. Then Agatha serenely closed the window, and drew down that blind also.

"Ah! she did not see me; it was evident she did not, and I was mistaken!" said the trembling farmer, hastily wiping his face, and mopping out the rills trickling down within his shirt-

collar as far as he could get at them, which was by no means
to their termination. "A pretty creature, and so innocent, too!
Watering her flowers; how I like a girl who is fond of flowers!
I wish she had spoken, and I wish I was younger. Yes, I know
what I'd do with the little mouse!" And the old gentleman
tapped emotionally upon the ground with his stick.

V

"Agatha, I suppose you have heard the news from somebody else by this time?" said her Uncle Humphrey some two
or three weeks later. "I mean what Farmer Lovill has been
talking to me about."

"No, indeed," said Agatha.

"He wants to marry ye if you be willing."

"O, I never!" said Agatha with dismay. "That old man!"

"Old? He's hale and hearty; and, what's more, a man very
well to do. He'll make you a comfortable home, and dress ye
up like a doll, and I'm sure you'll like that, or you baint a
woman of woman born."

"But it *can't be*, uncle!—other reasons—"

"What reasons?"

"Why, I've promised Oswald Winwood—years ago!"

"Promised Oswald Winwood years ago, have you?"

"Yes; surely you know it, Uncle Humphrey. And we write to
one another regularly."

"Well, I can just call to mind that ye are always scribbling
and getting letters from somewhere. Let me see—where is he
now? I quite forget."

"In India still. Is it possible that you don't know about him,
and what a great man he's getting? There are paragraphs
about him in our paper very often. The last was about some
translation from Hindostani that he'd been making. And he's
coming home for me."

"I very much question it. Lovill will marry you at once, he
says."

"Indeed, he will not."

"Well, I don't want to force you to do anything against your
will, Agatha, but this is how the matter stands. You know I am

a little behindhand in my dealings will Lovill—nothing serious, you know, if he gives me time—but I want to be free of him quite in order to go to Australia."

"Australia!"

"Yes. There's nothing to be done here. I don't know what business is coming to—can't think. But never mind that; this is the point: if you will marry Farmer Lovill, he offers to clear off the debt, and there will no longer be any delay about my own marriage; in short, away I can go. I mean to, and there's an end on't."

"What, and leave me at home alone?"

"Yes, but a married woman, of course. You see the children are getting big now. John is twelve and Nathaniel ten, and the girls are growing fast, and when I am married again I shall hardly want you to keep house for me—in fact, I must reduce our family as much as possible. So that if you could bring your mind to think of Farmer Lovill as a husband, why, 'twould be a great relief to me after having the trouble and expense of bringing you up. If I can in that way edge out of Lovill's debt I shall have a nice bit of money in hand."

"But Oswald will be richer even than Mr Lovill," said Agatha, through her tears.

"Yes, yes. But Oswald is not here, nor is he likely to be. How silly you be."

"But he will come, and soon, with his eleven hundred a year and all."

"I wish to Heaven he would. I'm sure he might have you."

"Now, you promise that, uncle, don't you?" she said, brightening. "If he comes with plenty of money before you want to leave, he shall marry me, and nobody else."

"Ay, if he comes. But, Agatha, no nonsense. Just think of what I've been telling you. And at any rate be civil to Farmer Lovill. If this man Winwood were here and asked for ye, and married ye, that would be a very different thing. I do mind now that I saw something about him and his doings in the papers; but he's a fine gentleman by this time, and won't think of stooping to a girl like you. So you'd better take the one who is ready; old men's darlings fare very well as the world goes. We shall be off in nine months, mind, that I've settled. And you must be a married woman afore that time, and wish us good-bye upon your husband's arm."

"That old arm couldn't support me."

"And if you don't agree to have him, you'll take a couple of hundred pounds out of my pocket; you'll ruin my chances altogether—that's the long and the short of it."

Saying which the gloury man turned his back upon her, and his footsteps became drowned in the rumble of the mill.

VI

Nothing so definite was said to her again on the matter for some time. The old yeoman hovered round her, but, knowing the result of the interview between Agatha and her uncle, he forbore to endanger his suit by precipitancy. But one afternoon he could not avoid saying, "Aggie, when may I speak to you upon a serious subject?"

"Next week," she replied, instantly.

He had not been prepared for such a ready answer, and it startled him almost as much as it pleased him. Had he known the cause of it his emotions might have been different. Agatha, with all the womanly strategy she was capable of, had written post-haste to Oswald after the conversation with her uncle, and told him of the dilemma. At the end of the present week his answer, if he replied with his customary punctuality, would be sure to come. Fortified with his letter she thought she could meet the old man. Oswald she did not doubt.

Nor had she any reason to. The letter came prompt to the day. It was short, tender, and to the point. Events had shaped themselves so fortunately that he was able to say he would return and marry her before the time named for the family's departure for Queensland.

She danced about for joy. But there was a postscript to the effect that she might as well keep this promise a secret for the present, if she conveniently could, that his intention might not become a public talk in Cloton. Agatha knew that he was a rising and aristocratic young man, and saw at once how proper this was.

So she met Mr Lovill with a simple flat refusal, at which her uncle was extremely angry, and her disclosure to him afterward of the arrival of the letter went but a little way in pacifying him. Farmer Lovill would put in upon him for the debt, he said, unless she could manage to please him for a short time.

"I don't want to please him," said Agatha. "It is wrong to encourage him if I don't mean it."

"Will you behave toward him as the Parson advises you?"

The Parson! That was a new idea, and, from her uncle, unexpected.

"I will agree to what Mr Davids advises about my mere daily behaviour before Oswald comes, but nothing more," she said. "That is, I will if you know for certain that he's a good man, who fears God and keeps the commandments."

"Mr Davids fears God, for sartin, for he never ventures to name Him outside the pulpit; and as for the commandments, 'tis knowed how he swore at the church-restorers for taking them away from the chancel."

"Uncle, you always jest when I am serious."

"Well, well! at any rate his advice on a matter of this sort is good."

"How is it you think of referring me to him?" she asked, in perplexity; "you so often speak slightingly of him."

"Oh—well," said Humphrey, with a faintly perceptible desire to parry the question, "I have spoken roughly about him once now and then; but perhaps I was wrong. Will ye go?"

"Yes, I don't mind," she said, languidly.

When she reached the Vicar's study Agatha began her story with reserve, and said nothing about the correspondence with Oswald; yet an intense longing to find a friend and confidant led her to indulge in more feeling than she had intended, and as a finale she wept. The genial incumbent, however, remained quite cool, the secret being that his heart was involved a little in another direction—one, perhaps, not quite in harmony with Agatha's interests—of which more anon.

"So the difficulty is," he said to her, "how to behave in this trying time of waiting for Mr Winwood, that you may please parties all round and give offence to none."

"Yes, Sir, that's it," sobbed Agatha, wondering how he could have realized her position so readily. "And uncle wants to go to Australia."

"One thing is certain," said the Vicar; "you must not hurt the feelings of Mr Lovill. Wonderfully sensitive man—a man I respect much as a godly doer."

"Do you, Sir?"

"I do. His earnestness is remarkable."

"Yes, in courting."

"The cue is: treat Mr Lovill gently—gently as a babe! Love opposed, especially an old man's, gets all the stronger. It is your policy to give him seeming encouragement, and so let his feelings expend themselves and die away."

"How am I to? To advise is so easy."

"Not by acting untruthfully, of course. You say your lover is sure to come back before your uncle leaves England."

"I know he will."

"Then pacify old Mr Lovill in this way: Tell him you'll marry him when your uncle wants to go, if Winwood doesn't come for you before that time. That will quite content Mr Lovill, for he doesn't in the least expect Oswald to return, and you'll see that his persecution will cease at once."

"Yes; I'll agree to it," said Agatha promptly.

Mr Davids had refrained from adding that neither did he expect Oswald to come, and hence his advice. Agatha on her part too refrained from stating the good reasons she had for the contrary expectation, and hence her assent. Without the last letter perhaps even her faith would hardly have been bold enough to allow this palpable driving of her into a corner.

"It would be as well to write Mr Lovill a little note, saying you agree to what I have advised," said the Parson evasively.

"I don't like writing."

"There's no harm. 'If Mr Winwood doesn't come I'll marry you,' &c. Poor Mr Lovill will be content, thinking Oswald will not come; you will be content, knowing he will come; your uncle will be content, being indifferent which of two rich men has you and relieves him of his difficulties. Then, if it's the will of Providence, you'll be left in peace. Here's a pen and ink; you can do it at once."

Thus tempted, Agatha wrote the note with a trembling hand. It really did seem upon the whole a nicely strategic thing to do in her present environed situation. Mr Davids took the note with the air of a man who did not wish to take it in the least, and placed it on the mantle-piece.

"I'll send it down to him by one of the children," said Aggy, looking wistfully at her note with a little feeling that she should like to have it back again.

"Oh, no, it is not necessary," said her pleasant adviser. He had rung the bell; the servant now came, and the note was sent off in a trice.

When Agatha got into the open air again her confidence returned, and it was with a mischievous sense of enjoyment that she considered how she was duping her persecutors by keeping secret Oswald's intention of a speedy return. If they only knew what a firm foundation she had for her belief in what they all deemed but an improbable contingency, what a life they would lead her; how the old man would worry her uncle for payment, and what general confusion there would be. Mr Davids' advice was very shrewd, she thought, and she was glad she had called upon him.

Old Lovill came that very afternoon. He was delighted, and danced a few bars of a hornpipe in entering the room. So lively was the antique boy that Agatha was rather alarmed at her own temerity when she considered what was the basis of his gaiety; wishing she could get from him some such writing as he had got from her, that the words of her promise might not in any way be tampered with, or the conditions ignored.

"I only accept you conditionally, mind," she anxiously said. "That is distinctly understood."

"Yes, yes," said the yeoman. "I am not so young as I was, little dear, and beggars musn't be choosers. With my ra-ta-ta—say, dear, shall it be the first of November?"

"It will really never be."

"But if he doesn't come, it shall be the first of November?" She slightly nodded her head.

"Clk!—I think she likes me!" said the old man aside to Aggy's uncle, which aside was distinctly heard by Aggy.

One of the younger children was in the room, drawing idly on a slate. Agatha at this moment took the slate from the child, and scribbled something on it.

"Now you must please me by just writing your name here," she said in a voice of playful indifference.

"What is it?" said Lovill, looking over and reading. "'If Oswald Winwood comes to marry Agatha Pollin before November, I agree to give her up to him without objection.' Well, that is cool for a young lady under six feet, upon my word—hee-hee!" He passed the slate to the miller, who read the writing and passed it back again.

"Sign—just in courtesy," she coaxed.

"I don't see why—"

"I do it to test your faith in me; and now I find you have none. Don't you think I should have rubbed it out instantly? Ah, perhaps I can be obstinate too!"

He wrote his name then. "Now I have done it, and shown my faith," he said, and at once raised his fingers as if to rub it out again. But with hands that moved like lightning she snatched up the slate, flew up stairs, locked it in her box, and came down again.

"Souls of men—that's sharp practice," said the old gentleman.

"Oh, it is only a whim—a mere memorandum," said she. "You had my promise, but I had not yours."

"Ise wants my slate," cried the child.

"I'll buy you a new one, dear," said Agatha, and soothed her.

When she had left the room old Lovill spoke to her uncle somewhat uneasily of the event, which, childish as it had been, discomposed him for the moment.

"Oh, that's nothing," said Miller Pollin assuringly; "only play—only play. She's a mere child in nater, even now, and she did it only to tease ye. Why, she overheard your whisper that you thought she liked ye, and that was her playful way of punishing ye for your confidence. You'll have to put up with these worries, farmer. Considering the difference in your ages, she is sure to play pranks. You'll get to like 'em in time."

"Ay, ay, faith, so I shall! I was always a Turk for sprees!—eh, Pollin? hee-hee!" And the suitor was merry again.

VII

Her life was certainly much pleasanter now. The old man treated her well, and was almost silent on the subject nearest his heart. She was obliged to be very stealthy in receiving letters from Oswald, and on this account was bound to meet the postman, let the weather be what it would. These transactions were easily kept secret from people out of the house, but it was a most difficult task to hide her movements from her uncle. And one day brought utter failure.

"How's this—out already, Agatha?" he said, meeting her in the lane at dawn on a foggy morning. She was actually reading a letter just received, and there was no disguising the truth.

"I've been for a letter from Oswald."

"Well, but that won't do. Since he don't come for ye, ye must think no more about him."

"But he's coming in six weeks. He tells me all about it in this very letter."

"What—really to marry you?" said her uncle incredulously.

"Yes, certainly."

"But I hear that he's wonderfully well off."

"Of course he is; that's why he's coming. He'll agree in a moment to be your surety for the debt to Mr Lovill."

"Has he said so?"

"Not yet; but he will."

"I'll believe it when I see him and he tells me so. It is very odd, if he means so much, that he hev never wrote a line to me."

"We thought—you would force me to have the other at once if he wrote to you," she murmured.

"Not I, if he comes rich. But it is rather a cock-and-bull story, and since he didn't make up his mind before now, I can't say I be much in his favour. Agatha, you had better not say a word to Mr Lovill about these letters; it will make things deuced unpleasant if he hears of such goings on. You are to reckon yourself bound by your word. Oswald won't hold water, I'm afeard. But I'll be fair. If he do come, proves his income, marries ye willy-nilly, I'll let it be, and the old man and I must do as we can. But barring that—you keep your promise to the letter."

"That's what it will be, uncle. Oswald will come."

"Write you must not. Lovill will smell it out, and he'll be sharper than you will like. 'Tis not to be supposed that you are to send love-letters to one man as if nothing was going to happen between ye and another man. The first of November is drawing nearer every day. And be sure and keep this a secret from Lovill for your own sake."

The more clearly that Agatha began to perceive the entire contrast of expectation as to issue between herself and the other party to the covenant, the more alarmed she became. She had not anticipated such a narrowing of courses as had occurred. A malign influence seemed to be at work without any visible human agency. The critical time drew nearer, and, though no ostensible preparation for the wedding was made, it was evident to all that Lovill was painting and papering his house for somebody's reception. He made a lawn where there had existed a nook of refuse; he bought furniture for a woman's room. The greatest horror was that he insisted upon her taking his arm one day, and there being no help for it she assented, though her distaste was unutterable. She felt the skinny arm through his sleeve, saw over the wry shoulders, looked upon the knobby feet, and shuddered. What if Oswald should not come; the time for her uncle's departure was really getting near. When she reached home she ran up to her bedroom.

On recovering from her dreads a little, Agatha looked from the window. The deaf lad John, who assisted in the mill, was quietly glancing toward her, and a gleam of friendship passed over his kindly face as he caught sight of her form. This reminded her that she had, after all, some sort of friend close at hand. The lad knew pretty well how events stood in Agatha's life, and he was always ready to do on her part whatever lay in his power. Agatha felt stronger, and resolved to bear up.

VIII

Heavens! how anxious she was! It actually wanted only ten days to the first of November, and no new letter had come from Oswald.

Her uncle was married, and Frances was in the house, and the preliminary steps for emigration to Queensland had been taken. Agatha surreptitiously obtained newspapers, scanned the Indian shipping news till her eyes ached, but all to no purpose, for she knew nothing either of route or vessel by which Oswald would return. He had mentioned nothing more than the month of his coming, and she had no way of making that single scrap of information the vehicle for obtaining more.

"In ten days, Agatha," said the old farmer. "There is to be no show or fuss of any kind; the wedding will be quite private, in consideration of your feelings and wishes. We'll go to church as if we were taking a morning walk, and nobody will be there to disturb you. Tweedledee!" He held up his arm and crossed it with his walking-stick, as if he were playing the fiddle, at the same time cutting a caper.

"He will come, and then I shan't be able to marry you, even th-th-though I may wish to ever so much," she faltered, shivering. "I have promised him, and I *must* have him, you know, and you have agreed to let me."

"Yes, yes," said Farmer Lovill, pleasantly. "But that's a misfortune you need not fear at all, my dear; he won't come at this late day and compel you to marry him in spite of your attachment to me. But, ah—it is only a joke to tease me, you little rogue! Your uncle says so."

"Agatha, come, cheer up, and think no more of that fellow," said her uncle when they chanced to be alone together. "'Tis ridiculous, you know. We always knew he wouldn't come."

The day passed. The sixth morning came, the noon, the evening. The fifth day came and vanished. Still no sound of Oswald. His friends now lived in London, and there was not a soul in the parish, save herself, that he corresponded with, or one to whom she could apply in such a delicate matter as this.

It was the evening before her wedding-day, and she was standing alone in the gloom of her bedchamber looking out on the plot in front of the mill. She saw a white figure moving below, and knew him to be the deaf miller lad, her friend. A sudden impulse animated Agatha. She had been making desperate attempts during the last two days to like the old man, and, since Oswald did not come, to marry him without further resistance, for the sheer good of the family of her uncle, to whom she was indeed indebted for much; but had only got so far in her efforts as not to positively hate him. Now rebelliousness came unsought. The lad knew her case, and upon this fact she acted. Gliding down stairs, she beckoned to him, and, as they stood together in the stream of light from the open mill door, she communicated her directions, partly by signs, partly by writing, for it was difficult to speak to him without being heard all over the premises.

He looked in her face with a glance of confederacy, and said that he understood it all. Upon this they parted.

The old man was at her house that evening, and when she withdrew wished her good-bye "for the present" with a dozen smiles of meaning. Agatha had retired early, leaving him still there, and when she reached her room, instead of looking at the new dress she was supposed to be going to wear on the morrow, busied herself in making up a small bundle of ordinary articles of clothing. Then she extinguished her light, lay down upon the bed without undressing, and waited for a preconcerted time.

In what seemed to her the dead of night, but which she concluded must be the time agreed upon—half-past five—there was a slight noise as of gravel being thrown against her window. Agatha jumped up, put on her bonnet and cloak, took up her bundle, and went down stairs without a light. At the bottom she slipped on her boots, and passed amid the chirping crickets to the door. It was unbarred. Her uncle, then, had risen, as she had half expected, and it necessitated a little more caution. The morning was dark as a cavern, not a star being visible; but knowing the bearings well, she went cautiously and in silence to the mill door. A faint light shone from inside, and the form of the mill-cart appeared without, the horse ready harnessed to it. Agatha did not see John for the moment, but concluded that he was in the mill with her uncle, who had just at this minute started the wheel for the day. She at once slipped into the vehicle and under the tilt, pulling some empty sacks over, as it had been previously agreed that she should do, to avoid the risk of discovery. After a few minutes of suspense she heard John coming from under the wall, where he had apparently been standing and watching her safely in, and mounting in front, away he drove at a walking pace.

Her scheme had been based upon the following particulars of mill business: Thrice a week it was the regular custom for John and another young man to start early in the morning, each with a horse and covered cart, and go in different directions to customers a few miles off, the carts being laden overnight. All that she had asked John to do this morning was to take her with him to a railway station about ten miles distant, where she might safely wait for an up train.

How will John act on returning—what will he say—how will he excuse himself? she thought as they jogged along. "John!" she said, meaning to ask him about these things; but he did not hear, and she was too confused and weary after her wakeful night to be able to think consecutively on any subject. But the relief of finding that her uncle did not look into the cart caused a delicious lull in her, and while listlessly watching the dark gray sky through the triangular opening between the curtains at the fore part of the tilt, and John's elbow projecting from the folds of one of them, showing where he was sitting on the outside, she fell asleep.

She awoke after a short interval—everything was just the same—jog, jog, on they went; there was the dim slit between the curtains in front, and, after slightly wondering that John had not troubled himself to see that she was comfortable, she dozed again. Thus Agatha remained until she had a clear consciousness of the stopping of the cart. It aroused her, and looking at once through a small opening at the back, she perceived in the dim dawn that they were turning right about; in another moment the horse was proceeding on the way back again.

"John, what are you doing?" she exclaimed, jumping up, and pulling aside the curtain which parted them.

John did not turn.

"How fearfully deaf he is!" she thought, "and how odd he looks behind, and he hangs forward as if he were asleep. His hair is snow-white with flour; does he never clean it, then?" She crept across the sacks, and slapped him on the shoulder. John turned then.

"Hee-hee, my dear!" said the blithe old gentleman; and the moisture of his aged eye glistened in the dawning light, as he turned and looked into her horrified face. "It is all right; I am John, and I have given ye a nice morning's airing to refresh ye for the uncommon duties of to-day; and now we are going back for the ceremony—hee-hee!"

He wore a miller's smock-frock on this interesting occasion, and had been enabled to play the part of John in the episode by taking the second cart and horse and anticipating by an hour the real John in calling her.

Agatha sank backward. How on earth had he discovered the scheme of escape so readily; he, an old and by no means suspicious man? But what mattered a solution! Hope was crushed, and her rebellion was at an end. Agatha was awakened from thought by another stopping of the horse, and they were again at the mill-door.

She dimly recognized her uncle's voice speaking in anger to her when the old farmer handed her out of the vehicle, and heard the farmer reply, merrily, that girls would be girls and have their freaks, that it didn't matter, and that it was a pleasant jest on this auspicious morn. For himself, there was nothing he had enjoyed all his life so much as a practical joke which did no harm. Then she had a sensation of being told to go into the house, have some food, and dress for her marriage with Mr Lovill, as she had promised to do on that day.

All this she did, and at eleven o'clock became the wife of the old man.

When Agatha was putting on her bonnet in the dusk that evening, for she would not illuminate her ghastly face by a candle, a rustling came against the door. Agatha turned. Her uncle's wife, Frances, was looking into the room, and Agatha could just discern upon her aunt's form the blue cloak which had ruled her destiny.

The sight was almost more than she could bear. If, as seemed likely, this effect was intended, the trick was certainly successful. Frances did not speak a word.

Then Agatha said in quiet irony, and with no evidence whatever of regret, sadness, or surprise at what the act revealed: "And so you told Mr Lovill of my flight this morning, and set him on the track? It would be amusing to know how you found out my plan, for he never could have done it by himself, poor old darling."

"Oh, I was a witness of your arrangement with John last night—that was all, my dear," said her aunt pleasantly. "I mentioned it then to Mr Lovill, and helped him to his joke of hindering you. . . . You remember the van, Agatha, and how you made use of my name on that occasion, years ago, now?"

"Yes, and did you hear our talk that night? I always fancied otherwise."

"I heard it all. It was fun to you; what do you think it was to me—fun, too?—to lose the man I longed for, and to become the wife of a man I care not an atom about?"

"Ah, no. And how you struggled to get him away from me, dear aunt!"

"And have done it, too."

"Not you, exactly. The Parson and fate."

"Parson Davids kindly persuaded you, because I kindly persuaded him, and persuaded your uncle to send you to him. Mr Davids is an old admirer of mine. Now do you see a wheel within a wheel, Agatha?"

Calmness was almost insupportable by Agatha now, but she managed to say: "Of course you have kept back letters from Oswald to me?"

"No, I have not done that," said Frances. "But I told Oswald, who landed at Southampton last night, and called here in great haste at seven this morning, that you had gone out for an early drive with the man you were to marry to-day, and that it might cause confusion if he remained. He looked very pale, and went away again at once to catch the next London train, saying something about having been prevented by a severe illness from sailing at the time he had promised and intended for the last twelvemonth."

The bride, though nearly slain by the news, would not flinch in the presence of her adversary. Stilling her quivering flesh, she said smiling: "That information is deeply interesting, but does not concern me at all, for I am my husband's darling now, you know, and I wouldn't make the dear man jealous for the world." And she glided down stairs to the chaise.

THE THIEVES WHO
COULDN'T HELP SNEEZING

Many years ago, when oak-trees now past their prime were about as large as elderly gentlemen's walking-sticks, there lived in Wessex a yeoman's son, whose name was Hubert. He was about fourteen years of age, and was as remarkable for his candour and lightness of heart as for his physical courage, of which, indeed, he was a little vain.

One cold Christmas Eve his father, having no other help at hand, sent him on an important errand to a small town several miles from home. He travelled on horseback, and was detained by the business till a late hour of the evening. At last, however, it was completed; he returned to the inn, the horse was saddled, and he started on his way. His journey homeward lay through the Vale of Blackmore, a fertile but somewhat lonely district, with heavy clay roads and crooked lanes. In those days, too, a great part of it was thickly wooded.

It must have been about nine o'clock when, riding along amid the overhanging trees upon his stout-legged cob Jerry, and singing a Christmas carol, to be in harmony with the season, Hubert fancied that he heard a noise among the boughs. This recalled to his mind that the spot he was travers-ing bore an evil name. Men had been waylaid there. He looked at Jerry, and wished he had been of any other colour than light grey; for on this account the docile animal's form was visible even here in the dense shade. "What do I care?" he said aloud, after a few minutes of reflection. "Jerry's legs are too nimble to allow any highwayman to come near me."

"Ha! ha! indeed," was said in a deep voice; and the next moment a man darted from the thicket on his right hand, another man from the thicket on his left hand, and another from a tree-trunk a few yards ahead. Hubert's bridle was seized, he was pulled from his horse, and although he struck out with all his might, as a brave boy would naturally do, he was overpowered. His arms were tied behind him, his legs bound tightly together, and he was thrown into the ditch. The

robbers, whose faces he could now dimly perceive to be arti-
ficially blackened, at once departed, leading off the horse.

As soon as Hubert had a little recovered himself, he found
that by great exertion he was able to extricate his legs from
the cord; but, in spite of every endeavour, his arms remained
bound as fast as before. All, therefore, that he could do was to
rise to his feet and proceed on his way with his arms behind
him, and trust to chance for getting them unfastened. He
knew that it would be impossible to reach home on foot that
night, and in such a condition; but he walked on. Owing to
the confusion which this attack caused in his brain, he lost his
way, and would have been inclined to lie down and rest till
morning among the dead leaves had he not known the danger of sleeping without wrappers in a frost so severe. So he
wandered further onwards, his arms wrung and numbed by
the cord which pinioned him, and his heart aching for the
loss of poor Jerry, who never had been known to kick, or bite,
or show a single vicious habit. He was not a little glad when he
discerned through the trees a distant light. Towards this he
made his way, and presently found himself in front of a large
mansion with flanking wings, gables, and towers, the battle-
ments and chimneys showing their shapes against the stars.

All was silent; but the door stood wide open, it being from
this door that the light shone which had attracted him. On
entering he found himself in a vast apartment arranged as a
dining-hall, and brilliantly illuminated. The walls were covered with a great deal of dark wainscoting, formed into
moulded panels, carvings, closet-doors, and the usual fittings
of a house of that kind. But what drew his attention most was
the large table in the midst of the hall, upon which was spread
a sumptuous supper, as yet untouched. Chairs were placed
around, and it appeared as if something had occurred to
interrupt the meal just at the time when all were ready to
begin.

Even had Hubert been so inclined, he could not have eaten
in his helpless state, unless by dipping his mouth into the
dishes, like a pig or cow. He wished first to obtain assistance;
and was about to penetrate further into the house for that
purpose when he heard hasty footsteps in the porch and the

words, "Be quick!" uttered in the deep voice which had reached him when he was dragged from the horse. There was only just time for him to dart under the table before three men entered the dining-hall. Peeping from beneath the hanging edges of the tablecloth, he perceived that their faces, too, were blackened, which at once removed any remaining doubts he may have felt that these were the same thieves.

"Now, then," said the first—the man with the deep voice— "let us hide ourselves. They will all be back again in a minute. That was a good trick to get them out of the house—eh?"

"Yes. You well imitated the cries of a man in distress," said the second.

"Excellently," said the third.

"But they will soon find out that it was a false alarm. Come, where shall we hide? It must be some place we can stay in for two or three hours, till all are in bed and asleep. Ah! I have it. Come this way! I have learnt that the further closet is not opened once in a twelvemonth; it will serve our purpose exactly."

The speaker advanced into a corridor which led from the hall. Creeping a little farther forward, Hubert could discern that the closet stood at the end, facing the dining-hall. The thieves entered it, and closed the door. Hardly breathing, Hubert glided forward, to learn a little more of their intention, if possible; and, coming close, he could hear the robbers whispering about the different rooms where the jewels, plate, and other valuables of the house were kept, which they plainly meant to steal.

They had not been long in hiding when a gay chattering of ladies and gentlemen was audible on the terrace without. Hubert felt that it would not do to be caught prowling about the house, unless he wished to be taken for a robber himself; and he slipped softly back to the hall, out at the door, and stood in a dark corner of the porch, where he could see everything without being himself seen. In a moment or two a whole troop of personages came gliding past him into the house. There were an elderly gentleman and lady, eight or nine young ladies, as many young men, besides half-a-dozen men-servants and maids. The mansion had apparently been quite emptied of its occupants.

"Now, children and young people, we will resume our meal," said the old gentleman. "What the noise could have been I cannot understand. I never felt so certain in my life that there was a person being murdered outside my door."

Then the ladies began saying how frightened they had been, and how they had expected an adventure, and how it had ended in nothing after all.

"Wait a while," said Hubert to himself. "You'll have adventure enough by-and-by, ladies."

It appeared that the young men and women were married sons and daughters of the old couple, who had come that day to spend Christmas with their parents.

The door was then closed, Hubert being left outside in the porch. He thought this a proper moment for asking their assistance; and, since he was unable to knock with his hands, began boldly to kick the door.

"Hullo! What disturbance are you making here?" said a footman who opened it; and, seizing Hubert by the shoulder, he pulled him into the dining-hall. "Here's a strange boy I have found making a noise in the porch, Sir Simon."

Everybody turned.

"Bring him forward," said Sir Simon, the old gentleman before mentioned. "What were you doing there, my boy?"

"Why, his arms are tied!" said one of the ladies.

"Poor fellow!" said another.

Hubert at once began to explain that he had been waylaid on his journey home, robbed of his horse, and mercilessly left in this condition by the thieves.

"Only to think of it!" exclaimed Sir Simon.

"That's a likely story," said one of the gentleman-guests, incredulously.

"Doubtful, hey?" asked Sir Simon.

"Perhaps he's a robber himself," suggested a lady.

"There is a curiously wild wicked look about him, certainly, now that I examine him closely," said the old mother.

Hubert blushed with shame; and, instead of continuing his story, and relating that robbers were concealed in the house, he doggedly held his tongue, and half resolved to let them find out their danger for themselves.

"Well, untie him," said Sir Simon. "Come, since it is Christmas Eve, we'll treat him well. Here, my lad; sit down in that empty seat at the bottom of the table, and make as good a meal as you can. When you have had your fill we will listen to more particulars of your story."

The feast then proceeded; and Hubert, now at liberty, was not at all sorry to join in. The more they eat and drank the merrier did the company become; the wine flowed freely, the logs flared up the chimney, the ladies laughed at the gentlemen's stories; in short, all went as noisily and as happily as a Christmas gathering in old times possibly could do.

Hubert, in spite of his hurt feelings at their doubts of his honesty, could not help being warmed both in mind and in body by the good cheer, the scene, and the example of hilarity set by his neighbours. At last he laughed as heartily at their stories and repartees as the old Baronet, Sir Simon, himself. When the meal was almost over one of the sons, who had drunk a little too much wine, after the manner of men in that century, said to Hubert, "Well, my boy, how are you? Can you take a pinch of snuff?" He held out one of the snuff-boxes which were then becoming common among young and old throughout the country.

"Thank you," said Hubert, accepting a pinch.

"Tell the ladies who you are, what you are made of, and what you can do," the young man continued, slapping Hubert upon the shoulder.

"Certainly," said our hero, drawing himself up, and thinking it best to put a bold face on the matter. "I am a travelling magician."

"Indeed!"

"What shall we hear next?"

"Can you call up spirits from the vasty deep, young wizard?"

"I can conjure up a tempest in a cupboard," Hubert replied.

"Ha—ha!" said the old Baronet, pleasantly rubbing his hands. "We must see this performance. Girls, don't go away: here's something to be seen."

"Not dangerous, I hope?" said the old lady.

Hubert rose from the table. "Hand me your snuff-box, please," he said to the young man who had made free with him. "And now," he continued, "without the least noise, follow me. If any of you speak it will break the spell."

They promised obedience. He entered the corridor, and, taking off his shoes, went on tiptoe to the closet door, the guests advancing in a silent group at a little distance behind him. Hubert next placed a stool in front of the door, and, by standing upon it, was tall enough to reach to the top. He then, just as noiselessly, poured all the snuff from the box along the upper edge of the door, and, with a few short puffs of breath, blew the snuff through the chink into the interior of the closet. He held up his finger to the assembly, that they might be silent.

"Dear me, what's that?" said the old lady, after a minute or two had elapsed.

A suppressed sneeze had come from inside the closet.

Hubert held up his finger again.

"How very singular," whispered Sir Simon. "This is most interesting."

Hubert took advantage of the moment to gently slide the bolt of the closet door into its place. "More snuff," he said, calmly.

"More snuff," said Sir Simon. Two or three gentlemen passed their boxes, and the contents were blown in at the top of the closet. Another sneeze, not quite so well suppressed as the first, was heard: then another, which seemed to say that it would not be suppressed under any circumstances whatever. At length there arose a perfect storm of sneezes.

"Excellent, excellent for one so young!" said Sir Simon. "I am much interested in this trick of throwing the voice—called, I believe, ventriloquism."

"More snuff," said Hubert.

"More snuff," said Sir Simon. Sir Simon's man brought a large jar of the best scented Scotch.

Hubert once more charged the upper chink of the closet, and blew the snuff into the interior, as before. Again he charged, and again, emptying the whole contents of the jar.

The tumult of sneezes became really extraordinary to listen to—there was no cessation. It was like wind, rain, and sea battling in a hurricane.

"I believe there are men inside, and that it is no trick at all!" exclaimed Sir Simon, the truth flashing on him.

"There are," said Hubert. "They are come to rob the house; and they are the same who stole my horse."

The sneezes changed to spasmodic groans. One of the thieves, hearing Hubert's voice, cried, "Oh! mercy! mercy! let us out of this!"

"Where's my horse?" said Hubert.

"Tied to the tree in the hollow behind Short's Gibbet. Mercy! mercy! let us out, or we shall die of suffocation!"

All the Christmas guests now perceived that this was no longer sport, but serious earnest. Guns and cudgels were procured; all the men-servants were called in, and arranged in position outside the closet. At a signal Hubert withdrew the bolt, and stood on the defensive. But the three robbers, far from attacking them, were found crouching in the corner, gasping for breath. They made no resistance; and, being pinioned, were placed in an out-house till the morning.

Hubert now gave the remainder of his story to the assembled company, and was profusely thanked for the services he had rendered. Sir Simon pressed him to stay over the night, and accept the use of the best bed-room the house afforded, which had been occupied by Queen Elizabeth and King Charles successively when on their visits to this part of the country. But Hubert declined, being anxious to find his horse Jerry, and to test the truth of the robbers' statements concerning him.

Several of the guests accompanied Hubert to the spot behind the gibbet, alluded to by the thieves as where Jerry was hidden. When they reached the knoll and looked over, behold! there the horse stood, uninjured, and quite unconcerned. At sight of Hubert he neighed joyfully; and nothing could exceed Hubert's gladness at finding him. He mounted, wished his friends "Good-night!" and cantered off in the direction they pointed out as his nearest way, reaching home safely about four o'clock in the morning.

AN INDISCRETION IN THE LIFE OF AN HEIRESS

PART I

CHAPTER I

When I would pray and think, I think and pray
To several subjects: heaven hath my empty words;
Whilst my invention, hearing not my tongue,
Anchors on Isabel.

The congregation in Tollamore Church were singing the evening hymn, the people gently swaying backwards and forwards like trees in a soft breeze. The heads of the village children, who sat in the gallery, were inclined to one side as they uttered their shrill notes, their eyes listlessly tracing some crack in the old walls, or following the movement of a distant bough or bird, with features rapt almost to painfulness.

In front of the children stood a thoughtful young man, who was plainly enough the schoolmaster; and his gaze was fixed on a remote part of the aisle beneath him. When the singing was over, and all had sat down for the sermon, his eyes still remained in the same place. There was some excuse for their direction, for it was in a straight line forwards; but their fixity was only to be explained by some object before them. This was a square pew, containing one solitary sitter. But that sitter was a young lady, and a very sweet lady was she.

Afternoon service in Tollamore parish was later than in many others in that neighbourhood; and as the darkness deepened during the progress of the sermon, the rector's pulpit-candles shone to the remotest nooks of the building, till at length they became the sole lights of the congregation. The lady was the single person besides the preacher whose face was turned westwards, the pew that she occupied being the only one in the church in which the seat ran all round. She reclined in her corner, her bonnet and dark dress growing by degrees invisible, and at last only her upturned face could be discerned, a solitary white spot against the black surface of the wainscot. Over her head rose a vast marble monument, erected to the memory of her ancestors, male and female; for she was one of high standing in that parish. The design consisted of a winged skull and two cherubim, supporting a pair of tall Corinthian columns, between which spread a broad slab, containing the roll of ancient names, lineages, and deeds, and surmounted by a pediment, with the crest of the family at its apex.

As the youthful schoolmaster gazed, and all these details became dimmer, her face was modified in his fancy, till it seemed almost to resemble the carved marble skull immediately above her head. The thought was unpleasant enough to arouse him from his half-dreamy state, and he entered on rational considerations of what a vast gulf lay between that lady and himself, what a troublesome world it was to live in where such divisions could exist, and how painful was the evil when a man of his unequal history was possessed of a keen susceptibility.

Now a close observer, who should have happened to be near the large pew, might have noticed before the light got low that the interested gaze of the young man had been returned from time to time by the young lady, although he, towards whom her glances were directed, did not perceive the fact. It would have been guessed that something in the past was common to both, notwithstanding their difference in social standing. What that was may be related in a few words.

One day in the previous week there had been some excitement in the parish on account of the introduction upon the farm of a steam threshing-machine for the first time, the date of these events being some thirty years ago. The machine had been hired by a farmer who was a relative of the schoolmaster's, and when it was set going all the people round about came to see it work. It was fixed in the corner of a field near the main road, and in the afternoon a passing carriage stopped outside the hedge. The steps were let down, and Miss Geraldine Allenville, the young woman whom we have seen sitting in the church pew, came through the gate of the field towards the engine. At that hour most of the villagers had been to the spot, had gratified their curiosity, and afterwards gone home again; so that there were only now left standing beside the engine the engine-man, the farmer, and the young schoolmaster, who had come like the rest. The labourers were at the other part of the machine, under the cornstack some distance off.

The girl looked with interest at the whizzing wheels, asked questions of the old farmer, and remained in conversation with him for some time, the schoolmaster standing a few paces distant, and looking more or less towards her. Suddenly the expression of his face changed to one of horror; he was by her side in a moment, and, seizing hold of her, he swung her round by the arm to a distance of several feet.

In speaking to the farmer she had inadvertently stepped backwards, and had drawn so near to the band which ran from the engine to the drum of the thresher that in another moment her dress must have been caught, and she would have been whirled round the wheel as a mangled carcase. As soon as the meaning of the young man's act was understood by her she turned deadly pale and nearly fainted. When she was well enough to walk, the two men led her to the carriage, which had been standing outside the hedge all the time.

"You have saved me from a ghastly death!" the agitated girl murmured to the schoolmaster. "Oh! I can never forget it!" and then she sank into the carriage and was driven away.

On account of this the schoolmaster had been invited to Tollamore House to explain the incident to the Squire, the young lady's only living parent. Mr Allenville thanked her preserver, inquired the history of his late father, a painter of good family, but unfortunate and improvident; and finally told his visitor that, if he were fond of study, the library of the house was at his service. Geraldine herself had spoken very impulsively to the young man—almost, indeed, with impru-dent warmth—and his tender interest in her during the church service was the result of the sympathy she had shown.

And thus did an emotion, which became this man's sole motive power through many following years, first arise and establish itself. Only once more did she lift her eyes to where he sat, and it was when they all stood up before leaving. This time he noticed the glance. Her look of recognition led his feelings onward yet another stage. Admiration grew to be attachment; he even wished that he might own her, not exactly as a wife, but as a being superior to himself—in the sense in which a servant may be said to own a master. He would have cared to possess her in order to exhibit her glories to the world, and he scarcely even thought of her ever loving him.

There were two other stages in his course of love, but they were not reached till some time after to-day. The first was a change from this proud desire to a longing to cherish. The last stage, later still, was when her very defects became rallying-points for defence, when every one of his senses became special pleaders for her; and that not through blindness, but from a tender inability to do aught else than defend her against all the world.

CHAPTER II

> She was active, stirring, all fire—
> Could not rest, could not tire—
> Never in all the world such an one!
> And here was plenty to be done,
> And she that could do it, great or small,
> She was to do nothing at all.

Five mornings later the same young man was looking out of the window of Tollamore village school in a fixed and absent manner. The weather was exceptionally mild, though scarcely to the degree which would have justified his airy situation at such a month of the year. A hazy light spread through the air, the landscape on which his eyes were resting being enlivened and lit up by the spirit of an unseen sun rather than by its direct rays. Every sound could be heard for miles. There was a great crowing of cocks, bleating of sheep, and cawing of rooks, which proceeded from all points of the compass, rising and falling as the origin of each sound was near or far away. There were also audible the voices of people in the village, interspersed with hearty laughs, the bell of a distant flock of sheep, a robin close at hand, vehicles in the neighbouring roads and lanes. One of these latter noises grew gradually more distinct, and proved itself to be rapidly nearing the school. The listener blushed as he heard it.

"Suppose it should be!" he said to himself.

He had said the same thing at every such noise that he had heard during the foregoing week, and had been mistaken in his hope. But this time a certain carriage did appear in answer to his expectation. He came from the window hastily; and in a minute a footman knocked and opened the school door.

"Miss Allenville wishes to speak to you, Mr Mayne."

The schoolmaster went to the porch—he was a very young man to be called a schoolmaster—his heart beating with excitement.

"Good morning," she said, with a confident yet girlish smile. "My father expects me to inquire into the school arrangements, and I wish to do so on my own account as well. May I come in?"

She entered as she spoke, telling the coachman to drive to the village on some errand, and call for her in half an hour.

Mayne could have wished that she had not been so thoroughly free from all apparent consciousness of the event of the previous week, of the fact that he was considerably more of a man than the small persons by whom the apartment was mainly filled, and that he was as nearly as possible at her own level in age, as wide in sympathies, and possibly more inflammable in heart. But he soon found that a sort of fear to entrust her voice with the subject of that link between them was what restrained her. When he had explained a few details of routine she moved away from him round the school.

He turned and looked at her as she stood among the children. To his eyes her beauty was indescribable. Before he had met her he had scarcely believed that any woman in the world could be so lovely. The clear, deep eyes, full of all tender expressions; the fresh, subtly-curved cheek, changing its tones of red with the fluctuation of each thought; the ripe tint of her delicate mouth, and the indefinable line where lip met lip; the noble bend of her neck, the wavy lengths of her dark brown hair, the soft motions of her bosom when she breathed, the light fall of her little feet, the elegant contrivances of her attire, all struck him as something he had dreamed of and was not actually seeing. Geraldine Allenville was, in truth, very beautiful; she was a girl such as his eyes had never elsewhere beheld; and her presence here before his face kept up a sharp struggle of sweet and bitter within him.

He had thought at first that the flush on her face was caused by the fresh air of the morning; but, as it quickly changed to a lesser hue, it occurred to Mayne that it might after all have arisen from shyness at meeting him after her narrow escape. Be that as it might, their conversation, which at first consisted of bald sentences, divided by wide intervals of time, became more frequent, and at last continuous. He was painfully soon convinced that her tongue would never have run so easily as it did had it not been that she thought him a person on whom she could vent her ideas without reflection or punctiliousness—a thought, perhaps, expressed to herself by such words as, "I will say what I like to him, for he is only our schoolmaster."

"And you have chosen to keep a school," she went on, with a shade of mischievousness in her tone, looking at him as if she thought that, had she been a man capable of saving people's lives, she would have done something much better than teaching. She was so young as to habitually think thus of other persons' courses.

"No," he said, simply; "I don't choose to keep a school in the sense you mean, choosing it from a host of pursuits, all equally possible."

"How came you here, then?"

"I fear more by chance than by aim."

"Then you are not very ambitious?"

"I have my ambitions, such as they are."

"I thought so. Everybody has nowadays. But it is a better thing not to be too ambitious, *I* think."

"If we value ease of mind, and take an economist's view of our term of life, it may be a better thing."

Having been tempted, by his unexpectedly cultivated manner of speaking, to say more than she had meant to say, she found it embarrassing either to break off or to say more, and in her doubt she stooped to kiss a little girl.

"Although I spoke lightly of ambition," she observed, without turning to him, "and said that easy happiness was worth most, I could defend ambition very well, and in the only pleasant way."

"And that way?"

"On the broad ground of the loveliness of any dream about future triumphs. In looking back there is a pleasure in contemplating a time when some attractive thing of the future appeared possible, even though it never came to pass."

Mayne was puzzled to hear her talk in this tone of maturity. That such questions of success and failure should have occupied his own mind seemed natural, for they had been forced upon him by the difficulties he had encountered in his pursuit of a career. He was not just then aware how very unpractical the knowledge of this sage lady of seventeen really was; that it was merely caught up by intercommunication with people of culture and experience, who talked before her of their theories and beliefs till she insensibly acquired their tongue.

The carriage was heard coming up the road. Mayne gave her the list of the children, their ages, and other particulars which she had called for, and she turned to go out. Not a word had been said about the incident by the threshing-machine, though each one could see that it was constantly in the other's thoughts. The roll of the wheels may or may not have reminded her of her position in relation to him. She said, bowing, and in a somewhat more distant tone: "We shall all be glad to learn that our schoolmaster is so—nice; such a philosopher." But, rather surprised at her own cruelty in uttering the latter words, she added one of the sweetest laughs that ever came from lips, and said, in gentlest tones, "Good morning; I shall *always* remember what you did for me. Oh! it makes me sick to think of that moment. I came on purpose to thank you again, but I could not say it till now!"

Mayne's heart, which had felt the rebuff, came round to her with a rush; he could have almost forgiven her for physically wounding him if she had asked him in such a tone not to notice it. He watched her out of sight, thinking in rather a melancholy mood how time would absorb all her beauty, as the growing distance between them absorbed her form. He then went in, and endeavoured to recall every word that he had said to her, troubling and racking his mind to the utmost of his ability about his imagined faults of manner. He remembered that he had used the indicative mood instead of the proper subjunctive in a certain phrase. He had given her to understand that an old idea he had made use of was his own, and so on through other particulars, each of which was an item of misery.

The place and the manner of her sitting were defined by the position of her chair, and by the books, maps, and prints scattered round it. Her "I shall always remember," he repeated to himself, aye, a hundred times; and though he knew the plain import of the words, he could not help toying with them, looking at them from all points, and investing them with extraordinary meanings.

CHAPTER III

> But what is this? I turn about
> And find a trouble in thine eye.

Egbert Mayne, though at present filling the office of village schoolmaster, had been intended for a less narrow path. His position at this time was entirely owing to the death of his father in embarrassed circumstances two years before. Mr Mayne had been a landscape and animal painter, and had settled in the village in early manhood, where he set about improving his prospects by marrying a small farmer's daughter. The son had been sent away from home at an early age to a good school, and had returned at seventeen to enter upon some professional life or other. But his father's health was at this time declining, and when the painter died, a year and a half later, nothing had been done for Egbert. He was now living with his maternal grandfather, Richard Broadford, the farmer, who was a tenant of Squire Allenville's. Egbert's ideas did not incline to painting, but he had ambitious notions of adopting a literary profession, or entering the Church, or doing something congenial to his tastes whenever he could set about it. But first it was necessary to read, mark, learn, and look around him; and, a master being temporarily required for the school until such time as it should be placed under Government inspection, he stepped in and made use of the occupation as a stop-gap for a while.

He lived in his grandfather's farmhouse, walking backwards and forwards to the school every day, in order that the old man, who would otherwise be living quite alone, might have the benefit of his society during the long winter evenings. Egbert was much attached to his grandfather, and so, indeed, were all who knew him. The old farmer's amiable disposition and kindliness of heart, while they had hindered him from enriching himself one shilling during the course of a long and laborious life, had also kept him clear of every arrow of antagonism. The house in which he lived was the same that he had been born in, and was almost a part of himself. It had been built by his father's father; but on the dropping of the lives for which it was held, some twenty years earlier, it had lapsed to the Squire.

Richard Broadford was not, however, dispossessed: after his father's death the family had continued as before in the house and farm, but as yearly tenants. It was much to Broadford's delight, for his pain at the thought of parting from those old sticks and stones of his ancestors, before it had been known if the tenure could be continued, was real and great.

On the evening of the day on which Miss Allenville called at the school Egbert returned to the farmhouse as usual. He found his grandfather sitting with his hands on his knees, and showing by his countenance that something had happened to disturb him greatly. Egbert looked at him inquiringly, and with some misgiving.

"I have got to go at last, Egbert," he said, in a tone intended to be stoical, but far from it. "He is my enemy after all."

"Who?" said Mayne.

"The Squire. He's going to take seventy acres of neighbour Greenman's farm to enlarge the park; and Greenman's acreage is to be made up to him, and more, by throwing my farm in with his. Yes, that's what the Squire is going to have done. . . . Well, I thought to have died here; but 'tisn't to be."

He looked as helpless as a child, for age had weakened him. Egbert endeavoured to cheer him a little, and vexed as the young man was, he thought there might yet be some means of tiding over this difficulty. "Mr Allenville wants seventy acres more in his park, does he?" he echoed mechanically. "Why can't it be taken entirely out of Greenman's farm? His is big enough, Heaven knows; and your hundred acres might be left you in peace."

"Well mayest say so! Oh, it is because he is tired of seeing old-fashioned farming like mine. He likes the young genera-tion's system best, I suppose."

"If I had only known this this afternoon," Egbert said.

"You could have done nothing."

"Perhaps not." Egbert was, however, thinking that he would have mentioned the matter to his visitor, and told her such circumstances as would have enlisted her sympathies in the case.

"I thought it would come to this," said old Richard, vehe-mently. "The present Squire Allenville has never been any real friend to me. It was only through his wife that I have stayed here so long. If it hadn't been for her, we should have gone the very year that my poor father died, and the house fell into hand. I wish we had now. You see, now she's dead, there's nobody to counteract him in his schemes; and so I am to be swept away."

They talked on thus, and by bed-time the old man was in better spirits. But the subject did not cease to occupy Egbert's mind, and that anxiously. Were the house and farm which his grandfather had occupied so long to be taken away, Egbert knew it would affect his life to a degree out of all proportion to the seriousness of the event. The transplanting of old people is like the transplanting of old trees; a twelvemonth usually sees them wither and die away.

The next day proved that his anticipations were likely to be correct, his grandfather being so disturbed that he could scarcely eat or drink. The remainder of the week passed in just the same way. Nothing now occupied Egbert's mind but a longing to see Miss Allenville. To see her would be bliss; to ask her if anything could be done by which his grandfather might retain the farm and premises would be nothing but duty. His hope of good results from the course was based on the knowledge that Allenville, cold and hard as he was, had some considerable affection for or pride in his daughter, and that thus she might influence him.

It was not likely that she would call at the school for a week or two at least, and Mayne therefore tried to meet with her elsewhere. One morning early he was returning from the remote hamlet of Hawksgate, on the further side of the parish, and the nearest way to the school was across the park. He read as he walked, as was customary with him, though at present his thoughts wandered incessantly. The path took him through a shrubbery running close up to a remote wing of the mansion. Nobody seemed to be stirring in that quarter, till, turning an angle, he saw Geraldine's own graceful figure close at hand, robed in fur, and standing at ease outside an open French casement.

She was startled by his sudden appearance, but her face soon betrayed a sympathetic remembrance of him. Egbert scarcely knew whether to stop or to walk on, when, casting her eyes upon his book, she said, "Don't let me interrupt your reading."

"I am glad to have—" he stammered, and for the moment could get no farther. His nervousness encouraged her to continue.

"What are you reading?" she said.

The book was, as may possibly be supposed by those who know the mood inspired by hopeless attachments, "Childe Harold's Pilgrimage," a poem which at that date had never been surpassed in congeniality to the minds of young persons in the full fever of virulent love. He was rather reluctant to let her know this; but as the inquiry afforded him an opening for conversation he held out the book, and her eye glanced over the page.

"Oh, thank you," she said hastily, "I ought not to have asked that—only I am interested always in books. Is your grandfather quite well, Mr Mayne? I saw him yesterday, and thought he seemed to be not in such good health as usual."

"His mind is disturbed," said Egbert.

"Indeed, why is that?"

"It is on account of his having to leave the farm. He is old, and was born in that house."

"Ah, yes, I have heard something of that," she said with a slightly regretful look. "Mr Allenville has decided to enlarge the park. Born in the house was he?"

"Yes. His grandfather built it. May I ask your opinion on the point, Miss Allenville? Don't you think it would be possible to enlarge the park without taking my grandfather's farm? Greenman has already five hundred acres."

She was perplexed how to reply, and evading the question said, "Your grandfather much wishes to stay?"

"He does, intensely—more than you can believe or think. But he will not ask to be let remain. I dread the effect of leaving upon him. If it were possible to contrive that he should not be turned out I should be grateful indeed."

"I—I will do all I can that things may remain as they are," she said with a deepened colour. "In fact, I am almost certain that he will not have to go, since it is so painful to him," she added in the sanguine tones of a child. "My father could not have known that his mind was so bent on staying."

Here the conversation ended, and Egbert went on with a lightened heart. Whether his pleasure arose entirely from having done his grandfather a good turn, or from the mere sensation of having been near her, he himself could hardly have determined.

CHAPTER IV

> Oh, for my sake, do you with fortune chide,
> The guilty goddess of my harmful deed
> That did not better for my life provide.

Now commenced a period during which Egbert Mayne's emotions burnt in a more unreasoning and wilder worship than at any other time in his life. The great condition of idealisation in love was present here, that of an association in which, through difference in rank, the petty human elements that enter so largely into life are kept entirely out of sight, and there is hardly awakened in the man's mind a thought that they appertain to her at all.

He deviated frequently from his daily track to the spot where the last meeting had been, till, on the fourth morning after, he saw her there again; but she let him pass that time with a bare recognition. Two days later the carriage drove down the lane to the village as he was walking away. When they met she told the coachman to stop.

"I am glad to tell you that your grandfather may be perfectly easy about the house and farm," she said; as if she took unfeigned pleasure in saying it. "The question of altering the park is postponed indefinitely. I have resisted it: I could do no less for one who did so much for me."

"Thank you very warmly," said Egbert so earnestly, that she blushed crimson as the carriage rolled away.

The spring drew on, and he saw and spoke with her several times. In truth he walked abroad much more than had been usual with him formerly, searching in all directions for her form. Had she not been unreflecting and impressionable— had not her life dragged on as uneventfully as that of one in gaol, through her residing in a great house with no companion but an undemonstrative father; and, above all, had not Egbert been a singularly engaging young man of that distracting order of beauty which grows upon the feminine gazer with every glance, this tender waylaying would have made little difference to anybody. But such was not the case. In return for Egbert's presence of mind at the threshing she had done him a kindness, and the pleasure that she took in the act shed an added interest upon the object of it. Thus, on both sides it had happened that a deed of solicitude casually performed gave each doer a sense of proprietorship in its recipient, and a wish still further to establish that position by other deeds of the same sort.

To still further kindle Geraldine's indiscreet interest in him, Egbert's devotion became perceptible ere long even to her inexperienced eyes; and it was like a new world to the young girl. At first she was almost frightened at the novelty of the thing. Then the fascination of the discovery caused her ready, receptive heart to palpitate in an ungovernable manner whenever he came near her. She was not quite in love herself, but she was so moved by the circumstance of her deliverer being in love, that she could think of nothing else. His appearing at odd places startled her; and yet she rather liked that kind of startling. Too often her eyes rested on his face; too often her thoughts surrounded his figure and dwelt on his conversation.

One day, when they met on a bridge, they did not part till after a long and interesting conversation on books, in which many opinions of Mayne's (crude and unformed enough, it must be owned) that happened to take her fancy, set her glowing with ardour to unfold her own.

After any such meeting as this, Egbert would go home and think for hours of her little remarks and movements. The day and minute of every accidental rencounter became registered in his mind with the indelibility of ink. Years afterwards he could recall at a moment's notice that he saw her at eleven o'clock on the third of April, a Sunday; at four on Tuesday, the twelfth; at a quarter to six on Thursday, the twenty-eighth; that on the ninth it rained at a quarter past two, when she was walking up the avenue; that on the seventeenth the grass was rather too wet for a lady's feet; and other calendrical and meteorological facts of no value whatever either to science or history.

On a Tuesday evening, when they had had several conversations out of doors, and when a passionate liking for his society was creeping over the reckless though pure girl, slowly, insidiously, and surely, like ripeness over fruit, she further committed herself by coming alone to the school. A heavy rain had threatened to fall all the afternoon, and just as she entered it began. School hours were at that moment over, but he waited a few moments before dismissing the children, to see if the storm would clear up. After looking round at the classes, and making sundry inquiries of the little ones in the usual manner of ladies who patronise a school, she came up to him.

"I listened outside before I came in. It was a great pleasure to hear the voices—three classes reading at three paces." She continued with a laugh: "There was a rough treble voice bowling easily along, an ambling sweet voice earnest about fishes in the sea, and a shrill voice spelling out letter by letter. Then there was a shuffling of feet—then you sang. It seemed quite a little poem."

"Yes," Egbert said. "But perhaps, like many poems, it was hard prose to the originators."

She remained thinking, and Mayne looked out at the weather. Judging from the sky and wind that there was no likelihood of a change that night, he proceeded to let the children go. Miss Allenville assisted in wrapping up as many of them as possible in the old coats and other apparel which Egbert kept by him for the purpose. But she touched both clothes and children rather gingerly, and as if she did not much like the contact.

Egbert's sentiments towards her that evening were vehement and curious. Much as he loved her, his liking for the peasantry about him—his mother's ancestry—caused him sometimes a twinge of self-reproach for thinking of her so exclusively, and nearly forgetting all his old acquaintance, neighbours, and his grandfather's familiar friends, with their rough but honest ways. To further complicate his feelings to-night there was the sight, on the one hand, of the young lady with her warm rich dress and glowing future, and on the other of the weak little boys and girls—some only five years old, and none more than twelve, going off in their different directions in the pelting rain, some for a walk of more than two miles, with the certainty of being drenched to the skin, and with no change of clothes when they reached their home. He watched the rain spots thickening upon the faded frocks, worn-out tippets, yellow straw hats and bonnets, and coarse pinafores of his unprotected little flock as they walked down the path, and was thereby reminded of the hopelessness of his attachment, by perceiving how much more nearly akin was his lot to theirs than to hers.

Miss Allenville, too, was looking at the children, and unfortunately she chanced to say, as they toddled off, "Poor little wretches!"

A sort of despairing irritation at her remoteness from his plane, as implied by her pitying the children so unmercifully, impelled him to remark, "Say poor little *children*, madam."

She was silent—awkwardly silent.

"I suppose I must walk home," she said, when about half a minute had passed. "Nobody knows where I am, and the carriage may not find me for hours."

"I'll go for the carriage," said Egbert readily.

But he did not move. While she had been speaking, there had grown up in him a conviction that these opportunities of seeing her would soon necessarily cease. She would get older, and would perceive the incorrectness of being on intimate terms with him merely because he had snatched her from danger. He would have to engage in a more active career, and go away. Such ideas brought on an irresistible climax to an intense and long-felt desire. He had just reached that point in the action of passion upon mind at which it masters judgment.

It was almost dark in the room, by reason of the heavy clouds and the nearness of the night. But the fire had just flamed up brightly in the grate, and it threw her face and form into ruddy relief against the grey wall behind.

Suddenly rushing towards her, he seized her hand before she comprehended his intention, kissed it tenderly, and clasped her in his arms. Her soft body yielded like wool under his embrace. As suddenly releasing her he turned, and went back to the other end of the room.

Egbert's feeling as he retired was that he had committed a crime. The madness of the action was apparent to him almost before it was completed. There seemed not a single thing left for him to do, but to go into life-long banishment for such sacrilege. He faced round and regarded her. Her features were not visible enough to judge of their expression. All that he could discern through the dimness and his own agitation was that for some time she remained quite motionless. Her state was probably one of suspension; as with Ulysses before Melanthus, she may have—

> Entertained a breast
> That in the strife of all extremes did rest.

In one, two, or five minutes—neither of them ever knew exactly how long—apparently without the motion of a limb, she glided noiselessly to the door and vanished.

Egbert leant himself against the wall, almost distracted. He could see absolutely no limit to the harm that he had done by his wild and unreasoning folly. "Am I a man to thus ill-treat the loveliest girl that ever was born? Sweet injured creature— how she will hate me!" These were some of the expressions that he murmured in the twilight of that lonely room.

Then he said that she certainly had encouraged him, which, unfortunately for her, was only too true. She had seen that he was always in search of her, and she did not put herself out of his way. He was sure that she liked him to admire her. "Yet, no," he murmured, "I will not excuse myself at all."

The night passed away miserably. One conviction by degrees overruled all the rest in his mind—that if she knew precisely how pure had been his longing towards her, she could not think badly of him. His reflections resulted in a resolve to get an interview with her, and make his defence and explanation in full. The decision come to, his impatience could scarcely preserve him from rushing to Tollamore House that very daybreak, and trying to get into her presence, though it was the likeliest of suppositions that she would never see him.

Every spare minute of the following days he hovered round the house, in hope of getting a glimpse of her; but not once did she make herself visible. He delayed taking the extreme step of calling, till the hour came when he could delay no longer. On a certain day he rang the bell with a mild air, and disguised his feelings by looking as if he wished to speak to her merely on copy-books, slates, and other school matters, the school being professedly her hobby. He was told that Miss Allenville had gone on a visit to some relatives thirty-five miles off, and that she would probably not return for a month.

As there was no help for it, Egbert settled down to wait as he best could, not without many misgivings lest his rash action, which a prompt explanation might have toned down and excused, would now be the cause of a total estrangement between them, so that nothing would restore him to the place he had formerly held in her estimation. That she had ever seriously loved him he did not hope or dream; but it was intense pain to him to be out of her favour.

CHAPTER V

So I soberly laid my last plan
To extinguish the man,
Round his creep-hole, with never a break
Ran my fires for his sake;
Over head did my thunder combine
With my underground mine:
Till I looked from my labour content
To enjoy the event.
When sudden—how think ye the end?

A week after the crisis mentioned above, it was secretly whispered to Egbert's grandfather that the park enlargement scheme was after all to be proceeded with; that Miss Allenville was extremely anxious to have it put in hand as soon as possible. Farmer Broadford's farm was to be added to Greenman's, as originally intended, and the old house that Broadford lived in was to be pulled down as an encumbrance.

"It is she this time!" murmured Egbert, gloomily. "Then I did offend her, and mortify her; and she is resentful."

The excitement of his grandfather again caused him much alarm, and even remorse. Such was the responsiveness of the farmer's physical to his mental state that in the course of a week his usual health failed, and his gloominess of mind was followed by dimness of sight and giddiness. By much persuasion Egbert induced him to stay at home for a day or two; but indoors he was the most restless of creatures, through not being able to engage in the pursuits to which he had been accustomed from his boyhood. He walked up and down, looking wistfully out of the window, shifting the positions of books and chairs, and putting them back again, opening his desk and shutting it after a vacant look at the papers, saying he should never get settled in another farm at his time of life, and evincing all the symptoms of nervousness and excitability.

Meanwhile Egbert anxiously awaited Miss Allenville's return, more resolved than ever to obtain audience of her, and beg her not to visit upon an unoffending old man the consequences of a young one's folly. Any retaliation upon himself he would accept willingly, and own to be well deserved.

At length, by making off-hand inquiries (for he dared not ask directly for her again) he learnt that she was to be at home on the Thursday. The following Friday and Saturday he kept a sharp look-out; and, when lingering in the park for at least the tenth time in that half-week, a sudden rise in the ground revealed her coming along the path.

Egbert stayed his advance, in order that, if she really objected to see him, she might easily strike off into a side path or turn back.

She did not accept the alternatives, but came straight on to where he lingered, averting her face waywardly as she approached. When she was within a few steps of him he could see that the trimmings of her dress trembled like leaves. He cleared his dry throat to speak.

"Miss Allenville," he said, humbly taking off his hat, "I should be glad to say one word to you, if I may."

She looked at him for just one moment, but said nothing; and he could see that the expression of her face was flushed, and her mood skittish. The place they were standing in was a remote nook, hidden by the trunks and boughs, so that he could afford to give her plenty of time, for there was no fear of their being observed or overheard. Indeed, knowing that she often walked that way, Egbert had previously surveyed the spot and thought it suitable for the occasion, much as Wellington antecedently surveyed the field of Waterloo.

Here the young man began his pleading speech to her. He dilated upon his sensations when first he saw her; and as he became warmed by his oratory he spoke of all his inmost perturbations on her account without the slightest reserve. He related with much natural eloquence how he had tried over and over again not to love her, and how he had loved her in spite of that trying; of his intention never to reveal his passion, till their situation on that rainy evening prompted the impulse which ended in that irreverent action of his; and earnestly asked her to forgive him—not for his feelings, since they were his own to commend or blame—but for the way in which he testified of them to one so cultivated and so beautiful.

Egbert was flushed and excited by the time that he reached this point in his tale.

Her eyes were fixed on the grass; and then a tear stole quietly from its corner, and wandered down her cheek. She tried to say something, but her usually adroit tongue was unequal to the task. Ultimately she glanced at him, and murmured, "I forgive you;" but so inaudibly, that he only recognised the words by their shape upon her lips.

She looked not much more than a child now, and Egbert thought with sadness that her tear and her words were perhaps but the result, the one of a transitory sympathy, the other of a desire to escape. They stood silent for some seconds, and the dressing-bell of the house began ringing. Turning slowly away without another word she hastened out of his sight.

When Egbert reached home some of his grandfather's old friends were gathered there, sympathising with him on the removal he would have to submit to if report spoke truly. Their sympathy was rather more for him to bear than their indifference; and as Egbert looked at the old man's bent figure, and at the expression of his face, denoting a wish to sink under the earth, out of sight and out of trouble, he was greatly depressed, and he said inwardly, "What a fool I was to ask forgiveness of a woman who can torture my only relative like this! Why do I feel her to be glorious? Oh that I had never seen her!"

The next day was Sunday, and his grandfather being too unwell to go out, Egbert went to the evening service alone. When it was over, the rector detained him in the churchyard to say a few words about the next week's undertakings. This was soon done, and Egbert turned back to leave the now empty churchyard. Passing the porch he saw Miss Allenville coming out of the door.

Egbert said nothing, for he knew not what to say; but she spoke. "Ah, Mr Mayne, how beautiful the west sky looks! It is the finest sunset we have had this spring."

"It is very beautiful," he replied, without looking westward a single degree. "Miss Allenville," he said reproachfully, "you might just have thought whether, for the sake of reaching one guilty person, it was worth while to deeply wound an old man."

"I do not allow you to say that," she answered with proud quickness. "Still, I will listen just this once."

"Are you glad you asserted your superiority to me by putting in motion again that scheme for turning him out?"

"I merely left off hindering it," she said.

"Well, we shall go now," continued Egbert, "and make room for newer people. I hope you forgive what caused it all."

"You talk in that strain to make me feel regrets; and you think that because you are read in a few books you may say or do anything."

"No, no. That's unfair."

"I will try to alter it—that your grandfather may not leave. Say that you forgive me for thinking he and yourself had better leave—as I forgive you for what you did. But remember, nothing of that sort ever again."

"Forgive you? Oh, Miss Allenville!" said he in a wild whisper, "I wish you had sinned a hundred times as much, that I might show how readily I can forgive all."

She had looked as if she would have held out her hand; but, for some reason or other, directly he had spoken with emotion it was not so well for him as when he had spoken to wound her. She passed on silently, and entered the private gate to the house.

A day or two after this, about three o'clock in the afternoon, and whilst Egbert was giving a lesson in geography, a lad burst into the school with the tidings that Farmer Broadford had fallen from a corn-stack they were threshing, and hurt himself severely.

The boy had borrowed a horse to come with, and Mayne at once made him gallop off with it for a doctor. Dismissing the children, the young man ran home full of forebodings. He found his relative in a chair, held up by two of his labouring-men. He was put to bed, and seeing how pale he was, Egbert gave him a little wine, and bathed the parts which had been bruised by the fall.

Egbert had at first been the more troubled at the event through believing that his grandfather's fall was the result of his low spirits and mental uneasiness; and he blamed himself for letting so infirm a man go out upon the farm till quite recovered. But it turned out that the actual cause of the accident was the breaking of the ladder that he had been standing on. When the surgeon had seen him he said that the external bruises were mere trifles; but that the shock had been great, and had produced internal injuries highly dangerous to a man in that stage of life.

His grandson was of opinion in later years that the fall only hastened by a few months a dissolution which would soon have taken place under any circumstances, from the natural decay of the old man's constitution. His pulse grew feeble and his voice weak, but he continued in a comparatively firm state of mind for some days, during which he talked to Egbert a great deal.

Egbert trusted that the illness would soon pass away; his anxiety for his grandfather was great. When he was gone not one of the family would be left but himself. But in spite of hope the younger man perceived that death was really at hand. And now arose a question. It was certainly a time to make confidences, if they were ever to be made; should he, then, tell his grandfather, who knew the Allenvilles so well, of his love for Geraldine? At one moment it seemed duty; at another it seemed a graceful act, to say the least.

Yet Egbert might never have uttered a word but for a remark of his grandfather's which led up to the very point. He was speaking of the farm and of the Squire, and thence he went on to the daughter.

"She, too," he said, "seems to have that reckless spirit which was in her mother's family, and ruined her mother's father at the gaming table, though she's too young to show much of it yet."

"I hope not," said Egbert fervently.

"Why? What be the Allenvilles to you—not that I wish the girl harm?"

"I think she is the very best being in the world. I—love her deeply."

His grandfather's eyes were set on the wall. "Well, well, my poor boy," came softly from his mouth. "What made ye think of loving her? Ye may as well love a mountain, for any return you'll ever get. Do she know of it?"

"She guesses it. It was my saving her from the threshing-machine that began it."

"And she checks you?"

"Well—no."

"Egbert," he said after a silence, "I am grieved, for it can but end in pain. Mind, she's an inexperienced girl. She never thinks of what trouble she may get herself into with her father and with her friends. And mind this, my lad, as another reason for dropping it; however honourable your love may be, you'll never get credit for your honour. Nothing you can do will ever root out the notion of people that where the man is poor and the woman is high-born he's a scamp and she's an angel."

"She's very good."

"She's thoughtless, or she'd never encourage you. You must try not to see her."

"I will never put myself in her way again."

The subject was mentioned no more then. The next day the worn-out old farmer died, and his last request to Egbert was that he would do nothing to tempt Geraldine Allenville to think of him further.

CHAPTER VI

> Hath misery made thee blind
> To the fond workings of a woman's mind?
> And must I say—albeit my heart rebel
> With all that woman feels but should not tell;
> Because, despite thy faults, that heart is moved—
> It feared thee, thank'd thee, pitied, madden'd, loved?

It was in the evening of the day after Farmer Broadford's death that Egbert first sat down in the house alone. The bandy-legged little man who had acted as his grandfather's groom of the chambers and stables simultaneously had gone into the village. The candles were not yet lighted, and Mayne abstractedly watched upon the pale wall the latter rays of sunset slowly changing into the white shine of a moon a few days old. The ancient family clock had stopped for want of winding, and the intense silence that prevailed seemed more like the bodily presence of some quality than the mere absence of sound.

He was thinking how many were the indifferent expressions which he had used towards the poor body lying cold upstairs—the only relation he had latterly had upon earth—which might as well have been left unsaid; of how far he had been from practically attempting to do what in theory he called best—to make the most of every pulse of natural affection; that he had never heeded or particularly inquired the meaning of the different pieces of advice which the kind old man had tendered from time to time; that he had never even thought of asking for any details of his grandfather's history.

His musings turned upon Geraldine. He had promised to seek her no more, and he would keep his promise. Her interest in him might only be that of an exceedingly romantic and freakish soul, awakened but through "lack of other idleness," and because sound sense suggested to her that it was a thing dangerous to do; for it seemed that she was ever and only moved by the superior of two antagonistic forces. She had as yet seen little or no society, she was only seventeen; and hence it was possible that a week of the town and fashion into which she would soon be initiated might blot out his very existence from her memory.

He was sitting with his back to the window, meditating in this minor key, when a shadow darkened the opposite moonlit wall. Egbert started. There was a gentle tap at the door; and he opened it to behold the well-known form of the lady in his mind.

"Mr Mayne, are you alone?" she whispered, full of agitation.

"Quite alone, excepting my poor grandfather's body upstairs," he answered, as agitated as she.

Then out it all came. "I couldn't help coming—I hope—
oh, I do so pray—that it was not through me that he died. Was
it I, indeed, who killed him? They say it was the effect of the
news that he was to leave the farm. I would have done anything to hinder his being turned out had I only reflected! And
now he is dead. It was so cruel to an old man like him; and
now you have nobody in the world to care for you, have you,
Egbert—except me?"

The ice was wholly broken. He took her hand in both his
own and began to assure her that her alarm was grounded on
nothing whatever. And yet he was almost reluctant to assure
her out of so sweet a state. And when he had said over and
over again that his grandfather's fall had nothing to do with
his mental condition, that the utmost result of her hasty
proceeding was a sadness of spirit in him, she still persisted, as
is the custom of women, in holding to that most painful
possibility as the most likely, simply because it wounded her
most. It was a long while before she would be convinced of
her own innocence, but he maintained it firmly, and she
finally believed.

They sat down together, restraint having quite died out
between them. The fine-lady portion of her existence, of
which there was never much, was in abeyance, and they spoke
and acted simply as a young man and woman who were beset
by common troubles, and who had like hopes and fears.

"And you will never blame me again for what I did?" said
Egbert.

"I never blamed you much," she murmured with arch
simplicity. "Why should it be wrong for me to be honest with
you now, and tell everything you want to know?"

Mayne was silent. That was a difficult question for a conscientious man to answer. Here was he nearly twenty-one years
of age, and with some experience of life, while she was a girl
nursed up like an exotic, with no real experience, and but
little over seventeen—though from the fineness of her figure
she looked more womanly than she really was. It plainly had
not crossed her young mind that she was on the verge of
committing the most horrible social sin—that of loving beneath her, and owning that she so loved. Two years thence

she might see the imprudence of her conduct, and blame him for having led her on. Ought he not, then, considering his grandfather's words, to say that it was wrong for her to be honest; that she should forget him, and fix her mind on matters appertaining to her order? He could not do it—he let her drift sweetly on.

"I think more of you than of anybody in the whole world," he replied. "And you will allow me to, will you not?—let me always keep you in my heart, and almost worship you?"

"That would be wrong. But you may think of me, if you like to, very much; it will give me great pleasure. I don't think my father thinks of me at all—or anybody, except you. I said the other day I would never think of you again, but I have done it, a good many times. It is all through being obliged to care for somebody whether you will or no."

"And you will go on thinking of me?"

"I will do anything to—oblige you."

Egbert, on the impulse of the moment, bent over her and raised her little hand to his lips. He reverenced her too much to think of kissing her cheek. She knew this, and was thrilled through with the delight of being adored as one from above the sky.

Up to this day of its existence their affection had been a battle, a species of antagonism wherein his heart and the girl's had faced each other, and been anxious to do honour to their respective parts. But now it was a truce and a settlement, in which each one took up the other's utmost weakness, and was careless of concealing his and her own.

Surely, sitting there as they sat then, a more unreasoning condition of mind as to how this unequal conjunction would end never existed. They swam along through the passing moments, not a thought of duty on either side, not a further thought on his but that she was the dayspring of his life, that he would die for her a hundred times; superadded to which was a shapeless uneasiness that she would in some manner slip away from him. The solemnity of the event that had just happened would have shown up to him any ungenerous feeling in strong colours—and he had reason afterwards to examine the epoch narrowly; but it only seemed to demonstrate how instinctive and uncalculating was the love that worked within him.

It was almost time for her to leave. She held up her watch to the moonlight. Five minutes more she would stay; then three minutes, and no longer. "Now I am going," she said. "Do you forgive me entirely?"

"How shall I say 'Yes' without assuming that there was something to forgive?"

"Say 'Yes.' It is sweeter to fancy I am forgiven than to think I have not sinned."

With this she went to the door. Egbert accompanied her through the wood, and across a portion of the park, till they were about a hundred yards from the house, when he was forced to bid her farewell.

The old man was buried on the following Sunday. During several weeks afterwards Egbert's sole consolation under his loss was in thinking of Geraldine, for they did not meet in private again till some time had elapsed. The ultimate issue of this absorption in her did not concern him at all: it seemed to be in keeping with the system of his existence now that he should have an utterly inscrutable to-morrow.

CHAPTER VII

Come forward, some great marshal, and organise equality in society.

The month of August came round, and Miss Allenville was to lay the foundation-stone of a tower or beacon which her father was about to erect on the highest hill of his estate, to the memory of his brother, the General. It was arranged that the school children should sing at the ceremony. Accordingly, at the hour fixed, Egbert was on the spot; a crowd of villagers had also arrived, and carriages were visible in the distance, wending their way towards the scene. When they had drawn up alongside and the visitors alighted, the master-mason appeared nervous.

"Mr Mayne," he said to Egbert, "you had better do what's to be done for the lady. I shall speak too loud, or too soft, or handle things wrong. Do you attend upon her, and I'll lower the stone."

Several ladies and gentlemen now gathered round, and presently Miss Allenville stood in position for her office, supported on one side by her father, a hard-featured man of five-and-forty, and some friends who were visiting at the house; and on the other by the school children, who began singing a song in keeping with the occasion. When this was done, Geraldine laid down the sealed bottle with its enclosed memorandum, which had been prepared for the purpose, and taking a trowel from her father's hand, dabbled confusedly in the mortar, accidentally smearing it over the handle of the trowel.

"Lower the stone," said Egbert, who stood close by, to the mason at the winch; and the stone began to descend.

The dainty-handed young woman was looking as if she would give anything to be relieved of the dirty trowel; but Egbert, the only one who observed this, was guiding the stone with both hands into its place, and could not receive the tool of her. Every moment increased her perplexity.

"Take it, take it, will you?" she impatiently whispered to him, blushing with a consciousness that people began to perceive her awkward handling.

"I must just finish this first," he said.

She was resigned in an instant. The stone settled down upon its base, when Egbert at once took the trowel, and her father came up and wiped her glove. Egbert then handed her the mallet.

"What must I do with this thing?" she whispered entreatingly, holding the mallet as if it might bite her.

"Tap with it, madam," said he.

She did as directed, and murmured the form of words which she had been told to repeat.

"Thank you," she said softly when all was done, restored to herself by the consciousness that she had performed the last part gracefully. Without lifting her eyes she added, "It was thoughtful of you to remember that I shouldn't know, and to stand by to tell me."

Her friends now moved away, but before she had joined them Egbert said, chiefly for the pleasure of speaking to her: "The tower, when it is built, will be seen many miles off."

"Yes," she replied in a discreet tone, for many eyes were upon her. "The view is very extensive." She glanced round upon the whole landscape stretched out before her, in the extreme distance of which was visible the town of Westcombe.

"How long does it take to go to Westcombe across this way?" she asked of him while they were bringing up the carriage.

"About two hours," he said.

"Two hours—so long as that, does it? How far is it away?"

"Eight miles."

"Two hours to drive eight miles—who ever heard of such a thing!"

"I thought you meant walking."

"Ah, yes; but one hardly means walking without expressly stating it."

"Well, it seems just the other way to me—that walking is meant unless you say driving."

That was the whole of their conversation. The remarks had been simple and trivial, but they brought a similar thought into the minds of both of them. On her part it spread a sudden gloom over her face, and it made him feel dead at heart. It was that horrid thought of their differing habits and of those contrasting positions which could not be reconciled.

Indeed, this perception of their disparity weighed more and more heavily upon him as the days went on. There was no doubt about their being lovers, though scarcely recognised by themselves as such; and, in spite of Geraldine's warm and unreflecting impulses, a sense of how little Egbert was accustomed to what is called society, and the polite forms which constant usage had made almost nature with her, would rise on occasion, and rob her of many an otherwise pleasant minute. When any little occurrence had brought this into more prominence than usual, Egbert would go away, wander about the lanes, and be kept awake a great part of the night by the distress of mind such a recognition brought upon him. How their intimacy would end, in what uneasiness, yearning, and misery, he could not guess. As for picturing a future of happiness with her by his side there was not ground enough upon which to rest the momentary imagination of it. Thus they mutually oppressed each other even while they loved.

In addition to this anxiety was another; what would be thought of their romance by her father, if he were to find it out? It was impossible to tell him, for nothing could come of that but Egbert's dismissal and Geraldine's seclusion; and how could these be borne?

He looked round anxiously for some means of deliverance. There were two things to be thought of, the saving of her dignity, and the saving of his and her happiness. That to accomplish the first he ought voluntarily to leave the village before their attachment got known, and never seek her again, was what he sometimes felt; but the idea brought such misery along with it that it died out under contemplation.

He determined at all events to put the case clearly before her, to heroically set forth at their next meeting the true bearings of their position, which she plainly did not realise to the full as yet. It had never entered her mind that the link between them might be observed by the curious, and instantly talked of. Yes, it was his duty to warn her, even though by so doing he would be heaping coals of fire on his own head. For by acting upon his hint she would be lost to him, and the charm that lay in her false notions of the world be for ever destroyed.

That they would ultimately be found out, and Geraldine be lowered in local estimation, was, indeed, almost inevitable. There was one grain of satisfaction only among this mass of distresses. Whatever should become public, only the fashionable side of her character could be depreciated; the natural woman, the specimen of English girlhood that he loved, no one could impugn or harm.

Meetings had latterly taken place between them without any pretence of accident, and these were facilitated in an amazing manner by the duty imposed upon her of visiting the school as the representative of her father. At her very next appearance he told her all he thought. It was when the children had left the room for the quarter of an hour's airing that he gave them in the middle of the morning.

She was quite hurt at being treated with justice, and a crowd of tears came into her sorrowful eyes. She had never thought of half that he feared, and almost questioned his kindness in enlightening her.

"Perhaps you are right," she murmured, with the merest motion of lip. "Yes, it is sadly true. Should our conduct become known, nobody will judge us fairly. 'She was a wild, weak girl,' they will say."

"To care for such a man—a village youth. They will even suppress the fact that his father was a painter of no mean power, and a gentleman by education, little as it would redeem us; and justify their doing so by reflecting that in adding to the contrast they improve the tale:

> And calumny meanwhile shall feed on us
> As worms devour the dead: what we have done
> None shall dare vouch, though it be truly known.

And they will continue, 'He was an artful fellow to win a girl's affections in that way—one of the mere scum of the earth,' they'll say."

"Don't, don't make it so bad!" she implored, weeping outright. "They cannot go so far. Human nature is not so wicked and blind. And they *dare* not speak so disrespectfully of me, or of any one I choose to favour." A slight haughtiness was apparent in these words. "But, oh, don't let us talk of it—it makes the time miserable."

However, she had been warned. But the difficulty which presented itself to her mind was, after all, but a small portion of the whole. It was how should they meet together without causing a convulsion in neighbouring society. His was more radical and complex. The only natural drift of love was towards marriage. But how could he picture, at any length of years ahead, her in a cottage as his wife, or himself in a mansion as her husband? He in the one case, she in the other, were alike painfully incredible.

But time had flown, and he conducted her to the door. "Good-bye, Egbert," she said tenderly.

"Good-bye, dear, dear madam," he answered; and she was gone.

Geraldine had never hinted to him to call her by her Christian name, and finding that she did not particularly wish it he did not care to do so. "Madam" was as good a name as any other for her, and by adhering to it and using it at the warmest moments it seemed to change its nature from that of a mere title to a soft pet sound. He often wondered in after days at the strange condition of a girl's heart which could allow so much in reality, and at the same time permit the existence of a little barrier such as that; how the keen intelligent mind of woman could be ever so slightly hoodwinked by a sound. Yet, perhaps, it was womanlike, after all, and she may have caught at it as the only straw within reach of that dignity or pride of birth which was drowning in her impetuous affection.

CHAPTER VIII

The world and its ways have a certain worth,
And to press a point while these oppose
Were a simple policy: best wait,
And we lose no friends, and gain no foes.

The inborn necessity of ransacking the future for a germ of hope led Egbert Mayne to dwell for longer and longer periods on the at first rejected possibility of winning and having her. And apart from any thought of marriage, he knew that Geraldine was sometimes a trifle vexed that their experiences contained so little in common—that he had never dressed for dinner, or made use of a carriage in his life; even though in literature he was her master, thanks to his tastes.

For the first time he seriously contemplated a visionary scheme which had been several times cursorily glanced at; a scheme almost as visionary as any ever entertained by a man not yet blinded to the limits of the possible. Lighted on by impulse, it was not taken up without long calculation, and it was one in which every link was reasoned out as carefully and as clearly as his powers would permit. But the idea that he would be able to carry it through was an assumption which, had he bestowed upon it one-hundredth part of the thought spent on the details of its working, he would have thrown aside as unfeasible.

To give up the school, to go to London or elsewhere, and there to try to rise to her level by years of sheer exertion, was the substance of this scheme. However his lady's heart might be grieved by his apparent desertion, he would go. A knowledge of life and of men must be acquired, and that could never be done by thinking at home.

Egbert's abstract love for the gigantic task was but small; but there was absolutely no other honest road to her sphere. That the habits of men should be so subversive of the law of nature as to indicate that he was not worthy to marry a woman whose own instincts said that he was worthy, was a great anomaly, he thought, with some rebelliousness; but this did not upset the fact or remove the difficulty.

He told his fair mistress at their next accidental meeting (much sophistry lay in their definition of "accidental" at this season) that he had determined to leave Tollamore. Mentally she exulted at his spirit, but her heart despaired. He solemnly assured her that it would be much better for them both in the end; and she became submissive, and entirely agreed with him. Then she seemed to acquire a sort of superior insight by virtue of her superior rank, and murmured, "You will expand your mind, and get to despise me for all this, and for my want of pride in being so easily won; and it will end unhappily."

Her imagination so affected her that she could not hinder the tears from falling. Nothing was more effective in checking his despair than the sight of her despairing, and he immediately put on a more hopeful tone.

"No," he said, taking her by the hand, "I shall rise, and become so learned and so famous that—." He did not like to say plainly that he really hoped to win her as his wife, but it is very probable that she guessed his meaning nearly enough.

"You have some secret resources!" she exclaimed. "Some help is promised you in this ambitious plan."

It was most painful to him to have to tell her the truth after this sanguine expectation, and how uncertain and unaided his plans were. However, he cheered her with the words, "Wait and see." But he himself had many misgivings when her sweet face was turned away.

Upon this plan he acted at once. Nothing of moment occurred during the autumn, and the time for his departure gradually came near. The sale of his grandfather's effects having taken place, and notice having been given at the school, there was very little else for him to do in the way of preparation, for there was no family to be consulted, no household to be removed. On the last day of teaching, when the afternoon lessons were over, he bade farewell to the school children. The younger ones cried, not from any particular reflection on the loss they would sustain, but simply because their hearts were tender to any announcement couched in solemn terms. The elder children sincerely regretted Egbert, as an acquaintance who had not filled the post of schoolmaster so long as to be quite spoilt as a human being.

On the morning of departure he rose at half-past three, for Tollamore was a remote nook of a remote district, and it was necessary to start early, his plan being to go by packet from Melport. The candle-flame had a sad and yellow look when it was brought into his bedroom by Nathan Brown, one of his grandfather's old labourers, at whose house he had taken a temporary lodging, and who had agreed to awake him and assist his departure. Few things will take away a man's confidence in an impulsive scheme more than being called up by candlelight upon a chilly morning to commence working it out. But when Egbert heard Nathan's great feet stamping spiritedly about the floor downstairs, in earnest preparation of breakfast, he overcame his weakness and bustled out of bed.

They breakfasted together, Nathan drinking the hot tea with rattling sips, and Egbert thinking as he looked at him that Nathan had never appeared so desirable a man to have about him as now when he was about to give him up.

"Well, good mornen, Mistur Mayne," Nathan said, as he opened the door to let Egbert out. "And mind this, sir; if they use ye bad up there, th'lt always find a hole to put thy head into at Nathan Brown's, I'll warrant as much."

Egbert stepped from the door, and struck across to the manor-house. The morning was dark, and the raw wind made him shiver till walking warmed him. "Good heavens, here's an undertaking!" he sometimes thought. Old trees seemed to look at him through the gloom, as they rocked uneasily to and fro; and now and then a dreary drop of rain beat upon his face as he went on. The dead leaves in the ditches, which could be heard but not seen, shifted their positions with a troubled rustle, and flew at intervals with a little rap against his walking-stick and hat. He was glad to reach the north stile, and get into the park, where, with an anxious pulse, he passed beneath the creaking limes.

"Will she wake soon enough; will she be forgetful, and sleep over the time?" He had asked himself this many times since he rose that morning, and still beset by the inquiry, he drew near to the mansion.

Her bedroom was in the north wing, facing towards the church, and on turning the brow of the hill a faint light in the window reassured him. Taking a few little stones from the path he threw them upon the sill, as they had agreed, and she instantly opened the window, and said softly, "The butler sleeps on the ground floor on this side, go to the bow-window in the shrubbery."

He went round among the bushes to the place mentioned, which was entirely sheltered from the wind. She soon appeared, bearing in her hand a wax taper, so small that it scarcely gave more light than a glowworm. She wore the same dress that she had worn when they first met on the previous Christmas, and her hair was loose, as at that time. Indeed, she looked throughout much as she had looked then, except that her bright eyes were red, as Egbert could see well enough.

"I have something for you," she said softly as she opened the window. "How much time is there?"

"Half-an-hour only, dearest."

She began a sigh, but checked it, at the same time holding out a packet to him.

"Here are fifty pounds," she whispered. "It will be useful to you now, and more shall follow."

Egbert felt how impossible it was to accept this. "No, my dear one," he said, "I cannot."

"I don't require it, Egbert. I wish you to have it; I have plenty. Come, do take it." But seeing that he continued firm on this point she reluctantly gave in, saying that she would keep it for him.

"I fear so much that papa suspects me," she said. "And if so, it was my own fault, and all owing to a conversation I began with him without thinking beforehand that it would be dangerous."

"What did you say?"

"I said," she whispered, "'Suppose a man should love me very much, would you mind my being acquainted with him if he were a very worthy man?' 'That depends upon his rank and circumstances,' he said. 'Suppose,' I said, 'that in addition to his goodness he had much learning, and had made his name famous in the world, but was not altogether rich?' I think I showed too much earnestness, and I wished that I could have recalled my words. 'When the time comes I will tell you,' he said, 'and don't speak or think of these matters again.'"

In consequence of this new imprudence of hers Egbert doubted if it would be right to correspond with her. He said nothing about it then, but it added a new shade to the parting.

"I think your decision a good and noble one," she murmured, smiling hopefully. "And you will come back some day a wondrous man of the world, talking of vast Schemes, radical Errors, and saying such words as the 'Backbone of Society,' the 'Tendency of Modern Thought,' and other things like that. When papa says to you, 'My Lord the Chancellor,' you will answer him with 'A tall man, with a deep-toned voice—I know him well.' When he says, 'Such and such were Lord Hatton's words, I think,' you will answer, 'No, they were Lord Tyrrell's; I was present on the occasion'; and so on in that way. You must get to talk authoritatively about vintages and their dates, and to know all about epicureanism, idleness, and fashion; and so you will beat him with his own weapons, for he knows nothing of these things. He will criticise you; then he will be nettled; then he will admire you."

Egbert kissed her hand devotedly, and held it long.

"If you cannot in the least succeed," she added, "I shall never think the less of you. The truly great stand on no middling ledge; they are either famous or unknown."

Egbert moved slowly away amongst the laurestines. Holding the light above her bright head she smiled upon him, as if it were unknown to her that she wept at the same time.

He left the park precincts, and followed the turnpike road to Melport. In spite of the misery of parting he felt relieved of a certain oppressiveness, now that his presence at Tollamore could no longer bring disgrace upon her. The threatening rain passed off by the time that he reached the ridge dividing the inland districts from the coast. It began to get light, but his journey was still very lonely. Ultimately the yellow shore-line of pebbles grew visible, and the distant horizon of water, spreading like a grey upland against the sky, till he could soon hear the measured flounce of the waves.

He entered the town at sunrise, just as the lamps were extinguished, and went to a tavern to breakfast. At half-past eight o'clock the boat steamed out of the harbour and reached London after a passage of five-and-forty hours.

PART II

CHAPTER I

He, like a captain who beleaguers round
Some strong-built castle on a rising ground,
Views all the approaches with observing eyes;
This and that other part in vain he tries,
And more on industry than force relies.

Since Egbert Mayne's situation is not altogether a new and unprecedented one, there will be no necessity for detailing in all its minuteness his attempt to scale the steeps of Fame. For notwithstanding the fact that few, comparatively, have reached the top, the lower tracts of that troublesome incline have been trodden by as numerous a company as any allegorical spot in the world.

The reader must then imagine five years to have elapsed, during which rather formidable slice of human life Egbert had been constantly striving. It had been drive, drive from month to month; no rest, nothing but effort. He had progressed from newspaper work to criticism, from criticism to independent composition of a mild order, from the latter to the publication of a book which nobody ever heard of, and from this to the production of a work of really sterling merit, which appeared anonymously. Though he did not set society in a blaze, or even in a smoke, thereby, he certainly caused a good many people to talk about him, and to be curious as to his name.

The luminousness of nature which had been sufficient to attract the attention and heart of Geraldine Allenville had, indeed, meant much. That there had been power enough in the presence, speech, mind, and tone of the poor painter's son to fascinate a girl of Geraldine's station was of itself a ground for the presumption that he might do a work in the world if he chose. The attachment to her was just the stimulus which such a constitution as his required, and it had at first acted admirably upon him. Afterwards the case was scarcely so happy.

He had investigated manners and customs no less than literature; and for awhile the experience was exciting enough. But several habits which he had at one time condemned in the ambitious classes now became his own. His original fondness for art, literature, and science was getting quenched by his slowly increasing habit of looking upon each and all of these as machinery wherewith to effect a purpose.

A new feeling began to animate all his studies. He had not the old interest in them for their own sakes, but a breathless interest in them as factors in the game of sink or swim. He entered picture galleries, not, as formerly, because it was his humour to dream pleasantly over the images therein expressed, but to be able to talk on demand about painters and their peculiarities. He examined Correggio to criticise his flesh shades; Angelico, to speak technically of the pink faces of his saints; Murillo, to say fastidiously that there was a certain silliness in the look of his old men; Rubens for his sensuous women; Turner for his Turneresqueness. Romney was greater than Reynolds because Lady Hamilton had been his model, and thereby hung a tale. Bonozzi Gozzoli was better worth study than Raffaelle, since the former's name was a learned sound to utter, and all knowledge got up about him would tell.

Whether an intense love for a woman, and that woman Geraldine, was a justifiable reason for this desire to shine it is not easy to say.

However, as has been stated, Egbert worked like a slave in these causes, and at the end of five full years was repaid with certain public applause, though, unfortunately, not with much public money. But this he hoped might come soon.

Regarding his love for Geraldine, the most noteworthy fact to be recorded of the period was that all correspondence with her had ceased. In spite of their fear of her father, letters had passed frequently between them on his first leaving home, and had been continued with ardour for some considerable time. The reason of its close will be perceived in the following note, which he received from her two years before the date of the present chapter:—

"Tollamore House.

"MY DEAR EGBERT,

"How shall I tell you what has happened! and yet how can I keep silence when sooner or later you must know all?

"My father has discovered what we feel for each other. He took me into his room and made me promise never to write to you, or seek you, or receive a letter from you. I promised in haste, for I was frightened and excited, and now he trusts me—I wish he did not—for he knows I would not be mean enough to lie. So don't write, poor Egbert, or expect to hear from miserable me. We must try to hope; yet it is a long dreary thing to do. But I *will* hope, and not be beaten. How could I help promising, Egbert, when he compelled me? He is my father. I cannot think what we shall do under it all. It is cruel of life to be like this towards us when we have done no wrong.

　　　*　　　*　　　*　　　*　　　*

"We are going abroad for a long time. I think it is because of you and me, but I don't know. He does not tell me where we shall go. Just as if a place like Europe could make me forget you. He doesn't know what's in me, and how I can think about you and cry at nights—he cannot. If he did, he must see how silly the plan is.

"Remember that you go to church on Sunday mornings, for then I think that perhaps we are reading in the same place at the same moment; and we are sometimes, no doubt. Last Sunday, when we came to this in the Psalms, 'And he shall be like a tree planted by the waterside that will bring forth his fruit in due season: his leaf also shall not wither; and look, whatsoever he doeth, it shall prosper,' I thought, 'That's Egbert in London.' I know you were reading that same verse in your church—I felt that you said it with us. Then I looked up to your old nook under the tower arch. It was a misery to see the wood and the stone just as good as ever, and you not there. It is not only that you are gone at these times, but a heavy creature—blankness—seems to stand in your place.

"But how can I tell you of these thoughts now that I am to write no more? Yet we will hope, and hope. Remember this, that should anything serious happen, I will break the bond and write. Obligation would end then. Good-bye for a time. I cannot put into words what I would finish with. Good-bye, good-bye.　　　　　　　　　"G. A.

"P.S. Might we not write just one line at very wide intervals? It is too much never to write at all."

On receiving this letter Egbert felt that he could not honourably keep up a regular correspondence with her. But a determination to break it off would have been more than he could have adhered to if he had not been strengthened by the hope that he might soon be able to give a plausible reason for renewing it. He sent her a line, bidding her to expect the best results from the prohibition, which, he was sure, would not be for long. Meanwhile, should she think it not wrong to send a line at very wide intervals, he would promptly reply.

But she was apparently too conscientious to do so, for nothing had reached him since. Yet she was as continually in his thought and heart as before. He felt more misgivings than he had chosen to tell her of on the ultimate effect of the prohibition, but could do nothing to remove it. And then he had learnt that Miss Allenville and her father had gone to Paris, as the commencement of a sojourn abroad.

These circumstances had burdened him with long hours of depression, till he had resolved to throw his whole strength into a production which should either give him a fair start towards fame, or make him clearly understand that there was no hope in that direction for such as he. He had begun the attempt, and ended it, and the consequences were fortunate to an unexpected degree.

CHAPTER II

Towards the loadstar of my one desire
I flitted like a dizzy moth, whose flight
Is as a dead leaf's in the owlet light.

Mayne's book having been launched into the world and well received, he found time to emerge from the seclusion he had maintained for several months, and to look into life again.

One warm, fashionable day, between five and six o'clock, he was walking along Piccadilly, absent-minded and unobservant, when an equipage approached whose appearance thrilled him through. It was the Allenville landau, newly-painted up. Egbert felt almost as if he had been going into battle; and whether he should stand forth visibly before her or keep in the background seemed a question of life or death.

He waited in unobserved retirement, which it was not difficult to do, his aspect having much altered since the old times. Coachman, footman, and carriage advanced, in graceful unity of glide, like a swan. Then he beheld her, Geraldine, after two years of silence, five years of waiting, and nearly three years of separation; for although he had seen her two or three times in town after he had taken up his residence there, they had not once met since the year preceding her departure for the Continent.

She came opposite, now passively looking round, then actively glancing at something which interested her. Egbert trembled a little, or perhaps a great deal, at sight of her. But she passed on, and the back of the carriage hid her from his view.

So much of the boy was left in him still that he could scarcely withhold himself from rushing after her, and jumping into the carriage. She had appeared to be well and blooming, and an instinctive vexation that their long separation had produced no perceptible effect upon her, speedily gave way before a more generous sense of gratification at her well-being. Still, had it been possible, he would have been glad to see some sign upon her face that she yet remembered him.

This sudden discovery that they were in town after their years of travel stirred his lassitude into excitement. He went back to his chambers to meditate upon his next step. A trembling on Geraldine's account was disturbing him. She had probably been in London ever since the beginning of the season, but she had not given him a sign to signify that she was so near; and but for this accidental glimpse of her he might have gone on for months without knowing that she had returned from abroad.

Whether she was leading a dull or an exciting life Egbert had no means of knowing. That night after night the arms of interesting young men rested upon her waist and whirled her round the ball-room he could not bear to think. That she frequented gatherings and assemblies of all sorts he calmly owned as very probable, for she was her father's only daughter, and likely to be made much of. That she had not written a line to him since their return was still the grievous point.

"If I had only risen one or two steps further," he thought, "how boldly would I seek her out. But only to have published one successful book in all these years—such grounds are slight indeed."

For several succeeding days he did nothing but look about the Park, and the streets, and the neighbourhood of Chevron Square, where their town-house stood, in the hope of seeing her again; but in vain. There were moments when his distress that she might possibly be indifferent about him and his affairs was unbearable. He fully resolved that he would on some early occasion communicate with her, and know the worst. Years of work remained to be done before he could think of appearing before her father; but he had reached a sort of half-way stage at which some assurance from herself that his track was a hopeful one was positively needed to keep him firm.

Egbert still kept on the look-out for her at every public place; but nearly a month passed, and she did not appear again. One Sunday evening, when he had been wandering near Chevron Square, and looking at her windows from a distance, he returned past her house after dusk. The rooms were lighted, but the windows were still open, and as he strolled along he heard notes from a piano within. They were the accompaniment to an air from the *Messiah,* though no singer's voice was audible. Egbert readily imagined who the player might be, for the *Messiah* was an oratorio which Geraldine often used to wax eloquent upon in days gone by. He had not walked far when he remembered that there was to be an exceptionally fine performance of that stirring composition during the following week, and it instantly occurred to him that Geraldine's mind was running on the same event, and that she intended to be one of the audience.

He resolved upon doing something at a venture. The next morning he went to the ticket-office, and boldly asked for a place as near as possible to those taken in the name of Allenville.

"There is no vacant one in any of those rows," the office-keeper said, "but you can have one very near their number on the other side of the division."

Egbert was astonished that for once in his life he had made a lucky hit. He booked his place, and returned home.

The evening arrived, and he went early. On taking his seat he found himself at the left-hand end of a series of benches, and close to a red cord, which divided the group of seats he had entered from stalls of a somewhat superior kind. He was passing the time in looking at the extent of orchestra space, and other things, when he saw two ladies and a gentleman enter and sit down in the stalls diagonally before his own, and on the other side of the division. It delighted and agitated him to find that one of the three was Geraldine; her two companions he did not know.

"Policy, don't desert me now," he thought; and immediately sat in such a way that unless she turned round to a very unlikely position she would not see him.

There was a certain half-pleasant misery in sitting behind her thus as a possibly despised lover. To-night, at any rate, there would be sights and sounds common to both of them, though they should not communicate to the extent of a word. Even now he could hear the rustle of her garments as she settled down in her seat, and the faint murmur of words that passed between her and her friends.

Never, in the many times that he had listened to that rush of harmonies, had they affected him as they did then; and it was no wonder, considering what an influence upon his own life had been and still was exercised by Geraldine, and that she now sat there before him. The varying strains shook and bent him to themselves as a rippling brook shakes and bends a shadow. The music did not show its power by attracting his attention to its subject; it rather dropped its own libretto and took up in place of that the poem of his life and love.

There was Geraldine still. They were singing the chorus "Lift up your heads," and he found a new impulse of thought in him. It was towards determination. Should every member of her family be against him he would win her in spite of them. He could now see that Geraldine was moved equally with himself by the tones which entered her ears.

"Why do the nations so furiously rage together" filled him with a gnawing thrill, and so changed him to its spirit that he believed he was capable of suffering in silence for his whole lifetime, and of never appearing before her unless she gave a sign.

The audience stood up, and the "Hallelujah Chorus" began. The deafening harmonies flying from this group and from that seemed to absorb all the love and poetry that his life had produced, to pour it upon that one moment, and upon her who stood so close at hand. "I will force Geraldine to be mine," he thought. "I will make that heart ache of love for me." The chorus continued, and her form trembled under its influence. Egbert was for seeking her the next morning and knowing what his chances were, without waiting for further results. The chorus and the personality of Geraldine still filled the atmosphere. "I will seek her to-night—as soon as we get out of this place," he said. The storm of sound now reached its climax, and Geraldine's power was proportionately increased. He would give anything for a glance this minute—to look into her eyes, she into his. "If I can but touch her hand, and get one word from her, I will," he murmured.

He shifted his position somewhat and saw her face. Tears were in her eyes, and her lips were slightly parted. Stretching a little nearer he whispered, "My love!"

Geraldine turned her wet eyes upon him, almost as if she had not been surprised, but had been forewarned by her previous emotion. With the peculiar quickness of grasp that she always showed under sudden circumstances, she had realised the position at a glance.

"Oh, Egbert!" she said; and her countenance flagged as if she would have fainted.

"Give me your hand," he whispered.

She placed her hand in his, under the cord, which it was easy to do without observation; and he held it tight.

"Mine, as before?" he asked.

"Yours now as then," said she.

They were like frail and sorry wrecks upon that sea of symphony, and remained in silent abandonment to the time, till the strains approached their close.

"Can you meet me to-night?" said Egbert.

She was half frightened at the request, and said, "Where?"

"At your own front door, at twelve o'clock." He then was at once obliged to gently withdraw himself, for the chorus was ended, and the people were sitting down.

The remainder was soon over, and it was time to leave. Egbert watched her and her party out of the house, and, turning to the other doorway, went out likewise.

CHAPTER III

Bright reason will mock thee,
Like the sun from a wintry sky.

When he reached his chambers he sat down and literally did
nothing but watch the hand of the mantel-clock minute by
minute, till it marked half-past eleven, scarcely removing his
eyes. Then going again into the street he called a cab, and was
driven down Park Lane and on to the corner of Chevron
Square. Here he alighted, and went round to the number
occupied by the Allenvilles.

A lamp stood nearly opposite the doorway, and by receding
into the gloom to the railing of the square he could see
whatever went on in the porch of the house. The lamps over
the doorways were nearly all extinguished, and everything
about this part was silent and deserted, except at a house on
the opposite side of the square, where a ball was going on.
But nothing of that concerned Egbert: his eyes had sought
out and remained fixed upon Mr Allenville's front door, in
momentary expectation of seeing it gently open.

The dark wood of the door showed a keen and distinct
edge upon the pale stone of the porch floor. It must have
been about two minutes before the hour he had named when
he fancied he saw a slight movement at that point, as of
something slipped out from under the door.

"It is but fancy," he said to himself.

He turned his eyes away, and turned them back again.
Some object certainly seemed to have been thrust under the
door. At this moment the four quarters of midnight began to
strike, and then the hour. Egbert could remain still no longer,
and he went into the porch. A note had been slipped under
the door from inside.

He took it to the lamp, turned it over, and saw that it was
directed only with initials,—" To E. M." Egbert tore it open
and glanced upon the page. With a shiver of disappointment
he read these words in her handwriting:—

" It was when under the influence of much emotion, kindled in
me by the power of the music, that I half assented to a meeting with

you to-night; and I believe that you also were excited when you asked for one. After some quiet reflection I have decided that it will be much better for us both if we do not see each other.

"You will, I know, judge me fairly in this. You have by this time learnt what life is; what particular positions, accidental though they may be, ask, nay, imperatively exact from us. If you say 'not imperatively,' you cannot speak from knowledge of the world.

"To be woven and tied in with the world by blood, acquaintance, tradition, and external habit, is to a woman to be utterly at the beck of that world's customs. In youth we do not see this. You and I did not see it. We were but a girl and a boy at the time of our meetings at Tollamore. What was our knowledge? A list of other people's words. What was our wisdom? None at all.

"It is well for you now to remember that I am not the unsophisticated girl I was when you first knew me. For better or for worse I have become complicated, exclusive, and practised. A woman who can speak, or laugh, or dance, or sing before any number of men with perfect composure may be no sinner, but she is not what I was once. She is what I am now. She is not the girl you loved. That woman is not here.

"I wish to write kindly to you, as to one for whom, in spite of the unavoidable division between our paths, I must always entertain a heartfelt respect. Is it, after this, out of place in me to remind you how contrasting are all our associations, how inharmonious our times and seasons? Could anything ever overpower this incongruity?

"But I must write plainly, and, though it may grieve you now, it will produce ultimately the truest ease. This is my meaning. If I could accept your addresses without an entire loss of position I would do so; but, since this cannot be, we must forget each other.

"Believe me to be, with wishes and prayers for your happiness,

"Your sincere friend,
"G. A."

Egbert could neither go home nor stay still; he walked off rapidly in any direction for the sole sake of vehement motion. His first impulse was to get into darkness. He went towards Kensington; thence threaded across to the Uxbridge Road, thence to Kensal Green, where he turned into a lane and followed it to Kilburn, and the hill beyond, at which spot he halted and looked over the vast haze of light extending to the length and breadth of London. Turning back and wandering among some fields by a way he could never afterwards recollect, sometimes sitting down, sometimes leaning on a stile, he lingered on until the sun had risen. He then slowly walked again towards London, and, feeling by this time very weary, he entered the first refreshment-house that he came to, and attempted to eat something. Having sat for some time over this meal without doing much more than taste it, he arose and set out for the street in which he lived. Once in his own rooms he lay down upon the couch and fell asleep.

When he awoke it was four o'clock. Egbert then dressed and went out, partook of a light meal at his club at the dismal hour between luncheon and dinner, and cursorily glanced over the papers and reviews. Among the first things that he saw were eulogistic notices of his own book in three different reviews, each the most prominent and weighty of its class. Two of them, at least, would, he knew, find their way to the drawing-room of the Allenvilles, for they were among the periodicals which the Squire regularly patronised.

Next, in a weekly review he read the subjoined note:—

"The authorship of the book —— ——, about which conjecture has lately been so much exercised, is now ascribed to Mr Egbert Mayne, whose first attempt in that kind we noticed in these pages some eighteen months ago."

He took up a daily paper, and presently lighted on the following paragraph:—

"It is announced that a marriage is arranged between Lord Bretton, of Tosthill Park, and Geraldine, only daughter of Foy Allenville, Esq., of Tollamore House, Wessex."

Egbert arose and went towards home. Arrived there he met the postman at the door, and received from him a small note. The young man mechanically glanced at the direction.

"From her," he mentally exclaimed. "What does it—"

This was what the letter contained:—

"Twelve o'clock.
"I have just learnt that the anonymous author of the book in which the world has been so interested during the past two months, and which I have read, is none other than yourself. Accept my congratulations. It seems almost madness in me to address you now. But I could not do otherwise on receipt of this news, and after writing my last letter. Let your knowledge of my nature prevent your misconstru-

ing my motives in writing thus on the spur of the moment. I need scarcely add, please keep it a secret for ever. I am not morally afraid, but other lives, hopes, and objects than mine have to be considered.

"The announcement of the marriage is premature, to say the least. I would tell you more, but dare not.

"G. A."

The conjunction of all this intelligence produced in Egbert's heart a stillness which was some time in getting aroused to excitement. His emotion was formless. He knew not what point to take hold of and survey his position from; and, though his faculties grew clearer with the passage of time, he failed in resolving on a course with any deliberateness. No sooner had he thought, "I will never see her again for my pride's sake," than he said, "Why not see her? she is a woman; she may love me yet."

He went downstairs and out of the house, and walked by way of the Park towards Chevron Square.

Probably nobody will rightly appreciate Mayne's wild behaviour at this juncture, unless, which is very unlikely, he has been in a somewhat similar position himself. It may always appear to cool critics, even if they are generous enough to make allowances for his feelings, as visionary and weak in the extreme. Yet it was scarcely to be expected, after the mental and emotional strain that he had undergone during the preceding five years, that he should have acted much otherwise.

He rang the bell and asked to see Mr Allenville. He, perhaps fortunately, was not at home. "Miss Allenville, then," said Mayne.

"She is just driving out," said the footman dubiously.

Egbert then noticed for the first time that the carriage was at the door, and almost as soon as the words were spoken Geraldine came downstairs.

"The madness of hoping to call that finished creature, wife!" he thought.

Geraldine recognised him, and looked perplexed.

"One word, Miss Allenville," he murmured.

She assented, and he followed her into the adjoining room.

"I have come," said Egbert. "I know it is hasty of me; but I must hear my doom from your own lips. Five years ago you

spurred me on to ambition. I have followed but too closely
the plan I then marked out, for I have hoped all along for a
reward. What am I to think? Have you indeed left off feeling
what you once felt for me?"

"I cannot speak of it now," she said hurriedly. "I told you in
my letter as much as I dared. Believe me I cannot speak—in
the way you wish. I will always be your friend."

"And is this the end? Oh, my God!"

"And we shall hope to see you to dinner some day, now you
are famous," she continued, pale as ashes. "But I—cannot be
with you as we once were. I was such a child at that time, you
know."

"Geraldine, is this all I get after this lapse of time and heat
of labour?"

"I am not my own mistress—I have my father to please," she
faintly murmured. "I must please him. There is no help for
this. Go from me—do go!"

Egbert turned and went, for he felt that he had no longer
a place beside her.

CHAPTER IV

Then I said in my heart, "As it happeneth to the fool, so it
happeneth even to me; and why was I then more wise?"

Mayne was in rather an ailing state for several days after the
above-mentioned event. Yet the lethean stagnation which
usually comes with the realisation that all is over allowed him
to take some deep sleeps, to which he had latterly been a
stranger.

The hours went by, and he did the best he could to dismiss
his regrets for Geraldine. He was assisted to the very little
success that he attained in this by reflecting how different a
woman she must have become from her old sweet self of five
or six years ago.

"But how paltry is my success now she has vanished!" he
said. "What is it worth? What object have I in following it up
after this?" It rather startled him to see that the root of his

desire for celebrity having been Geraldine, he now was a man who had no further motive in moving on. Town life had for some time been depressing to him. He began to doubt whether he could ever be happy in the course of existence that he had followed through these later years. The perpetual strain, the lack of that quiet to which he had been accustomed in early life, the absence of all personal interest in things around him, was telling upon his health of body and of mind.

Then revived the wish which had for some time been smouldering in his secret heart—to leave off, for the present, at least, his efforts for distinction; to retire for a few months to his old country nook, and there to meditate on his next course.

To set about this was curiously awkward to him. He had planned methods of retrogression in case of defeat through want of ability, want of means, or lack of opportunity; but to retreat because his appetite for advance had gone off was what he had never before thought of.

His reflections turned upon the old home of his mother's family. He knew exactly how Tollamore appeared at that time of the year. The trees with their half-ripe apples, the bees and butterflies lazy from the heat; the haymaking over, the harvest not begun, the people lively and always out of doors. He would visit the spot, and call upon some old and half-forgotten friends of his grandfather in an adjoining parish.

Two days later he left town. The fine weather, his escape from that intricate web of effort in which he had been bound these five years, the sensation that nobody in the world had any claims upon him, imparted some buoyancy to his mind; and it was in a serene if sad spirit that he entered Tollamore Vale, and smelt his native air.

He did not at once proceed to the village, but stopped at Fairland, the parish next adjoining. It was now evening, and he called upon some of the old cottagers whom he knew. Time had set a mark upon them all since he had last been there. Middle-aged men were a little more round-shouldered, their wives had taken to spectacles, young people had grown up out of recognition, and old men had passed into second childhood.

Egbert found here, as he had expected, precisely such a lodging as a hermit would desire. It was in an ivy-covered detached house which had been partly furnished for a tenant who had never come, and it was kept clean by an old woman living in a cottage near. She offered to wait upon Egbert whilst he remained there, coming in the morning and leaving in the afternoon, thus giving him the house to himself during the latter part of the day.

When it grew dusk he went out, wishing to ramble for a little time. The gibbous moon rose on his right, the stars showed themselves sleepily one by one, and the far distance turned to a mysterious ocean of grey. He instinctively directed his steps towards Tollamore, and when there towards the school. It looked very little changed since the year in which he had had the memorable meetings with her there, excepting that the creepers had grown higher.

He went on towards the Park. Here was the place whereon he had used to await her coming—he could be sure of the spot to a foot. There was the turn of the hill around which she had appeared. The sentimental effect of the scenes upon him was far greater than he had expected, so great that he wished he had never been so reckless as to come here. "But this is folly," he thought. "The betrothed of Lord Bretton is a woman of the world in whose thoughts, hopes, and habits I have no further interest or share."

In the lane he heard the church-bells ringing out their five notes, and meeting a shepherd Egbert asked him what was going on.

"Practising," he said, in an uninterested voice. "'Tis against young Miss's wedding, that their hands may be thoroughly in by the day for't."

He presently came to where his grandfather's old house had stood. It was pulled down, the ground it covered having become a shabby, irregular spot, half grown over with trailing plants. The garden had been grassed down, but the old appletrees still remained, their trunks and stems being now sheeted on one side with moonlight. He entertained himself by guessing where the front door of the house had been, at which Geraldine had entered on the memorable evening when she came to him full of grief and pity, and a tacit avowal of love was made on each side. Where they had sat together was now but a heap of broken rubbish half covered with grass. Near this melancholy spot was the cottage once inhabited by Nathan Brown. But Nathan was dead now, and his wife and family had gone elsewhere.

Finding the effect of memory to be otherwise than cheerful, Mayne hastened from the familiar spot, and went on to the parish of Fairland in which he had taken his lodging.

It soon became whispered in the neighbourhood that Miss Allenville's wedding was to take place on the 17th of October. Egbert heard few particulars of the matter beyond the date, though it is possible that he might have known more if he had tried. He preferred to fortify himself by dipping deeply into the few books he had brought with him; but the most obvious plan of escaping his thoughts, that of a rapid change of scene by travel, he was unaccountably loth to adopt. He felt that he could not stay long in this district; yet an indescribable fascination held him on day after day, till the date of the marriage was close at hand.

CHAPTER V

How all the other passions fleet to air,
As doubtful thoughts, and rash-embraced despair
And shudd'ring fear, and green-eyed jealousy!

On the eve of the wedding the people told Mayne that arches and festoons of late summer-flowers and evergreens had been put up across the path between the church porch at Tollamore and the private gate to the Squire's lawn, for the procession of bride and bridesmaids. Before it got dark several villagers went on foot to the church to look at and admire these decorations. Egbert had determined to see the ceremony over. It would do him good, he thought, to be witness of the sacrifice.

Hence he, too, went along the path to Tollamore to inspect

the preparations. It was dusk by the time that he reached the churchyard, and he entered it boldly, letting the gate fall together with a loud slam, as if he were a man whom nothing troubled. He looked at the half-completed bowers of green, and passed on into the church, never having entered it since he first left Tollamore.

He was standing by the chancel-arch, and observing the quantity of flowers which had been placed around the spot, when he heard the creaking of a gate on its hinges. Two figures entered the church, and Egbert stepped behind a canopied tomb.

The persons were females, and they appeared to be servants from the neighbouring mansion. They brought more flowers and festoons, and were talking of the event of the morrow. Coming into the chancel they threw down their burdens with a remark that it was too dark to arrange more flowers that night.

"This is where she is to kneel," said one, standing with her arms akimbo before the altar-railing. "And I wish 'twas I instead, Lord send if I don't."

The two girls went on gossiping till other footsteps caused them to turn.

"I won't say 'tisn't she. She has been here two or three times to day. Let's go round this way."

And the servants went towards the door by a circuitous path round the aisle, to avoid meeting with the new-comer.

Egbert, too, thought he would leave the place now that he had heard and seen thus much; but from carelessness or design he went straight down the nave. An instant afterwards he was standing face to face with Geraldine. The servants had vanished.

"Good evening," she said serenely, not knowing him, and supposing him to be a parishioner.

Egbert returned the words hastily, and, in standing aside to let her pass, looked clearly into her eyes and pale face, as if there never had been a time at which he would have done anything on earth for her sake.

She knew him, and started, uttering a weak exclamation. When he reached the door he turned his head, and saw that

she was irresolutely holding up her hand, as if to beckon to
him to come back.

"One word, since I have met you," she said in unequal half-
whispered tones. "I have felt that I was one-sided in my haste
on the day you called to see me in London. I misunderstood
you."

Egbert could at least out-do her in self-control, and, astonished that she should have spoken, he answered in a yet
colder tone,

"I am sorry for that; very sorry, madam."

"And you excuse it?"

"Of course I do, readily. And I hope you, too, will pardon
my intrusion on that day, and understand the—circumstances."

"Yes, yes. Especially as I am most to blame for those indiscreet proceedings in our early lives which led to it."

"Certainly you were not most to blame."

"How can you say that?" she answered with a slight laugh,
"when you know nothing of what my motives and feelings
were?"

"I know well enough to judge, for I was the elder. Let me
just recall some points in your own history at that time."

"No."

"Will you not hear a word?"

"I cannot. . . . . Are you writing another book?"

"I am doing nothing. I am idling at Monk's Hut."

"Indeed!" she said, slightly surprised. "Well, you will always
have my good wishes, whatever you may do. If any of my
relatives can ever help you—"

"Thank you, madam, very much. I think, however, that I
can help myself."

She was silent, looking upon the floor; and Egbert spoke
again, successfully hiding the feelings of his heart under a
light and untrue tone. "Miss Allenville, you know that I loved
you devotedly for many years, and that that love was the
starting point of all my ambition. My sense of it makes this
meeting rather awkward. But men survive almost anything.
I have proved it. Their love is strong while it lasts, but it
soon withers at sight of a new face. I congratulate you on

your coming marriage. Perhaps I may marry some day, too."

"I hope you will find some one worth your love. I am sorry I ever—inconvenienced you as I did. But one hardly knows at that age—"

"Don't think of it for a moment—I really entreat you not to think of that." What prompted the cruelty of his succeeding words he never could afterwards understand. "It was a hard matter at first for me to forget you, certainly; but perhaps I was helped in my wish by the strong prejudice I originally had against your class and family. I have fixed my mind firmly upon the differences between us, and my youthful fancy is pretty fairly overcome. Those old silly days of devotion were pretty enough, but the devotion was entirely unpractical, as you have seen, of course."

"Yes, I have seen it," she faltered.

"It was scarcely of a sort which survives accident and division, and is strengthened by disaster."

"Well, perhaps not, perhaps not. You can scarcely care much now whether it was or not; or, indeed, care anything about me or my happiness."

"I do care."

"How much? As you do for that of any other wretched human being?"

"Wretched? No!"

"I will tell you—I must tell you!" she said with rapid utterance. "This is my secret, this. I don't love the man I am going to marry; but I have agreed to be his wife to satisfy my friends. Say you don't hate me for what I have told. I could not bear that you should not know!"

"Hate you? Oh, Geraldine!"

A hair's-breadth further, and they would both have broken down.

"Not a word more. Now you know my unhappy state, and I shall die content."

"But, darling—my Geraldine!"

"It is too late. Good-night—good-bye!" She spoke in a hurried voice, almost like a low cry, and rushed away.

Here was a revelation. Egbert moved along to the door, and up the path, in a condition in which his mind caused his very body to ache. He gazed vacantly through the railings of the lawn, which came close to the churchyard; but she was gone. He still moved mechanically on. A little further and he was overtaken by the parish clerk, who, addressing a few words to him, soon recognised his voice.

The clerk's talk, too, was about the wedding. "Is the marriage likely to be a happy one?" asked Egbert, aroused by the subject.

"Well, between you and me, Mr Mayne, 'tis a made up affair. Some says she can't bear the man."

"Lord Bretton?"

"Yes. I could say more if I dared; but what's the good of it now!"

"I suppose none," said Egbert wearily.

He was glad to be again alone, and went on towards Fairland slowly and heavily. Had Geraldine forgotten him, and loved elsewhere with a light heart, he could have borne it; but this sacrifice at a time when, left to herself, she might have listened to him, was an intolerable misery. Her inconsistent manner, her appearance of being swayed by two feelings, her half-reservations, were all explained. "Against her wishes," he said; "at heart she may still be mine. Oh, Geraldine, my poor Geraldine, is it come to this!"

He bitterly regretted his first manner towards her, and turned round to consider whether he could not go back, endeavour to find her, and ask if he could be of any possible use. But all this was plainly absurd. He again proceeded homeward as before.

Reaching Fairland he sat awhile in his empty house without a light, and then went to bed. Owing to the distraction of his mind he lay for three or four hours meditating, and listening to the autumn wind, turning restlessly from side to side, the blood throbbing in his temples and singing in his ears, and the ticking of his watch waxing apparently loud enough to stun him. He conjured up the image of Geraldine in her various stages of preparation on the following day. He saw her coming in at the well-known door, walking down the aisle in a floating cloud of white, and receiving the eyes of the assembled crowd without a flush, or a sign of consciousness; utter-

ing the words, "I take thee to my wedded husband," as quietly
as if she were dreaming them. And the husband? Egbert
shuddered. How could she have consented, even if her
memories stood their ground only half so obstinately as
his own? As for himself, he perceived more clearly than
ever how intricately she had mingled with every motive in
his past career. Some portion of the thought, "marriage
with Geraldine," had been marked on every day of his
manhood.

Ultimately he fell into a fitful sleep, when he dreamed of
fighting, wading, diving, boring, through innumerable multi-
tudes, in the midst of which Geraldine's form appeared
flitting about, in the usual confused manner of dreams—
sometimes coming towards him, sometimes receding, and
getting thinner and thinner till she was a mere film tossed
about upon a seething mass.

He jumped up in the bed, damp with a cold perspiration,
and in an agony of disquiet. It was a minute or two before he
could collect his senses. He went to the window and looked
out. It was quite dark, and the wind moaned and whistled
round the corners of the house in the heavy intonations
which seem to express that ruthlessness has all the world to
itself.

"Egbert, do, do come to me!" reached his ears in a faint
voice from the darkness.

There was no mistaking it: it was assuredly the tongue of
Geraldine.

He half dressed himself, ran down stairs, and opened the
front door, holding the candle above his head. Nobody was
visible.

He set down the light, hastened round the back of the
house, and saw a dusky figure turning the corner to get to the
gate. He then ran diagonally across the plot, and intercepted
the form in the path. "Geraldine!" he said, "can it indeed be
you?"

"Yes, it is, it is!" she cried wildly, and fell upon his shoulder.

The hot turmoil of excitement pervading her hindered her
from fainting, and Egbert placed his arm round her, and led
her into the house, without asking a question, or meeting

with any resistance. He assisted her into a chair as soon as they reached the front room.

"I have run away from home, Egbert, and to you!" she sobbed. "I am not insane: they and you may think so, but I am not. I came to find you. Such shocking things have happened since I met you just now. Can Lord Bretton come and claim me?"

"Nobody on earth can claim you, darling, against your will. Now tell it all to me."

She spoke on between her tears. "I have loved you ever since, Egbert; but such influences have been brought to bear upon me that at last I have hardly known what I was doing. At last, I thought that perhaps, after all, it would be better to become a lady of title, with a large park and houses of my own, than the wife of any man of genius who was poor. I loved you all the time, but I was half ashamed that I loved you. I went out continually, that gaiety might obscure the past. And then dark circles came round my eyes—I grew worn and tired. I am not nearly so nice to look at as at that time when we used to meet in the school, nor so healthy either . . . I think I was handsome then." At this she smiled faintly, and raised her eyes to his, with a sparkle of their old mischief in them.

"And now and ever," he whispered.

"How innocent we were then! Fancy, Egbert, our unreserve would have been almost wrong if we had known the canons of behaviour we learnt afterwards. Ah! who at that time would have thought I was to yield to what I did? I wish now that I had met you at the door in Chevron Square, as I promised. But I feared to—I had promised Lord Bretton—and I that evening received a lecturing from my father, who saw you at the concert—he was in a seat further behind. And then, when I heard of your great success, how I wished I had held out a little longer! for I knew your hard labour had been on my account. When we met again last night it seemed awful, horrible—what I had done. Yet how could I tell you plainly? When I got indoors I felt I should die of misery, and I went to my father, and said I could not be married to-morrow. Oh, how angry he was, and what a dreadful scene occurred!" She covered her face with her hands.

"My poor Geraldine!" said Egbert, supporting her with his arm.

"When I was in my room this came into my mind, 'Better is it that thou shouldest not vow, than that thou shouldest vow and not pay.' I could bear it no longer. I was determined not to marry him, and to see you again, whatever came of it. I dressed, and came down stairs noiselessly, and slipped out. I knew where your house was, and I hastened here."

"You will never marry him now?"

"Never. Yet what can I do? Oh! what can I do? If I go back to my father—no, I cannot go back now—it is too late. But if they should find me, and drag me back, and compel me to perform my promise!"

"There is one simple way to prevent that, if, beloved Geraldine, you will agree to adopt it."

"Yes."

"By becoming *my* wife, at once. We would return to London as soon as the ceremony was over; and there you may defy them all."

"Oh, Egbert! I have thought of this—"

"You will have no reason to regret it. Perhaps I can introduce you to as intellectual, if odd-mannered and less aristocratic, society than that you have been accustomed to."

"Yes, I know it—I reflected on it before I came . . . I will be your wife," she replied tenderly. "I have come to you, and to you I will cling."

Egbert kissed her lips then for the first time in his life. He reflected for some time, if that process could be called reflection which was accompanied with so much excitement.

"The parson of your parish would perhaps refuse to marry us, even if we could get to the church secretly," he said, with a cloud on his brow. "That's a difficulty."

"Oh, don't take me there! I cannot go to Tollamore. I shall be seen, or we shall be parted. Don't take me there."

"No, no; I will not, love. I was only thinking. Are you known in this parish?"

"Well, yes; not, however, to the clergyman. He is a young man—old Mr Keene is dead, you know."

"Then I can manage it." Egbert clasped her in his arms in

the delight of his heart. "Now this is our course. I am first going to the surrogate's, and then further; and while I am gone you must stay in this house absolutely alone, and lock yourself in for safety. There is food in the house, and wine in that cupboard; you must stay here in hiding till I come back. It is now five o'clock. I will be here again at latest by eleven. If anybody knocks, remain silent, and the house will be supposed empty, as it lately has been so for a long time. My old servant and waitress must not come here to-day—I will manage that. I will light a fire, which will have burnt down by daylight, so that the room will be warmed for you. Sit there while I set about it."

He lit the fire, placed on the table all the food the house afforded, and went away.

CHAPTER VI

Hence will I to my ghostly father's cell;
His help to crave, and my dear hap to tell.

In half an hour Egbert returned, leading a horse.

"I have borrowed this from an old neighbour," he said, "and I have told the woman who waits upon me that I am going on a journey, and shall lock up the house to-day, so that she will not be wanted. And now, dearest, I want you to lend me something."

"Whatever it may be, you know it is yours."

"It is that," he answered, lightly touching with the tip of his finger a sparkling ring she wore on hers—the same she had used to wear at their youthful meetings in past years. "I want it as a pattern for the size."

She drew it off and handed it to him, at the same time raising her eyelids and glancing under his with a little laugh of confusion. His heart responded, and he kissed her; but he could not help feeling that she was by far too fair a prize for him.

She accompanied him to the door, and Mayne mounted the horse. They parted, and, waiting to hear her lock herself in, he cantered off by a bridle-path towards a town about five miles off.

It was so early that the surrogate on whom he called had not yet breakfasted, but he was very willing to see Mayne, and took him at once to the study. Egbert briefly told him what he wanted; that the lady he wished to marry was at that very moment in his house, and could go nowhere else for shelter—hence the earliness and urgency of his errand.

The surrogate seemed to see rather less interest in the circumstances than Mayne did himself; but he at once pre-pared the application for a license. When it was done, he made it up into a letter, directed it, and placed it on the mantelpiece. "It shall go by this evening's post," he said.

"But," said Egbert, "considering the awkward position this lady is in, cannot a special messenger be sent for the license? It is only seven or eight miles to ——, and yet otherwise I must wait for two days' posts."

"Undoubtedly; if anybody likes to pay for it, a special mes-senger may be sent."

"There will be no paying; I am willing to go myself. Do you object?"

"No; if the case is really serious, and the lady is dangerously compromised by every delay."

Mayne left the vicarage of the surrogate and again rode off; this time it was towards a well-known cathedral town. He felt bewildering sensations during this stroke for happiness, and went on his journey in that state of mind which takes cogni-sance of little things, without at the time being conscious of them, though they return vividly upon the memory long after.

He reached the city after a ride of seven additional miles, and soon obtained the precious document, and all else that he required. Returning to the inn where the horse had been rested, rubbed down, and fed, he again crossed the saddle, and at ten minutes past eleven he was back at Fairland. Before going to Monk's Hut, where Geraldine was immured, he hastened straight to the parsonage.

The young clergyman looked curiously at him, and at the bespattered and jaded horse outside. "Surely you are too rash in the matter," he said.

"No," said Egbert; "there are weighty reasons why I should be in such haste. The lady has at present no home to go to. She has taken shelter with me. I am doing what I consider best in so awkward a case."

The parson took down his hat, and said, "Very well; I will go to the church at once. You must be quick if it is to be done to-day."

Mayne left the horse for the present in the parson's yard, ran round to the clerk, thence to Monk's Hut, and called Geraldine.

It was, indeed, a hasty preparation for a wedding ceremony that these two made that morning. She was standing at the window, quite ready, and feverish with waiting. Kissing her gaily and breathlessly he directed her by a slightly circuitous path to the church; and, when she had been gone about two minutes, proceeded thither himself by the direct road, so that they met in the porch. Within, the clergyman, clerk, and clerk's wife had already gathered; and Geraldine and Egbert advanced to the communion railing.

Thus they became man and wife.

"Now he cannot claim me anyhow," she murmured when the service was ended, as she sank almost fainting upon the arm of Mayne.

"Mr Mayne," said the clergyman, aside to him in the vestry, "what is the name of the family at Tollamore House?"

"Strangely enough, Allenville—the same as hers," said he, coolly.

The parson looked keenly and dubiously at Mayne, and Egbert returned the look, whereupon the other turned aside and said nothing.

Egbert and Geraldine returned to their hermitage on foot, as they had left it; and, by rigorously excluding all thoughts of the future, they felt happy with the same old unreasoning happiness as of six years before, now resumed for the first time since that date.

But it was quite impossible that the hastily-married pair should remain at Monk's Hut unseen and unknown, as they fain would have done. Almost as soon as they had sat down in the house they came to the conclusion that there was no alternative for them but to start at once for Melport, if not for London. The difficulty was to get a conveyance. The only horse obtainable here, though a strong one, had already been tired down by Egbert in the morning, and the nearest village at which another could be had was about two miles off.

"I can walk as far as that," said Geraldine.

"Then walk we will," said Egbert. "It will remove all our difficulty." And, first packing up a small valise, he locked the door and went off with her upon his arm, just as the church clock struck one.

That walk through the woods was as romantic an experience as any they had ever known in their lives, though Geraldine was far from being quite happy. On reaching the village, which was larger than Fairland, they were fortunate enough to secure a carriage without any trouble. The village stood on the turnpike road, and a fly, about to return to Melport, where it had come from, was halting before the inn. Egbert hired it at once, and in little less than an hour and a half bridegroom and bride were comfortably housed in a quiet hotel of the seaport town above mentioned.

CHAPTER VII

How small a part of time they share
That are so wondrous sweet and fair!

They remained three days at Melport without having come to any decision on their future movements.

On the third day, at breakfast, Egbert took up the local newspaper which had been published that morning, and his eye presently glanced upon a paragraph headed "The Tollamore Elopement."

Before reading it he considered for a moment whether he should lay the journal aside, and for the present hide its contents from the tremulous creature opposite. But deeming this unadvisable, he gently prepared her for the news, and read the paragraph aloud.

It was to the effect that the village of Tollamore and its neighbourhood had been thrown into an unwonted state of excitement by the disappearance of Miss Allenville on the eve of the preparations for her marriage with Lord Bretton, which had been alluded to in their last number. Simultaneously there had disappeared from a neighbouring village, whither he had come for a few months' retirement, a gentleman named Mayne, of considerable literary reputation in the metropolis, and apparently an old acquaintance of Miss Allenville's. Efforts had been made to trace the fugitives by the young lady's father and the distracted bridegroom, Lord Bretton, but hitherto all their exertions had been unavailing.

Subjoined was another paragraph, entitled "Latest particulars."

"It has just been discovered that Mr Mayne and Miss Allenville are already man and wife. They were boldly married at the parish church of Fairland, before any person in the village had the least suspicion who or what they were. It appears that the lady joined her intended husband early that morning at the cottage he had taken for the season, that they went to the church by different paths, and after the ceremony walked out of the parish by a route as yet unknown. In consequence of this intelligence Lord Bretton has returned to London, and her father is left alone to mourn the young lady's rashness."

Egbert lifted his eyes and watched Geraldine as he finished reading. On perceiving his look she tried to smile. The smile thinned away, for there was not cheerfulness enough to support it long, and she said faintly, "Egbert, what must be done?"

"We must, I suppose, leave this place, darling; charming as our life is here."

"Yes; I fear we must."

"London seems to be the spot for us at once, before we attract the attention of the people here."

"How well everything might end," she said, "if my father were induced to welcome you, and make the most of your reputation! I wonder, wonder if he would! In that case there would be little amiss."

Mayne, after some reflection, said, "I think that I will go to your father before we leave for town. We are certain to be discovered by somebody or other, either here or in London, and that would bring your father, and there would possibly result a public meeting between him and myself at which words might be uttered which could not be forgotten on either side; so that a private meeting and explanation is safest, before anything of that sort can happen."

"I think," she said, looking to see if he approved of her words as they fell, "I think that a still better course would be for me to go to him—alone."

Mayne did not care much about this plan at first; but further discussion gave it a more feasible aspect, since Allenville, though stern and proud, was fond of his daughter, and had never crossed her, except when her whims interfered, as he considered, with her interests. Nothing could unmarry them; and Geraldine's mind would be much more at ease after begging her father's forgiveness. The journey was therefore decided on. They waited till nearly evening, and then, ordering round a brougham, Egbert told the man to drive to Tollamore.

The journey to Geraldine was tedious and oppressive to a degree. When, after two hours' driving, they drew near the park precincts, she said shivering,

"I don't like to drive up to the house, Egbert."

"I will do just as you like. What do you propose?"

"To let him wait in the road, under the three oak trees, while you and I walk to the house."

Egbert humoured her in everything; and when they reached the designated spot the driver was stopped, and they alighted. Carefully wrapping her up he gave her his arm, and they started for Tollamore House at an easy pace through the moonlit park, avoiding the direct road as much as possible.

Geraldine spoke but little during the walk, especially when they neared the house, and passed across the smooth broad glade which surrounded it. At sight of the door she seemed to droop, and leant heavily upon him. Egbert more than ever wished to confront Mr Allenville himself; morally and socially it appeared to him the right thing to do. But Geraldine trembled when he again proposed it; and he yielded to her entreaty thus far, that he would wait a few minutes till she had entered and seen her father privately, and prepared the way for Egbert to follow, which he would then do in due course.

The spot in which she desired him to wait was a summer-house under a tree about fifty yards from the lawn front of the house, and commanding a view of the door on this side. She was to enter unobserved by the servants, and go straight to her father, when, should he listen to her with the least show of mildness, she would send out for Egbert to follow. If the worst were to happen, and he were to be enraged with her, refusing to listen to entreaties or explanations, she would hasten out, rejoin Egbert, and depart.

In this little summer-house he embraced her, and bade her adieu, after their honeymoon of three short days. She trembled so much that she could scarcely walk when he let go her hand.

"Don't go alone—you are not well," said Egbert.

"Yes, yes, dearest, I am—and I will soon return, so soon!" she answered; and he watched her crossing the grass and advancing, a mere dot, towards the mansion. In a short time the appearance of an oblong of light in the shadowy expanse of wall denoted to him that the door was open: her outline appeared on it; then the door shut her in, and all was shadow as before. Even though they were husband and wife the line of demarcation seemed to be drawn again as rigidly as when he lived at the school.

Egbert waited in the solitude of this place minute by minute, restlessly swinging his foot when seated, at other times walking up and down, and anxiously watching for the arrival of some messenger. Nearly half an hour passed, but no messenger came.

The first sign of life in the neighbourhood of the house was in the shape of a man on horseback, galloping from the stable entrance. Egbert saw this by looking over the wall at the back of the summer-house; and the man passed along the open drive, vanishing in the direction of the lodge. Mayne, not without some presentiment of ill, wondered what it could mean, but thought it just possible that the horseman was a special messenger sent to catch the late post at the nearest town, as was sometimes done by Squire Allenville. So he curbed his impatience for Geraldine's sake.

Next he observed lights moving in the upper windows of the building. "It has been made known to them all that she is come, and they are preparing a room," he thought hopefully.

But nobody came from the door to welcome him; his existence was apparently forgotten by the whole world. In another ten minutes he saw the Melport brougham that had brought them, creeping slowly up to the house. Egbert went round to the man, and told him to drive to the stables and wait for orders.

From the length of Geraldine's absence, Mayne could not help concluding that the impression produced on her father was of a doubtful kind, not quite favourable enough to warrant her in telling him at once that her husband was in waiting. Still, a sense of his dignity as her husband might have constrained her to introduce him as soon as possible, and he had only agreed to wait a few minutes. Something unexpected must, after all, have occurred. And this supposition was confirmed a moment later by the noise of a horse and carriage coming up the drive. Egbert again looked over into the open park, and saw the vehicle reach the carriage entrance, where somebody alighted and went in.

"Her father away from home perhaps, and now just returned," he said.

He lingered yet another ten minutes, and then could endure no longer. Before he could reach the lawn door through which Geraldine had disappeared it opened. A person came out and, without shutting the door, hastened across to where Egbert stood. The man was a servant, without a hat on, and the moment that he saw Mayne he ran up to him.

"Mr Mayne?" he said.

"It is," said Egbert.

"Mr Allenville desires that you will come with me. There is something serious the matter. Miss Allenville is taken dangerously ill, and she wishes to see you."

"What has happened to her?" gasped Egbert breathlessly.

"Miss Allenville came unexpectedly home just now, and

directly she saw her father it gave her such a turn that she fainted, and ruptured a blood-vessel internally, and fell upon the floor. They have put her to bed, and the doctor has come, but we are afraid she won't live over it. She has suffered from it before."

Egbert did not speak, but walked hastily beside the man-servant. The only recollection that he ever had in after years of entering that house was a vague idea of stags' antlers in a long row on the wall, and a sense of great breadth in the stone staircase as he ascended it. Everything else was in a mist.

Mr Allenville, on being informed of his arrival, came out and met him in the corridor.

Egbert's mind was so entirely given up to the one thought that the life of his Geraldine was in danger, that he quite forgot the peculiar circumstances under which he met Allenville, and the peculiar behaviour necessary on that account. He seized her father's hand, and said abruptly,

"Where is she? Is the danger great?"

Allenville withdrew his hand, turned, and led the way into his daughter's room, merely saying in a low hard tone, "Your wife is in great danger, sir."

Egbert rushed to the bedside and bent over her in agony not to be described. Allenville sent the attendants from the room, and closed the door.

"Father," she whispered feebly, "I cannot help loving him. Would you leave us alone? We are very dear to each other, and perhaps I shall soon die."

"Anything you wish, child," he said with stern anguish; "and anything can hardly include more." Seeing that she looked hurt at this, he spoke more pleasantly. "I am glad to please you—you know I am, Geraldine—to the utmost." He then went out.

"They would not have let you know if Dr Williams had not insisted," she said. "I could not speak to explain at first—that's how it is you have been left there so long."

"Geraldine, dear, dear Geraldine, why should all this have come upon us?" he said in broken accents.

"Perhaps it is best," she murmured. "I hardly knew what I

was doing when I entered the door, or how I could explain to my father, or what could be done to reconcile him to us. He kept me waiting a little time before he would see me, but at last he came into the room. I felt a fulness on my chest, I could not speak, and then this happened to me. Papa has asked no questions."

A silence followed, interrupted only by her fitful breathing:

> A silence which doth follow talk, that causes
> The baffled heart to speak with sighs and tears.

"Do you love me very much now, Egbert?" she said. "After all my vacillation, do you?"

"Yes—how can you doubt?"

"I do not doubt. I know you love me. But will you stay here till I get better? You must stay. Papa is sure to be friendly with you now."

"Don't agitate yourself, dearest, about me. All is right with me here. Your health is the one thing to be anxious about now."

"I have only been taken ill like this once before in my life, and I thought it would never be again."

As she was not allowed to speak much, he remained holding her hand; and after some time she sank into a light sleep. Egbert then went from the chamber for a moment, and asked the physician, who was in the next room, if there was good hopé for her life.

"It is a dangerous attack, and she is very weak," he replied, concealing, though scarcely able to conceal, the curiosity with which he regarded Egbert; for the marriage had now become generally known.

The evening and night wore on. Great events in which he could not participate seemed to be passing over Egbert's head; a stir was in progress, of whose results he grasped but small and fragmentary notions. And, on the other hand, it was mournfully strange to notice her father's behaviour during these hours of doubt. It was only when he despaired that he looked upon Egbert with tolerance. When he hoped, the young man's presence was hateful to him.

Not knowing what to do when out of her chamber, having nobody near him to whom he could speak on intimate terms, Egbert passed a wretched time of three long days. After watching by her for several hours on the third day, he went downstairs, and into the open air. There intelligence was brought him that another effusion, more violent than any which preceded it, had taken place. Egbert rushed back to her room. Powerful remedies were applied, but none availed. A fainting-fit followed, and in two or three hours it became plain to those who understood that there was no Geraldine for the morrow.

Sometimes she was lethargic, and as if her spirit had already flown; then her mind wandered; but towards the end she was sensible of all that was going on, though unable to speak, her strength being barely enough to enable her to receive an idea.

It was a gentle death. She was as acquiescent as if she had been a saint, which was not the least striking and uncommon feature in the life of this fair and unfortunate lady. Her husband held one tiny hand, remaining all the time on the right side of the bed in a nook beside the curtains, while her father and the rest remained on the left side, never raising their eyes to him, and scarcely ever addressing him.

Everything was so still that her weak act of trying to live seemed a silent wrestling with all the powers of the universe. Pale and hopelessly anxious they all waited and watched the heavy shadows close over her. It might have been thought that death felt for her and took her tenderly. She sighed twice or three times; then her heart stood still; and this strange family alliance was at an end for ever.

OUR EXPLOITS AT WEST POLEY

A Story for Boys

CHAPTER I

On a certain fine evening of early autumn—I will not say how many years ago—I alighted from a green gig, before the door of a farmhouse at West Poley, a village in Somersetshire. I had reached the age of thirteen, and though rather small for my age, I was robust and active. My father was a schoolmaster, living about twenty miles off. I had arrived on a visit to my Aunt Draycot, a farmer's widow, who, with her son Stephen, or Steve, as he was invariably called by his friends, still managed the farm, which had been left on her hands by her deceased husband.

Steve promptly came out to welcome me. He was two or three years my senior, tall, lithe, ruddy, and somewhat masterful withal. There was that force about him which was less suggestive of intellectual power than (as Carlyle said of Cromwell) "Doughtiness—the courage and faculty to do."

When the first greetings were over, he informed me that his mother was not indoors just then, but that she would soon be home. "And, do you know, Leonard," he continued, rather mournfully, "she wants me to be a farmer all my life, like my father."

"And why not be a farmer all your life, like your father?" said a voice behind us.

We turned our heads, and a thoughtful man in a threadbare, yet well-fitting suit of clothes, stood near, as he paused for a moment on his way down to the village.

"The straight course is generally the best for boys," the speaker continued, with a smile. "Be sure that professions you know little of have as many drudgeries attaching to them as those you know well—it is only their remoteness that lends them their charm." Saying this he nodded and went on.

"Who is he?" I asked.

"Oh—he's nobody," said Steve. "He's a man who has been all over the world, and tried all sorts of lives, but he has never got rich, and now he has retired to this place for quietness. He calls himself the Man who has Failed."

After this explanation I thought no more of the Man who had Failed than Steve himself did; neither of us was at that time old enough to know that the losers in the world's battle are often the very men who, too late for themselves, have the clearest perception of what constitutes success; while the successful men are frequently blinded to the same by the tumult of their own progress.

To change the subject, I said something about the village and Steve's farm-house—that I was glad to see the latter was close under the hills, which I hoped we might climb before I returned home. I had expected to find these hills much higher, and I told Steve so without disguise.

"They may not be very high, but there's a good deal inside 'em," said my cousin, as we entered the house, as if he thought me hypercritical, "a good deal more than you think."

"Inside 'em?" said I, "stone and earth, I suppose."

"More than that," said he. "You have heard of the Mendip Caves, haven't you?"

"But they are nearer Cheddar," I said.

"There are one or two in this place, likewise," Steve answered me. "I can show them to you to-morrow. People say there are many more, only there is no way of getting into them."

Being disappointed in the height of the hills, I was rather incredulous about the number of the caves; but on my saying so, Steve rejoined, "Whatever you may think, I went the other day into one of 'em—Nick's Pocket—that's the cavern nearest here, and found that what was called the end was not really the end at all. Ever since then I've wanted to be an explorer, and not a farmer; and in spite of that old man, I think I am right."

At this moment my aunt came in, and soon after we were summoned to supper; and during the remainder of the evening nothing more was said about the Mendip Caves. It would have been just as well for us two boys if nothing more had been said about them at all; but it was fated to be otherwise, as I have reason to remember.

Steve did not forget my remarks, which, to him, no doubt, seemed to show a want of appreciation for the features of his native district. The next morning he returned to the subject, saying, as he came indoors to me suddenly, "I mean to show ye a little of what the Mendips contain, Leonard, if you'll come with me. But we must go quietly, for my mother does not like me to prowl about such places, because I get muddy. Come here, and see the preparations I have made."

He took me into the stable, and showed me a goodly supply of loose candle ends; also a bit of board perforated with holes, into which the candles would fit, and shaped to a handle at one extremity. He had provided, too, some slices of bread and cheese, and several apples. I was at once convinced that caverns which demanded such preparations must be something larger than the mere gravel-pits I had imagined; but I said nothing beyond assenting to the excursion.

It being the time after harvest, while there was not much to be attended to on the farm, Steve's mother could easily spare him, "to show me the neighbourhood," as he expressed it, and off we went, with our provisions and candles.

A quarter of a mile, or possibly a little more—for my recollections on matters of distance are not precise—brought us to the mouth of the cave called Nick's Pocket, the way thither being past the village houses, and the mill, and across the mill-stream, which came from a copious spring in the hillside some distance further up. I seem to hear the pattering of that mill-wheel when we walked by it, as well as if it were going now; and yet how many years have passed since the sound beat last upon my ears.

The mouth of the cave was screened by bushes, the face of the hill behind being, to the best of my remembrance, almost vertical. The spot was obviously well known to the inhabitants, and was the haunt of many boys, as I could see by footprints; though the cave, at this time, with others thereabout, had been but little examined by tourists and men of science.

We entered unobserved, and no sooner were we inside, than Steve lit a couple of candles and stuck them into the board. With these he showed the way. We walked on over a somewhat uneven floor, the novelty of the proceeding impressing me, at first, very agreeably; the light of the candles was sufficient, at first, to reveal only the nearer stalactites, remote nooks of the cavern being left in well-nigh their original mystic shadows. Steve would occasionally turn, and accuse me, in arch tones, of being afraid, which accusation I (as a boy would naturally do) steadfastly denied; though even now I can recollect that I experienced more than once some sort of misgiving.

"As for me—I have been there hundreds of times," Steve said proudly. "We West Poley boys come here continually to play 'I spy,' and think nothing of running in with no light of any sort. Come along, it is home to me. I said I would show you the inside of the Mendips, and so I will."

Thus we went onward. We were now in the bowels of the Mendip hills—a range of limestone rocks stretching from the shores of the Bristol Channel into the middle of Somersetshire. Skeletons of great extinct beasts, and the remains of prehistoric men have been found thereabouts since that time; but at the date of which I write science was not so ardent as she is now, in the pursuit of the unknown; and we boys could only conjecture on subjects in which the boys of the present generation are well-informed.

The dim sparkle of stalactite, which had continually appeared above us, now ranged lower and lower over our heads, till at last the walls of the cave seemed to bar further progress.

"There, this spot is what everybody calls the end of Nick's Pocket," observed Steve, halting upon a mount of stalagmite, and throwing the beams of the candles around. "But let me tell you," he added, "that here is a little arch, which I and some more boys found the other day. We did not go under it, but if you are agreed we will go in now and see how far we can get, for the fun of the thing. I brought these pieces of candle on purpose." Steve looked what he felt—that there was a certain grandeur in a person like himself, to whom such mysteries as caves were mere playthings, because he had been born close alongside them. To do him justice, he was not altogether wrong, for he was a truly courageous fellow, and could look dangers in the face without flinching.

"I think we may as well leave fun out of the question," I said, laughing; "but we will go in."

Accordingly he went forward, stooped, and entered the low archway, which, at first sight, appeared to be no more than a slight recess. I kept close at his heels. The arch gave access to a narrow tunnel or gallery, sloping downwards, and presently terminating in another cave, the floor of which spread out into a beautiful level of sand and shingle, interspersed with pieces of rock. Across the middle of this subterranean shore, as it might have been called, flowed a pellucid stream. Had my thoughts been in my books, I might have supposed we had descended to the nether regions, and had reached the Stygian shore; but it was out of sight, out of mind, with my classical studies then.

Beyond the stream, at some elevation, we could see a delightful recess in the crystallized stone work, like the apse of a Gothic church.

"How tantalizing!" exclaimed Steve, as he held the candles above his head, and peered across. "If it were not for this trickling riband of water, we could get over and climb up into that arched nook, and sit there like kings on a crystal throne!"

"Perhaps it would not look so wonderful if we got close to it," I suggested. "But, for that matter, if you had a spade, you could soon turn the water out of the way, and into that hole." The fact was, that just at that moment I had discovered a low opening on the left hand, like a human mouth, into which the stream would naturally flow, if a slight barrier of sand and pebbles were removed.

On looking there also, Steve complimented me on the sharpness of my eyes. "Yes," he said, "we could scrape away that bank, and the water would go straight into the hole surely enough. And we will. Let us go for a spade!"

I had not expected him to put the idea into practice; but it was no sooner said than done. We retraced our steps, and in a few minutes found ourselves again in the open air, where the sudden light overpowered our eyes for awhile.

"Stay here, while I run home," he said. "I'll not be long."

I agreed, and he disappeared. In a very short space he came back with a spade in his hand, and we again plunged in. This time the candles had been committed to my charge. When we had passed down the gallery into the second cave, Steve directed me to light a couple more of the candles, and stick them against a piece of rock, that he might have plenty of light to work by. This I did, and my stalwart cousin began to use the spade with a will, upon the breakwater of sand and stones.

The obstacle, which had been sufficient to turn the stream at a right angle, possibly for centuries, was of the most fragile description. Such instances of a slight obstruction diverting a sustained onset often occur in nature on a much larger scale. The Chesil Bank, for example, connecting the peninsula of Portland, in Dorsetshire, with the mainland, is a mere string of loose pebbles; yet it resists, by its shelving surface and easy curve, the mighty roll of the Channel seas, when urged upon the bank by the most furious southwest gales.

In a minute or two a portion of the purling stream discovered the opening Steve's spade was making in the sand, and began to flow through. The water assisted him in his remaining labours, supplementing every spadeful that he threw back, by washing aside ten. I remember that I was child enough, at that time, to clap my hands at the sight of larger and larger quantities of the brook tumbling in the form of a cascade down the dark chasm, where it had possibly never flowed before, or at any rate, never within the human period of the earth's history. In less than twenty minutes the whole stream trended off in this new direction, as calmly as if it had coursed there always. What had before been its bed now gradually drained dry, and we saw that we could walk across dryshod, with ease.

We speedily put the possibility into practice, and so reached the beautiful, glistening niche, that had tempted us to our engineering. We brought up into it the candles we had stuck against the rockwork further down, placed them with the others around the niche, and prepared to rest awhile, the spot being quite dry.

"That's the way to overcome obstructions!" said Steve, triumphantly. "I warrant nobody ever got so far as this before—at least, without wading up to his knees, in crossing that watercourse."

My attention was so much attracted by the beautiful natural ornaments of the niche, that I hardly heeded his remark. These covered the greater part of the sides and roof; they were flesh-coloured, and assumed the form of frills, lace, coats of mail; in many places they quaintly resembled the skin of geese after plucking, and in others the wattles of turkeys. All were decorated with water crystals.

"Well," exclaimed I, "I could stay here always!"

"So could I," said Steve, "if I had victuals enough. And some we'll have at once."

Our bread and cheese and apples were unfolded, and we speedily devoured the whole. We then tried to chip pieces from the rock, and but indifferently succeeded, though while doing this we discovered some curious stones, like axe and arrow heads, at the bottom of the niche; but they had become partially attached to the floor by the limestone deposit, and could not be extracted.

"This is a long enough visit for to-day," said my cousin, jumping up as one of the candles went out. "We shall be left in the dark if we don't mind, and it would be no easy matter to find our way out without a light."

Accordingly we gathered up the candles that remained, descended from the niche, recrossed the deserted bed of the stream, and found our way to the open air, well pleased enough with the adventure, and promising each other to repeat it at an early day. On which account, instead of bringing away the unburnt candles, and the wood candlestick, and the spade, we laid these articles on a hidden shelf near the entrance, to be ready at hand at any time.

Having cleaned the tell-tale mud from our boots, we were on the point of entering the village, when our ears were attracted by a great commotion in the road below.

"What is it?" said I, standing still.

"Voices, I think," replied Steve. "Listen!"

It seemed to be a man in a violent frenzy. "I think it is somebody out of his mind," continued my cousin. "I never heard a man rave so in my life."

"Let us draw nearer," said I.

We moved on, and soon came in sight of an individual, who, standing in the midst of the street, was gesticulating distractedly, and uttering invectives against something or other, to several villagers that had gathered around.

"Why, 'tis the miller!" said Steve. "What can be the matter with him?"

We were not kept long in suspense, for we could soon hear his words distinctly. "The money I've sunk here!" he was saying; "the time—the honest labour—all for nothing! Only beggary afore me now! One month it was a new pair of millstones; then the back wall was cracked with the shaking, and had to be repaired; then I made a bad speculation in corn and dropped money that way! But 'tis nothing to this! My own freehold—the only staff and dependence o' my family—all useless now—all of us ruined!"

"Don't you take on so, Miller Griffin," soothingly said one who proved to be the Man who had Failed. "Take the ups with the downs, and maybe 'twill come right again."

"Right again!" raved the miller; "how can what's gone forever come back again as 'twere afore—that's what I ask my wretched self—how can it?"

"We'll get up a subscription for ye," said a local dairyman.

"I don't drink hard; I don't stay away from church, and I only grind into Sabbath hours when there's no getting through the work otherwise, and I pay my way like a man!"

"Yes—you do that," corroborated the others.

"And yet, I be brought to ruinous despair, on this sixth day of September, Hannah Dominy; as if I were a villain! Oh, my mill, my mill wheel—you'll never go round any more—never more!" The miller flung his arms upon the rail of the bridge, and buried his face in his hands.

"This raving is but making a bad job worse," said the Man who had Failed. "But who will listen to counsel on such matters."

By this time we had drawn near, and Steve said, "What's the cause of all this?"

"The river has dried up—all on a sudden," said the dairy-man, "and so his mill won't go any more."

I gazed instantly towards the stream, or rather what had been the stream. It was gone; and the mill wheel, which had pattered so persistently when we entered the cavern, was silent. Steve and I instinctively stepped aside.

"The river gone dry!" Steve whispered.

"Yes," said I. "Why, Steve, don't you know why?"

My thoughts had instantly flown to our performance of turning the stream out of its channel in the cave, and I knew in a moment that this was the cause. Steve's silence showed me that he divined the same thing, and we stood gazing at each other in consternation.

CHAPTER II

How We Shone in the Eyes of the Public.

As soon as we had recovered ourselves we walked away, unconsciously approaching the river-bed, in whose hollows lay the dead and dying bodies of loach, sticklebacks, dace, and other small fry, which before our entrance into Nick's Pocket had raced merrily up and down the waterway. Further on we perceived numbers of people ascending to the upper part of the village, with pitchers on their heads, and buckets yoked to their shoulders.

"Where are you going?" said Steve to one of these.

"To your mother's well for water," was the answer. "The river we have always been used to dip from is dried up. Oh, mercy me, what with the washing and cooking and brewing I don't know what we shall do to live, for 'tis killing work to bring water on your back so far!"

As may be supposed, all this gave me still greater concern than before, and I hurriedly said to Steve that I was strongly of opinion that we ought to go back to the cave immediately, and turn the water into the old channel, seeing what harm we had unintentionally done by our manœuvre.

"Of course we'll go back—that's just what I was going to say," returned Steve. "We can set it all right again in half an hour, and the river will run the same as ever. Hullo—now you are frightened at what has happened! I can see you are."

I told him that I was not exactly frightened, but that it seemed to me we had caused a very serious catastrophe in the village, in driving the miller almost crazy, and killing the fish, and worrying the poor people into supposing they would never have enough water again for their daily use without fetching it from afar. "Let us tell them how it came to pass," I suggested, "and then go and set it right."

"Tell 'em—not I!" said Steve. "We'll go back and put it right, and say nothing about it to any one, and they will simply think it was caused by a temporary earthquake, or something of that sort." He then broke into a vigorous whistle, and we retraced our steps together.

It occupied us but a few minutes to rekindle a light inside the cave, take out the spade from its nook, and penetrate to the scene of our morning exploit. Steve then fell to, and first rolling down a few large pieces of stone into the current, dexterously banked them up with clay from the other side of the cave, which caused the brook to swerve back into its original bed almost immediately. "There," said he, "it is all just as it was when we first saw it—now let's be off."

We did not dally long in the cavern; but when we gained the exterior we decided to wait there a little time till the villagers should have discovered the restoration of their stream, to watch the effect. Our waiting was but temporary; for in quick succession there burst upon our ears a shout, and then the starting of the mill-wheel patter.

At once we walked into the village street with an air of unconcern. The miller's face was creased with wrinkles of satisfaction; the countenances of the blacksmith, shoemaker, grocer and dairyman were perceptibly brighter. These, and many others of West Poley, were gathered on the bridge over the mill-tail, and they were all holding a conversation with the parson of the parish, as to the strange occurrence.

Matters remained in a quiet state during the next two days. Then there was a remarkably fine and warm morning, and we proposed to cross the hills and descend into East Poley, the next village, which I had never seen. My aunt made no objection to the excursion, and we departed, ascending the hill in a straight line, without much regard to paths. When we had reached the summit, and were about half way between the two villages, we sat down to recover breath. While we sat a man overtook us, and Steve recognized him as a neighbour.

"A bad job again for West Poley folks!" cried the man, without halting.

"What's the matter now?" said Steve, and I started with curiosity.

"Oh, the river is dry again. It happened at a quarter past ten this morning, and it is thought it will never flow any more. The miller he's gone crazy, or all but so. And the washer-woman, she will have to be kept by the parish, because she can't get water to wash with; aye, 'tis a terrible time that's come. I'm off to try to hire a water-cart, but I fear I shan't hear of one."

The speaker passed by, and on turning to Steve I found he was looking on the ground. "I know how that's happened," he presently said. "We didn't make our embankment so strong as it was before, and so the water has washed it away."

"Let's go back and mend it," said I; and I proposed that we should reveal where the mischief lay, and get some of the labourers to build the bank up strong, that this might not happen again.

"No," said Steve, "since we are half way we will have our day's pleasure. It won't hurt the West Poley people to be out of water for one day. We'll return home a little earlier than we intended, and put it all in order again, either ourselves, or by the help of some men."

Having gone about a mile and a half further we reached the brow of the descent into East Poley, the place we had come to visit. Here we beheld advancing towards us a stranger whose actions we could not at first interpret. But as the distance between us and him lessened we discerned, to our surprise, that he was in convulsions of laughter. He would laugh until he was tired, then he would stand still gazing on the ground, as if quite preoccupied, then he would burst out laughing again and walk on. No sooner did he see us two boys than he placed his hat upon his walking-stick, twirled it and cried "Hurrah!"

I was so amused that I could not help laughing with him; and when he came abreast of us Steve said, "Good morning; may I ask what it is that makes you laugh so?"

But the man was either too self-absorbed or too supercilious to vouchsafe to us any lucid explanation. "What makes me laugh?" he said. "Why, good luck, my boys! Perhaps when you are as lucky, you will laugh too." Saying which he walked on and left us; and we could hear him exclaiming to himself, "Well done—hurrah!" as he sank behind the ridge.

Without pausing longer we descended towards the village, and soon reached its outlying homesteads. Our path intersected a green field dotted with trees, on the other side of which was an inn. As we drew near we heard the strains of a fiddle, and presently perceived a fiddler standing on a chair outside the inn door; whilst on the green in front were several people seated at a table eating and drinking, and some younger members of the assembly dancing a reel in the background.

We naturally felt much curiosity as to the cause of the merriment, which we mentally connected with that of the man we had met just before. Turning to one of the old men feasting at the table, I said to him as civilly as I could, "Why are you all so lively in this parish, sir?"

"Because we are in luck's way just now, for we don't get a new river every day. Hurrah!"

"A new river?" said Steve and I in one breath.

"Yes," said one of our interlocutors, waving over the table a ham-bone he had been polishing. "Yesterday afternoon a river of beautiful water burst out of the quarry at the higher end of this bottom; in an hour or so it stopped again. This morning, about a quarter past ten, it burst out again, and it is running now as if it would run always."

"It will make all land and houses in this parish worth double as much as afore," said another; "for want of water is the one thing that has always troubled us, forcing us to sink deep wells, and even then being hard put to, to get enough for our cattle. Now we have got a river, and the place will grow to a town."

"It is as good as two hundred pounds to me!" said one who looked like a grazier.

"And two hundred and fifty to me!" cried another, who seemed to be a brewer.

"And sixty pound a year to me, and to every man here in the building trade!" said a third.

As soon as we could withdraw from the company, our thoughts found vent in words.

"I ought to have seen it!" said Steve. "Of course if you stop a stream from flowing in one direction, it must force its way out in another."

"I wonder where their new stream is," said I.

We looked round. After some examination we saw a depression in the centre of a pasture, and, approaching it, beheld the stream meandering along over the grass, the current not having had as yet sufficient time to scour a bed. Walking down to the brink, we were lost in wonder at what we had unwittingly done, and quite bewildered at the strange events we had caused. Feeling, now, that we had walked far enough from home for one day, we turned, and, in a brief time, entered a road pointed out by Steve, as one that would take us to West Poley by a shorter cut than our outward route.

As we ascended the hill, Steve looked round at me. I suppose my face revealed my thoughts, for he said, "You are amazed, Leonard, at the wonders we have accomplished without knowing it. To tell the truth, so am I."

I said that what staggered me was this—that we could not turn back the water into its old bed now, without doing as much harm to the people of East Poley by taking it away, as we should do good to the people of West Poley by restoring it.

"True," said Steve, "that's what bothers me. Though I think we have done more good to these people than we have done harm to the others; and I think these are rather nicer people than those in our village, don't you?"

I objected that even if this were so, we could have no right to take water away from one set of villagers and give it to another set without consulting them.

Steve seemed to feel the force of the argument; but as his mother had a well of her own he was less inclined to side with his native place than he might have been if his own household had been deprived of water, for the benefit of the East Poleyites. The matter was still in suspense, when, weary with our day's pilgrimage, we reached the mill.

The mill-pond was drained to its bed; the wheel stood motionless; yet a noise came from the interior. It was not the noise of machinery, but of the nature of blows, followed by bitter expostulations. On looking in, we were grieved to see that the miller, in a great rage, was holding his apprentice by the collar, and beating him with a strap.

The miller was a heavy, powerful man, and more than a match for his apprentice and us two boys besides; but Steve reddened with indignation, and asked the miller, with some spirit, why he served the poor fellow so badly.

"He says he'll leave," stormed the frantic miller. "What right hev he to say he'll leave, I should like to know!"

"There is no work for me to do, now the mill won't go," said the apprentice, meekly; "and the agreement was that I should be at liberty to leave if work failed in the mill. He keeps me here and don't pay me; and I be at my wits' end how to live."

"Just shut up!" said the miller. "Go and work in the garden! Mill-work or no mill-work, you'll stay on."

Job, as the miller's boy was called, had won the good-will of Steve, and Steve was now ardent to do him a good turn. Looking over the bridge, we saw, passing by, the Man who had Failed. He was considered an authority on such matters as these, and we begged him to come in. In a few minutes the miller was set down, and it was proved to him that, by the terms of Job's indentures, he was no longer bound to remain.

"I have to thank you for this," said the miller, savagely, to Steve. "Ruined in every way! I may as well die!"

But my cousin cared little for the miller's opinion, and we came away, thanking the Man who had Failed for his interference, and receiving the warmest expressions of gratitude from poor Job; who, it appeared, had suffered much ill-treatment from his irascible master, and was overjoyed to escape to some other employment.

We went to bed early that night, on account of our long walk; but we were far too excited to sleep at once. It was scarcely dark as yet, and the nights being still warm the window was left open as it had been left during the summer. Thus we could hear everything that passed without. People were continually coming to dip water from my aunt's well; they gathered round it in groups, and discussed the remarkable event which had latterly occurred for the first time in parish history.

"My belief is that witchcraft have done it," said the shoemaker, "and the only remedy that I can think o', is for one of us to cut across to Bartholomew Gann, the white wizard, and get him to tell us how to counteract it. 'Tis a long pull to his house for a little man, such as I be, but I'll walk it if nobody else will."

"Well, there's no harm in your going," said another. "We can manage by drawing from Mrs Draycot's well for a few days; but something must be done, or the miller'll be ruined, and the washerwoman can't hold out long."

When these personages had drawn water and retired, Steve spoke across from his bed to me in mine. "We've done more good than harm, that I'll maintain. The miller is the only man seriously upset, and he's not a man to deserve consideration. It has been the means of freeing poor Job, which is another good thing. Then, the people in East Poley that we've made happy are two hundred and fifty, and there are only a hundred in this parish, even if all of 'em are made miserable."

I returned some reply, though the state of affairs was, in truth, one rather suited to the genius of Jeremy Bentham than to me. But the problem in utilitarian philosophy was shelved by Steve exclaiming, "I have it! I see how to get some real glory out of this!"

I demanded how, with much curiosity.

"You'll swear not to tell anybody, or let it be known anyhow that we are at the bottom of it all?"

I am sorry to say that my weak compunctions gave way under stress of this temptation; and I solemnly declared that I would reveal nothing, unless he agreed with me that it would be best to do so. Steve made me swear, in the tone of Hamlet to the Ghost, and when I had done this, he sat up in his bed to announce his scheme.

"First, we'll go to Job," said Steve. "Take him into the secret; show him the cave; give him a spade and pickaxe; and tell him to turn off the water from East Poley at, say, twelve o'clock, for a little while. Then we'll go to the East Poley boys and declare ourselves to be magicians."

"Magicians?" I said.

"Magicians, able to dry up rivers, or to make 'em run at will," he repeated.

"I see it!" I almost screamed, in my delight.

"To show our power, we'll name an hour for drying up theirs, and making it run again after a short time. Of course we'll say the hour we've told Job to turn the water in the cave. Won't they think something of us then?"

I was enchanted. The question of mischief or not mischief was as indifferent to me now as it was to Steve—for which indifference we got rich deserts, as will be seen in the sequel.

"And to look grand and magical," continued he, "we'll get some gold lace that I know of in the garret, on an old coat my grandfather wore in the Yeomanry Cavalry, and put it round our caps, and make ourselves great beards with horse-hair. They will look just like real ones at a little distance off."

"And we must each have a wand!" said I, explaining that I knew how to make excellent wands, white as snow, by peeling a couple of straight willows; and that I could do all that in the morning while he was preparing the beards.

Thus we discussed and settled the matter, and at length fell asleep—to dream of to-morrow's triumphs among the boys of East Poley, till the sun of that morrow shone in upon our faces and woke us. We arose promptly and made our preparations, having carte blanche from my Aunt Draycot to spend the days of my visit as we chose.

Our first object on leaving the farmhouse was to find Job Tray, apprise him of what it was necessary that he should know, and induce him to act as confederate. We found him outside the garden of his lodging; he told us he had nothing to do till the following Monday, when a farmer had agreed to hire him. On learning the secret of the river-head, and what we proposed to do, he expressed his glee by a low laugh of amazed delight, and readily promised to assist as bidden. It took us some little time to show him the inner cave, the tools, and to arrange candles for him, so that he might enter without difficulty just after eleven and do the trick. When this was all settled we put Steve's watch on a ledge in the cave, that Job might know the exact time, and came out to ascend the hills that divided the eastern from the western village.

For obvious reasons we did not appear in magician's guise till we had left the western vale some way behind us. Seated on the limestone ridge, removed from all observation, we set to work at preparing ourselves. I peeled the two willows we had brought with us to be used as magic wands, and Steve pinned the pieces of old lace round our caps, congratulating himself on the fact of the lace not being new, which would thus convey the impression that we had exercised the wizard's calling for some years. Our last adornments were the beards; and, finally equipped, we descended on the other side.

Our plan was now to avoid the upper part of East Poley, which we had traversed on the preceding day, and to strike into the parish at a point further down, where the humble cottages stood, and where we were both absolutely unknown. An hour's additional walking brought us to this spot, which, as the crow flies, was not more than half so far from West Poley as the road made it.

The first boys we saw were some playing in an orchard near the new stream, which novelty had evidently been the attraction that had brought them there. It was an opportunity for opening the campaign, especially as the hour was long after eleven, and the cessation of water consequent on Job's performance at a quarter past might be expected to take place as near as possible to twelve, allowing the five and forty minutes from eleven-fifteen as the probable time that would be occupied by the stream in travelling to the point we had reached.

I forget at this long distance of years the exact words used by Steve in addressing the strangers; but to the best of my recollection they were, "How d'ye do, gentlemen, and how does the world use ye?" I distinctly remember the sublimity he threw into his gait, and how slavishly I imitated him in the same.

The boys made some indifferent answer, and Steve continued, "You will kindly present us with some of those apples, I presume, considering what we are?"

They regarded us dubiously, and at last one of them said, "What are you, that you should expect apples from us?"

"We are travelling magicians," replied Steve. "You may have heard of us, for by our power this new river has begun to flow. Rhombustas is my name, and this is my familiar Balcazar."

"I don't believe it," said an incredulous one from behind.

"Very well, gentlemen; we can't help that. But if you give us some apples we'll prove our right to the title."

"Be hanged if we will give you any apples," said the boy who held the basket; "since it is already proved that magicians are impossible."

"In that case," said Steve, "we—we—"

"Will perform just the same," interrupted I, for I feared Steve had forgotten that the time was at hand when the stream would be interrupted by Job, whether we willed it or not.

"We will stop the water of your new river at twelve o'clock this day, when the sun crosses the meridian," said Rhombustas, "as a punishment for your want of generosity."

"Do it!" said the boys incredulously.

"Come here, Balcazar," said Steve. We walked together to the edge of the stream; then we muttered, *Hi, hae, haec, horum, harum, horum,* and stood waving our wands.

"The river do run just the same," said the strangers derisively.

"The spell takes time to work," said Rhombustas, adding in an aside to me, "I hope that fellow Job has not forgotten, or we shall be hooted out of the place."

There we stood, waving and waving our white sticks, hoping and hoping we should succeed; while still the river flowed.

Seven or ten minutes passed thus; and then, when we were nearly broken down by ridicule, the stream diminished its volume. All eyes were instantly bent on the water, which sank so low as to be in a short time but a narrow rivulet. The faithful Job had performed his task. By the time that the clock of the church tower struck twelve the river was almost dry.

The boys looked at each other in amazement, and at us with awe. They were too greatly concerned to speak except in murmurs to each other.

"You see the result of your conduct, unbelieving strangers," said Steve, drawing boldly up to them. "And I seriously ask that you hand over those apples before we bring further troubles upon you and your village. We give you five minutes to consider."

"We decide at once!" cried the boys. "The apples be yours and welcome."

"Thank you, gentlemen," said Steve, while I added, "For your readiness the river shall run again in two or three minutes' time."

"Oh—ah, yes," said Steve, adding heartily in undertones, "I had forgotten that!"

Almost as soon as the words were spoken we perceived a little increase in the mere dribble of water which now flowed, whereupon he waved his wand and murmured more words. The liquid thread swelled and rose; and in a few minutes was the same as before. Our triumph was complete; and the suspension had been so temporary that probably nobody in the village had noticed it but ourselves and the boys.

CHAPTER III

How We Were Caught in Our Own Trap.

At this acme of our glory who should come past but a hedger whom Steve recognized as an inhabitant of West Poley; unluckily for our greatness the hedger also recognized Steve.

"Well, Maister Stevey, what be you doing over in these parts then? And yer little cousin, too, upon my word! And beards— why ye've made yerselves ornamental! haw, haw!"

In great trepidation Steve moved on with the man, endeavouring thus to get him out of hearing of the boys.

"Look here," said Steve to me on leaving that outspoken rustic; "I think this is enough for one day. We'd better go further before they guess all."

"With all my heart," said I. And we walked on.

"But what's going on here?" said Steve, when, turning a corner of the hedge, we perceived an altercation in progress hard by. The parties proved to be a poor widow and a corn-factor, who had been planning a water-wheel lower down the stream. The latter had dammed the water for his purpose to such an extent as to submerge the poor woman's garden, turning it into a lake.

"Indeed, sir, you need not ruin my premises so!" she said with tears in her eyes. "The mill-pond can be kept from overflowing my garden by a little banking and digging; it will be just as well for your purpose to keep it lower down, as to let it spread out into a great pool here. The house and garden are yours by law, sir; that's true. But my father built the house, and, oh, sir, I was born here, and I should like to end my days under its roof!"

"Can't help it, mis'ess," said the corn-factor. "Your garden is a mill-pond already made, and to get a hollow further down I should have to dig at great expense. There is a very nice cottage up the hill, where you can live as well as here. When your father died the house came into my hands; and I can do what I like with my own."

The woman went sadly away indoors. As for Steve and myself, we were deeply moved as we looked at the pitiable sight of the poor woman's garden, the tops of the gooseberry bushes forming small islands in the water, and her few apple trees standing immersed half-way up their stems.

"The man is a rascal," said Steve. "I perceive that it is next to impossible, in this world, to do good to one set of folks without doing harm to another."

"Since we have not done all good to these people of East Poley," said I, "there is a reason for restoring the river to its old course through West Poley."

"But then," said Steve, "if we turn back the stream, we shall be starting Miller Griffin's mill; and then, by the terms of his

'prenticeship, poor Job will have to go back to him and be
beaten again! It takes good brains no less than a good heart to
do what's right towards all."

Quite unable to solve the problem into which we had
drifted, we retraced our steps, till, at a stile, within half a mile
of West Poley, we beheld Job awaiting us.

"Well, how did it act?" he asked with great eagerness. "Just
as the hands of your watch got to a quarter past eleven, I
began to shovel away, and turned the water in no time. But
I didn't turn it where you expected—not I—'twould have
started the mill for a few minutes, and I wasn't going to do
that."

"Then where did you turn it?" cried Steve.

"I found another hole," said Job.

"A third one?"

"Ay, hee, hee! a third one! So I pulled the stones aside from
this new hole, and shovelled the clay, and down the water
went with a gush. When it had run down there a few minutes,
I turned it back to the East Poley hole, as you ordered me to
do. But as to getting it back to the old West Poley hole, that
I'd never do."

Steve then explained that we no more wished the East
village to have the river than the West village, on account of
our discovery that equal persecution was going on in the one
place as in the other. Job's news of a third channel solved our
difficulty. "So we'll go at once and send it down this third
channel," concluded he.

We walked back to the village, and, as it was getting late,
and we were tired, we decided to do nothing that night, but
told Job to meet us in the cave on the following evening, to
complete our work there.

All next day my cousin was away from home, at market for
his mother, and he had arranged with me that if he did not
return soon enough to join me before going to Nick's Pocket,
I should proceed thither, where he would meet me on his way
back from the market-town. The day passed anxiously enough
with me, for I had some doubts of a very grave kind as to our
right to deprive two parishes of water on our own judgment,
even though that should be, as it was, honestly based on our

aversion to tyranny. However, dusk came on at last, and Steve not appearing from market, I concluded that I was to meet him at the cave's mouth.

To this end I strolled out in that direction, and there being as yet no hurry, I allowed myself to be tempted out of my path by a young rabbit, which, however, I failed to capture. This divergence had brought me inside a field, behind a hedge, and before I could resume my walk along the main road, I heard some persons passing along the other side. The words of their conversation arrested me in a moment.

" 'Tis a strange story if it's true," came through the hedge in the tones of Miller Griffin. "We know that East Poley folk will say queer things; but the boys wouldn't say that it was the work of magicians if they hadn't some ground for it."

"And how do they explain it?" asked the shoemaker.

"They say that these two young fellows passed down their lane about twelve o'clock, dressed like magicians, and offered to show their power by stopping the river. The East Poley boys challenged 'em; when, by George, they did stop the river! They said a few words, and it dried up like magic. Now mark my words, my suspicion is this: these two gamesters have somehow got at the river head, and been tampering with it in some way. The water that runs down East Poley bottom is the water that ought, by rights, to be running through my mill."

"A very pretty piece of mischief, if that's the case!" said the shoemaker. "I've never liked them lads, particularly that Steve—for not a boot or shoe hev he had o' me since he's been old enough to choose for himself—not a pair, or even a mending. But I don't see how they could do all this, even if they had got at the river head. 'Tis a spring out of the hill, isn't it? And how could they stop the spring?"

It seemed that the miller could offer no explanation, for no answer was returned. My course was clear: to join Job and Steve at Nick's Pocket immediately; tell them that we were suspected, and to get them to give over further proceedings, till we had stated our difficulties to some person of experience—say the Man who had Failed.

I accordingly ran like a hare over the clover inside the hedge, and soon was far away from the interlocutors. Drawing near the cave, I was relieved to see Steve's head against the sky. I joined him at once, and recounted to him, in haste, what had passed.

He meditated. "They don't even now suspect that the secret lies in the cavern," said he.

"But they will soon," said I.

"Well, perhaps they may," he answered. "But there will be time for us to finish our undertaking, and turn the stream down the third hole. When we've done that we can consider which of the villages is most worthy to have the river, and act accordingly."

"Do let us take a good wise man into our confidence," I said.

After a little demurring, he agreed that as soon as we had completed the scheme we would state the case to a competent adviser, and let it be settled fairly. "And now," he said, "where's Job; inside the cave, no doubt, as it is past the time I promised to be here."

Stepping inside the cave's mouth, we found that the candles and other things which had been deposited there were removed. The probability being that Job had arrived and taken them in with him, we groped our way along in the dark, helped by an occasional match which Steve struck from a box he carried. Descending the gallery at the further end of the outer cavern, we discerned a glimmer at the remote extremity, and soon beheld Job working with all his might by the light of one of the candles.

"I've almost got it into the hole that leads to neither of the Poleys, but I wouldn't actually turn it till you came," he said, wiping his face.

We told him that the neighbours were on our track, and might soon guess that we performed our tricks in Nick's Pocket, and come there, and find that the stream flowed through the cave before rising in the spring at the top of the village; and asked him to turn the water at once, and be off with us.

"Ah!" said Job, mournfully, "then 'tis over with me! They will be here to-morrow, and will turn back the stream, and the mill will go again, and I shall have to finish my time as 'prentice to the man who did this!" He pulled up his shirt sleeve, and showed us on his arm several stripes and bruises— black and blue and green—the tell-tale relics of old blows from the miller.

Steve reddened with indignation. "I would give anything to stop up the channels to the two Poleys so close that they couldn't be found again!" he said. "Couldn't we do it with stones and clay? Then if they came here 'twould make no difference, and the water would flow down the third hole forever, and we should save Job and the widow after all."

"We can but try it," said Job, willing to fall in with anything that would hinder his recall to the mill. "Let's set to work."

Steve took the spade, and Job the pickaxe. First they finished what Job had begun—the turning of the stream into the third tunnel or crevice, which led to neither of the Poleys. This done, they set to work jamming stones into the other two openings, treading earth and clay around them, and smoothing over the whole in such a manner that nobody should notice they had ever existed. So intent were we on completing it that—to our utter disaster—we did not notice what was going on behind us.

I was the first to look round, and I well remember why: my ears had been attracted by a slight change of tone in the purl of the water down the new crevice discovered by Job, and I was curious to learn the reason of it. The sight that met my gaze might well have appalled a stouter and older heart than mine. Instead of pouring down out of sight, as it had been doing when we last looked, the stream was choked by a rising pool into which it boiled, showing at a glance that what we had innocently believed to be another outlet for the stream was only a blind passage or *cul de sac*, which the water, when first turned that way by Job, had not been left long enough to fill before it was turned back again.

"Oh, Steve—Job!" I cried, and could say no more.

They gazed round at once, and saw the situation. Nick's Pocket had become a cauldron. The surface of the rising pool stood, already, far above the mouth of the gallery by which we had entered, and which was our only way out—stood far above the old exit of the stream to West Poley, now sealed up;

far above the second outlet to East Poley, discovered by Steve, and also sealed up by our fatal ingenuity. We had been spending the evening in making a closed bottle of the cave, in which the water was now rising to drown us.

"There is one chance for us—only one," said Steve in a dry voice.

"What one?" we asked in a breath.

"To open the old channel leading to the mill," said Steve.

"I would almost as soon be drowned as do that," murmured Job gloomily. "But there's more lives than my own, so I'll work with a will. Yet how be we to open any channel at all?"

The question was, indeed, of awful aptness. It was extremely improbable that we should have power to reopen either conduit now. Both those exits had been funnel-shaped cavities, narrowing down to mere fissures at the bottom; and the stones and earth we had hurled into these cavities had wedged themselves together by their own weight. Moreover— and here was the rub—had it been possible to pull the stones out while they remained unsubmerged, the whole mass was now under water, which enlarged the task of reopening the channel to Herculean dimensions.

But we did not know my cousin Steve as yet. "You will help me here," he said authoritatively to Job, pointing to the West Poley conduit. "Lenny, my poor cousin," he went on, turning to me, "we are in a bad way. All you can do is to stand in the niche, and make the most of the candles by keeping them from the draught with your hat, and burning only one at a time. How many have we, Job?"

"Ten ends, some long, some short," said Job.

"They will burn many hours," said Steve. "And now we must dive, and begin to get out the stones."

They had soon stripped off all but their drawers, and, laying their clothes on the dry floor of the niche behind me, stepped down into the middle of the cave. The water here was already above their waists, and at the original gulley-hole leading to West Poley spring was proportionately deeper. Into this part, nevertheless, Steve dived. I have recalled his appearance a hundred—aye, a thousand—times since that day, as he came up—his crown bobbing into the dim candle-light like a floating apple. He stood upright, bearing in his arms a stone as big as his head.

"That's one of 'em!" he said as soon as he could speak. "But there are many, many more!"

He threw the stone behind; while Job, wasting no time, had already dived in at the same point. Job was not such a good diver as Steve, in the sense of getting easily at the bottom; but he could hold his breath longer, and it was an extraordinary length of time before his head emerged above the surface, though his feet were kicking in the air more than once. Clutched to his chest, when he rose, was a second large stone, and a couple of small ones with it. He threw the whole to a distance; and Steve, having now recovered breath, plunged again into the hole.

But I can hardly bear to recall this terrible hour even now, at a distance of many years. My suspense was, perhaps, more trying than that of the others, for, unlike them, I could not escape reflection by superhuman physical efforts. My task of economizing the candles, by shading them with my hat, was not to be compared, in difficulty, to theirs; but I would gladly have changed places, if it had been possible to such a small boy, with Steve and Job, so intolerable was it to remain motionless in the desperate circumstances.

Thus I watched the rising of the waters, inch by inch, and on that account was in a better position than they to draw an inference as to the probable end of the adventure.

There were a dozen, or perhaps twenty, stones to extract before we could hope for an escape of the pent mass of water; and the difficulty of extracting them increased with each successive attempt in two ways: by the greater actual remoteness of stone after stone, and by its greater relative remoteness through the rising of the pool. However, the sustained, gallant struggles of my two comrades succeeded, at last, in raising the number of stones extracted to seven. Then we fancied that some slight passage had been obtained for the stream; for, though the terrible pool still rose higher, it seemed to rise less rapidly.

After several attempts, in which Steve and Job brought up nothing, there came a declaration from them that they could do no more. The lower stones were so tightly jammed between the sides of the fissure that no human strength seemed able to pull them out.

Job and Steve both came up from the water. They were exhausted and shivering, and well they might be. "We must try some other way," said Steve.

"What way?" asked I.

Steve looked at me. "You are a very good little fellow to stand this so well!" he said, with something like tears in his eyes.

They soon got on their clothes; and, having given up all hope of escape downward, we turned our eyes to the roof of the cave, on the chance of discovering some outlet there.

There was not enough light from our solitary candle to show us all the features of the vault in detail; but we could see enough to gather that it formed anything but a perfect dome. The roof was rather a series of rifts and projections, and high on one side, almost lost in the shades, there was a larger and deeper rift than elsewhere, forming a sort of loft, the back parts of which were invisible, extending we knew not how far. It was through this overhanging rift that the draught seemed to come which had caused our candle to gutter and flare.

To think of reaching an opening so far above our heads, so advanced into the ceiling of the cave as to require a fly's power of walking upside down to approach it, was mere waste of time. We bent our gaze elsewhere. On the same side with the niche in which we stood there was a small narrow ledge quite near at hand, and to gain it my two stalwart companions now exerted all their strength.

By cutting a sort of step with the pickaxe, Job was enabled to obtain a footing about three feet above the level of our present floor, and then he called to me.

"Now, Leonard, you be the lightest. Do you hop up here, and climb upon my shoulder, and then I think you will be tall enough to scramble to the ledge, so as to help us up after you."

I leapt up beside him, clambered upon his stout back as he bade me, and, springing from his shoulder, reached the ledge. He then handed up the pickaxe, directed me how to make its point firm into one of the crevices on the top of the ledge; next, to lie down, hold on to the handle of the pickaxe and give him my other hand. I obediently acted, when he sprang up, and turning, assisted Steve to do likewise.

We had now reached the highest possible coign of vantage left to us, and there remained nothing more to do but wait and hope that the encroaching water would find some unseen outlet before reaching our level.

Job and Steve were so weary from their exertions that they seemed almost indifferent as to what happened, provided they might only be allowed to rest. However, they tried to devise new schemes, and looked wistfully over the surface of the pool.

"I wonder if it rises still?" I said. "Perhaps not, after all."

"Then we shall only exchange drowning for starving," said Steve.

Job, instead of speaking, had endeavoured to answer my query by stooping down and stretching over the ledge with his arm. His face was very calm as he rose again. "It will be drowning," he said almost inaudibly, and held up his hand, which was wet.

CHAPTER IV

How Older Heads than Ours Became Concerned.

The water had risen so high that Job could touch its surface from our retreat.

We now, in spite of Job's remark, indulged in the dream that, provided the water would stop rising, we might, in the course of time, find a way out somehow, and Job by-and-by said, "Perhaps round there in the dark may be places where we could crawl out, if we could only see them well enough to swim across to them. Couldn't we send a candle round that way?"

"How?" said I and Steve.

"By a plan I have thought of," said he. Taking off his hat, which was of straw, he cut with his pocket-knife a little hole in the middle of the crown. Into this he stuck a piece of candle, lighted it, and lying down to reach the surface of the water as before, lowered the hat till it rested afloat.

There was, as Job had suspected, a slight circular current in the apparently still water, and the hat moved on slowly. Our six eyes became riveted on the voyaging candle as if it were a thing of fascination. It travelled away from us, lighting up in its progress unsuspected protuberances and hollows, but revealing to our eager stare no spot of safety or of egress. It went further and yet further into darkness, till it became like a star alone in a sky. Then it crossed from left to right. Then it gradually turned and enlarged, was lost behind jutting crags, reappeared, and journeyed back towards us, till it again floated under the ledge on which we stood, and we gathered it in. It had made a complete circuit of the cavern, the circular motion of the water being caused by the inpour of the spring, and it had showed us no means of escape at all.

Steve spoke, saying solemnly, "This is all my fault!"

"No," said Job. "For you would not have tried to stop the millstream if it had not been to save me."

"But I began it all," said Steve, bitterly. "I see now the foolishness of presumption. What right had I to take upon myself the ordering of a stream of water that scores of men three times my age get their living by?"

"I thought overmuch of myself, too," said Job. "It was hardly right to stop the grinding of flour that made bread for a whole parish, for my poor sake. We ought to ha' got the advice of some one wi' more experience than ourselves."

We then stood silent. The impossibility of doing more pressed in upon our senses like a chill, and I suggested that we should say our prayers.

"I think we ought," said Steve, and Job assenting, we all three knelt down. After this a sad sense of resignation fell on us all, and there being now no hopeful attempt which they could make for deliverance, the sleep that excitement had hitherto withstood overcame both Steve and Job. They leant back and were soon unconscious.

Not having exerted myself to the extent they had done I felt no sleepiness whatever. So I sat beside them with my eyes wide open, holding and protecting the candle mechanically, and wondering if it could really be possible that we were doomed to die.

I do not know how or why, but there came into my mind during this suspense the words I had read somewhere at school, as being those of Flaminius, the consul, when he was penned up at Thrasymene: "Friends, we must not hope to get out of this by vows and prayers alone. 'Tis by fortitude and strength we must escape." The futility of any such resolve in my case was apparent enough, and yet the words were sufficient to lead me to scan the roof of the cave once more.

When the opening up there met my eye I said to myself, "I wonder where that hole leads to?" Picking up a stone about the size of my fist I threw it with indifference, though with a good aim, towards the spot. The stone passed through the gaping orifice, and I heard it alight within like a tennis ball.

But its noise did not cease with its impact. The fall was succeeded by a helter-skelter kind of rattle which, though it receded in the distance, I could hear for a long time with distinctness, owing, I suppose, to the reflection or echo from the top and sides of the cave. It denoted that on the other side of that dark mouth yawning above me there was a slope downward—possibly into another cave, and that the stone had ricocheted down the incline. "I wonder where it leads?" I murmured again aloud.

Something greeted my ears at that moment of my pronouncing the words "where it leads" that caused me well nigh to leap out of my shoes. Even now I cannot think of it without experiencing a thrill. It came from the gaping hole.

If my readers can imagine for themselves the sensations of a timid bird, who, while watching the approach of his captors to strangle him, feels his wings loosening from the tenacious snare, and flight again possible, they may conceive my emotions when I realized that what greeted my ears from above were the words of a human tongue, direct from the cavity.

"Where, in the name of fortune, did that stone come from?"

The voice was the voice of the miller.

"Be dazed if I know—but 'a nearly broke my head!" The reply was that of the shoemaker.

"Steve—Job!" said I. They awoke with a start and exclamation. I tried to shout, but could not. "They have found us—up there—the miller—shoemaker!" I whispered, pointing to the hole aloft.

Steve and Job understood. Perhaps the sole ingredient, in this sudden revival of our hopes, which could save us from fainting with joy, was the one actually present—that our discoverer was the adversary whom we had been working to circumvent. But such antagonism as his weighed little in the scale with our present despairing circumstances.

We all three combined our voices in one shout—a shout which roused echoes in the cavern that probably had never been awakened since the upheaval of the Mendips, in whose heart we stood. When the shout died away we listened with parted lips.

Then we heard the miller speak again. "Faith, and believe me—'tis the rascals themselves! A-throwing stones—a-trying to terrify us off the premises! Did man ever know the like impudence? We have found the clue to the water mystery at last—may be at their pranks at this very moment! Clamber up here; and if I don't put about their backs the greenest stick that ever growed, I'm no grinder o' corn!"

Then we heard a creeping movement from the orifice over our heads, as of persons on their hands and knees; a puffing, as of fat men out of breath; sudden interjections, such as can be found in a list in any boys' grammar-book, and, therefore, need not be repeated here. All this was followed by a faint glimmer, about equal to that from our own candle, bursting from the gap on high, and the cautious appearance of a head over the ledge.

It was the visage of the shoemaker. Beside it rose another in haste, exclaiming, "Urrr—r! The rascals!" and waving a stick. Almost before we had recognized this as the miller, he, climbing forward with too great impetuosity, and not perceiving that the edge of the orifice was so near, was unable to check himself. He fell over headlong, and was precipitated a distance of some thirty feet into the whirling pool beneath.

Job's face, which, until this catastrophe, had been quite white and rigid at sight of his old enemy, instantly put on a more humane expression. "We mustn't let him drown," he said.

"No," said Steve, "but how can we save him in such an awkward place?"

There was, for the moment, however, no great cause for anxiety. The miller was a stout man, and could swim, though but badly—his power to keep afloat being due rather to the adipose tissues which composed his person, than to skill. But his immersion had been deep, and when he rose to the surface he was bubbling and sputtering wildly.

"Hu, hu, hu, hu! O, ho—I am drownded!" he gasped. "I am a dead man and miller—all on account of those villainous— I mean good boys!—If Job would only help me out I would give him such a dressing—blessing I would say—as he never felt the force of before. Oh, bub, bub, hu, hu, hu!"

Job had listened to this with attention. "Now, will you let me rule in this matter?" he said to Steve.

"With all my heart," said Steve.

"Look here, Miller Griffin," then said Job, speaking over the pool, "you can't expect me or my comrades to help ye until you treat us civilly. No mixed words o' that sort will we stand. Fair and square, or not at all. You must give us straight-forward assurance that you will do us no harm; and that if the water runs in your stream again, and the mill goes, and I finish out my 'prenticeship, you treat me well. If you won't promise this, you are a dead man in that water to-night."

"A master has a right over his 'prentice, body and soul!" cried the miller, desperately, as he swam round, "and I have a right over you—and I won't be drownded!"

"I fancy you will," said Job, quietly. "Your friends be too high above to get at ye."

"What must I promise ye, then, Job—hu—hu—hu—bub, bub, bub!"

"Say, If I ever strike Job Tray again, he shall be at liberty to leave my service forthwith, and go to some other employ, and this is the solemn oath of me, Miller Griffin. Say that in the presence of these witnesses."

"Very well—I say it—bub, bub—I say it." And the miller repeated the words.

"Now I'll help ye out," said Job. Lying down on his stomach he held out the handle of the shovel to the floating miller, and hauled him towards the ledge on which we stood. Then Steve took one of the miller's hands, and Job the other, and he mounted up beside us.

"Saved,—saved!" cried Miller Griffin.

"You must stand close in," said Steve, "for there isn't much room on this narrow shelf."

"Ay, yes I will," replied the saved man gladly. "And now, let's get out of this dark place as soon as we can—Ho!—Cobbler Jones!—here we be coming up to ye—but I don't see him!"

"Nor I," said Steve. "Where is he?"

The whole four of us stared with all our vision at the opening the miller had fallen from. But his companion had vanished.

"Well—never mind," said Miller Griffin, genially; "we'll follow. Which is the way?"

"There's no way—we can't follow," answered Steve.

"*Can't follow!*" echoed the miller, staring round, and perceiving for the first time that the ledge was a prison. "What—*not saved!*" he shrieked. "Not able to get out from here?"

"We be not saved unless your friend comes back to save us," said Job. "We've been calculating upon his help—otherwise things be as bad as they were before. We three have clung here waiting for death these two hours, and now there's one more to wait for death—unless the shoemaker comes back."

Job spoke stoically in the face of the cobbler's disappearance, and Steve tried to look cool also; but I think they felt as much discouraged as I, and almost as much as the miller, at the unaccountable vanishing of Cobbler Jones.

On reflection, however, there was no reason to suppose that he had basely deserted us. Probably he had only gone to bring further assistance. But the bare possibility of disappointment at such times is enough to take the nerve from any man or boy.

"He *must* mean to come back!" the miller murmured lugubriously, as we all stood in a row on the ledge, like sparrows on the moulding of a chimney.

"I should think so," said Steve, "if he's a man."

"Yes—he must!" the miller anxiously repeated. "I once said he was a two-penny sort of workman to his face—I wish I hadn't said it, oh—how I wish I hadn't; but 'twas years and years ago, and pray heaven he's forgot it! I once called him a stingy varmint—that I did! But we've made that up, and been friends ever since. And yet there's men who'll carry a snub in their buzzoms; and perhaps he's going to punish me now!"

"'Twould be very wrong of him," said I, "to leave us three to die because you've been a wicked man in your time, miller."

"Quite true," said Job.

"Zounds take your saucy tongues!" said Griffin. "If I had elbow room on this miserable perch I'd—I'd—"

"Just do nothing," said Job at his elbow. "Have you no more sense of decency, Mr Griffin, than to go on like that, and the waters rising to drown us minute by minute?"

"Rising to drown us—hey?" said the miller.

"Yes, indeed," broke in Steve. "It has reached my feet."

CHAPTER V

How We Became Close Allies with the Villagers.

Sure enough, the water—to which we had given less attention since the miller's arrival—had kept on rising with silent and pitiless regularity. To feel it actually lapping over the ledge was enough to paralyze us all. We listened and looked, but no shoemaker appeared. In no very long time it ran into our boots, and coldly encircled our ankles.

Miller Griffin trembled so much that he could scarcely keep his standing. "If I do get out of this," he said, "I'll do good—lots of good—to everybody! Oh, oh—the water!"

"Surely you can hold your tongue if this little boy can bear it without crying out!" said Job, alluding to me.

Thus rebuked, the miller was silent; and nothing more happened till we heard a slight sound from the opening which was our only hope, and saw a slight light. We watched, and the light grew stronger, flickering about the orifice like a smile on parted lips. Then hats and heads broke above the

edge of the same—one, two, three, four—then candles, arms
and shoulders; and it could be seen then that our deliverers
were provided with ropes.

"Ahoy—all right!" they shouted, and you may be sure we
shouted back a reply.

"Quick, in the name o' goodness!" cried the miller.

A consultation took place among those above, and one of
them shouted, "We'll throw you a rope's end and you must
catch it. If you can make it fast, and so climb up one at a time,
do it.

"If not, tie it round the first one, let him jump into the
water; we'll tow him across by the rope till he's underneath us,
and then haul him up."

"Yes, yes, that's the way!" said the miller. "But do be quick—
I'm dead drowned up to my thighs. Let me have the rope."

"Now, miller, that's not fair!" said one of the group above—
the Man who had Failed, for he was with them. "Of course
you'll send up the boys first—the little boy first of all."

"I will—I will—'twas a mistake," Griffin replied with
contrition.

The rope was then thrown; Job caught it, and tied it round
me. It was with some misgiving that I flung myself on the
water; but I did it, and, upheld by the rope, I floated across to
the spot in the pool that was perpendicularly under the opening, when the men all heaved, and I felt myself swinging in the
air, till I was received into the arms of half the parish. For the
alarm having been given, the attempt at rescue was known all
over the lower part of West Poley.

My cousin Steve was now hauled up. When he had gone the
miller burst into a sudden terror at the thought of being left
till the last, fearing he might not be able to catch the rope. He
implored Job to let him go up first.

"Well," said Job; "so you shall—on one condition."

"Tell it, and I agree."

Job searched his pockets, and drew out a little floury
pocket-book, in which he had been accustomed to enter sales
of meal and bran. Without replying to the miller, he stooped
to the candle and wrote. This done he said, "Sign this, and I'll
let ye go."

The miller read: I hereby certify that I release from this time forth Job Tray, my apprentice, by his wish, and demand no further service from him whatever. "Very well—have your way," he said; and taking the pencil subscribed his name. By this time they had untied Steve and were flinging the rope a third time; Job caught it as before, attached it to the miller's portly person, shoved him off, and saw him hoisted. The dragging up on this occasion was a test to the muscles of those above; but it was accomplished. Then the rope was flung back for the last time, and fortunate it was that the delay was no longer. Job could only manage to secure himself with great difficulty, owing to the numbness which was creeping over him from his heavy labours and immersions. More dead than alive he was pulled to the top with the rest.

The people assembled above began questioning us, as well they might, upon how we had managed to get into our peril-ous position. Before we had explained, a gurgling sound was heard from the pool. Several looked over. The water whose rising had nearly caused our death was sinking suddenly; and the light of the candle, which had been left to burn itself out on the ledge, revealed a whirlpool on the surface. Steve, the only one of our trio who was in a condition to observe any-thing, knew in a moment what the phenomenon meant.

The weight of accumulated water had completed the task of reopening the closed tunnel or fissure which Job's and Steve's diving had begun; and the stream was rushing rapidly down the old West Poley outlet, through which it had run from geological times. In a few minutes—as I was told, for I was not an eye-witness of further events this night—the water had drained itself out, and the stream could be heard trickling across the floor of the lower cave as before the check.

In the explanations which followed our adventure, the following facts were disclosed as to our discovery by the neighbours.

The miller and the shoemaker, after a little further discus-sion in the road where I overheard them, decided to investi-gate the caves one by one. With this object in view they got a lantern, and proceeded, not to Nick's Pocket, but to a well-known cave nearer at hand called Grim Billy, which to them seemed a likely source for the river.

This cave was very well known up to a certain point. The floor sloped upwards, and eventually led to the margin of the hole in the dome of Nick's Pocket; but nobody was aware that it was the inner part of Nick's Pocket which the treacherous opening revealed. Rather was the unplumbed depth beneath supposed to be the mouth of an abyss into which no human being could venture. Thus when a stone ascended from this abyss (the stone I threw) the searchers were amazed, till the miller's intuition suggested to him that we were there. And, what was most curious, when we were all delivered, and had gone home, and had been put into warm beds, neither the miller nor the shoemaker knew for certain that they had lighted upon the source of the mill stream. Much less did they suspect the contrivance we had discovered for turning the water to East or West Poley, at pleasure.

By a piece of good fortune, Steve's mother heard nothing of what had happened to us till we appeared dripping at the door, and could testify to our deliverance before explaining our perils.

The result which might have been expected to all of us, followed in the case of Steve. He caught cold from his prolonged duckings, and the cold was followed by a serious illness.

The illness of Steve was attended with slight fever, which left him very weak, though neither Job nor I suffered any evil effects from our immersion.

The mill-stream having flowed back to its course, the mill was again started, and the miller troubled himself no further about the river-head; but Job, thanks to his ingenuity, was no longer the miller's apprentice. He had been lucky enough to get a place in another mill many miles off, the very next day after our escape.

I frequently visited Steve in his bed-room, and, on one of these occasions, he said to me, "Suppose I were to die, and you were to go away home, and Job were always to stay away in another part of England, the secret of that mill-stream head would be lost to our village; so that if by chance the vent this way were to choke, and the water run into the East Poley channel, our people would not know how to recover it. They saved our lives, and we ought to make them the handsome return of telling them the whole manœuvre."

This was quite my way of thinking, and it was decided that Steve should tell all as soon as he was well enough. But I soon found that his anxiety on the matter seriously affected his recovery. He had a scheme, he said, for preventing such a loss of the stream again.

Discovering that Steve was uneasy in his mind, the doctor— to whom I explained that Steve desired to make personal reparation—insisted that his wish be gratified at once— namely, that some of the leading inhabitants of West Poley should be brought up to his bedroom, and learn what he had to say. His mother assented, and messages were sent to them at once.

The villagers were ready enough to come, for they guessed the object of the summons, and they were anxious, too, to know more particulars of our adventures than we had as yet had opportunity to tell them. Accordingly, at a little past six that evening, when the sun was going down, we heard their footsteps ascending the stairs, and they entered. Among them there were the blacksmith, the shoemaker, the dairyman, the Man who had Failed, a couple of farmers; and some men who worked on the farms were also admitted.

Some chairs were brought up from below, and, when our visitors had settled down, Steve's mother, who was very anxious about him, said, "Now, my boy, we are all here. What have you to tell?"

Steve began at once, explaining first how we had originally discovered the inner cave, and how we walked on till we came to a stream.

"What we want to know is this," said the shoemaker, "is that great pool we fetched you out of, the head of the mill-stream?"

Steve explained that it was not a natural pool, and other things which the reader already knows. He then came to the description of the grand manœuvre by which the stream could be turned into either the east or the west valley.

"But how did you get down there?" asked one. "Did you walk in through Giant's Ear, or Goblin's Cellar, or Grim Billy?"

"We did not enter by either of these," said Steve. "We entered by Nick's Pocket."

"Ha!" said the company, "that explains all the mystery."

"'Tis amazing," said the miller, who had entered, "that folks should have lived and died here for generations, and never ha' found out that Nick's Pocket led to the river spring!"

"Well, that isn't all I want to say," resumed Steve. "Suppose any people belonging to East Poley should find out the secret, they would go there and turn the water into their own vale; and, perhaps, close up the other channel in such a way that we could scarcely open it again. But didn't somebody leave the room a minute ago?—who is it that's going away?"

"I fancy a man went out," said the dairyman looking round. One or two others said the same, but dusk having closed in it was not apparent which of the company had gone away.

Steve continued: "Therefore before the secret is known, let somebody of our village go and close up the little gallery we entered by, and the upper mouth you look in from. Then there'll be no danger of our losing the water again."

The proposal was received with unanimous commendation, and after a little more consultation, and the best wishes of the neighbours for Steve's complete recovery, they took their leave, arranging to go and stop the cave entrances the next evening.

As the doctor had thought, so it happened. No sooner was his sense of responsibility gone, than Steve began to mend with miraculous rapidity. Four and twenty hours made such a difference in him that he said to me, with animation, the next evening: "Do, Leonard, go and bring me word what they are doing at Nick's Pocket. They ought to be going up there about this time to close up the gallery. But 'tis quite dark—you'll be afraid."

"No—not I," I replied, and off I went, having told my aunt my mission.

It was, indeed, quite dark, and it was not till I got quite close to the mill that I found several West Poley men had gathered in the road opposite thereto. The miller was not among them, being too much shaken by his fright for any active enterprise. They had spades, pickaxes, and other tools, and were just preparing for the start to the caves.

I followed behind, and as soon as we reached the outskirts of West Poley, I found they all made straight for Nick's Pocket as planned. Arrived there they lit their candles and we went into the interior. Though they had been most precisely informed by Steve how to find the connecting gallery with the inner cavern, so cunningly was it hidden by Nature's hand that they probably would have occupied no small time in lighting on it, if I had not gone forward and pointed out the nook.

They thanked me, and the dairyman, as one of the most active of the group, taking a spade in one hand, and a light in the other, prepared to creep in first and foremost. He had not advanced many steps before he reappeared in the outer cave, looking as pale as death.

CHAPTER VI

How all Our Difficulties Came to an End.

"What's the matter!" said the shoemaker.

"Somebody's there!" he gasped.

"It can't be," said a farmer. "Till those boys found the hole, not a being in the world knew of such a way in."

"Well, come and harken for yourselves," said the dairyman.

We crept close to the gallery mouth and listened. Peck, peck, peck; scrape, scrape, scrape, could be heard distinctly inside.

"Whoever they call themselves, they are at work like the busy bee!" said the farmer.

It was ultimately agreed that some of the party should go softly round into Grim Billy, creep up the ascent within the cave, and peer through the opening that looked down through the roof of the cave before us. By this means they might learn, unobserved, what was going on.

It was no sooner proposed than carried out. The baker and shoemaker were the ones that went round, and, as there was nothing to be seen where the others waited, I thought I would bear them company. To get to Grim Billy, a circuit of considerable extent was necessary; moreover, we had to cross the mill-stream. The mill had been stopped for the night, some time before, and, hence, it was by a pure chance we noticed that the river was gradually draining itself out. The misfortune initiated by Steve was again upon the village.

"I wonder if the miller knows it?" murmured the shoemaker. "If not, we won't tell him, or he may lose his senses outright."

"Then the folks in the cave are enemies!" said the farmer.

"True," said the baker, "for nobody else can have done this—let's push on."

Grim Billy being entered, we crawled on our hands and knees up the slope, which eventually terminated at the hole above Nick's Pocket—a hole that probably no human being had passed through before we were hoisted up through it on the evening of our marvellous escape. We were careful to make no noise in ascending, and, at the edge, we gazed cautiously over.

A striking sight met our view. A number of East Poley men were assembled below on the floor, which had been for awhile submerged by our exploit; and they were working with all their might to build and close up the old outlet of the stream towards West Poley, having already, as it appeared, opened the new opening towards their own village, discovered by Steve. We understood it in a moment, and, descending with the same softness as before, we returned to where our comrades were waiting for us in the other cave, where we told them the strange sight we had seen.

"How did they find out the secret?" the shoemaker inquired under his breath. "We have guarded it as we would ha' guarded our lives."

"I can guess!" replied the baker. "Have you forgot how somebody went away from Master Steve Draycot's bedroom in the dusk last night, and we didn't know who it was? Half an hour after, such a man was seen crossing the hill to East Poley;

I was told so to-day. We've been surprised, and must hold our own by main force, since we can no longer do it by stealth."

"How, main force?" asked the blacksmith and a farmer simultaneously.

"By closing the gallery they went in by," said the baker. "Then we shall have them in prison, and can bring them to book rarely."

The rest being all irritated at having been circumvented so slily and selfishly by the East Poley men, the baker's plan met with ready acceptance. Five of our body at once chose hard boulders from the outer cave, of such a bulk that they would roll about half-way into the passage or gallery—where there was a slight enlargement—but which would pass no further. These being put in position, they were easily wedged there, and it was impossible to remove them from within, owing to the diminishing size of the passage, except by more powerful tools than they had, which were only spades. We now felt sure of our antagonists, and in a far better position to argue with them than if they had been free. No longer taking the trouble to preserve silence, we, of West Poley, walked in a body round to the other cave—Grim Billy—ascended the inclined floor like a flock of goats, and arranged ourselves in a group at the opening that impended over Nick's Pocket.

The East Poley men were still working on, absorbed in their labour, and were unconscious that twenty eyes regarded them from above like stars.

"Let's halloo!" said the baker.

Halloo we did with such vigour that the East Poley men, taken absolutely unawares, well nigh sprang into the air at the shock it produced on their nerves. Their spades flew from their hands, and they stared around in dire alarm, for the echoes confused them as to the direction whence their hallooing came. They finally turned their eyes upwards, and saw us individuals of the rival village far above them, illuminated with candles, and with countenances grave and stern as a bench of unmerciful judges.

"Men of East Poley," said the baker, "we have caught ye in the execution of a most unfair piece of work. Because of a temporary turning of our water into your vale by a couple of

meddlesome boys—a piece of mischief that was speedily repaired—you have thought fit to covet our stream. You have
sent a spy to find out its secret, and have meanfully come here
to steal the stream for yourselves forever. This cavern is in our
parish, and you have no right here at all."

"The waters of the earth be as much ours as yours," said one
from beneath. But the remainder were thunderstruck, for
they knew that their chance had lain entirely in strategy and
not in argument.

The shoemaker then spoke: "Ye have entered upon our
property, and diverted the water, and made our parish mill
useless, and caused us other losses. Do ye agree to restore it to
its old course, close up the new course ye have been at such
labour to widen—in short, to leave things as they have been
from time immemorial?"

"No-o-o-o!" was shouted from below in a yell of defiance.

"Very well, then," said the baker, "we must make you. Gentlemen, ye are prisoners. Until you restore that water to us,
you will bide where you be."

The East Poley men rushed to escape by the way they had
entered. But half way up the tunnel a barricade of adaman-
tine blocks barred their footsteps. "Bring spades!" shouted
the foremost. But the stones were so well wedged, and the
passage so small, that, as we had anticipated, no engineering
force at their disposal could make the least impression upon
the blocks. They returned to the inner cave disconsolately.

"D'ye give in?" we asked them.

"Never!" said they doggedly.

"Let 'em sweat—let 'em sweat," said the shoemaker, placidly. "They'll tell a different tale by to-morrow morning. Let
'em bide for the night, and say no more."

In pursuance of this idea we withdrew from our position,
and, passing out of Grim Billy, went straight home. Steve was
excited by the length of my stay, and still more when I told
him the cause of it. "What—got them prisoners in the cave?"
he said. "I must go myself to-morrow and see the end of this!"

Whether it was partly due to the excitement of the occasion, or solely to the recuperative powers of a strong constitution, cannot be said; but certain it is that next morning, on

hearing the villagers shouting and gathering together, Steve sprang out of bed, declaring that he must go with me to see what was happening to the prisoners. The doctor was hastily called in, and gave it as his opinion that the outing would do Steve no harm, if he were warmly wrapped up; and soon away we went, just in time to overtake the men who had started on their way.

With breathless curiosity we entered Grim Billy, lit our candles and clambered up the incline. Almost before we reached the top, exclamations ascended through the chasm to Nick's Pocket, there being such words as, "We give in!" "Let us out!" "We give up the water forever!"

Looking in upon them, we found their aspect to be very different from what it had been the night before. Some had extemporized a couch with smock-frocks and gaiters, and jumped up from a sound sleep thereon; while others had their spades in their hands, as if undoing what they had been at such pains to build up, as was proved in a moment by their saying eagerly, "We have begun to put it right, and shall finish soon—we are restoring the river to his old bed—give us your word, good gentlemen, that when it is done we shall be free!"

"Certainly," replied our side with great dignity. "We have said so already."

Our arrival stimulated them in the work of repair, which had hitherto been somewhat desultory. Then shovels entered the clay and rubble like giants' tongues; they lit up more candles, and in half an hour had completely demolished the structure raised the night before with such labour and amazing solidity that it might have been expected to last forever. The final stone rolled away, the much tantalized river withdrew its last drop from the new channel, and resumed its original course once more.

While the East Poley men had been completing this task, some of our party had gone back to Nick's Pocket, and there, after much exertion, succeeded in unpacking the boulders from the horizontal passage admitting to the inner cave. By the time this was done, the prisoners within had finished their work of penance, and we West Poley men, who had remained to watch them, rejoined our companions. Then we all stood back, while those of East Poley came out, walking between their vanquishers, like the Romans under the Caudine Forks, when they surrendered to the Samnites. They glared at us with suppressed rage, and passed without saying a word.

"I see from their manner that we have not heard the last of this," said the Man who had Failed, thoughtfully. He had just joined us, and learnt the state of the case.

"I was thinking as much," said the shoemaker. "As long as that cave is known in Poley, so long will they bother us about the stream."

"I wish it had never been found out," said the baker bitterly. "If not now upon us, they will be playing that trick upon our children when we are dead and gone."

Steve glanced at me, and there was sadness in his look.

We walked home considerably in the rear of the rest, by no means at ease. It was impossible to disguise from ourselves that Steve had lost the good feeling of his fellow parishioners by his explorations and their results.

As the West Poley men had predicted, so it turned out. Some months afterwards, when I had gone back to my home and school, and Steve was learning to superintend his mother's farm, I heard that another midnight entry had been made into the cave by the rougher characters of East Poley. They diverted the stream as before, and when the miller and other inhabitants of the west village rose in the morning, behold, their stream was dry! The West Poley folk were furious, and rushed to Nick's Pocket. The mischief-makers were gone, and there was no legal proof as to their identity, though it was indirectly clear enough where they had come from. With some difficulty the water was again restored, but not till Steve had again been spoken of as the original cause of the misfortunes.

About this time I paid another visit to my cousin and aunt. Steve seemed to have grown a good deal older than when I had last seen him, and, almost as soon as we were alone, he began to speak on the subject of the mill-stream.

"I am glad you have come, Leonard," he said, "for I want to talk to you. I have never been happy, you know, since the adventure; I don't like the idea that by a freak of mine our village should be placed at the mercy of the East Poleyites; I shall never be liked again unless I make that river as secure from interruption as it was before."

"But that can't be," said I.

"Well, I have a scheme," said Steve musingly. "I am not so sure that the river may not be made as secure as it was before."

"But how? What is the scheme based on?" I asked, incredulously.

"I cannot reveal to you at present," said he. "All I can say is, that I have injured my native village, that I owe it amends, and that I'll pay the debt if it's a possibility."

I soon perceived from my cousin's manner at meals and elsewhere that the scheme, whatever it might be, occupied him to the exclusion of all other thoughts. But he would not speak to me about it. I frequently missed him for spaces of an hour or two, and soon conjectured that these hours of absence were spent in furtherance of his plan.

The last day of my visit came round, and to tell the truth I was not sorry, for Steve was so preoccupied as to be anything but a pleasant companion. I walked up to the village alone, and soon became aware that something had happened.

During the night another raid had been made upon the river head—with but partial success, it is true; but the stream was so much reduced that the mill-wheel would not turn, and the dipping pools were nearly empty. It was resolved to repair the mischief in the evening, but the disturbance in the village was very great, for the attempt proved that the more unscrupulous characters of East Poley were not inclined to desist.

Before I had gone much further, I was surprised to discern in the distance a figure which seemed to be Steve's, though I thought I had left him at the rear of his mother's premises.

He was making for Nick's Pocket, and following thither I reached the mouth of the cave just in time to see him enter.

"Steve!" I called out. He heard me and came back. He was pale, and there seemed to be something in his face which I had never seen there before.

"Ah—Leonard," he said, "you have traced me. Well, you are just in time. The folks think of coming to mend this mischief as soon as their day's work is over, but perhaps it won't be necessary. My scheme may do instead."

"How—do instead?" asked I.

"Well, save them the trouble," he said with assumed carelessness. "I had almost decided not to carry it out, though I have got the materials in readiness, but the doings of the night have stung me; I carry out my plan."

"When?"

"Now—this hour—this moment. The stream must flow into its right channel, and stay there, and no man's hands must be able to turn it elsewhere. Now good-bye, in case of accidents."

To my surprise, Steve shook hands with me solemnly, and wringing from me a promise not to follow, disappeared into the blackness of the cave.

For some moments I stood motionless where Steve had left me, not quite knowing what to do. Hearing footsteps behind my back, I looked round. To my great pleasure I saw Job approaching, dressed up in his best clothes, and with him the Man who had Failed.

Job was glad to see me. He had come to West Poley for a holiday, from the situation with the farmer which, as I now learned for the first time, the Man who had Failed had been the means of his obtaining. Observing, I suppose, the perplexity upon my face, they asked me what was the matter, and I, after some hesitation, told them of Steve. The Man who had Failed looked grave.

"Is it serious?" I asked him.

"It may be," said he, in that poetico-philosophic strain which, under more favouring circumstances, might have led him on to the intellectual eminence of a Coleridge or an Emerson. "Your cousin, like all such natures, is rushing into another extreme, that may be worse than the first. The opposite of error is error still; from careless adventuring at other people's expense he may have flown to rash self-sacrifice. He contemplates some violent remedy, I make no doubt. How long has he been in the cave? We had better follow him."

Before I could reply, we were startled by a jet of smoke, like that from the muzzle of a gun, bursting from the mouth of Nick's Pocket; and this was immediately followed by a deadened rumble like thunder underground. In another moment a duplicate of the noise reached our ears from over the hill, in the precise direction of Grim Billy.

"Oh—what can it be?" said I.

"Gunpowder," said the Man who had Failed, slowly.

"Ah—yes—I know what he's done—he has blasted the rocks inside!" cried Job. "Depend upon it, that's his plan for closing up the way to the river head."

"And for losing his life into the bargain," said our companion. "But no—he may be alive. We must go in at once—or as soon as we can breathe there."

Job ran for lights, and before he had returned we heard a familiar sound from the direction of the village. It was the patter of the mill-wheel. Job came up almost at the moment, and with him a crowd of the village people.

"The river is right again," they shouted. "Water runs better than ever—a full, steady stream, all on a sudden—just when we heard the rumble underground."

"Steve has done it!" I said.

"A brave fellow," said the Man who had Failed. "Pray that he is not hurt."

Job had lighted the candles, and, when we were entering, some more villagers, who at the noise of the explosion had run to Grim Billy, joined us. "Grim Billy is partly closed up inside!" they told us. "Where you used to climb up the slope to look over into Nick's Pocket, 'tis all altered. There's no longer any opening there; the whole rock has crumbled down as if the mountain had sunk bodily."

Without waiting to answer, we, who were about to enter Nick's Pocket, proceeded on our way. We soon had penetrated to the outer approaches, though nearly suffocated by the sulphurous atmosphere; but we could get no further than the first cavern. At a point somewhat in advance of the little gallery to the inner cave, Nick's Pocket ceased to exist. Its roof had sunk. The whole superimposed mountain, as it seemed, had quietly settled down upon the hollow places beneath it, closing like a pair of bellows, and barring all human entrance.

But alas, where was Steve? "I would liever have had no water in West Poley forevermore than have lost Steve!" said Job.

"And so would I!" said many of us.

To add to our terror, news was brought into the cave at that moment that Steve's mother was approaching; and how to meet my poor aunt was more than we could think.

But suddenly a shout was heard. A few of the party, who had not penetrated so far into the cave as we had done, were exclaiming, "Here he is!" We hastened back, and found they were in a small side hollow, close to the entrance, which we had passed by unheeded. The Man who had Failed was there, and he and the baker were carrying something into the light. It was Steve—apparently dead, or unconscious.

"Don't be frightened," said the baker to me. "He's not dead; perhaps not much hurt."

As he had declared, so it turned out. No sooner was Steve in the open air, than he unclosed his eyes, looked round with a stupefied expression, and sat up.

"Steve—Steve!" said Job and I, simultaneously.

"All right," said Steve, recovering his senses by degrees. "I'll tell—how it happened—in a minute or two."

Then his mother came up, and was at first terrified enough, but on seeing Steve gradually get upon his legs, she recovered her equanimity. He soon was able to explain all. He said that the damage to the village by his tampering with the stream had weighed upon his mind, and led him to revolve many schemes for its cure. With this in view he had privately made examination of the cave; when he discovered that the whole superincumbent mass, forming the roof of the inner cave, was divided from the walls of the same by a vein of sand, and, that it was only kept in its place by a slim support at one corner. It seemed to him that if this support could be removed, the upper mass would descend by its own weight, like the brick of a brick-trap when the peg is withdrawn.

He laid his plans accordingly; procuring gunpowder, and scooping out holes for the same, at central points in the rock. When all this was done, he waited a while, in doubt as to the effect; and might possibly never have completed his labours, but for the renewed attempt upon the river. He then made up his mind, and attached the fuse. After lighting it, he would have reached the outside safely enough but for the accident of stumbling as he ran, which threw him so heavily on the ground, that, before he could recover himself and go forward, the explosion had occurred.

All of us congratulated him, and the whole village was joyful, for no less than three thousand, four hundred and fifty tons of rock and earth—according to calculations made by an experienced engineer a short time afterwards—had descended between the river's head and all human interference, so that there was not much fear of any more East Poley manœuvres for turning the stream into their valley.

The inhabitants of the parish, gentle and simple, said that Steve had made ample amends for the harm he had done; and their good-will was further evidenced by his being invited to no less than nineteen Christmas and New Year's parties during the following holidays.

As we left the cave, Steve, Job, Mrs Draycot and I walked behind the Man who had Failed.

"Though this has worked well," he said to Steve, "it is by the merest chance in the world. Your courage is praiseworthy, but you see the risks that are incurred when people go out of their way to meddle with what they don't understand. Exceptionally smart actions, such as you delight in, should be carefully weighed with a view to their utility before they are begun. Quiet perseverance in clearly defined courses is, as a rule, better than the erratic exploits that may do much harm."

Steve listened respectfully enough to this, but he said to his mother afterwards: "He has failed in life, and how can his opinions be worth anything?"

"For this reason," said she. "He is one who has failed, not from want of sense, but from want of energy; and people of that sort, when kindly, are better worth attending to than those successful ones, who have never seen the seamy side of things. I would advise you to listen to him."

Steve probably did; for he is now the largest gentleman-farmer of those parts, remarkable for his avoidance of anything like speculative exploits.

OLD MRS CHUNDLE

The curate had not been a week in the parish, but the autumn morning proving fine he thought he would make a little water-colour sketch, showing a distant view of the Corvsgate ruin two miles off, which he had passed on his way hither. The sketch occupied him a longer time than he had anticipated. The luncheon hour drew on, and he felt hungry.

Quite near him was a stone-built old cottage of respectable and substantial build. He entered it, and was received by an old woman.

"Can you give me something to eat, my good woman?" he said.

She held her hand to her ear.

"Can you give me something for lunch?" he shouted. "Bread-and-cheese—anything will do."

A sour look crossed her face, and she shook her head. "That's unlucky," murmured he.

She reflected and said more urbanely: "Well, I'm going to have my own bit o' dinner in no such long time hence. 'Tis taters and cabbage, boiled with a scantling o' bacon. Would ye like it? But I suppose 'tis the wrong sort, and that ye would sooner have bread-and-cheese?"

"No, I'll join you. Call me when it is ready. I'm just out here."

"Ay, I've seen ye. Drawing the old stones, baint ye? Sure 'tis well some folk have nothing better to do with their time. Very well. I'll call ye, when I've dished up."

He went out and resumed his painting; till in about seven or ten minutes the old woman appeared at her door and held up her hand. The curate washed his brush, went to the brook, rinsed his hands and proceeded to the house.

"There's yours" she said, pointing to the table. "I'll have my bit here." And she denoted the settle.

"Why not join me?"

"Oh, faith, I don't want to eat with my betters—not I." And she continued firm in her resolution, and eat apart.

The vegetables had been well cooked over a wood fire—the only way to cook a vegetable properly—and the bacon was well-boiled. The curate ate heartily: he thought he had never tasted such potatoes and cabbage in his life, which he probably had not, for they had been just brought in from the garden, so that the very freshness of the morning was still in them. When he had finished he asked her how much he owed for the repast, which he had much enjoyed.

"Oh, I don't want to be paid for that bit of snack 'a b'lieve!"

"But really you must take something. It was an excellent meal."

"'Tis all my own growing, that's true. But I don't take money for a bit o' victuals. I've never done such a thing in my life."

"I should feel much happier if you would."

She seemed unsettled by his feeling, and added as by compulsion, "Well, then; I suppose twopence won't hurt ye?"

"Twopence?"

"Yes. Twopence."

"Why, my good woman, that's no charge at all. I am sure it is worth this, at least." And he laid down a shilling.

"I tell 'ee 'tis *twopence*, and no more!" she said firmly. "Why, bless the man, it didn't cost me more than three halfpence, and that leaves me a fair quarter profit. The bacon is the heaviest item; that may perhaps be a penny. The taters I've got plenty of, and the cabbage is going to waste."

He thereupon argued no further, paid the limited sum demanded, and went to the door. "And where does that road lead?" he asked, by way of engaging her in a little friendly conversation before parting, and pointing to a white lane which branched from the direct highway near her door.

"They tell me that it leads to Enckworth."

"And how far is Enckworth?"

"Three mile, they say. But God knows if 'tis true."

"You haven't lived here long, then?"

"Five-and-thirty year come Martinmas."

"And yet you have never been to Enckworth?"

"Not I. Why should I ever have been to Enckworth? I never had any business there—a great mansion of a place, holding people that I've no more doings with than with the people of the moon. No: there's on'y two places I ever go to from year's end to year's end: that's once a fortnight to Anglebury, to do my bit o' marketing; and once a week to my parish church."

"Which is that?"

"Why, Kingscreech."

"Oh—then you are in my parish?"

"Maybe. Just on the outskirts."

"I didn't know the parish extended so far. I'm a new comer. Well, I hope we may meet again. Good afternoon to you."

When the curate was next talking to his rector he casually observed: "By the way, that's a curious old soul who lives out towards Corvsgate—old Mrs—I don't know her name—a deaf old woman."

"You mean old Mrs Chundle, I suppose."

"She tells me she's lived there five-and-thirty years, and has never been to Enckworth, three miles off. She goes to two places only, from year's end to year's end—to the market town, and to church on Sundays."

"To church on Sundays. H'm. She rather exaggerates her travels, to my thinking. I've been rector here thirteen years, and I have certainly never seen her at church in my time."

"A wicked old woman. What can she think of herself for such deception!"

"She didn't know you belonged here when she said it, and could find out the untruth of her story. I warrant she wouldn't have said it to me!" And the rector chuckled.

On reflection the curate felt that this was decidedly a case for his ministrations, and on the first spare morning he strode across to the cottage beyond the ruin. He found its occupant of course at home.

"Drawing picters again?" she asked, looking up from the hearth, where she was scouring the fire-dogs.

"No. I come on more important matters, Mrs Chundle. I am the new curate of this parish."

"You said you was last time. And after you had told me and went away I said to myself, he'll be here again sure enough, hang me if I didn't. And here you be."

"Yes. I hope you don't mind?"

"Oh, no. You find us a roughish lot, I make no doubt?"

"Well, I won't go into that. But I think it was a very culpable—unkind thing of you to tell me you came to church every
Sunday, when I find you've not been seen there for years."

"Oh—did I tell 'ee that?"

"You certainly did."

"Now I wonder what I did that for?"

"I wonder too."

"Well, you could ha' guessed, after all, that I didn't come to
any service. Lord, what's the good o' my lumpering all the way
to church and back again, when I'm as deaf as a plock? Your
own commonsense ought to have told 'ee that 'twas but a
figure o' speech, seeing you was a pa'son."

"Don't you think you could hear the service if you were to
sit close to the reading-desk and pulpit?"

"I'm sure I couldn't. O no—not a word. Why I couldn't
hear anything even at that time when Isaac Coggs used to cry
the Amens out loud beyond anything that's done nowadays,
and they had the barrel-organ for the tunes—years and years
agone, when I was stronger in my narves than now."

"H'm—I'm sorry. There's one thing I could do, which I
would with pleasure, if you'll use it. I could get you an ear-
trumpet. Will you use it?"

"Ay, sure. That I woll. I don't care what I use—'tis all the
same to me."

"And you'll come?"

"Yes. I may as well go there as bide here, I suppose."

The ear-trumpet was purchased by the zealous young man,
and the next Sunday, to the great surprise of the parishioners
when they arrived, Mrs Chundle was discovered in the front
seat of the nave of Kingscreech Church, facing the rest of the
congregation with an unmoved countenance.

She was the centre of observation through the whole morning service. The trumpet, elevated at a high angle, shone and
flashed in the sitters' eyes as the chief object in the sacred
edifice.

The curate could not speak to her that morning, and called
the next day to inquire the result of the experiment. As soon
as she saw him in the distance she began shaking her head.

"No; no;" she said decisively as he approached. "I knowed 'twas all nonsense."

"What?"

"'Twasn't a mossel o' good, and so I could have told 'ee before. A wasting your money in jimcracks upon a' old 'ooman like me."

"You couldn't hear? Dear me—how disappointing."

"You might as well have been mouthing at me from the top o' Creech Barrow."

"That's unfortunate."

"I shall never come no more—never—to be made such a fool of as that again."

The curate mused. "I'll tell you what, Mrs Chundle. There's one thing more to try, and only one. If that fails I suppose we shall have to give it up. It is a plan I have heard of, though I have never myself tried it; it's having a sound-tube fixed, with its lower mouth in the seat immediately below the pulpit, where you would sit, the tube running up inside the pulpit with its upper end opening in a bell-mouth just beside the book-board. The voice of the preacher enters the bell-mouth, and is carried down directly to the listener's ear. Do you understand?"

"Exactly."

"And you'll come, if I put it up at my own expense?"

"Ay, I suppose. I'll try it, e'en though I said I wouldn't. I may as well do that as do nothing, I reckon."

The kind-hearted curate, at great trouble to himself, obtained the tube and had it fixed vertically as described, the upper mouth being immediately under the face of whoever should preach, and on the following Sunday morning it was to be tried. As soon as he came from the vestry the curate perceived to his satisfaction Mrs Chundle in the seat beneath, erect and at attention, her head close to the lower orifice of the sound-pipe, and a look of great complacency that her soul required a special machinery to save it, while other people's could be saved in a commonplace way. The rector read the prayers from the desk on the opposite side, which part of the service Mrs Chundle could follow easily enough by the help of the prayer-book; and in due course the curate mounted the eight steps into the wooden octagon, gave out his text, and began to deliver his discourse.

It was a fine frosty morning in early winter, and he had not got far with his sermon when he became conscious of a steam rising from the bell-mouth of the tube, obviously caused by Mrs Chundle's breathing at the lower end, and it was accompanied by a suggestion of onion-stew. However he preached on awhile, hoping it would cease, holding in his left hand his finest cambric handkerchief kept especially for Sunday morning services. At length, no longer able to endure the odour, he lightly dropped the handkerchief into the bell of the tube, without stopping for a moment the eloquent flow of his words; and he had the satisfaction of feeling himself in comparatively pure air.

He heard a fidgeting below; and presently there arose to him over the pulpit-edge a hoarse whisper: "The pipe's chokt!"

"Now, as you will perceive, my brethren," continued the curate, unheeding the interruption; "by applying this test to ourselves, our discernment of—"

"The pipe's chokt!" came up in a whisper yet louder and hoarser.

"Our discernment of actions as morally good, or indifferent, will be much quickened, and we shall be materially helped in our—"

Suddenly came a violent puff of warm wind, and he beheld his handkerchief rising from the bell of the tube and floating to the pulpit-floor. The little boys in the gallery laughed, thinking it a miracle. Mrs Chundle had, in fact, applied her mouth to the bottom end, blown with all her might, and cleared the tube. In a few seconds the atmosphere of the pulpit became as before, to the curate's great discomfiture. Yet stop the orifice again he dared not, lest the old woman should make a still greater disturbance and draw the attention of the congregation to this unseemly situation.

"If you carefully analyze the passage I have quoted," he continued in somewhat uncomfortable accents, "you will perceive that it naturally suggests three points for consideration—"

("It's not onions: it's peppermint," he said to himself.)

"Namely, mankind in its unregenerate state—"

("And cider.")

"The incidence of the law, and lovingkindness or grace, which we will now severally consider—"

("And pickled cabbage. What a terrible supper she must have made!")

"Under the twofold aspect of external and internal consciousness."

Thus the reverend gentleman continued strenuously for perhaps five minutes longer: then he could stand it no more. Desperately thrusting his thumb into the hole he drew the threads of his distracted discourse together, the while hearing her blow vigorously to dislodge the plug. But he stuck to the hole, and brought his sermon to a premature close.

He did not call on Mrs Chundle the next week, a slight cooling of his zeal for her spiritual welfare being manifest; but he encountered her at the house of another cottager whom he was visiting; and she immediately addressed him as a partner in the same enterprize.

"I could hear beautiful!" she said. "Yes; every word! Never did I know such a wonderful machine as that there pipe. But you forgot what you was doing once or twice, and put your handkercher on the top o' en, and stopped the sound a bit. Please not to do that again, for it makes me lose a lot. Howsomever, I shall come every Sunday morning reg'lar now, please God."

The curate quivered internally.

"And will ye come to my house once in a while and read to me?"

"Of course."

Surely enough the next Sunday the ordeal was repeated for him. In the evening he told his trouble to the rector. The rector chuckled.

"You've brought it upon yourself" he said. "You don't know this parish so well as I. You should have left the old woman alone."

"I suppose I should!"

"Thank Heaven, she thinks nothing of my sermons, and doesn't come when I preach. Ha, ha!"

"Well," said the curate somewhat ruffled, "I must do something. I cannot stand this. I shall tell her not to come."

"You can hardly do that."

"And I've half-promised to go and read to her. But—I shan't go."

"She's probably forgotten by this time that you promised."

A vision of his next Sunday in the pulpit loomed horridly before the young man, and at length he determined to escape the experience. The pipe should be taken down. The next morning he gave directions, and the removal was carried out.

A day or two later a message arrived from her, saying that she wished to see him. Anticipating a terrific attack from the irate old woman he put off going to her for a day, and when he trudged out towards her house on the following afternoon it was in a vexed mood. Delicately nurtured man as he was he had determined not to re-erect the tube, and hoped he might hit on some new *modus vivendi*, even if at any inconvenience to Mrs Chundle, in a situation that had become intolerable as it was last week.

"Thank Heaven, the tube is gone," he said to himself as he walked; "and nothing will make me put it up again!"

On coming near he saw to his surprise that the calico curtains of the cottage windows were all drawn. He went up to the door, which was ajar; and a little girl peeped through the opening.

"How is Mrs Chundle?" he asked blandly.

"She's dead, sir" said the girl in a whisper.

"Dead? . . . Mrs Chundle dead?"

"Yes, sir."

A woman now came. "Yes, 'tis so, sir. She went off quite sudden-like about two hours ago. Well, you see, sir, she was over seventy years of age, and last Sunday she was rather late in starting for church, having to put her bit o' dinner ready before going out; and was very anxious to be in time. So she hurried overmuch, and runned up the hill, which at her time of life she ought not to have done. It upset her heart, and she's been poorly all the week since, and that made her send for 'ee. Two or three times she said she hoped you would come soon, as you'd promised to, and you were so staunch and faithful in wishing to do her good, that she knew 'twas not by your own wish you didn't arrive. But she would not let us send again, as it might trouble 'ee too much, and there might be other poor folks needing you. She worried to think she might not be able to listen to 'ee next Sunday, and feared you'd be hurt at it, and think her remiss. But she was eager to hear you again later on. However, 'twas ordained otherwise for the poor soul, and she was soon gone. 'I've found a real friend at last,' she said. 'He's a man in a thousand. He's not ashamed of a' old woman, and he holds that her soul is worth saving as well as richer people's.' She said I was to give you this."

It was a small folded piece of paper, directed to him and sealed with a thimble. On opening it he found it to be what she called her will, in which she had left him her bureau, case-clock, settle, four-post bedstead, and framed sampler—in fact all the furniture of any account that she possessed.

The curate went out, like Peter at the cock-crow. He was a meek young man, and as he went his eyes were wet. When he reached a lonely place in the lane he stood still thinking, and kneeling down in the dust of the road rested his elbow in one hand and covered his face with the other. Thus he remained some minute or so, a black shape on the hot white of the sunned trackway; till he rose, brushed the knees of his trousers, and walked on.

THE DOCTOR'S LEGEND

I

"Not more than half-a-dozen miles from the Wessex coast" (said the doctor) "is a mansion which appeared newer in the last century than it appears at the present day after years of neglect and occupation by inferior tenants. It was owned by a man of five-and-twenty, than whom a more ambitious person-age never surveyed his face in a glass. His name I will not mention out of respect to those of his blood and connections who may remain on earth, if any such there be. In the words of a writer of that time who knew him well, he was 'one whom anything would petrify but nothing would soften'.

"This worthy gentleman was of so elevated and refined a nature that he never gave a penny to women who uttered bad words in their trouble and rage, or who wore dirty aprons in view of his front door. On those misguided ones who did not pull the fore-lock to him in passing, and call him 'your Hon-our' and 'Squire', he turned the shoulder of scorn, especially when he wore his finer ruffles and gold seals.

"Neither his personal nor real estate at this time was large; but the latter he made the most of by jealously guarding it, as of the former by his economies. Yet though his fields and woods were well-watched by his gamekeepers and other de-pendants, such was his dislike to intrusion that he never ceased to watch the watchers. He stopped footpaths and en-closed lands. He made no exception to these sentiments in the case of his own villagers, whose faces were never to be seen in his private grounds except on pressing errands.

"Outside his garden-wall, near the entrance to the park, there lived a poor woman with an only child. This child had been so unfortunate as to trespass upon the Squire's lawn on more than one occasion, in search of flowers; and on this incident, trivial as it was, hung much that was afterwards of concern to the house and lineage of the Squire. It seems that the Squire had sent a message to the little girl's mother concerning the nuisance; nevertheless, only a few days afterwards, he saw the child there again. This unwarrantable impertinence, as the owner and landlord deemed it to be, irritated him exceedingly; and, with his walking cane elevated, he began to pursue the child to teach her by chastisement what she would not learn by exhortation.

"Naturally enough, as soon as the girl saw the Squire in pursuit of her she gave a loud scream, and started off like a hare; but the only entrance to the grounds being on the side which the Squire's position commanded, she could not escape, and endeavoured to elude him by winding, and doubling in her terrified course. Finding her, by reason of her fleetness, not so easy to chastise as he had imagined, her assailant lost his temper—never a very difficult matter—and the more loudly she screamed the more angrily did he pursue. A more untoward interruption to the peace of a beautiful and secluded spot was never seen.

"The race continued, and the Squire, now panting with rage and exertion, drew closer to his victim. To the horrified eyes of the child, when she gazed over her shoulder, his face appeared like a crimson mask set with eyes of fire. The glance sealed her fate in the race. By a sudden start forward he caught hold of her by the skirt of her short frock flying behind. The clutch so terrified the child that, with a louder shriek than ever, she leapt from his grasp, leaving the skirt in his hand. But she did not go far; in a few more moments she fell on the ground in an epileptic fit.

"This strange, and, but for its painfulness, even ludicrous scene, was witnessed by one of the gardeners who had been working near, and the squire haughtily directed him to take the prostrate and quivering child home; after which he walked off, by no means pleased with himself at the unmanly and undignified part which a violent temper had led him to play.

"The mother of the girl was in great distress when she saw her only child brought home in such a condition: she was still more distressed, when in the course of a day or two, it became doubtful if fright had not deprived the girl entirely of her reason, as well as of her health. In the singular, nervous malady which supervened the child's hair came off, and her teeth fell from her gums; till no one could have recognised in the mere scare-crow that she appeared, the happy and laughing youngster of a few weeks before.

"The mother was a woman of very different mettle from her poor child. Impassioned and determined in character, she was not one to provoke with impunity. And her moods were as enduring as they were deep. Seeing what a wreck her darling had become she went on foot to the manor-house, and, contrary to the custom of the villagers, rang at the front door, where she asked to see that ruffian the master of the mansion who had ruined her only child. The Squire sent out a reply that he was very sorry for the girl, but that he could not see her mother, accompanying his message by a *solatium* of five shillings.

"In the bitterness of her hate, the woman threw the five-shilling-piece through the panes of the dining-room window, and went home to brood again over her idiotized child.

"One day a little later, when the girl was well enough to play in the lane, she came in with a bigger girl who took care of her.

"'Death's Head—I be Death's Head—hee, hee!' said the child.

"'What?' said her mother, turning pale.

"The girl in charge explained that the other children had nick-named her daughter 'Death's Head' since she had lost her hair, from her resemblance to a skull.

"When the elder girl was gone the mother carefully regarded the child from a distance. In a moment she saw how cruelly apt the *sobriquet* was. The bald scalp, the hollow cheeks—by reason of the absence of teeth—and the saucer eyes, the cadaverous hue, had, indeed, a startling likeness to that bony relic of mortality.

"At this time the Squire was successfully soliciting in marriage a certain Lady Cicely, the daughter of an ancient and noble house in that county. During the ensuing summer their nuptials were celebrated, and the young wife brought home amid great rejoicing, and ringing of bells, and dancing on the green, followed by a bonfire after dark on the hill. The woman whose disfigured child was as the apple of her eye to her, saw all this, and the greater the good fortune that fell to the Squire, the more envenomed did she become.

"The newly-wedded lady was much liked by the villagers in general, to whom she was very charitable, intelligently entering into their lives and histories, and endeavouring to relieve their cares. On a particular evening of the ensuing Autumn when she had been a wife but a few months, after some parish-visiting, she was returning homeward to dinner on foot, her way to the mansion lying by the churchyard-wall. It was barely dusk, but a full harvest moon was shining from the east. At this moment of the Lady Cicely's return, it chanced that the widow with her afflicted girl was crossing the churchyard by the footpath from gate to gate. The churchyard was in obscurity, being shaded by the yews. Seeing the lady in the adjoining highway, the woman hastily left the footpath with the child, crossed the graves to the shadow of the wall outside which the lady was passing, and pulled off the child's hood so that the baldness was revealed. Whispering to the child, 'Grin at her my deary!' she held up the little girl as high as she could, which was just sufficient to disclose her face over the coping of the wall to a person on the other side.

"The moonlight fell upon the sepulchral face and head, intensifying the child's daytime aspect till it was only too much like that which had suggested the nickname. The unsuspecting and timid lady—a perfect necrophobist by reason of the care with which everything unpleasant had been kept out of her dainty life—saw the death-like shape, and, shrieking with sudden terror, fell to the ground. The lurking woman with her child disappeared in another direction, and passed through the churchyard gate homeward.

"The Lady Cicely's shriek brought some villagers to the spot. They found her quivering, but not senseless; and she was taken home. There she lay prostrate for some time under the doctor's hands.

II

"It was the following spring, and the time drew near when an infant was to be born to the Squire. Great was the anxiety of all concerned, by reason of the fright and fall from which the Lady Cicely had suffered in the latter part of the preceding year. However the event which they were all expecting took place, and, to the joy of her friends, no evil consequences seemed to have ensued from the terrifying incident before-mentioned. The child of Lady Cicely was a son and heir.

"Meanwhile the mother of the afflicted child watched these things in silence. Nothing—not even malevolent tricks upon those dear to him—seemed to interrupt the prosperity of the Squire. An Uncle of his, a money-lender in some northern city, died childless at this time, and left an immense fortune to his nephew the Lady Cicely's husband; who, fortified by this acquisition, now bethought himself of a pedigree as a necessity, so as to be no longer beholden to his wife for all the ancestral credit that his children would possess. By searching in the County history he happily discovered that one of the knights who came over with William the Conqueror bore a name which somewhat resembled his own, and from this he constructed an ingenious and creditable genealogical tree; the only rickety point in which occurred at a certain date in the previous century. It was the date whereat it became necessary to show that his great-grandfather (in reality a respectable village tanner) was the indubitable son of a scion of the knightly family before alluded to, despite the fact that this scion had lived in quite another part of the county. This little artistic junction, however, was satisfactorily manipulated, and the grafting was only to be perceived by the curious.

"His upward progress was uninterrupted. His only son grew to be an interesting lad, though, like his mother, exceedingly timid and impressionable. With his now great wealth, the Squire began to feel that his present modest country-seat was insufficient, and there being at this time an Abbey and its estates in the market, by reason of some dispute in the family hitherto its owners, the wealthy gentleman purchased it. The Abbey was of large proportions, and stood in a lovely and fertile valley surrounded by many attached estates. It had a situation fit for the home of a prince, still more for that of an Archbishop. This historic spot, with its monkish associations, its fish-ponds, woods, village, abbey-church, and Abbots' bones beneath their incised slabs, all passed into the possession of our illustrious self-seeker.

"Meeting his son when the purchase was completed, he smacked the youth on the shoulder.

"'We've estates, and rivers, and hills, and woods, and a beautiful Abbey unrivalled in the whole of Wessex—Ha, ha!' he cried.

"'I don't care about Abbeys,' said the gentle son. 'They are gloomy; this one particularly.'

"'Nonsense!' said his father. 'And we've a village, and the Abbey church into the bargain.'

"'Yes.'

"'And dozens of mitred Abbots in their stone coffins underground, and tons of monks—all for the same money. . . . Yes the very dust of those old rascals is mine! Ho-ho!'

"The son turned pale. 'Many were holy men,' he murmured, 'despite the errors in their creed.'

" 'D— ye, grow up, and get married, and have a wife who'll disabuse you of that ghostly nonsense!' cried the Squire.

"Not more than a year after this, several new peers were created for political reasons with which we have no concern. Among them was the subject of this legend; much to the chagrin of some of his neighbours, who considered that such rapid advancement was too great for his deserts. On this point I express no opinion.

"He now resided at the Abbey, outwardly honoured by all in his vicinity, though perhaps less honoured in their hearts; and many were the visitors from far and near. In due course his son grew to manhood and married a beautiful woman, whose beauty nevertheless was no greater than her taste and accomplishments. She could read Latin and Greek, as well as one or two modern languages; above all she had great skill as a sculptress in marble and other materials.

"The poor widow in the other village seemed to have been blasted out of existence by the success of her long-time enemy. The two could not thrive side by side. She declined and died; her death having, happily, been preceded by that of her child.

"Though the Abbey, with its little cells, and quaint turnings, satisfied the curiosity of visitors, it did not satisfy the noble lord (as the Squire had now become). Except the Abbot's Hall, the rooms were miserably small for a baron of his wealth, who expected soon to be an Earl, and the parent of a line of Earls.

"Moreover the village was close to his very doors—on his very lawn, and he disliked the proximity of its inhabitants, his old craze for seclusion remaining with him still. On Sundays they sat at service in the very Abbey Church which was part of his own residence. Besides, as his son had said, the conventual buildings formed a gloomy dwelling, with its dark corridors, monkish associations, and charnel-like smell.

"So he set to work, and did not spare his thousands. First, he carted the village bodily away to a distance of a mile or more, where he built new, and, it must be added, convenient cottages, and a little barn-like church. The spot on which the old village had stood was now included in his lawn. But the villagers still intruded there, for they came to ring the Abbey-Church bells—a fine peal, which they professed (it is believed truly) to have an immemorial right to chime.

"As the natives persistently came and got drunk in the ringing-loft, the peer determined to put a stop to it. He sold the ring of bells to a founder in a distant city, and to him one day the whole beautiful set of them was conveyed on waggons away from the spot on which they had hung and resounded for so many centuries, and called so many devout souls to prayer. When the villagers saw their dear bells going off in procession, never to return, they stood at their doors and shed tears.

"It was just after this time that the first shadow fell upon the new lord's life. His wife died. Yet the renovation of the residence went on apace. The Abbey was pulled down wing by wing, and a fair mansion built on its site. An additional lawn was planned to extend over the spot where the cloisters had been, and for that purpose the ground was to be lowered and levelled. The flat tombs covering the Abbots were removed one by one, as a necessity of the embellishment, and the bones dug up.

"Of these bones it seemed as if the excavators would never reach the end. It was necessary to dig ditches and pits for them in the plantations, and from their quantity there was not much respect shown to them in wheeling them away.

III

"One morning, when the family were rising from breakfast, a message was brought to my lord that more bones than ever had been found in clearing away the ground for the ballroom, and for the foundations of the new card-parlour. One of the skeletons was that of a mitred abbot—evidently a very holy person. What were they to do with it?

"'Put him into any hole,' says my lord.

"The foreman came a second time, 'There is something strange in those bones, my lord,' he said; 'we remove them by barrowfuls, and still they seem never to lessen. The more we carry away, the more there are left behind.'

"The son looked disturbed, rose from his seat and went out of the room. Since his mother's death he had been much depressed, and seemed to suffer from nervous debility.

"'Curse the bones!' said the peer, angry at the extreme sensitiveness of his son, whose distress and departure he had observed. 'More, do .ye say? Throw the wormy rubbish into any ditch you can find!'

"The servants looked uneasily at each-other, for the old Catholicism had not at that time ceased to be the religion of these islands so long as it has now, and much of its superstition and weird fancy still lingered in the minds of the simple folk of this remote nook.

"The son's wife, the bright and accomplished woman aforesaid, to enliven the subject told her father-in-law that she was designing a marble tomb for one of the London churches, and the design was to be a very artistic allegory of Death and the Resurrection; the figure of an Angel on one side, and that of Death on the other (according to the extravagant symbolism of that date, when such designs as this were much in vogue). Might she, the lady asked, have a skull to copy in marble for the head of Death?

"She might have them all, and welcome, her father-in-law said. He would only be too glad.

"She went out to the spot where the new foundations were being dug, and from the heap of bones chose the one of those sad relics which seemed to offer the most perfect model for her chisel.

" 'It is the last Abbot's, my lady,' said the clerk of the works.

" 'It will do,' said she; and directed it to be put into a box and sent to the house in London where she and her husband at present resided.

"When she met her husband that day he proposed that they should return to town almost immediately. 'This is a gloomy place,' said he. 'And if ever it comes into my hands I shan't live here much. I've been telling the old man of my debts, too, and he says he won't pay them . . . be hanged if he will, until he has a grandson at least. . . . So let's be off.'

"They returned to town. This young man the son and heir, though quiet and nervous, was not a very domestic character; he had many friends of both sexes with whom his refined and accomplished wife was unacquainted. Therefore she was thrown much upon her own resources; and her gifts in carving were a real solace to her. She proceeded with her design for the tomb of her acquaintance; and the Abbot's skull having duly arrived, she made use of it as her model as she had planned.

"Her husband being as usual away from home, she worked at her self-imposed task till bed-time—and then retired. When the house had been wrapped in sleep for some hours the front door was opened, and the absent one entered, a little the worse for liquor—for drinking in those days was one of a nobleman's accomplishments. He ascended the stairs, candle in hand, and feeling uncertain whether his wife had gone to bed or no, entered her studio to look for her. Holding the candle unsteadily above his head, he perceived a heap of modelling clay; behind it a sheeted figure with a death's-head above it—this being in fact the draped dummy arrangement that his wife had built up to be ultimately copied in marble for the allegory she had designed to support the mural tablet.

"The sight seemed to overpower the gazer with horror; the candle fell from his hand; and in the darkness he rushed downstairs and out of the house.

"'I've seen it before!' he cried in mad and maudlin accents. 'Where? when?'

"At four o'clock the next morning news was brought to the house that my lord's heir had shot himself dead with a pistol at a tavern not far off.

"His reason for the act was absolutely inexplicable to the outer world. The heir to an enormous property and a high title, the husband of a wife as gifted as she was charming; of all the men in English society he seemed to be the last likely to undertake such a desperate deed.

"Only a few persons—his wife not being one of them, though his father was—knew of the sad circumstance in the life of the suicide's mother the late Lady Cicely, a few months before his birth—in which she was terrified nearly to death by the woman who held up poor little 'Death's-Head', over the churchyard wall.

"Then people said that in this there was retribution upon the ambitious lord for his wickedness, particularly that of cursing the bones of the holy men of God. I give the superstition for what it is worth. It is enough to add, in this connection, that the old lord died, some say like Herod, of the characteristics he had imputed to the inoffensive human remains. However that may be in a few years the title was extinct, and now not a relative or scion remains of the family that bore his name.

"A venerable dissenter, a fearless ascetic of the neighbourhood, who had been deprived of his opportunities through some objections taken by the peer, preached a sermon the Sunday after his funeral, and mentioning no names, significantly took as his text, Isaiah XIV. 10–23:—

"'Art thou also become weak as we? Art thou become like unto us? Thy pomp is brought down to the grave, and the noise of thy viols: the worm is spread under thee, and the worms cover thee. How art thou fallen from Heaven, O Lucifer, son of the morning! How art thou cut down to the ground, which didst weaken the nations. . . . I will rise up against him, saith the Lord of hosts, and cut off from Babylon the name, and remnant, and son, and nephew, saith the Lord.'

"Whether as a Christian moralist he was justified in doing this I leave others to judge."

Here the doctor concluded his story, and the thoughtfulness which it had engendered upon his own features spread over those of his hearers, as they sat with their eyes fixed upon the fire.

THE SPECTRE OF THE REAL
An end-of-the-century Narrative

I

A certain March night of this present "waning age" had settled down upon the woods and the park and the parapets of Ambrose Towers. The harsh stable-clock struck a quarter-to-ten. Thereupon a girl in light evening attire and wraps came through the entrance-hall, opened the front door and the small wrought-iron gate beyond it which led to the terrace, and stepped into the moonlight. Such a person, such a night, and such a place were unexceptionable materials for a scene in that poetical drama of two which the world has often beheld; which leads up to a contract that causes a slight sinking in the poetry, and a perceptible lack of interest in the play.

She moved so quietly that the alert birds resting in the great cedar-tree never stirred. Gliding across its funereal shadow over a smooth plush of turf, as far as to the Grand Walk whose pebbles shone like the floor-stones of the Apocalyptic City, she paused and looked back at the old brick walls—red in the daytime, sable now—at the shrouded mullions, the silhouette of the tower; though listening rather than seeing seemed her object in coming to the pause. The clammy wings of a bat brushed past her face, startling her and making her shiver a little. The stamping of one or two horses in their stalls surprised her by its distinctness and isolation. The servants' offices were on the other side of the house, and the lady who, with the exception of the girl on the terrace, was its only occupant, was resting on a sofa behind one of the curtained windows. So Rosalys went on her way unseen, trod the margin of the lake, and plunged into the distant shrubberies.

The clock had reached ten. As the last strokes of the hour rang out a young man scrambled down the sunk-fence bordering the pleasure-ground, leapt the iron railing within, and joined the girl who stood awaiting him. In the half-light he could not see how her full under-lip trembled, or the fire of joy that kindled in her eyes. But perhaps he guessed, from daylight experiences, since he passed his arm round her shoulders with assurance, and kissed her ready mouth many times. Her head still resting against his arm they walked towards a bench, the rough outlines of which were touched at one end only by the moon-rays. At the dark end the pair sat down.

"I cannot come again" said the girl.

"Oh?" he vaguely returned. "This is new. What has happened? I thought you said your mother supposed you to be working at your Harmony, and would never imagine our meeting here?" The voice sounded just a trifle hard for a lover's.

"No, she would not. And I still detest deceiving her. I would do it for no one but you, Jim. But what I meant was this: I feel that it can all lead to nothing. Mother is not a bit more worldly than most people, but she naturally does not want her only child to marry a man who has nothing but the pay of an officer in the Line to live upon. At her death (you know she has only a life-interest here), I should have to go away unless my uncle, who succeeds, chose to take me to stay with him. I have no fortune of my own beyond a mere pittance. Two hundred a year."

Jim's reply was something like a sneer at the absent lady:

"You may as well add to the practical objection the sentimental one; that she wouldn't allow you to change your fine old crusted name for mine, which is merely the older one of the little freeholder turned out of this spot by your ancestor when he came."

"Dear, dear Jim, don't say those horrid things! As if *I* had ever even thought of that for a moment!"

He shook her hand off impatiently, and walked out into the moonlight. Certainly as far as physical outline went he might have been the direct product of a line of Paladins or hereditary Crusaders. He was tall, straight of limb, with an aquiline nose, and a mouth fitfully scornful. Rosalys sat almost motionless, watching him. There was no mistaking the ardour of her feelings; her power over him seemed to be lessened by his consciousness of his influence upon the lower and weaker side of her nature. It gratified him as a man to feel it; and though she was beautiful enough to satisfy the senses of the critical, there was perhaps something of contempt inwoven with his love. His victory had been too easy, too complete.

"Dear Jim, you are not going to be vexed? It really isn't my fault that I can't come out here again! Mother will be downstairs to-morrow, and then she might take it into her head to look at any time into the schoolroom and see how the Harmony gets on."

"And you are going off to London soon?" said Jim, still speaking gloomily.

"I am afraid so. But couldn't you come there too? I know your leave is not up for a great many weeks?"

He was silent for longer than she had ever known him at these times. Rosalys left her seat on the bench and threw her arms impulsively round him.

"I *can't* go away unless you will come to London when we do, Jim!"

"I will; but on one condition."

"What condition? You frighten me!"

"That you will marry me when I do join you there."

The quick breath that heaved in Rosalys ebbed silently; and she leant on the rustic bench with one hand, a trembling being apparent in her garments.

"You really—mean it, Jim darling?"

He swore that he did; that life was quite unendurable to him as he then experienced it. When she was once his wife nothing could come between them; but of course the marriage need not be known for a time—indeed must not. He could not take her abroad. The climate of Burmah would be too trying for her; and, besides, they really would not have enough to live upon.

"Couldn't we get on as other people do?" said Rosalys, trying not to cry at these arguments. "I am so tired of concealment, and I don't like to marry privately! It seems to me, much as I love being with you, that there is a sort of—well—vulgarity in our clandestine meetings, as we now enjoy them. Therefore how should I ever have strength enough to hide the fact of my being your wife, to face my mother day after day with the shadow of this secret between us?"

For all answer Jim kissed her, and stroked her silky brown curls.

"I suppose I shall end in agreeing with you—I always do!" she said, her mouth quivering. "Though I *can* be very dogged and obstinate too, Jim! Do you know that all my governesses have said I was the most stubborn child they ever came across? But then, in that case, my temper must be really aroused. You have never seen me as I am when angry. Perhaps, Jim, you would get to hate me?" She looked at him wistfully with her wet eyes.

"I shall never cease to love you desperately, as I do now!" declared the young man. "How lovely you look, little Rosalys, with that one moonbeam making your forehead like pure white marble. But time is passing. You must go back, my darling, I'm afraid. And you won't fail me in London? I shall make all the plans. Good-bye—good-bye!"

One clinging, intermittent kiss; and then from the shadow in which he stood Jim watched her light figure past the lake, and hurrying along in the shelter of the yew hedges towards the great house, asleep under the reaching deeps of sky, and the vacant gaze of the round white moon.

II

When clouds are iron-grey above the prim drab houses, and a hard east wind blows flakes of dust, stable-straws, scraps of soiled newspaper, and sharp pieces of grit into the eyes of foot-passengers, a less inviting and romantic dwelling-spot than Eaton Place can hardly be experienced.

But the Prince's daughter of the Canticles, emerging from her palace to see the vine flourish and the pomegranates bud forth with her Beloved, could not have looked more unconscious of grime than Rosalys Ambrose as she came down the steps of one of the tall houses in the aforesaid highly respectable place of residences. Her cheeks were hotly pink, her eyes shining, her lips parted. Having once made up her mind, "Qualms of prudence, pride and pelf" had died within her passionate little heart. After to-day she would belong absolutely to Jim, be his alone, through all the eternities, as it seemed; and of what account was anything else in the world? The entirely physical character of his affection for her, and perhaps of hers for him, was an unconjectured element herein which might not render less transitory the most transitory of sweet things. Thus hopefully she stepped out of the commonplace home that would, in one sense, be hers no more.

The raw wind whistled up the street, and deepened the colour in her face. She was plainly dressed in grey, and wore a rather thick veil, natural to the dusty day: it could not however conceal the sparkle of her eyes: veils, even thick ones, happily, never do. Hailing a hansom she told the driver to take her to the corner of the Embankment.

In the midst of her pre-occupation she noticed as the cab turned the corner out of Eaton Place that the bony chestnut-horse went lame. Rosalys was superstitious as well as tender-hearted, and she deemed that some stroke of ill-luck might befall her if she drove to be married behind a suffering animal. She alighted and paid off the man, and in her excitement gave him three times his fare. Hurrying forward on foot she heard her name called, and received a cordial greeting from a tall man with grey whiskers, in whom she recognized Mr Durrant, Jim's father. It occurred to her for a second that he might have discovered the plot and have lain in wait to prevent it. However, he spoke in his usual half-respectful, half-friendly tones, not noticing her frightened face. Mr Durrant was a busy man. Besides holding several very important land-agencies in the county where Rosalys lived, he had business in the city to transact at times. He explained to Miss Ambrose that some urgent affairs he was supervising for a client of his, Lord Parkhurst, had now brought him up to London for a few weeks.

"Lord Parkhurst is away?" she asked, to say something. "I hear of him sometimes through his uncle Colonel Lacy."

"Yes. A thorough sailor. Mostly afloat," Mr Durrant replied. "Well—we're rather out of the way in Porchester Terrace; otherwise, my wife would be so pleased if you would come to tea, Miss Ambrose? My son Jim, lazy young beggar, is up here now, too—going to plays and parties. Well, well, it's natural he should like to amuse himself before he leaves for Burmah, poor boy. Are you looking for a hansom? Yes? Hi!" And he waved his stick.

"Thank you so much" said Miss Ambrose. "And I will tell Mamma where you and Mrs Durrant are staying."

She was surprised at her own composure. Her unconscious father-in-law elect helped her into the cab, took off his hat, and walked rapidly away. Rosalys felt her heart stand still when she drew up at the place of meeting. She saw Jim, very blooming and very well-dressed, awaiting her, outwardly calm, at any rate. He jumped into her vehicle and they drove on city-wards.

"You are only ten minutes late, dearest," he said. "Do you know, I was half afraid you might have failed me at the last moment?"

"You don't believe it, Jim!"

"Well, I sometimes think I ought not to expect you to keep engagements with me so honestly as you do. Good, brave, little Rosalys!"

They moved on through the press of struggling omnibuses, gigantic vans, covered carts, and foot-passengers who darted at imminent risk of their lives amid the medley of wheels, horses, and shouting drivers. The noise jarred Rosalys' head, and she began to be feverishly anxious.

The church stood in the neighbourhood of a great meat-market, and the pavement was crowded by men in blue linen blouses, their clothes sprinkled with crimson stains. The young girl gave a shiver of disgust.

"How revolting it must be to have a butcher for a husband! They can't have hearts like other men. . . . What a gloomy part of London this is to be married in, Jim!"

"Ah—yes! Everything looks gloomy with the east wind blowing. Now, here we are! Jump out, little woman!"

He handed money to the driver, who went off with the most cursory thoughts of the part that he had played in this little excursion of a palpitating pair into the unknown.

"Jimmy darling; oughtn't you, or one of us, to have lived here for fifteen days?" she said as they entered the fine old

Norman porch, to which she was quite blind in her pre-occupation.

Durrant laughed. "I have declared that I did," he answered coolly. "I hope, in the circumstances, that it's a forgivable lie. Cheer up, Rosalys; don't all of a sudden look so solemn!"

There were tears in her eyes. The gravity of the step she was about to take had begun to frighten her.

They had some time to wait before the clergyman conde-scended to come out of the vestry and perform the ceremony which was to unite her to Jim. Two or three other couples were also in the church on the same errand: a haggard woman in a tawdry white bonnet, hanging on to the arm of a short crimson-faced man, who had evidently been replenish-ing his inside with gin to nerve himself to the required pitch for the ordeal: a girl with a coarse, hard face, accompanied by a slender youth in shabby black: a tall man, of refined aspect, in very poor clothes, whose hollow cough shook his thin shoulders and chest, and told his bride that her happiness, such as it was, would probably last but the briefest space.

Rosalys glanced absently at the beautiful building, with its Norman apse and transverse arches of horse-shoe form, and the massive curves and cushion-capitals that supported the tower-end; the whole impression left by the church being one of singular harmony, loveliness, and above all, repose—which struck even her by its great contrast with her experiences just then. As the clergyman emerged from the vestry a shaft of sunlight smote the altar, touched the quaint tomb where the founder of the building lay in his dreamless sleep, and quivered on the darned clothes of the consumptive bride-groom.

Jim and Rosalys moved forward, and then the light shone for a moment, too, upon his yellow hair and handsome face. To the woman who loved him it seemed that "From the crown of his head even to the sole of his foot there was no blemish in him."

The curate looked sharply at the four couples; angrily, Rosalys fancied, at her. But it was only because the east-wind had given him an acute tooth-ache that his gaze was severe, and his reading spiritless.

The four couples having duly contracted their inviolable unities, and slowly gone their ways through the porch, Jim and Rosalys adjourned to a fashionable hotel on the Embankment, where in a room all to themselves they had luncheon, over which Rosalys presided with quite a housewifely air.

"When shall I see you again?" he said, as he put her into a cab two or three hours later on in the afternoon.

"*You* must arrange all that, Jim. Somehow I feel so dreadfully sad and sinful now, all of a sudden! Have I been wicked? I don't know!"

Her tone changed as she met his passionate gaze, and she said very low, with a lump in her throat:

"O my dear darling! I care for nothing in the whole wide world, now that I belong to you!"

III

The London weeks went by with all their commonplaces, all their novelties. Mr Durrant, senior, had finished his urgent business, and returned to his square and uninteresting country-house. But Jim lingered on in town, although conscious of some subtle change in himself and his view of things. He and Rosalys met whenever it was possible, which was pretty frequently. Often they contrived to do so at hastily arranged luncheons and teas in the private rooms of hotels; sometimes, when Mrs Ambrose was suddenly called away, at Jim's own rooms. Sometimes they adventured to queer suburban restaurants.

In the lapse of these weeks the twain began somehow to lose a little of their zest for each other's society. Jim himself was aware of it before he had yet discovered that something of the same disappointment was dulling her heart too. On his own side it was the usual lowering of the fire—the slackening of a man's passion for a woman when she becomes his property. On hers it was a more mixed feeling. No doubt her love for Jim had been of but little higher quality than his for her. She had thoroughly abandoned herself to his good looks, his recklessness, his eagerness; and, now that the sensuous part of her character was satisfied, her fervour also began to burn itself down. But beyond, above, this, the concealment of her marriage was repugnant to Rosalys. When the rapture of the early meetings had died away she began to loathe the sordid deceit which these involved: the secretly despatched letters, the unavoidably brazen lies to her mother, who, if she attached overmuch importance to money and birth, yet loved her daughter in all good faith and simplicity. Then once or twice Jim was late at their interviews. He seemed indifferent and pre-occupied. His manner stung Rosalys into impatient utterance at the end of a particular meeting in which this mood was unduly prominent.

"You forget all I have given up for you!" she cried. "You make a fool of me in allowing me to wait here for you. It is humiliating and vulgar! I hate myself for behaving as I do!"

"The renunciations are not all on your side," he answered caustically. "You forget all that the loss of his freedom means to a man!"

Her heart swelled, and she had great difficulty in keeping back her tears. But she took refuge in sullenness.

"Unfortunately we can't undo our folly!" she murmured. "You will have to make the best of it as well as I. I suppose the awakening to a sense of our idiocy was bound to come sooner or later. But—I didn't think it would come so soon! Jim, look at me! Are you really angry? Don't for God's sake go and leave me like this!"

He was walking slowly towards the great iron gate leading out of Kensington Gardens; a dogged cast on his now familiar countenance.

"Don't make a scene in public, for Heaven's sake, Rosalys!" Feeling that he had spoken too brutally he suddenly paused, and changed:

"I am sorry, little woman, if I was cross! But things have combined to harass me lately. Of course we won't part from one another in anger."

Jim glanced at her straight profile with its full under-lip and firmly curved chin, at the lashes on either lid, and the glossy brown hair twisted in coils under her hat. But the sight of this loveliness, now all his own, failed to arouse the old emotions. He simply contemplated her approvingly from an artistic point of view.

They had reached the gateway, and she placed her hand on his arm.

"Good-bye. When shall we next meet? To-day is Tuesday. Shall it be Friday?"

"I am afraid I must go out of London on Thursday for a day or two. I'll write, dear. Let me call a hansom."

She thanked him in a cold voice again, and with a last handshake, and a smile that hovered on sorrow, left him and drove away towards Belgravia.

Once or twice later on they met; the next interview being shorter and sadder perhaps than the last. The one that followed it ended in bitterness.

"This had better be our long good-bye, I suppose?" said she.

"Perhaps it had. . . . You seem to be always looking out for causes of reproach, Rosalys. I don't know what has come over you."

"It is *you* who have changed!" she cried, with a little stamp. "And you are by far the most to blame of us two. You forget that I should never have contemplated marriage as a possibility! You have made me lie to my mother, do things of which I am desperately ashamed, and now you don't attempt to disguise your weariness of me!"

It was Jim's turn to lose his temper now. "You forget that *you* gave me considerable encouragement! Most girls would not have come out again and again to surreptitious meetings with a man who was in love with them,—girls brought up as you have been!"

She started as in a spasm. A momentary remorse seized him. He realized that he had been betrayed into speaking as no man of kindly good-feeling could speak. He made a tardy, scarcely gracious apology, and they parted. A few days afterwards he wrote a letter full of penitence for having hurt her, and she answered almost affectionately. But each knew that their short-lived romance was dead as the wind-flowers that had blossomed at its untimely birth.

IV

In August this pair of disappointed people met once more amid their old surroundings. Perhaps their enforced absence from one another gave at first some zest to their reunion. Jim was at times tender, and like his former self; Rosalys, if sad and subdued, less sullen and reproachful than she had been in London.

Mrs Ambrose had fallen into delicate health, and her daughter was in consequence able to dispose of her time outside the house as she wished. The moonlight meetings with Jim were discontinued, but husband and wife went for long strolls sometimes in the remoter nooks of the park, through winding walks in the distant shrubberies, and down paths hidden by high yew-hedges from intruding eyes that might look with suspicion on their being together.

On one especially beautiful August day they paced side by side, talking at moments with something of their old tenderness. The sky above the dark-green barriers on either hand was a bottomless deep of blue. The yew-boughs were covered in curious profusion by the handiwork of energetic spiders, who had woven their glistening webs in every variety of barbaric pattern. In shape some resembled hammocks, others ornamental purses, others deep bags, in the middle of which a large yellow insect remained motionless and watchful.

"Shall we sit for a little while in the summer-house?" said Rosalys at last, in flat accents, for a tête-à-tête with Jim had long ceased to give her any really strong beats of pleasure. "I want to talk to you further about plans; how often we had better write, and so on."

They sat down, in an arbour made of rustic logs, which overlooked the mere. The wood-work had been left rough within, and dusty spider-webs hung in the crevices; here and there the bark had fallen away in strips; above, on the roof, there were clumps of fungi, looking like tufts of white fur.

"This is a sunless, queer sort of place you have chosen," he said, looking round critically.

The boughs had grown so thickly in the foreground that the glittering margin of water was hardly perceptible between their interlacing twigs, and no visible hint of a human habitation was given, though the rustic shelter had been originally built with the view of affording a picturesque glimpse of the handsome old brick house wherein the Ambroses had lived for some three centuries.

"You might have found a more lively scene for what will be, perhaps, our last interview for years," Jim went on.

"Are you really going so soon?" she asked, passing over the complaint.

"Next week. And my father has made all sorts of arrangements for me. Besides, he is beginning to suspect that you and I are rather too intimate. And your mother knows, somehow or other, that I have been up here several times of late. We must be careful."

"I suppose so," she answered absently, looking out under the log roof at a chaffinch swinging himself backwards and forwards on a larch bough. A sort of dreary indifference to her surroundings; a sense of being caged and trapped had begun to take possession of Rosalys. The present was full of perplexity, the future objectless. Now and then, when she looked at Jim's lithe figure, and healthy, virile face, she felt that perhaps she might have been able to love him still if only he had cared for her with a remnant of his former passionate devotion. But his indifference was even more palpable than her own. They sat and talked on within the dim arbour for a little while. Then Jim made one of the unfortunate remarks that always galled her to the quick. She rose in anger, answered him with cold sarcasm, and hastened away down the little wood. He followed, a rather ominous light shining in his eyes.

"Your temper is really growing insufferable, Rosalys!" he cried, and clenched his hand roughly on her arm to detain her.

"How dare you!" said the girl. "For God's sake leave me, and don't come back again! I rejoice to think that in a few days it will not be in your power to insult me any more!"

"Damn it—I am going to leave you, am I not! I only want to keep you here for a moment to come to some understanding! . . . Indeed you'll be surprised to find how very much I am going to leave you, when you hear what I mean! My ideas have grown considerably emancipated of late, and therefore I tell you that there is no reason on earth why any soul should ever know of that miserable mistake we made in the spring."

She winced a little; it was an unexpected move; and her eyes lingered uneasily on a copper-coloured butterfly playing a game of hide-and-seek with a little blue companion.

"Who," he continued, "is ever going to search the register of that old East-London church? We must philosophically look on the marriage as an awkward fact in our lives, which won't prevent our loving elsewhere when we feel inclined. In my opinion this early error will carry one advantage with it— that we shall be unable to extinguish any love we may each feel for another person by a sordid matrimonial knot— unless, indeed, after seven years of obliviousness to one another's existence."

"I'll—try to—emancipate myself likewise," she said slowly. "It will be well to forget this tragedy of our lives! And the most tragic part of it is—that we are not even sorry that we don't love each other any more!"

"The truest words you ever spoke!"

"And the surest event that was ever to come, given your nature—"

"And yours!"

She hastened on down the grass walk into the broad gravelled path leading to the house. At the corner stood Mrs Ambrose, who was better, and had come out for a stroll— assuming as an invalid the privilege of wearing a singular scarlet gown and a hat in which a number of black quills stood startlingly erect.

"Ah—Rosy!" she cried. "Oh, and Mr Durrant? What a colour you have got, child!"

"Yes. Mr Durrant and I have been having a furious political discussion, mamma. I have grown quite hot over it. He is more unreasonable than ever. But when he gets abroad he won't be as he is now. A few years of India will change all that." And to carry on the idea of her unconcern she turned to whistle to a bold robin that had flitted down from a larch tree, perched on the yew hedge, and looked inquiringly at her, answering her whistle with his pathetic little pipe.

Durrant had come up behind. "Yes," he said cynically. "One never knows how an enervating country may soften one's brains."

He bade them a cool good-bye and left. She watched his retreating figure, the figure of the active, the strong, the handsome animal, who had scarcely won the better side of her nature at all. He never turned his head. So this was the end!

The bewildering bitterness of it well-nigh paralysed Rosalys for a few moments. Why had they been allowed—he and she—to love one another with that eager, almost unholy, passion, and then to part with less interest in each other than ordinary friends? She felt ashamed of having ceded herself to him. If her mother had not been beside her she would have screamed out aloud in her exasperating pain.

Mrs Ambrose lifted up her voice. "What are you looking at, child? . . . My dear, I want a little word with you. Are you attending? When you pout your lip like that, Rosalys, I always know that you are in a bad frame of mind. . . . The vicar has been here; and he has made me a little unhappy."

"I should have thought he was too stupid to give anyone a pang! Why do they put such simpletons into the churches!"

"Well—he says that people are chattering about you and that young Durrant. And I must tell you that—that, from a marrying point of view, he is impossible. You know that. And I don't want him to make up to you. Now, Rosalys, my darling, tell me honestly—I feel I have not looked after you lately as I ought to have done—tell me honestly: Is he in love with you?"

"He is not, mother, to my certain knowledge."

"Are you with him?"

"No. That I swear."

V

Seven years and some months had passed since Rosalys spoke as above-written. And never a sound of Jim.

As she had mentally matured under the touch of the gliding seasons, Miss Ambrose had determined to act upon the
hint Jim had thrown out to her as to the practical nullity of
their marriage-contract if they simply kept in different hemi-
spheres without a word. She had never written to him a line;
and he had never written a line to her.

He might be dead for all that she knew: he possibly was
dead. She had taken no steps to ascertain anything about
him, though she had been aware for years that he was no
longer in the Army-list. Dead or alive he was completely cut
off from the county in which he and she had lived, for his
father had died a long time before this, his house and properties had been sold, and not a scion of the line of Durrant
remained in that part of England.

Rosalys had readily imbibed his ideas of their mutual inde-
pendence; and now, after the lapse of all these years, had
acted upon them with the surprising literalness of her sex
when they act upon advice at all.

Mrs Ambrose, who had distinguished herself no whit during her fifty years of life saving by the fact of having brought
a singularly beautiful girl into the world, had passed quietly
out of it. Rosalys' uncle had succeeded his sister-in-law in the
possession of the old house with its red tower, and the broad
paths and garden-lands; he had been followed by an unsatis-
factory son of his, last in the entail, and thus unexpectedly
Rosalys Ambrose found herself sole mistress of the spot of her
birth.

People marvelled somewhat that she continued to call herself Miss Ambrose. Though a woman now getting on for thirty
she was distinctly attractive both in face and in figure, and
could confront the sunlight as well as the moonbeams still. In
the manner of women who are yet sure of their charms she
was fond of representing herself as much older than she really
was. Perhaps she would have been disappointed if her friends
had not laughed and contradicted her, and told her that she
was still lovely and looked like a girl. Lord Parkhurst, anyhow,
was firmly of that contradictory opinion; and perhaps she
cared more for his views than for anyone else's at the present
time.

That distinguished sailor had been but one of many suitors; but he stirred her heart as none of the others could do. It was not merely that he was brave, and pleasing, and had returned from a late campaign in Egypt with a hero's reputation; but that his chivalrous feelings towards women, originating perhaps in the fact that he knew very little about them, were sufficient to gratify the most exacting of the sex.

His rigid notions of duty and honour, both towards them and from them, made the blood of Rosalys run cold when she thought of a certain little episode of her past life, notwithstanding that, or perhaps because, she loved him dearly.

"He is not the least bit of a flirt, like most sailors," said Miss Ambrose to her cousin and companion, Miss Jennings, on a particular afternoon in this eighth year of Jim Durrant's obliteration from her life. It was an afternoon with an immense event immediately ahead of it; no less an event than Rosalys' marriage with Lord Parkhurst, which was to take place on the very next day.

The local newspaper had duly announced the coming wedding in proper terms as "the approaching nuptials of the beautiful and wealthy Miss Ambrose of Ambrose Towers with a distinguished naval officer, the Lord Parkhurst." There followed an ornamental account of the future bridegroom's heroic conduct during the late war. "The handsome face and figure of Lord Parkhurst," wound up the honest paragraphist, "are not altogether unknown to us in this vicinity, as he has recently been visiting his uncle, Colonel Lacy, High Sheriff of the County. We wish all prosperity to the happy couple, who have doubtless a brilliant and cloudless future before them."

This was the way in which her acceptance of Durrant's views had worked themselves out. He had said; "After seven years of mutual oblivion we can marry again if we choose."

And she had chosen.

Rosalys almost wished that Lord Parkhurst had been a flirt, or at least had won experience as the victim of one, or many, of those precious creatures, and had not so implicitly trusted her. It would have brought things more nearly to a level.

"A flirt! I should think not," said Jane Jennings. "In fact, Rosalys, he is almost alarmingly strict in his ideas. It is a mistake to believe that so many women are angels, as he does. He is too simple. He is bound to be disappointed some day."

Miss Ambrose sighed nervously. "Yes," she said.

"I don't mean by you to-morrow! God forbid!"

"No."

Miss Ambrose sighed again, and a silence followed, during which, while recalling unutterable things of the past, Rosalys gazed absently out of the window at the lake, that some men were dredging, the mud left bare by draining down the water being imprinted with hundreds of little footmarks of plovers feeding there. Eight or nine herons stood further away, one or two composedly fishing, their grey figures reflected with unblurred clearness in the mirror of the pool. Some little water-hens waddled with a fussy gait across the sodden ground in front of them, and a procession of wild geese came through the sky, and passed on till they faded away into a row of black dots.

Suddenly the plovers rose into the air, uttering their customary wails, and dispersing like a group of stars from a rocket; and the herons drew up their flail-like legs, and flapped themselves away. Something had disturbed them; a carriage, sweeping round to the other side of the house.

"There's the door-bell!" Rosalys exclaimed, with a start. "That's he, for certain! Is my hair untidy Jane? I've been rumpling it awfully, leaning back on the cushions. And do see if my gown is all right at the back—it never did fit well."

The butler flung open the folding-doors and announced in the voice of a man who felt that it was quite time for this nonsense of calling to be put an end to by the more compact arrangement of the morrow:

"Lord Parkhurst!"

A man of middle size, with a fair and pleasant face, and a short beard, entered the room. His blue eyes smiled rather more than his lips as he took the little hand of his hostess in his own with the air of one verging on proprietorship of the same, and said: "Now, darling; about what we have to settle before the morning! I have come entirely on business, as you perceive!"

Rosalys tenderly smiled up at him. Miss Jennings left the room, and Rosalys' sailor silently kissed and admired his betrothed, till he continued:

"Ah—my beautiful one! I have nothing to give you in return for the immeasurable gift you are about to bestow on me—excepting such love as no man ever felt before! I almost wish you were not quite so good and perfect and innocent as you are! And I wish you were a poorer woman—as poor as I— and had no lovely home such as this. To think you have kept yourself from all other men for such an unworthy fellow as me!"

Rosalys looked away from him along the green vistas of chestnuts and beeches stretching far down outside the windows.

"Oswald—I know how much you care for me: and that is why I—hope you won't be disappointed—after you have taken me to-morrow for good and all! I wonder if I shall hinder and hamper you in your profession. Perhaps you ought to marry a girl much younger than yourself—your nature is so young—not a maturing woman like me."

For all answer he smiled at her with the confiding, fearless gaze that she loved.

Lord Parkhurst stayed on through a paradisical hour till Miss Jennings came to tell them that tea was in the library. Presently they were reminded by the same faithful relative and dependent that on that evening of all evenings they had promised to drive across to the house of Colonel Lacy, Lord Parkhurst's uncle, and one of Rosalys' near neighbours, and dine there quietly with two or three intimate friends.

VI

When Rosalys entered Colonel Lacy's drawing-room before dinner, the eyes of the few guests assembled there were naturally enough fixed upon her.

"By Jove, she's better looking than ever—though she's not more than a year or two under thirty!" whispered young Lacy to a man standing in the shadow behind a high lamp.

The person addressed started, and did not answer for a moment. Then he laughed and said forcedly,

"Yes, wonderful for her age, she certainly is."

As he spoke his hostess, a fat and genial lady, came blandly towards him.

"Mr Durrant, I'm so sorry we've no lady for you to take in to-night. One or two people have thrown us over. I want to introduce you to Miss Ambrose. Isn't she lovely? O, how stupid I am! Of course you grew up in this neighbourhood, and must have known all about her as a girl."

Jim Durrant it was, in the flesh; once the soldier, now the "traveller and explorer" of the little known interiors of Asiatic countries; to use the words in which he described himself. His foreign-looking and sun-dried face was rather pale and set as he walked last into the dining-room with young Lacy. He had only arrived on that day at an hotel in the nearest town, where he had been accidentally met and recognized by that young man, and asked to dinner off-hand.

Smiling, and apparently unconscious, he sat down on the left side of his hostess, talking calmly to her and across the table to the one or two he knew. Rosalys heard his voice as the phantom of a dead sound mingling with the usual trivial words and light laughter of the rest, Lord Parkhurst's conversation about Egyptian finance, and Mrs Lacy's platitudes about the Home-Rule question, as if she were living through a curiously incoherent dream.

Suddenly during the progress of the dinner Mrs Lacy looked across with a glance of solicitude towards the other end of the table, and said in a low voice:

"I am afraid Miss Ambrose is rather overstrained—as she may naturally be? She looks *so* white and tired. Do you think, Parkhurst, that she finds this room too hot? I will have the window opened at the top."

"She does look pale," Lord Parkhurst murmured, and as he spoke glanced anxiously and tenderly towards his betrothed. "I think too, she has a little over-taxed herself—she don't usually get so white as this."

Rosalys felt his eyes upon her, looked across at him, and smiled strangely.

When dinner was ended Rosalys still seemed not quite herself, whereupon she was taken in hand by her good and fussy hostess; sal-volatile was brought, and she was given the most comfortable chair and the largest cushions the house afforded. It seemed to Rosalys as if hours had elapsed before the men joined the ladies and there came that general moving of places like the shuffling of a pack of cards. She heard Jim's voice speaking close to her ear:

"I want to have a word with you."

"I can't!" she faltered.

"Did you get my letter?"

"No!" said she.

"I wonder how that was! Well—I'll be at the door of Ambrose Towers while the stable-clock is striking twelve to-night. Be there to meet me. I'll not detain you long. We must have an understanding."

"For God's sake how do you come here?"

"I saw in the newspapers that you were going to marry. What could I do otherwise than let you know I was alive?"

"O, you might have done it less cruelly!"

"Will you be at the door?"

"I *must*, I suppose! . . . Don't tell him here—before these people! It will be such an agonising disturbance that—"

"Of course I shan't. Be there."

This was all they could say. Lord Parkhurst came forward, and observing to Durrant, "They are wanting you for bézique," sat down beside Rosalys.

She had intended to go home early: and went even earlier than she had planned. At half-past ten she found herself in her own hall, not knowing how she had got there, or when she had bidden adieu to Lord Parkhurst, or what she had said to him.

Jim's letter was lying on the table awaiting her.

As soon as she had got upstairs and slipped into her dressing-gown, had dispatched her maid, and ascertained that all the household had retired, she read her husband's note, which briefly informed her that he had led an adventurous life since they had parted, and had come back to see if she were living, when he suddenly heard that she was going to be married. Then Rosalys sat down at her writing-table to begin somehow a letter to Lord Parkhurst. To write that was an imperative duty before she slept. It need not be said that awful indeed to her was its object, the letting Lord Parkhurst know that she had a husband, and had seen him that day. But she could not shape a single line, and the visioned aspect that she would wear in his eyes as soon as he discovered this truth of her history, was so terrible to her that she burst into hysterical sobbing over the paper as she sat.

The clock crept on to twelve before Rosalys had written a word. The labour seemed Herculean—insuperable. Why had she not told him face to face?

Twelve o'clock it was; and nothing done; and controlling herself as women can, when they must, she went down to the door. Softly opening it a little way she saw against the iron gate immediately without it the form of her husband, Jim Durrant—upon the whole much the same form that she had known eight years ago.

"Here I am," said he.

"Yes," said she.

"Open this iron thing."

A momentary feeling of aversion caused her to hesitate.

"Do you hear—do you mean to say—Rosalys!" he began.

"No—no. Of course I will!" She opened the grille and he came up and touched her hand lightly.

"Kissing not allowed, I suppose," he observed, with mock solemnity, "in view of the fact that you are to be married to-morrow?"

"You know better!" she said. "Of course I'm not going to commit bigamy! The wedding is not to be."

"Have you explained to him?"

"N-no—not yet. I was just writing it when—"

"Ha—you haven't! Good. Woman's way. Shall I give him a friendly call to-morrow morning?"

"O no, no—let me do it!" she implored. "I love him so well, and it will break his poor heart if it is not done gently! O God—if I could only die to-night, while he still believes in me! You don't know what affection I have felt for him!" she continued miserably, not caring what Jim thought. "He has been my whole world! And he—he believes me to be so good! He has all the old-fashioned ideas of marriage that people of your fast sets smile at! He knows nothing of any kind of former acquaintance between you and me. I ought not to have done it—kept him in the dark! I tried not to. But I was so fearfully lonely! And now I've lost him! . . . If I could only have got at that register in that City church, how I would have torn out the leaf!" she added vehemently.

"That's a pleasant remark to make to a husband!"

"Well—that was my feeling; I may as well be honest! I didn't know you were coming back any more; and you yourself suggested that I might be able to re-marry!"

"You'd better do it—I shan't tell. And if anybody else did, the punishment is not heavy nowadays. The judges are beginning to discountenance informers on previous marriages, if the new-assorted parties themselves are satisfied to forget them."

"Don't insult me so. You've not forgotten how to do that in all these years!"

There was a silence, in which she regarded with passive gloom the familiar scene before her. The inquisitive jays, the pensive wood-doves, that lodged at their ease thereabout, as if knowing that their proprietor was a gunless woman, all slept calmly; and not a creature was conscious of the presence of these two but a little squirrel they had disturbed in a beech near the shady wall. Durrant remained gazing at her; then he spoke, in a changed and richer voice:

"Rosalys!"

She looked vaguely at his face without answering.

"How pretty you look in this star-light—much as you did when we used to meet out here nine or ten years ago!"

"Ah! But—"

The sentence was broken by his abrupt movement forward. He seized her firmly in his arms, and kissed her repeatedly before she was aware.

"Don't—don't!" she said, struggling.

"Why?"

"I don't like you—I don't like you!"

"What rot! Yes, you do! Come—damn you, dear—put up your face as you used to! Now, I'm not going off in a huff—I'm determined I won't; nor shall you either! . . . Let me sit down in your hall, or somewhere, Rosalys! I've come a long way to-day, and I'm tired. And after eight years!"

"I don't know what to say to it—there's no light downstairs! The servants may hear us too—it is not so very late!"

"We can whisper. And suppose they do? They must know to-morrow!"

She gasped a sigh, and preceded him in through the door; and the squirrel saw nothing more.

VII

It was three-hours-and-half later when they re-appeared. The lawn was as silent as when they had left it, though the sleep of things had weakened to a certain precarious slightness; and round the corner of the house a low line of light showed the dawn.

"Now, good-bye, dear," said her husband, lightly. "You'll let him know at once?"

"Of course."

"And send to me directly after?"

"Yes."

"And now for my walk across the fields to the hotel. These boots are thin, but I know the old way well enough. By Jove, I wonder what Mélanie—"

"Who?"

"O—what Mélanie will think, I was going to say. It slipped out—I didn't mean to hurt your feelings at all."

"Mélanie—who is she?"

"Well—she's a French lady. You know, of course, Rosalys, that I thought you were perhaps dead—and—so this lady passes as Mrs Durrant."

Rosalys started.

"In fact I found her in the East, and took pity upon her—that's all. Though if it had happened that you had not been living now I have got back, I should of course, have married her at once."

"Is—she, then, here with you at the hotel?"

"O no—I wouldn't bring her on here till I knew how things were."

"Then where is she?"

"I left her at my rooms in London. O, it will be all right—I shall see her safely back to Paris, and make a little provision for her. Nobody in England knows anything of her existence."

"When—did you part from her?"

"Well, of course, at breakfast-time."

Rosalys bowed herself against the doorway. "O—O—what have I done! What a fool—what a weak fool!" she moaned. "Go away from me—go away!"

Jim was almost distressed when he saw the distortion of her agonized face.

"Now why should you take on like this! There's nothing in it. People do these things. Living in a prim society here you don't know how the world goes on!"

"O, but to think it didn't occur to me that the sort of man—"

Jim, though anxious, seemed to awaken to something humorous in the situation, and vented a momentary chuckle. "Well, it is rather funny that I should have let it out. But still—"

"Don't make a deep wrong deeper by cruel levity! Go away!"

"You'll be in a better mood to-morrow, mark me, and then I'll tell you all my history. There—I'm gone! *Au revoir!*"

He disappeared under the trees. Rosalys, rousing herself, closed the gate and fastened the door, and sat down in one of the hall chairs, her teeth shut tight, and her little hands clenched. When she had passed this mood, and returned upstairs, she regarded the state of her room sadly, and bent again over her writing-table, murmuring "O, how weak, how weak was I!"

But in a few minutes she found herself nerved to an unexpected and passionate vigour of action; and began writing her letter to Lord Parkhurst with great rapidity. Sheet after sheet she filled, and, having read them over, she sealed up the letter and placed it on the mantelpiece to be given to a groom and dispatched by hand as soon as the morning was a little further advanced.

With cold feet and a burning head she flung herself upon the bed just as she was, and waited for the day without the power to sleep. When she had lain nearly two hours, and the

morning had crept in, and she could hear from the direction
of the stables that the men were astir, she rang for her maid,
and taking the letter in her hand stood with it in an attitude
of suspense as the woman entered. The latter looked full of
intelligence.

"Are any of the men about?" asked Rosalys.

"O yes, ma'am. There've been such an accident in the
meads this past night—about half-a-mile down the river—and
Jones ran up from the lodge to call for help quite early; and
Benton and Peters went as soon as they were dressed. A
gentleman drowned—yes—it's Mr James Durrant—the son of
old Mr Durrant who died some years ago. He came home only
yesterday, after having been heard nothing of for years and
years. He left Mrs Durrant, who they say is a French lady,
somewhere in London, but they have telegraphed and found
her, and she's coming. They say she's quite distracted. The
poor gentleman left the Three Lions last night and went out
to dinner, saying he would walk home, as it was a fine night
and not very far: and it is supposed he took the old short cut
across the moor where there used to be a path when he was a
lad at home, crossing the big river by a plank. There is only a
rail now, and he must have tried to get across upon it, for it
was broken in two, and his body found in the water-weeds just
below."

"Is he—dead?"

"O yes. They had a great trouble to get him out. The men
have just come in from carrying him to the hotel. It will be sad
for his poor wife when she gets there!"

"His poor wife—yes."

"Travelling all the way from London on such a call!"

Rosalys had allowed the hand in which she held the letter
to Lord Parkhurst to drop to her side: she now put it in the
pocket of her dressing-gown.

"I was wishing to send somewhere," she said. "But I think I
will wait till later."

The house was astir betimes on account of the wedding,
and Rosalys' companion in particular, who was not sad because she was going to live on with the bride. When Miss
Jennings saw her cousin's agitation she said she looked ill,

and insisted upon sending for the doctor. He, who was the local practitioner, arrived at breakfast time; very proud to attend such an important lady, who mostly got doctored in London. He said Rosalys certainly was not quite in her usual state of health; prescribed a tonic, and declared that she would be all right in an hour or two. He then informed her that he had been suddenly called up that morning to the case of which they had possibly heard—the drowning of Mr Durrant.

"And you could do nothing?" asked Rosalys.

"O no. He'd been under water too long for any human aid. Dead and stiff. . . . It was not so very far down from here. . . . Yes, I remember him quite as a boy. But he has had no relations hereabout for years past—old Durrant's property was sold to pay his debts, if you recollect; and nobody expected to see the son again. I think he has lived in the East Indies a good deal. Much better for him if he had not come—poor fellow!"

When the doctor had left Rosalys went to the window, and remained for some time thinking. There was the lake from which the water had flowed down the river that had drowned Jim after visiting her last night—as a mere interlude in his continuous life of caresses with the Frenchwoman Mélanie. She turned, took from her dressing-gown pocket the renunciatory letter to her intended husband Lord Parkhurst, thrust it through the bars of the grate, and watched it till it was entirely consumed.

The wedding had been fixed for an early hour in the afternoon, and as the morning wore on Rosalys felt increasing strength, mental and physical. The doctor's dose had been a powerful one: the image of "Mélanie", too, had much to do with her recuperative mood; more still, Rosalys' innate qualities; and nerve of the woman who nine years earlier had gone to the city to be married as if it were a mere shopping expedition; most of all, she loved Lord Parkhurst; he was the man among all men she desired. Rosalys allowed things to take their course.

Soon the dressing began; and she sat through it quite calmly. When Lord Parkhurst rode across for a short visit that day he only noticed that she seemed strung-up, nervous, and that the flush of love which mantled her cheek died away to pale rather quickly.

On the way to church the road skirted the low-lying ground where the river was, and about a dozen men were seen in the bright green meadow, standing beside the deep central stream, and looking intently at a broken rail.

"Who are those men?" said the bride.

"O—they are the coroner's jury, I think," said Miss Jennings; "come to view the place where that unfortunate Mr Durrant lost his life last night. It was curious that, by the merest accident, he should have been at Mrs Lacy's dinner,— since they hardly know him at all."

"It was—I saw him there," said Rosalys.

They had reached the church. Ten minutes later she was kneeling against the altar-railings, with Lord Parkhurst on her right hand.

The wedding was by no means a gay one, and there were few people invited, Rosalys, for one thing, having hardly any relations. The newly united pair got away from the house very soon after the ceremony. When they drove off there was a group of people round the door, and some among the by-standers asked how far they were going that day.

"To Dover. They cross the Channel to-morrow, I believe."

To-morrow came, and those who had gathered together at the wedding went about their usual duties and amusements, Colonel Lacy among the rest. As he and his wife were return-ing home by the late afternoon train after a short journey up the line, he bought a copy of an evening paper, and glanced at the latest telegrams.

"My good God!" he cried.

"What?" said she, starting towards him.

He tried to read—then handed the paper; and she read for herself:

"D O V E R.—DEATH OF LORD PARKHURST, R.N.—

"We regret to announce that this distinguished nobleman "and heroic naval officer, who arrived with Lady Parkhurst "last evening at the Lord Chamberlain Hotel in this town,

"preparatory to starting on their wedding-tour, entered his
"dressing-room very early this morning, and shot himself
"through the head with a revolver. The report was heard
"shortly after dawn, none of the inmates of the hotel being
"astir at the time. No reason can be assigned for the rash act."

BLUE JIMMY:
THE HORSE STEALER

Blue Jimmy stole full many a steed
Ere his last fling he flung.

The name of "Blue Jimmy"—a passing allusion to whose
career is quoted above from Mr Thomas Hardy's ballad "A
Trampwoman's Tragedy"—is now nearly forgotten even in
the West of England. Yet he and his daring exploits were on
the tongues of old rustics in that district down to twenty or
thirty years ago, and there are still men and women living who
can recall their fathers' reminiscences of him.

To revive the adventures of any notorious horse-thief may
not at first sight seem edifying; but in the present case, if
stories may be believed, the career of the delinquent discloses
that curious feature we notice in the traditions of only some
few of the craft—a mechanical persistence in a series of actions as if by no will or necessity of the actor, but as if under
some external or internal compulsion against which reason
and a foresight of sure disaster were powerless to argue.

Jimmy is said to have been, in one account of him, "worth
thousands," in another a "well-to-do" farmer, and in all a man
who found or would have found no difficulty in making an
honest income. Yet this could not hinder him from indulging
year after year in his hazardous pursuit, or recreation, as it
would seem to have been, till he had reft more than a hundred horses from their owners, and planted them profitably
on innocent purchasers.

This was in full view of the fact that in those days the
sentence for horse-stealing was, as readers will hardly need to
be reminded, death without hope of mitigation. It is usually
assumed that the merciless judicial sentence, however lacking
in Christian loving-kindness towards the criminal, had at least
the virtue always of being in the highest degree deterrent; yet
at that date, when death was the penalty for many of what we
should now consider minor crimes, their frequency was ex-

traordinary. This particular offence figures almost continually in the calendar at each assize, and usually there were several instances at each town on a circuit. Jimmy must have known this well enough; but the imminent risk of his neck for a few pounds in each case did not deter him.

He stood nineteen times before my lord judge ere the final sentence came—no verdict being previously returned against him for the full offence through lack of sufficient evidence.

Of this long string of trials we may pass over the details till we reach the eighteenth—a ticklish one for Jimmy—in which he escaped, by a hair's breadth only, the doom that overtook him on the nineteenth for good and all. What had happened was as follows:—

On a December day in 1822 a certain John Wheller, living near Chard, in Somerset, was standing at his door when Jimmy—whose real name was James Clace—blithely rode by on a valuable mare.

They "passed the time of day" to each other, and then, without much preface:

"A fine morning," says Jimmy cheerfully.

"'Tis so," says Mr Wheller.

"We shall have a dry Christmas," Jimmy continues.

"I think we shall so," answers Wheller.

Jimmy pulled rein. "Now do you happen to want a good mare that I bought last week at Stratton Fair?" And he turned his eye on the flank of the animal.

"I don't know that I do."

"The fact is a friend of mine bought one for me at the same time without my knowledge and, as I don't want two, I must get rid of this one at any sacrifice. You shall have her for fourteen pounds."

Wheller shook his head, but negotiation proceeded. Another man, one named Wilkins, a nephew of Wheller, happening to pass just then, assured Wheller that he knew the seller well, and that he was a farmer worth thousands who lived at Tiverton. Eventually the mare was exchanged for a cart-horse of Wheller's and three pounds in money.

Curiously enough Wheller did not suspect that anything was wrong till he found the next day that the animal was what he called "startish"—and, having begun to reflect upon the transaction, he went to his nephew Wilkins, who also lived at Chard, half a mile from Wheller, and asked him how he knew that the vendor of the mare was a farmer at Tiverton? The reply was vague and unsatisfying—in short the strange assurance of Wilkins, Wheller's own nephew, was never explained—and Wheller wished he had had nothing to do with the "man worth thousands." He went in search of him, and eventually found him at that ancient hostel "The Golden Heart" at Coombe St. Nicholas, placidly smoking a long clay pipe in the parlour over a tankard of ale.

"I have been looking for you," said Mr Wheller with severe suddenness.

"To get another such bargain, no doubt," says Jimmy with the bitter air of a man who has been a too generous fool in his dealings.

"Not at all. I suspect that you did not come honestly by that mare, and request to have back my money and cart-horse, when I'll return her."

"Good news for me!" says Jimmy, "for that I'm quite willing to do. Here, landlady! A pipe and ale for this gentleman. I've sent my man out to bring round my gig; and you can go back to my farm with me, and have your horse this very afternoon, on your promising to bring mine to-morrow. Whilst you are drinking I'll see if my man is getting ready."

Blue Jimmy went out at the back, and Wheller saw him go up the stable-yard, half-regretting that he had suspected such a cheerful and open man of business. He smoked and drank and waited, but his friend did not come back; and then it occurred to him to ask the landlady where her customer, the farmer, lived.

"What farmer?" said the landlady.

"He who has gone out to the stables—I forget his name—to get his horse put-to."

"I don't know that he's a farmer. He's got no horse in our stables—he's quite a stranger here."

"But he keeps the market here every week?"

"I never saw him before in my life. And I'll trouble you to pay for your ale, and his likewise, as he didn't."

When Wheller reached the yard the "farmer" had vanished, and no trace of him was discoverable in the town.

This looked suspicious, yet after all it might have meant only that the man who sold him the mare did not wish to reopen the transaction. So Wheller went home to Chard, resolving to say nothing, but to dispose of the mare on the first opportunity. This he incontinently did to Mr Loveridge, a neighbour, at a somewhat low price, rubbed his hands, and devoutly hoped that no more would be heard of the matter. And nothing was for some while.

We now take up the experience of Mr Loveridge with the animal. He had possessed her for some year or two when it was rumoured in Chard that a Mr Thomas Sheppard, of Stratton, in Cornwall, had been making inquiries about the mare.

Mr Loveridge felt uneasy, and spoke to Wheller, of whom he had bought her, who seemed innocence itself, and who certainly had not stolen her; and by and by another neighbour who had just heard of the matter came in with the information that handbills were in circulation in Cornwall when he was last there, offering a reward for a particular mare like Mr Loveridge's, which disappeared at Stratton Fair.

Loveridge felt more and more uncomfortable, and began to be troubled by bad dreams. He grew more and more sure, although he had no actual proof, that the horse in his possession was the missing one, until, valuable to him as his property was for hauling and riding, his conscience compelled him to write a letter to the said Mr Sheppard, the owner of the lost animal.

In a few days W. Yeo, an emissary of Mr Sheppard, appeared at Mr Loveridge's door. "What is the lost mare like?" said Mr Loveridge cautiously.

"She has four black streaks down her right fore-foot, and her tail is 'stringed' so"—here he described the shades, gave the particular manner in which the tail had been prepared for the fair, and, adding other descriptive details, was certain it was the same mare that had been brought to Chard. He had broken it in for Mr Sheppard, and never before had known a mare so peculiarly marked.

The end of the colloquy was that Mr Loveridge gave up the animal, and found himself the loser of the money he had paid for it. For being richer than his worthy neighbour Wheller who had sold it to him, he magnanimously made up their temporary quarrel on the declaration of Wheller that he did not know of the theft, and had honestly bought the horse. Together then they vowed vengeance against the thief, and with the assistance of Mr Sheppard he was ultimately found at Dorchester. He was committed for the crime, and proving to be no less a personage than the already notorious Blue Jimmy, tried at the Taunton Assizes on March 28, 1825, before Mr Justice Park.

During the trial all the crowd in court thought that this was to be the end of famous Blue Jimmy; but an odd feature in the evidence against him was that the prosecutor, Mr Sheppard, when cross-examined on the marks described by his assistant Yeo, declared that he could not swear positively to any of them.

The learned Judge, in summing up, directed the jury to consider whether the identity of the mare had been so indubitably proved as to warrant them in pronouncing the prisoner guilty, and suggested that the marks described by the witness Yeo might be found upon many horses. "It was remarkable," his Lordship observed, "that Wilkins, who was present when Wheller bought the horse, although the nephew of the latter, and living within half a mile of him, had not been brought into court to give evidence, though witnesses from so considerable a distance as Cornwall had been examined."

In spite of this summing-up people in court were all expecting that Blue Jimmy would swing for his offences this time; yet the verdict was "Not Guilty," and we may well imagine the expression of integrity on Blue Jimmy's countenance as he walked out of the dock, although, as later discoveries proved, he had, as a matter of fact, stolen the mare.

But the final scene for Blue Jimmy was not long in maturing itself. Almost exactly two years later he stood at the bar in the same assize court at Taunton, indicted for a similar offence. This time the loser was one Mr Holcombe, of Fitzhead, and the interest in the trial was keener even than in the previous one.

Jimmy's first question had been, "Who is the judge?" and the answer came that it was Mr Justice Park, who had tried him before.

"Then I'm a dead man!" said Jimmy, and closed his lips, and appeared to consider his defence no longer.

It was also a mare on this occasion, a bay one, and the evidence was opened by the prosecutor, Mr Holcombe, who stated that the last time he saw his mare in the field from which he had lost her was on the 8th of the preceding October; on the 10th he missed her; he did not see her again till the 21st, when she was in a stall of Mr Oliver's, at the King's Arms, Dorchester.

Cross-examined by Mr Jeremy: The field from which the mare was stolen was adjoining the public road; he had never known the mare to escape; it was not possible for her to leave the field unless she was taken out.

Elizabeth Mills examined. Her husband kept the Crown and Anchor at Mosterton, Somerset; the prisoner came to her house about four o'clock on October 9. He had two horses with him. He asked for some person to put them in the stable; another man was in his company, and eventually the other man put them in the stable himself. The prisoner was riding the mare on his arrival; it was a bay one. Her husband returned about nine at night. (Cross-examined by Mr Jeremy.) Prisoner bargained with her husband for the horses; Pierce, the constable, was there while prisoner and her husband were talking; prisoner left next morning.

Robert Mills, husband of the last witness, examined. He reached home about nine o'clock on October 9. He went with Pierce the constable into the stable and saw a blood mare; also a pony mare. Constable and witness took two bridles and a saddle belonging to the horses into the house, having a mistrust that the animals were not honestly acquired. Prisoner called for his horses next morning, and asked what he had to pay. Witness, who now began to recognise him, said: "Jimmy, I don't think you came by these horses straight." He replied, "I don't know why you address me by the familiar

name of Jimmy, since it is not mine. I chopped the mare at
Alphington Fair for a black cart-horse." Prisoner spoke of the
pedigree of the mare, and asked twenty-five guineas for it, and
twelve for the pony. Witness offered twelve for the mare.
Prisoner refused, paid his reckoning and ordered his horses.
While the saddle was being put on, witness cut two marks in
the hair under the mane. Prisoner then left the house. The
other man had gone away before witness returned the night
before. The pony was left. Witness saw the mare afterwards,
on the 22nd, in Mr Holcombe's possession. He examined the
mare and found the private marks he had made on her under
the mane. He had never seen the prisoner between the time
the latter put up at his house and when he saw him in
Tiverton Prison. (Cross-examined by Mr Jeremy.) The morning after prisoner brought the horses to his house he asked
for some beer, though he was accustomed to wine, he remarked, and said that he was going to Bridport Fair to spend
a score of bank-notes or so by way of killing time.

A witness named Gillard, as he was walking to church on
the morning of the 8th (the morning before the robbery was
committed) saw the prisoner in a lane three miles from
Fitzhead, sitting on the ground between two camps of gipsies.

The prisoner said nothing in his defence, merely shaking
his head with a grim smile. The verdict was Guilty.

His Lordship, in passing sentence of death, entreated the
prisoner to make the best use of the short time he would have
to live in this world. The prisoner had been two years since
brought before him and in 1823 he had been convicted by his
learned Brother Hullock for a similar offence. The full weight
of the punishment awarded to his crime must now fall upon
him, without the least hope of mitigation.

Such was horse-stealing in the 'twenties of the last century,
and such its punishment.

How Jimmy acquired his repute for blueness—whether the
appellative was suggested to some luminous mind by his
clothes, or by his complexion, or by his morals, has never
been explained, and never will be now by any historian.

About a month later, in the same old *County Chronicle*, one
finds a tepid and unemotional account of the end of him at

Ilchester, Somerset, where then stood the county gaol—till lately remembered, though now removed—on the edge of a wide expanse of meadow-land, spread at that season of the year with a carpet of butter-cups and daisies. The account appears under the laconic heading, "Execution, Wednesday, April 25, 1827: James Clace, better known by the name of Blue Jimmy, suffered the extreme sentence of the law upon the new drop at Ilchester . . . Clace appears to have been a very notorious character" (this is a cautious statement of the reporter's, quite unlike the exuberant reporting of the present day: the culprit was notorious indubitably). "He is said to have confessed to having stolen an enormous number of horses, and he had been brought to the bar nineteen times for that class of offence. . . . In early life he lived as a postboy at Salisbury; afterwards he joined himself to some gipsies for the humour of the thing, and at length began those practices which brought him to an untimely end; aged 52."

A tradition was till lately current as to his hanging. When on the gallows he stated blandly that he had followed the strict rule of never stealing horses from people who were more honest than himself, but only from skinflints, taskmasters, lawyers, and parsons. Otherwise he might have stolen a dozen where he had only stolen one.

The same newspaper paragraph briefly alludes to a young man who was hanged side by side with Blue Jimmy, upon the "new drop":—

"William Hazlett—aged 25—for having stolen some sheep and some lambs. The miserable man, after being condemned, seemed to imagine that his *was a very hard case.*"

The *County Chronicle* prints the last few words in italics, appearing to hold up its hands in horror at the ingratitude of the aforesaid William Hazlett. For was not he provided with a "new drop," and had he not for his fellow voyager into futurity that renowned Wessex horse-thief, Blue Jimmy, who doubtless "flung his last fling" more boldly than many of his betters?

THE UNCONQUERABLE

I

There were times when Philip Fadelle acknowledged to himself with a sense of amusement not untinged with bitterness that even death had scarce succeeded in tempering the force of that inflexible will which he had ever recognised as an essential part of the being of his friend Roger Wingate. From the time when they were schoolboys together it had been a goad to urge him into paths whither he would not, the more effective in that it was wielded with the semblance of good-fellowship. The compelling pressure on his arm had been so much the friendly grip of one whose mastery of circumstance has given him the right to hale his friend, by the hair if need be, into ways of prosperity, that now when these fingers were cold and relaxed the moral force remained as potent as ever.

Among other things he remembered that, when he had spoken or rather hinted, of his intention to ask Gertrude Norton to be his wife, this same good friend had revealed the fact that there would be rivalry between them, but in mitigation, he had dwelt insistingly, his hand meanwhile pressing Philip's shoulder somewhat more heavily than usual, upon the fact that Gertrude Norton had been framed by Nature, obviously, to be the wife of himself, the astute and rising young politician, rather than to be the divinity of the struggling man of letters. Upon this occasion, Fadelle was glad to remember, he had refused to grant the premises, not that this was of great moment, seeing that some weeks later Roger Wingate was the accepted suitor of the girl whose gay looks and bounding spirits had seemed to merit some orbit of their own, instead of suffering eclipse by the luminous and self-sufficient personality of a too eminent husband.

He remembered also, with less of gratitude, that if he had acted more promptly and had omitted to confide in his friend, all might have gone differently. When, at length, he had decided to go to her he had broken his journey to linger irresolutely a day or two in an old Cathedral town, within the peaceful close and under the shadow of one of the most notable piles of Mediaeval architecture in England. His dallying had led to his arrival at the home of the woman he wished to make his wife a few hours after her engagement to Roger Wingate.

Had he been earlier, he fancied, he might have won her, for a gleam in her eyes seemed to reproach him. He found scant comfort from the recollection that it had always been Wingate's way to supersede him, even when they were at school together.

Five years after Roger Wingate's marriage, at a time when his career had seemed secure against mischance, he had succumbed with appalling swiftness to a few days' illness and an operation from which he never rallied. It was difficult for those who had known him to contemplate the idea of the extinction of one so vital. The force which had emanated from him had seemed imperishable.

The news, revealed in course of time by the widow, that it had been Wingate's definitely expressed wish that some memoir of himself should be compiled by his friend was to Philip Fadelle another, perhaps the last, manifestation of that overpowering will. Though none else had contemplated Wingate's death, he himself had done so, and in providing that his friend's hand should raise him a memorial lucent and rare, he had linked to this evidence of his friend's literary gift a sense of his own domination.

"Of course, had he lived longer, the biography would have been a work of importance; but as it is, with his letters— unique in their way, I believe—something not unworthy might be done." Gertrude had hesitated at this point, and then, in a lower key, had given her tribute to that unseen power:

"One feels, somehow, constrained to obey what one knows to have been his wish."

In this the man of letters had acquiesced, with a sigh that had a groan at its heart. He knew that the telling of that brief though redundant life might with safety be left in his hands, and he was prepared to offer what slight fame he had already garnered as incense to his dead comrade's memory.

"You have always been a most dear and generous friend to us both," she added, with a smile that had in it as much of tenderness (it seemed) for the living, as regret for the dead.

The memory of the past bloomed between them like some wan flower of which both inhaled the faint perfume; till Fadelle suddenly remembered that his friend had now been dead for nearly six months, and that the time would soon be at hand when he might make that proposal so long delayed. His face brightened and a shadow passed from his eyes: he spoke of the memoir with interest, even with pleasure. "It will be the last token that friendship can offer," he said almost with emotion, and to himself he added that it would be in the nature of a seal set upon Wingate's tomb.

As weeks passed and he gave himself wholeheartedly to the work he had undertaken he began to realize that here, under his hand, Wingate's character was developing into such complexities as hitherto he had not suspected! Besides those sterner qualities which had impelled him onward in his chosen career there were suggestions of mystery, definite shades, of romance it might be, almost incredible in one who had mastered the hard facts of life so unshrinkingly. More wonderful still was the presumption that this side of that forcible character had been revealed to no-one! Gertrude, so far as he could gather, had never seen it.

The biography, he judged, would do full justice to a personality almost unique in its qualities of ingenuous comradeship allied to a wellnigh overwhelming dominance: a rare enough combination.

The summer following Wingate's death had nearly passed when Fadelle decided to visit Gertrude, who had been living for some time with her mother in the country. He had refrained from accepting the invitation, often and pressingly repeated, until he had almost finished the biography. Now that this had been accomplished for all practical purposes, and the anniversary of Roger Wingate's death had come and gone, the way seemed clear for the furtherance of his chief desire. He was filled with a pleasing certainty as his train carried him on to his destination, and when he alighted at a little country station he accepted it as a good omen that she was there to meet him.

She had changed greatly. He remembered that after a few months of married life she had seemed subdued to that strong will, had been absorbed into that overwhelming personality with which she had been mated. Now, as she sat in the dog-cart, waiting to drive her guest to her house, he noted with a leaping heart that the Gertrude of her maiden days had been reincarnated. In her bright face was all the arch vivacity of unfettered girlhood, and as they were carried swiftly between green hedgerows he rejoiced to hear again the gay inconsequence that Roger had always tacitly suppressed.

Glancing at her charming profile he wondered, once again, if she had ever plumbed that hidden well of sentiment which he fancied he had discovered in the secret writings of his friend. Some day he might ask,—but not yet.

"I have a heap of things to show you," she assured him triumphantly, "and ever so much to discuss. It is easier to talk, don't you think, than to write?"

"About what?"

"Oh, about the biography, of course."

His gaze fastened itself upon the bracken at the side of the lane down which they were passing and sought out the flecks of golden brown among the green.

"Ah, yes."

When he turned to her again there was something so unwidow-like in her grey tweed, in the small jaunty plume of her hat, and her business-like dog-skin gloves that a smile hovered where doubt had been.

"Ah, that biography! It will need days and days of discussion. Of course it must be a tremendous thing."

"Of course it must, but do you know—" her eyes sought his with laughing embarrassment, "sometimes I am afraid that it is going to be something of an obsession."

His glance held hers with amused assurance.

"I'm not quite sure that I have not found it something of that sort already."

Then mysteriously, a sense of loyalty to the dear husband
and friend descended between them and froze their gaiety.

"Of course it must be great—powerful—like himself."

"Of course." He spoke dully and his mobile jaw grew rigid.
Twice already, within one brief hour, he had met with an
invisible rebuff; yet the hand that dealt it was one that he had
thought bereft of power.

They passed a tiny lodge and swept up a drive.

"Here is the house; rather small; but a haven of rest for
tired souls. It is rather sweet, isn't it?"

He thought it was, as he saw it nestling among the trees,
grey walled and red roofed, and in front, walking on the wide
gravel sweep before the door, as if to lend the final touch of
domesticity, a mushroom-hatted and lace-shawled lady,
Gertrude's mother, who turned at the sound of wheels to
greet her visitor.

The days of his visit passed, and deliberate and continued
observation confirmed Philip Fadelle in the assurance that to
Gertrude Wingate the past thirteen months had brought a
virtual renewal of blithe girlhood; but when she discussed
with him the biography she became preternaturally solemn,
and assumed a delightfully important manner as of one in
whose small hands weighty affairs of state have been placed.

At such times the author noticed, with a sense of irritated
amusement, that his work had sufficed to raise Wingate on to
a loftier pedestal than he had, in his wife's estimation, previously occupied. She was pleased to be Fadelle's divinity, but
there were moments when he told himself bitterly that in
spirit she remained Wingate's slave.

This intuition, however, did not suffice to rob his holiday of
any perceptible amount of charm, since Gertrude Wingate, as
she rambled with him through woods and fields, betrayed the
gaiety of a child who has escaped from the durance of a stern
school. When she referred to her late husband it was in notes
of eulogy rather than of regretful reminiscence.

"This immaculate man has only just begun to live," Fadelle
told himself with chagrin. "He was born in the first chapter of
the biography."

Nevertheless he worked assiduously at his task: every stone
set into that destined memorial must be polished and

repolished, even though it were with bleeding hands. There was something in Gertrude's bright friendship that sustained him. Often when she turned from the subject of the biography to discuss his other more personal work she unconsciously gained in vividness, and her eyes beamed with a kindlier interest. She was quickly appreciative of subtle intangible moods, she was swift to catch a meaning, and was there, with him, in a moment, when women of a more pronounced intellectuality would have been labouring painfully behind.

The best minutes of the day to him were those when, after dinner, they together paced up and down before the lighted windows of the house. As they turned again and again in their steady pacing, one luminous rectangle, which showed the calm figure of Gertrude's mother knitting beside a shaded lamp, was to them a link with civilization; for, on the other hand, the lawn sloped away to a whispering darkness full of primeval mystery.

"You know, of course, that I took no part in the political life that Roger led," she said suddenly one evening when walking thus. "I might have understood, I suppose, all that there was; but I could never have really cared. I belong more to that." She thrust her hand through the darkness and waved it at the shrouded woods and fields beyond.

"Listen!"

There was a fair in the village some distance away, hidden behind the woods. A hoarse murmur reached them faintly, and on the sky one sullen patch betrayed the reflected light of the flaming naptha-lamps that hung on the booths, and the screaming merry-go-round.

They pierced, venturously, further into the darkness, walking some way down the avenue, while the ghostly branches waved blackly overhead. It was then, he afterwards felt, that he should have spoken but, unlike his erstwhile friend and school-fellow, he let the decisive moment fall away. Together they returned to the house and the warm and lighted sanity of the drawingroom, to discuss a chapter dealing with a political crisis in which the inflexible will and insistent personality of Roger Wingate had not been found wanting.

It was, as Fadelle had imagined it would be, during one of those late evening strollings and communings that he asked

Gertrude to be his wife. When she slowly and reluctantly gave a refusal she tempered it with explanations of an unsuspected character, so that the listener, peering bewilderedly at a totally strange aspect of Roger Wingate, almost missed the sense of his own loss.

"If there was one thing that he hated, one thing which always worried and upset him," she explained, "it was the idea, suggested to him in some way that I cannot understand, of my marrying again in the event of his early death. To him it seemed betrayal of the basest kind, utterly unforgiveable."

"I remember," she continued, "how he urged upon me the idea that the one who survived should remain faithful to the memory of the deceased. I—" here she flushed and lowered her eyes, "gave no actual pledge; but still—"

"Then I—" he returned with pale severity, "can say no more,—if you think you are in any way bound by an implied consent."

This strangely enough, she disclaimed, faltering and hesitating: she was not bound, in one sense, she believed, but a sense of loyalty stood as such a bond. Had her husband been less true, for that he was made of truth no-one could deny, it would have been quite simple, for she had given no pledge. It might even be, she hinted, that in time to come she would feel her obligation less strongly.

"It is the biography, partly, I believe," she uttered, laying her hand on his arm with a soft impulsiveness, "I don't think that I ever—I am almost ashamed to say it—I don't think I ever fully realized before I read what you have written, how strong, how true, how utterly loyal he was to me."

There was the cadence of tears in her voice as she urged this point of view upon him. He had raised in her a finer appreciation of Wingate's qualities, and this being so she could not repay loyalty with disloyalty: she felt that he would agree with her in that.

They stood together at the edge of the gravel sweep where it touched the darker line of the grass: beside them reared itself a tall yew, stern against the sombre purple of the sky. He watched, and through his sense of this outward beauty there pierced the knowledge that he was conquered, overwhelmed by a far reaching power, and he knew how well his friend had gauged, weighed, and estimated his tendency to idealize, and how well he had made use of it. Wingate had been working through himself as if he were still alive.

There seemed, under the circumstances, little that need be said, but as they moved slowly back to the opened and lighted porch Gertrude walked beside him, and, holding up her white skirt in one of the pretty ways she had at her command, pleaded that nothing should be altered, and that he must always be her dear and close friend. Fadelle felt the groan he was too heartsick to utter aloud. Yes, all was to remain as before; had not Wingate willed it so?

II

It was not later than the next morning that he announced in the worn formula that pressing affairs demanded his quick return to Town. Mrs Norton, benignly presiding over the breakfast table, was puzzled and mildly reproachful: her daughter looked conscience-stricken, and her eyes, for an instant, grew wider and brighter as if with unshed tears.

"Is there nothing I can say?" she asked softly when they were alone together. "Nothing that I can say to persuade you to remain with us a little longer?"

He feared not, unless—this with a poor smile,—she could induce his publishers to wait upon him here, in the country, and the authorities of the British Museum to send him several parcels of books and papers.

"And the biography?" she asked without the least pretence of accepting the laboured joke.

That, he replied, was practically finished, and he proceeded to enlarge upon the subject with much deliberation, while Gertrude listened with weary blankness. Her interest in the biography seemed to have passed.

"There is something," she said with sudden remembrance, "something that I have forgotten to tell you. I should have spoken about it before." She told him that she had discovered an accumulation of papers and letters in an old bureau which had been sent down from her town house, together with other furniture. If he cared to look through them, he might be able to tell whether the letters were of any consequence. They were tied up carefully, dated and docketed, she thought, and a few minutes would doubtless serve to determine their importance.

"I had no idea until a day or two ago that there were any letters there," she said. "The bureau was in a room where Roger kept old books that he never used, but evidently did not wish to destroy or give away; his school trunks, sets of games and other boyish treasures. Indeed I did not know that he used the bureau at all for he always kept the room locked up."

They went together to a spare room and she showed him the letters and papers, all neatly ranged in various drawers and pigeon-holes.

"I would have gone through these myself," she said in a low tone; "but just now it seems beyond me."

He threw an enquiring glance towards her and noticed her air of depression, and the weary look in her eyes. She left him when he had assured her that he could run through the letters more expeditiously without her aid. Taking a packet from the top drawer and slipping off an elastic band he began to read.

He had been through quite half a dozen letters before the meaning of their so careful concealment in the bureau struck home to his puzzled senses. Here, he felt, his hand was on a clue which, followed up, would explain much of the hidden side of Wingate's character that he had suspected but never clearly viewed. Reading on and on he drew deep breaths of bewilderment as packet after packet revealed a hitherto un-known Wingate, one to whom base trickery and unholy alli-ances had not been too mean weapons for gaining desired ends. No laudatory biography could have been written had these circumstances been revealed before. He remembered bitterly one chapter that he had filled with an exposition of Wingate's loyalty to a party, which, as these letters showed, he had basely sold. There was no proof of any great, overwhelm-ing temptation and sudden, pitiable fall, such as the heart of any understanding man might have forgiven. He had lied and cheated in a calm deliberate manner, using, as in all other circumstances of his life, that unconquerable will, which it seemed had awed his accomplices into lasting silence.

Fadelle, in reading, wondered why Wingate should have piled together and preserved this mass of evidence now before him, for had these letters and papers, all damning records, been burnt, the high integrity of his character would have remained undoubted. An ordinary man, with little of statecraft and nothing of Wingate's ability, would have taken this ordinary precaution. Nevertheless, people did such things as keep compromising papers, and, it was not out of accord with Wingate's character that he should have hurled his own image from its pedestal thus violently. No gradual descent would have served that supreme wilfulness.

The last packet of letters gave the final blow, and Fadelle put his hand to his head mechanically, as if amazed at the dull numbing pain it had sustained. Up to this moment he had held that his friend had carried, as a well of sweetening waters in the inviolable recesses of his heart, deep and unstained reverence for a domestic ideal, but these letters spoke of the deepest treachery, not to his party this time but to his wife.

He put them down and rested his aching head on his hands. Gradually the dubious haze and confusion cleared away and a tiny ray of light, no more than a pin-point at first—pierced the darkness and grew and grew until his mind was illuminated by one vast idea. He, Philip Fadelle, had triumphed at last: his adversary, after long years of victory, had met with one finally decisive stroke, for Fate had taken up arms against her erstwhile favourite on Fadelle's behalf.

One thing seemed plain enough to him: the biography could hardly be published now, at any rate not as he had written it. Gertrude would share the disillusionment, and not, so he dared to think, too regretfully. There was no reason now for her keeping faith with the memory of one who had been so unfaithful to her as she must be made to know. Things grew clearer and clearer to him, and at length he was serenely contented. He seemed to be holding out a cynically good-natured hand to Wingate across the dividing stream.

"I've won at last, old friend. You made a good fight of it always; but now, like the sportsman you always were, you must confess yourself beaten."

Strange that even now, with that confuting pile of letters before him, he should still cherish the idea of Wingate's straightness.

A slight noise made him start, and he turned to see that Gertrude had entered the room. In her hand she held some unfolded pages. She had been looking in a writing case that had belonged to her husband, one that had been used only when he was travelling, and in it she had found a letter, unfinished. "Addressed to me," she said with a slight tremor in her voice. "From the date I imagine that it was written while he was out of Town, during that last short holiday he took before his death. I remember that he was called back suddenly, and that is, probably, why this letter was never finished."

He asked, somewhat bewildered, if she wished him to read it.

"I thought you would like to, as he speaks very beautifully of you. I was greatly touched. It is like a message from the dead."

Fadelle's eyes lingered for a moment upon the letters spread before him on the bureau: there, too, was a message, but of a different cast. "Have you found anything there of importance?" asked Gertrude, her glance following his.

Moved by a sudden impulse, strange even to himself, he answered hurriedly that there was nothing; he supposed that the letters had been put there so that they might, after an interval, be destroyed. Of their nature he said nothing, and Gertrude then left him.

When he was alone he wondered why he had failed to reveal that which must be made known at some time: the opportunity had presented itself so aptly, and yet he had omitted to make use of it. Wingate, he was sure, had never hesitated to grasp the slightest chance; and here was he, in the moment of victory, acknowledging his weakness.

With a sigh he gathered together the letters of the last packet and slipped around them their elastic band, having done which he took up the written sheets which Gertrude had left.

"I have been wondering who would be the best man for this purpose, and I have come to the conclusion that there is only one of all my host of acquaintances in whom I am able to place implicit trust, and that one is Philip Fadelle. I am sorry that we have seen so little of him lately, but that has not been my fault. Indeed, as years pass, I realize more fully the loyalty of his friendship; he has been the same from boyhood, your friend and my friend, and I am certain that if I call upon him now to do me this service he will not fail me. I am going to ask him—"

The letter ended abruptly, leaving Fadelle in ignorance concerning the request that his dead friend would have made. With a steady hand he laid it on the top of the bureau. It was, indeed, a message from the dead, a supplication rather, an appeal, to which he could not but respond.

"He will not fail me." He repeated the words: they were uncanny now. Yes, Wingate had judged him well, he could not fail him; could not reveal. Once more his glance fell upon the packets of betraying letters, ranged in drawer and pigeon-hole, and then he walked back to one of the windows. Below, in the sunlight, he saw the figure of Gertrude moving among the flaming torch-lilies and flaunting golden-rod in the long garden at the side of the house. Some distance behind her, at the end of the kitchen garden, arose a thin blue column of smoke from a pile of burning weeds; the sight suggested to him a course of action and he went down.

As he drew near to her he saw in her eyes that she wished to know how the letter had affected him, but of that he had determined he would not speak.

"I have looked through the letters in the bureau," he said steadily. "They relate mostly to private political matters, and were evidently meant to be destroyed. Perhaps it would be better for me to take them away with me to look through them again more leisurely than I have time to do now. If I find nothing in them that needs preserving I suppose I have your permission to destroy them. I suppose that you do not wish to read them?"

He waited in strained suspense for her answer, which came as he had thought.

"No thank you. I would much rather not, if you do not think it necessary. I think there can be nothing more depressing than reading such letters, and I hope that I have seen the last of them."

As they sauntered in the garden she again approached, almost shyly, the question of his departure, and it was evident that she wished him to remain longer. These tentative advances were disregarded by Fadelle. All that he wished now was to free himself as quickly as possible from the burden of obligation to his dead friend, which pressed upon his shoulders with ever increasing weight.

When the time arrived for him to go to the station and Gertrude appeared, ready to drive him in her dogcart, it was clear, even to his dulled bachelor perceptions, that her costume of thick cream serge and hat to match had no suggestion of widowhood; and the light tendrils of hair that blew across her brow were almost virginal in their significance.

As they drove along he remarked dully that the bracken was taking to itself deeper tints of brown and gold. A strange silence fell between them, a silence that seemed ever at breaking point. He felt that at a word from Gertrude the whole face of his mental world might have changed for ever, but the word was not spoken, though he seemed to see its shadow on her lips and in her eyes. At the same quiet wayside station where she had met him upon his arrival the pony drew up, and he found that there was the briefest possible space in which to wait for the train; he wondered, even then, what the interval might bring forth, but its sliding moments proved barren. Gertrude spoke of the bright flowers of early autumn that were beginning to bloom in the neat little station-garden, and she stooped and petted a serious station-cat which strolled leisurely among the luggage. Then the train rushed in.

Fadelle had made his farewell and taken his seat when she moved suddenly forward, her lips eagerly parted.

"Goodbye, Goodbye!" He leaned from the window as the train started, and his voice drowned what she might have said.

She took a few quick steps, not half a dozen in all, by the side of the moving carriage, and he knew that she had something to say then that might never again be said.

"Goodbye!" He dropped back in his seat and saw her left behind, the light dying out of her face as she stood still.

It was not until the train had pulsed and rattled onward for some miles, and he felt himself being carried to pastures unstained by memory, that he uttered to himself a comment which was to him the final token of the affair—that from the other side of the grave Wingate had played his last card and won.

EXPLANATORY NOTES

ABBREVIATIONS

Collected Letters	*The Collected Letters of Thomas Hardy*, ed. Richard Little Purdy and Michael Millgate, 7 vols. (Oxford: Clarendon Press, 1978–88).
Excluded and Collaborative Stories	*Thomas Hardy: The Excluded and Collaborative Stories*, ed. Pamela Dalziel (Oxford: Clarendon Press, 1992).
HW	The *Harper's Weekly* text of 'An Indiscretion in the Life of an Heiress', 29 June–27 July 1878.
Life	*The Life and Work of Thomas Hardy*, ed. Michael Millgate (London: Macmillan, 1984).
NQM	The *New Quarterly Magazine* text of 'An Indiscretion in the Life of an Heiress', July 1878.
PersN	*The Personal Notebooks of Thomas Hardy*, ed. Richard H. Taylor (London: Macmillan, 1979).
TH	Thomas Hardy.

Unless otherwise indicated, quotations from TH's fiction collected during his lifetime are from the Wessex Edition (London: Macmillan, 1912–14); quotations from Shakespeare are from *The Dramatic Works of William Shakespeare* (London: Bell and Daldy, 1856), a 10-vol. set purchased by TH in 1863, but for ease of reference act, scene, and line numbers are included from *The Riverside Shakespeare* (Boston: Houghton Mifflin, 1974).

5   *Euclid*: Athenian mathematician of the third century BC; his *Elements* is the basis for the most common type of geometry.

6   *tenth commandment*: 'Thou shalt not covet thy neighbour's house, thou shalt not covet thy neighbour's wife, nor his manservant, nor his maidservant, nor his ox, nor his ass, nor any thing that is thy neighbour's' (Exod. 20: 17).

8   *Monument*: a pillar, 202 ft. in height, erected in 1671–7 in Pudding Lane to commemorate the Great Fire of London in 1666; see *Collected Letters*, i. 2.

    St George's Hospital: a famous London hospital located (until recently) at Hyde Park Corner.

9　　*royal letters extraordinary kitchen-range*: for the widespread ap-
propriation of royal allusions and images by Victorian advertis-
ers, see John May, *Victoria Remembered: A Royal History
1817–1861* (London: Heinemann, 1983) and, for later in the
century, Thomas Richards, 'The Image of Victoria in the Year
of the Jubilee', *Victorian Studies*, 31 (1987), 7–32.

10　*Martinmas summer*: St Martin's summer, a period of fine
weather sometimes occurring around 11 November (St
Martin's day).

11　*Maiden-Newton*: Dorset village; in later works given the
'Wessex' name (see n. to p. 36) of Chalk Newton.

　　　Weymouth: Dorset seaport; in later works given the 'Wessex'
name of Budmouth.

　　　Beaminster: Dorset village; in later works given the 'Wessex'
name of Emminster.

　　　Cloton: the only fictional place-name in the story; the village is
presumably based on Netherbury, Dorset.

　　　Helen: in classical mythology the most beautiful woman in the
world; her abduction by Paris led to the 10-year Trojan war.

12　*Portland*: Dorset peninsula; in later works given the 'Wessex'
name of the Isle of Slingers.

14　*staying at Beaminster*: 'Beaminster' is presumably TH's slip for
Maiden Newton; the carrier has just arrived *in* Beaminster.

15　*Macaulay*: Thomas Babington Macaulay (1800–59, historian
and politician) vigorously supported the India Bill introduced
by Sir Charles Wood in 1853. The bill embodied clauses originally introduced by Macaulay in 1833 for opening Indian civil
service appointments to competition.

16　*public school and college men*: men educated at endowed private
schools (e.g. Eton, Harrow) and at Oxford or Cambridge
colleges.

　　　Such a case occurs sometimes: Oswald Winwood's examination
success is to some extent based on that of Hooper Tolbort,
TH's Dorchester friend and rival during the late 1850s and
early 1860s. Tolbort, a brilliant linguist, was encouraged to sit
the Oxford Middle Class and Indian Civil Service examination
by his former schoolmaster, William Barnes, and by Horace
Moule, arguably the most significant—in both intellectual and

emotional terms—of TH's male friends. Tolbort took first place in both examinations, in 1859 and 1862 respectively, and TH was later to recall Moule's telling him of the latter success and producing 'a copy of the *Times*, where our friend's name stood at the head of the list, followed by 200 of lower rank' ('The Late Mr. T. W. H. Tolbort, B.C.S.', *Dorset County Chronicle*, 16 Aug. 1883).

19 *lifting his fingers . . . scale*: almost a direct quotation of Henery Fray's response to Bathsheba's unexpected gift of ten shillings in *Far from the Madding Crowd* (88; ch. 10).

20 *Bess*: baby-talk for 'Bless'.

straightening himself yet an inch taller: cf. Mountclere in *The Hand of Ethelberta*, who straightens himself 'to ten years younger' (261; ch. 31). The external resemblance between Lovill and Mountclere is quite marked: Lovill is 'really and fairly old—sixty-five years of age at least', Mountclere 'Sixty-five at least' (249; ch. 30), yet both cling to the things of youth, are perpetually and somewhat absurdly merry, and punctuate their speech with 'hee-hee' (a characteristic shared by another elderly suitor, Heddegan in 'A Mere Interlude'). Mountclere, whose speciously 'dignified aspect' is revealed as 'jocund slyness upon nearer view' (261; ch. 31), is, however, an altogether more sinister figure than the merely foolish and doting Lovill.

22 *to go to Australia*: subsequently identified more specifically as Queensland, to which one of TH's cousins, Martha Sparks, had emigrated with her husband in 1870.

23 *gloury*: Wright's *English Dialect Dictionary* defines 'glowery' as 'out of temper, cross, surly' and *OED* lists 'glour' as an alternative spelling of 'glower'.

33 *a pleasant jest . . . harm*: cf. Mountclere's response to Ethelberta's attempted flight in *The Hand of Ethelberta*: 'A very pleasant joke, my dear—hee-hee! And no more than was to be expected on this merry, happy day of our lives. Nobody enjoys a good jest more than I do: I always enjoyed a jest—hee-hee!' (443-4; ch. 47). The escape attempts in the two works are basically the same: the overheard plans for a flight to the nearest railway station, the anticipated time (for departure or for receiving a note of instructions), the mistaken identity of the 'accomplice', the woman's increasing puzzlement at his silence, the unexpected stop, and the consequent revelation—

accompanied by the elderly lover's characteristic 'hee-hee' and the bride's horrified dismay.

36   *Wessex*: one of the seven kingdoms into which England was divided in Anglo-Saxon times; TH adopted the name for what he defined as the 'partly real, partly dream country' of his fiction (1895 Preface to *Far from the Madding Crowd*), which approximately corresponded to the south-western English counties of Devon, Somerset, Wiltshire, Berkshire, Hampshire, and Dorset, especially the last. TH first used the name in *Far from the Madding Crowd* (1874) and by 1877 it was already gaining acceptance as a regional designation.

Blackmore: an alternative spelling of Blakemoor or Blackmoor, in north Dorset; the description of the Vale's being 'thickly wooded' perhaps provides a clue to the period of the story, since the Vale was enclosed and deforested during the course of the seventeenth century, and especially during the reign of Charles I. (Cf. the description of the Vale in *Tess of the d'Urbervilles* as having remained densely wooded down to 'comparatively recent times' (10; ch. 2).) The reference to the period when snuff-boxes were 'becoming common among young and old throughout the country' suggests, however, a late seventeenth-century or early eighteenth-century dating.

40   *Can you call . . . deep*: 'I can call spirits from the vasty deep' (Shakespeare, *1 Henry IV*, III. i. 52).

tempest in a cupboard: an allusion to the proverbial expression 'a tempest in a teacup', derived from the title of William Bayle Bernard's popular farce, *A Storm in a Tea Cup* (1854).

42   *Short's Gibbet*: apparently an invented name and place, although gibbets were common enough in the English countryside throughout the eighteenth century (see *Collected Letters*, v. 269).

Queen Elizabeth and King Charles: the Vale of Blackmoor was apparently never visited by Elizabeth or by either Charles I or Charles II. Elizabeth never went to Dorset; Charles I seems to have gone only in order to hunt on Cranborne Chase; while Charles II spent nineteen days hidden in a manor-house in south-west Dorset after his defeat at the battle of Worcester in 1651.

43   *When I would . . . Isabel*: Shakespeare, *Measure for Measure*, II. iv. 1–4.

43 *The congregation . . . painfulness*: cf. the description of the Carriford afternoon service in *Desperate Remedies*:

> The people were singing the Evening Hymn. . . . She looked at all the people as they stood and sang, waving backwards and forwards like a forest of pines swayed by a gentle breeze; then at the village children singing too, their heads inclined to one side, their eyes listlessly tracing some crack in the old walls, or following the movement of a distant bough or bird with features petrified almost to painfulness. (259; ch. 12)

The parallelism can be attributed to the fact that *Desperate Remedies*, like 'Indiscretion', was derived in part from *The Poor Man and the Lady*; see Pamela Dalziel, 'Exploiting the *Poor Man*: The Genesis of Hardy's *Desperate Remedies*', *Journal of English and Germanic Philology* (forthcoming).

Tollamore Church: presumably based on Stinsford Church (Mellstock in TH's 'Wessex'), familiar to TH from childhood; the monument to Geraldine's ancestors certainly shares many features with the Grey monument in Stinsford (see *An Inventory of Historical Monuments in the County of Dorset* (London: Royal Commission on Historical Monuments, 1970), iii. 253 and plate 203).

44 *unequal history*: *HW* reads 'no social standing'. The revision is one of several which TH introduced in *NQM* in order to reduce somewhat the difference in social position between Egbert and Geraldine, perhaps in response to the publisher Alexander Macmillan's comment that *The Poor Man and the Lady*, from which 'Indiscretion' derived, lacked the '*modesty of nature* of fact': 'King Cophetua & the beggar maid make a pretty tale in an old ballad; but make a story in which the Duke of Edinburgh takes in lawful wedlock even a private gentlemans [*sic*] daughter! . . . Given your characters, could it happen in the present day?' (10 Aug. 1868 letter, Dorset County Museum).

44–5 *Now a close observer . . . establish itself*: the sensational threshing-machine episode was evidently added to *NQM* in proof. *HW* has a much more prosaic account of the lovers' first meeting:

> That afternoon an emotion, which composed the young man's sole motive power through many following years, first arose and established itself in his breast. It was the second Sunday after Christmas, and he had lately come there to teach. This

was the second time in his life that he had set eyes on the only daughter and heiress of the family at Tollamore House; the first was when he arrived, a week earlier, and had been obliged to take up his quarters in the mansion, because the school-house was not quite ready. She had spoken very kindly to him—almost with imprudent kindness; and his gaze at her during the church service was the result of their acquaintance.

In *HW* there is thus no romantic stimulus for Geraldine's attraction to Egbert, which consequently seems less credible, as, indeed, does her unease during her first visit to the school or her desire to prevent the eviction of Egbert's grandfather. The *HW* account of the lovers' meeting also conflicts with the later narrative: not only does Egbert never live in the school-house but he could have stayed with his grandfather that first week as well as later. For the relationship between the *HW* version and *The Poor Man and the Lady*, see *Excluded and Collaborative Stories*, 74.

45   *Tollamore House*: presumably based on Kingston Maurward House, in the Dorset parish of Stinsford; known to TH since childhood, it appears as Knapwater House in *Desperate Remedies*.

46   *She was active . . . all*: Browning, 'The Flight of the Duchess', st. viii; TH omitted the four lines which follow 'tire'.

47   *Mayne could have wished . . . week*: cf. the *HW* version ('Mayne could have wished that she had not been so thoroughly free from all apparent consciousness that they had met before') and the account of Dick Dewy's feelings in *Under the Greenwood Tree*: 'Dick could have wished her manner had not been so entirely free from all apparent consciousness of those accidental meetings of theirs' (100; part II, ch. 6). The parallelism can be attributed to the fact that much of *Under the Greenwood Tree*, like *Desperate Remedies* and 'Indiscretion' itself, was derived from *The Poor Man and the Lady*; see Simon Gatrell, *Hardy the Creator: A Textual Biography* (Oxford: Clarendon Press, 1989), 12–14.

47–8   *The clear, deep eyes . . . attire*: cf. this passage and Egbert's response to Geraldine's beauty ('[his] heart . . . came round to her with a rush') with Dick's perception of Fancy in *Under the Greenwood Tree*: 'An easy bend of neck and graceful set of head; full and wavy bundles of dark-brown hair; light fall of little feet; pretty devices on the skirt of the dress; clear deep eyes . . .

Dick's heart went round to her with a rush' (121; part III, ch. 1).

48   *a person*: *HW* reads 'an innocent nobody'; see n. to p. 44.

"No," he said . . . possible: cf. Knight's response to Elfride in *A Pair of Blue Eyes*: 'No, I don't choose to do it in the sense you mean; choosing from a whole world of professions, all possible' (177; ch. 17). The parallelism suggests that *A Pair of Blue Eyes* was also in part derived from *The Poor Man and the Lady*, though to a lesser extent than *Desperate Remedies, Under the Greenwood Tree*, and 'Indiscretion'; see Michael Millgate, *Thomas Hardy: His Career as a Novelist* (London: The Bodley Head, 1971), 20–1, 364.

50   *Her "I shall . . . meanings*: cf. Cytherea's musing in *Desperate Remedies*: 'His parting words, "Don't forget me," she repeated to herself a hundred times, and though she thought their import was probably commonplace, she could not help toying with them,—looking at them from all points, and investing them with meanings of love and faithfulness' (34; ch. 3).

But what is this . . . eye: Tennyson, *In Memoriam*, sect. LXVIII; in the second line the correct reading is 'I find'.

51   *placed under Government inspection*: once the school was recognized for government funding it would become subject to an annual inspection and its teachers required to be appropriately trained and 'certificated'—as Egbert was not.

dropping of the lives: under a form of copyhold lease (of feudal origin but still widely used in nineteenth-century Dorset) many village tenancies were held 'on lives', the lease remaining in effect until the death of the longest lived of up to three persons, usually the current tenant, his wife, and eldest son; see Joan Brocklebank, *Affpuddle in the County of Dorset A.D. 987–1953* (Bournemouth: Horace G. Commin, 1968), 9–10. TH's birthplace in Higher Bockhampton was held on a lifehold tenancy and the system provides significant plot elements in several of his works, most notably *The Woodlanders* and 'Netty Sargent's Copyhold'.

53   *the nearest way . . . casement*: cf. this passage and subsequent descriptions of Egbert's behaviour (e.g. 'The spring drew on, and . . . he walked abroad much more than had been usual with him formerly', 'Egbert would go home and think for hours of her little remarks and movements') with 'Passing by the School' in *Under the Greenwood Tree*:

as the spring advanced Dick walked abroad much more frequently than had hitherto been usual with him, and was continually finding that his nearest way to or from home lay by the
road which skirted the garden of the school. . . . [T]urning the
angle . . . he saw Miss Fancy's figure, clothed in a dark-gray
dress, looking from a high open window . . . [H]e meditated
on her every little movement for hours after it was made. (67;
part II, ch. 1)

53 *Childe Harold's Pilgrimage*: Byron's poem; TH's marked copy
    (Halifax: Milner and Sowerby, 1865) is in the Dorset County
    Museum.

54 *Oh, for my sake . . . provide*: Shakespeare, Sonnet 111; the only
    alteration of wording is 'deed' for 'deeds'. In *HW* the epi-
    graph is 'Then flashed the living lightning from her eyes'
    (Pope, 'The Rape of the Lock', III. 155), presumably altered
    for *NQM* because it conflicted both with the description of
    Geraldine's motionlessness after Egbert's impulsive embrace
    and with her subsequent account of her feelings.

56 *the third of April . . . twenty-eighth*: TH is using here either the
    calendar for 1870 or, more probably, the 1864 calendar fol-
    lowed in the first half of *Desperate Remedies*.

    when a passionate . . . school: not present in *HW*; its addition is
    one of several revisions which TH introduced in *NQM* in order
    to emphasize Geraldine's thoughtlessness and impulsiveness.

58 *Ulysses . . . Melanthus . . . rest*: Melanthus, properly Melanthius,
    is the goatherd who sides with the suitors and insults Ulysses
    when the latter arrives in Ithaca disguised as a beggar. The
    quotation, from Chapman's translation of Homer's *Odyssey*
    (17. 313–14), describes Ulysses' reaction to his servant's
    abuse.

59 *disguised his feelings . . . matters*: cf. the description of Dick's
    visit to the school in *Under the Greenwood Tree*: 'He disguised his
    feelings . . . by endeavouring to appear like a man in a great
    hurry of business, who wished to leave the handkerchief and
    have done with such trifling errands' (63; part I, ch. 9).

60 *So I soberly . . . end?*: Browning, 'Instans Tyrannus', sts. vi–vii.

61 *Wellington . . . Waterloo*: Waterloo, south of Brussels, was the
    battlefield on which Napoleon was finally defeated by the
    British general, the Duke of Wellington, in 1815.

63 *we shall go . . . people*: since the park-enlargement scheme in-

volved tearing down the Broadford farmhouse and giving the farm to a current tenant, its enactment would not in fact 'make room for newer people'—nor, indeed, would it necessitate Egbert's own departure since he was only a temporary inhabitant of the farmhouse, living there to give his grandfather the 'benefit of his society during the long winter evenings'. The inconsistency is presumably attributable to the reworking of *Poor Man and the Lady* material for 'Indiscretion'.

63 *But remember, nothing . . . again*: *HW* reads: 'It was perhaps narrow-minded to do as I have done.' The revision is one of several TH introduced in *NQM* in order to reduce Geraldine's responsibility for the revival of the park-enlargement scheme and eliminate any suggestion of a class-determined motivation for her response. TH's revisions were not, however, comprehensive: the 'Instans Tyrannus' epigraph, beginning 'So I soberly laid my last plan | To extinguish the man' insists on Geraldine's active opposition, reiterated by the village rumour that it is she who is 'extremely anxious' to have the scheme put in hand as soon as possible.

65 *Hath misery . . . loved?*: Byron, *The Corsair*, III. viii. 3; in the fifth line the correct reading is 'despite thy crimes'.

66 *lack of other idleness*: correctly, 'want of other idleness', Shakespeare, *Twelfth Night*, I. v. 64.

67 *I would have done anything . . . reflected*: *HW* reads: 'I would not have done any thing tending to turn him out for all the world, had I only known.' See n. to p. 63.

69 *How shall I say 'Yes' . . . sinned*: cf. Manston's reply to Cytherea's request for forgiveness in *Desperate Remedies*: 'How shall I say "Yes" without judging you? . . . I'll say "Yes" . . . It is sweeter to fancy we are forgiven, than to think we have not sinned' (261–2; ch. 12).

Come forward . . . society: Thackeray, *The Book of Snobs*, 'Chapter Last' [45], 11th paragraph.

lay the foundation-stone: this scene is based on a ceremony TH attended with his employer, the architect Arthur Blomfield, in 1865 and described in his notebook. As recorded in *Life* (50) the note reads:

Blomfield handed her [the then Crown Princess of Germany] the trowel, and during the ceremony she got her glove daubed with the mortar. In her distress she handed the trowel back to him with an impatient whisper of 'Take it, take it!'

71 *Westcombe*: TH seems to have had no specific 'original' in mind.

73 *And calumny . . . known*: Shelley, 'The Revolt of Islam', IX. xxxi; TH omitted the two lines which precede 'what we have done'. This stanza is marked in TH's copy of *Queen Mab, and Other Poems* (Halifax: Milner and Sowerby, 1865) in the Frederick B. Adams collection.

74 *The world and its ways . . . foes*: Browning, 'The Statue and the Bust', ll. 138–41; the text of the 1849 edn. of *Poems* (apparently TH's source) does not include 'we' in the final line. TH used this quotation in several other works, including *Desperate Remedies*, 'The Waiting Supper', and *Jude the Obscure*.

75 *so subversive . . . instincts*: HW reads 'utterly' subversive, 'at once' worthy, and 'purest' instincts. The revision is one of several which TH introduced in *NQM* in order to moderate its social criticism, perhaps in the hope of avoiding the charges of exaggeration and excessiveness that had been levied against *The Poor Man and the Lady* (see *Excluded and Collaborative Stories*, 76).

76 *Melport*: Weymouth, Dorset; in later works given the 'Wessex' name of Budmouth.

77 *met on the previous Christmas*: Geraldine and Egbert in fact met at harvest-time; TH apparently failed to notice the inconsistency created by his revision of the account of the lovers' first meeting (see n. to pp. 44–5).

78 *Lord Hatton's . . . Lord Tyrrell's*: invented names.

79 *The truly great . . . unknown*: the same observation is made by Cytherea in *Desperate Remedies* (49; ch. 3).

He, like a captain . . . relies: Dryden, *The Works of Virgil, Aeneis*, v. 587–91; the quotation is accurate except for the substitution of 'He' for 'And'. These lines are marked in TH's copy (London: T. Allman & Son, n.d.), an early gift from his mother and now in the Dorset County Museum; the quotation also occurs in *Desperate Remedies*.

80 *He had investigated*: in HW preceded by: 'At first he had unflinchingly worked sixteen hours a day; but finding this to be a mistaken policy, he reduced the number to thirteen.'

81 *Correggio*: Italian painter (1494–1534); a reference to his flesh shades is also included in *Desperate Remedies*. All of the artists mentioned in this paragraph were studied by TH himself dur-

ing his early London years. His 'Schools of Painting' notebook, dated 12 May 1863, includes under '*School of Parma*' an entry for '*Antonio Allegri—da Correggio*':

b.1494. very original—poor—rose up, no one knows how—assumption of the Virgin, in the cathl. of Parma his great work in wh. he equalled M.A. & R. Mengs, in his estimate of Italian genius gives the 1st. place to Raphael, 2nd. Corregio [*sic*] 3rd. Titian—"An ideal beauty, with not so much of heaven as in Raphl. yet surpassing that of nature, but not too lofty for our love." great knowlge. of lights & shades. (*PersN* 108–9)

81 *Angelico*: Italian painter (1387–1455), usually known as Fra Angelico. In his notebook TH wrote: '*B. Giovanni Angelico*, a monk—remarkable beauty in his angels—' (*PersN* 105).

Murillo: Bartolomé-Esteban Murillo, Spanish painter (bap. 1618, d. 1682). TH's notebook entry reads: 'the chief boast of Spain b 1613 his holy family in N.G. equals Da Vinci, Raphl. & Correggio in sweetness of col: & freedom of touch. often coarse, never mean. often incorrect, never weak in character. d 1682' (*PersN* 111).

Rubens: Flemish painter, identified accurately and described by TH as '*Peter Paul Rubens* 1577—majesty & pomp—warmth of colour—deficient in soft and sublime inspiration consps: in Italian painters. Living life. voluptuousness—beauty of expression rather than form. d 1640' (*PersN* 112).

Turner: Joseph Mallord William Turner, English painter (1775–1851; *DNB*), whose work TH especially admired: see, e.g., *Life*, 192, 225–6.

Romney . . . Reynolds . . . Lady Hamilton: George Romney (1734–1802; *DNB*), like Sir Joshua Reynolds (1723–92; *DNB*) a very successful portrait-painter, was said to have had an affair with his beautiful model, Emma Hart, the future Lady Hamilton (née Amy Lyon, 1761?–1815; *DNB*), who later became Nelson's mistress. TH's notebook includes entries for both painters: '*Sir Joshua Reynolds* 1723. gt. power in portraits, correct taste—little imagination . . . Romney. 1746 [*sic*]. Lady Hamilton his chief model' (*PersN* 113).

Bonozzi Gozzoli: correctly, Benozzo Gozzoli, Italian painter (1420–97). The immediate source for the misspelling was presumably TH's notebook entry (also incorrect in its date): '*Bonozzi Gozzoli*—studied under Angelico died 1478' (*PersN* 105).

Raffaelle: Italian painter and architect (1483–1520). TH's

notebook entry reads: '*Raphael*—b. 1483. ideal beauty, lofti-
ness, & volupts. . the rival of M. Angelo.—chief glory, his
Transfiguration—in emulation of Michel Angelo's cold. by
Sebastiano, in the chapel of St Peter' (*PersN* 107).

82 *And he shall be like a tree . . . prosper*: Ps. 1: 3–4 (*Book of Common
Prayer*); TH also quoted the Tate and Brady metrical version of
these verses (also from the *Book of Common Prayer*) in *Desperate
Remedies*.

83 *Towards the loadstar . . . light*: Shelley, 'Epipsychidion', ll.
219–21; TH omitted the initial 'And' in the first line.

84 *Chevron Square*: perhaps to be identified with Belgrave Square;
the location is certainly Belgravia and the choice of name
could have been suggested by the unusual lozenge shape and
diagonal organization of this particular square. Chevron
Square is also the Swancourts' London address in *A Pair of Blue
Eyes*.

85 *Messiah*: Handel's oratorio. The words of the first chorus and
aria referred to are:

Lift up your heads, O ye gates; and be ye lift up, everlasting
doors; and the King of Glory shall come in. Who is the King
of Glory? The Lord strong and mighty, the Lord mighty in
battle. . . .
Why do the nations so furiously rage together, and why do the
people imagine a vain thing? The kings of the earth rise up,
and the rulers take counsel together against the Lord, and
against His Anointed.

86 *The varying strains . . . gnawing thrill*: cf. the description of
Cytherea's response to Manston's organ playing in *Desperate
Remedies*:

The varying strains . . . shook and bent her to themselves, as a
gushing brook shakes and bends a shadow cast across its surface. The power of the music did not show itself so much by
attracting her attention to the subject of the piece, as by taking
up and developing as its libretto the poem of her own life and
soul . . . [N]ew impulses of thought came with new harmonies,
and entered into her with a gnawing thrill. (155; ch. 8)

Cf. also Edmund Gosse's account of the *Poor Man and the Lady*
scene from which these two passages evidently derived:

there was given a concert, at which the Lady happened to be
seated alone at the last row of the expensive places, and the

architect immediately behind her in the front row of the cheap
places. Both were extremely moved by the emotion of the
music, and as she chanced to put her hand on the back of her
seat, he took it in his, and held it till the end of the performance. ('T. Hardy and "The Poor Man"', Brotherton Collection, University of Leeds)

88 *Bright reason . . . sky*: Shelley, 'Lines' ('When the lamp is shat-
tered'), st. iv; TH also used this quotation in *Desperate Remedies*.

89 *Kilburn, and the hill beyond*: where TH lodged when he first
went to London in 1862; see *Life*, 44.

92 *Then I said . . . wise?*: Eccles. 2: 15; the verse in fact begins
'Then said I'.

    Mayne was in rather an ailing state: *HW* includes the phrase
'not being physically the strongest of men'.

93 *Fairland*: TH perhaps had the Dorset hamlet of Higher
Bockhampton approximately in mind.

    Time had set a mark . . . childhood: cf. TH's reflections on revisit-
ing Hatfield. His 6 June 1866 note as recorded in *Life* (56)
reads: 'Changed since my early visit. . . . Pied rabbits in the
Park, descendants of those I knew. The once children are
quite old inhabitants.'

95 *How all the other passions . . . jealousy!*: Shakespeare, *The Merchant
of Venice*, III. ii. 108–10.

97 *not most to blame*: *HW* reads 'most to blame'.

99 *turning restlessly . . . ears*: in *Desperate Remedies* (233; ch. 11)
Edward's restless night on account of Cytherea is described in
the same terms.

102 *Better is it . . . pay*: Eccles. 5: 5.

103 *Hence will I . . . tell*: Shakespeare, *Romeo and Juliet*, II. ii. 188–9.

104 *a well-known cathedral town*: presumably Salisbury, Wiltshire
(Melchester in TH's 'Wessex'), though TH has greatly reduced the distances involved.

    that state of mind . . . after: cf. ch. 11 of *Desperate Remedies*: 'that
absent mood which takes cognizance of little things without
being conscious of them at the time, though they appear in the
eye afterwards as vivid impressions' (224).

106 *How small a part . . . fair!*: Edmund Waller, 'Go, Lovely Rose!'
The epigraph in *HW*, 'These violent delights have violent ends,
| And in their triumph die' (Shakespeare, *Romeo and Juliet*, II.

vi. 9–10), was presumably altered for *NQM* in order to avoid a
second reference to *Romeo and Juliet* (see n. to p. 103) and
because the Waller quotation both prefigures Geraldine's
death and suggests that her happiness with Egbert would in
any case have proved ephemeral.

109 *when he lived at the school*: Egbert never did live at the school;
see n. to pp. 44–5.

111 *directly she saw her father . . . before*: cf. Miss Aldclyffe's response
to the news of Manston's death in *Desperate Remedies*: 'she
shrieked—broke   a   blood-vessel—and   fell   upon   the
floor. . . . They say she is sure to get over it . . . She has suffered
from it before' (439; ch. 21).

112 *A silence . . . tears*: Shelley, 'The Revolt of Islam', VI. xxxi; 'A' is
an alteration of 'In'. This stanza is marked in TH's copy of
Queen Mab, and Other Poems (Halifax: Milner and Sowerby,
1865) in the Frederick B. Adams collection.

dangerous attack: *HW* reads 'dangerous hemorrhage'. The
heroine of *The Poor Man and the Lady* presumably died in much
the same fashion; George Brereton Sharpe, a distant relation
of TH's and former physician, advised him that 'Hemorrage
[*sic*] of the lungs' would be the best way to dispose of her
quickly and unexpectedly while at the same time allowing her
to retain possession of her faculties to the very end (21 Jan.
1868 letter, Dorset County Museum). TH also exploited this
convenient mode of death in *Desperate Remedies*.

113 *Everything was so still . . . universe*: in *Desperate Remedies* (440; ch.
21) Miss Aldclyffe's last moments are described in the same
terms.

and this strange . . . ever: not present in *HW*; presumably added
by TH in *NQM* in order to forestall any optimistic—and, as the
narrative makes abundantly clear, unrealistic—speculation
about a future reconciliation.

114 *A Story for Boys*: the subtitle was probably added by the *Household* editor to identify the story as designed for young readers
rather than for the 'AMERICAN HOUSEWIFE'. When initially
submitting the story to the *Youth's Companion* TH suggested
that it be subtitled 'A tale of the Mendips' (*Collected Letters*, i.
123).

West Poley: it seems impossible to identify the location much
more specifically than the narrator does himself, as 'a village in
Somersetshire', though one within the Mendip region (see

preceding note). That TH was not thinking of a place famous for its caves—such as Wookey, where the 1985 film version of the story was apparently shot—is made clear by Leonard's initial scepticism as to the existence of caves in the West Poley hills, the Mendip Caves, as he points out, being nearer Cheddar. Nick's Pocket, Grim Billy, Giant's Ear, and Goblin's Cellar do not appear to be actual cave names, and the use of 'twin' village names in Somerset—e.g. West and East Pennard or, indeed, West and East Coker—is too common to suggest any specific identification.

114 *though rather small for my age*: Richard Purdy suggested that in the presentation of Leonard there might be 'a reminiscence of Hardy himself and his boyhood' (Introduction to *Our Exploits at West Poley* [limited edn.] (London: Geoffrey Cumberlege, Oxford University Press, 1952), p. xii), and 'Our Exploits', with its moralizing upon the theme of prudence, may indeed represent an attempt to justify TH's own youthful passivity. There can be no doubt, however, that the doughty and 'truly courageous' Steve emerges more sympathetically than his cautious cousin, and it seems in fact unlikely that TH had in mind a specific 'original'—himself or anyone else—for either of the two boys. There appears to be no firm basis for Robert Gittings's association of the story with the family of TH's cousin Emma Cary, who lived in Faulkland, a small village in the Somerset parish of Hemington (*The Older Hardy* (London: Heinemann, 1978), 39). Gittings claimed that the ages of the Cary boys corresponded to those of Leonard (13) and Steve (15 or 16), but the 1881 census returns for Faulkland show that at that date—two years before 'Our Exploits' was written—the eldest Cary son was 19, the second 12, and the third 8. Nor does Faulkland itself seem a likely setting for the story: though within the Mendip region, the area is geographically quite distinct from that around Wookey and Cheddar—by the 1880s, when the Carys emigrated to Australia, Faulkland itself had become predominantly a coal-mining village—and offers little in the way of the topographical features exploited in TH's narrative.

Carlyle . . . do: in Lecture VI of *On Heroes, Hero-Worship, and the Heroic in History*. The 1841 first edn. (352) reads: 'Virtue, *Virtus*, manhood, *hero*-hood, is not fairspoken immaculate regularity; it is first of all, what the Germans well name it, *Tugend* (*Taugend, dow*-ing or *Dough*tiness), Courage and the Faculty to *do*.'

115 *the Man who has Failed*: Michael Millgate (*Thomas Hardy: A Biography* (Oxford: Oxford University Press, 1982), 238–9), noting that 'Our Exploits' was written at a difficult moment in TH's career, sees an autobiographical element in the cautionary figure of the Man who had Failed, especially since his failure is attributed to that very 'want of energy' to which TH himself occasionally confessed.

118 *nether regions . . . shore*: in classical mythology the Styx is one of the rivers forming the expanse of water which had to be crossed by the souls of the dead before reaching the kingdom of Hades.

119 *Chesil Bank*: also known as Chesil Beach and Pebble Bank or Beach.

     Portland: see n. to p. 12.

121 *Hannah Dominy*: i.e. anno Domini.

123 *mill-tail*: 'The water which runs away from a mill-wheel' (*OED*).

125 *Yesterday afternoon*: on the preceding page two days are said to have passed before the boys visit East Poley. The inconsistency is one of several in the story, presumably the results of authorial oversight or perhaps editorial excision (the *Household* text appears to have been abridged, the first two instalments referring to eight chapters rather than to the six actually published, and chs. IV and V being considerably shorter than the others).

128 *Jeremy Bentham*: political philosopher (1748–1832; *DNB*) who believed that utility was the touchstone of morality and that the greatest increase of happiness for the largest number of people should be the guiding principle of conduct.

129 *Hamlet to the Ghost*:

                         Remember thee?
            Ay, thou poor ghost, while memory holds a seat
         In this distracted globe. Remember thee?
         Yea, from the table of my memory
         I'll wipe away all trivial fond records,
         All saws of books, all forms, all pressures past,
         That youth and observation copied there;
         And thy commandment all alone shall live
         Within the book and volume of my brain,
         Unmix'd with baser matter: yes, yes, by heaven.
                    Shakespeare, *Hamlet*, I. v. 95–104

131 *Rhombustas . . . Balcazar*: invented names.

131   *Hi, hae . . . horum*: schoolboy Latin; the nominative and geni-
tive plurals of *hic* ('this').

133   *When your father . . . hands*: yet another example of an expired
lifehold tenancy (see n. to p. 51); cf. also the widow's desire to
stay in the family-built house with Broadford's similar wish in
'Indiscretion'.

138   *discovered by Steve*: in ch. I it is Leonard who discovers the
second hole; the inconsistency (repeated in ch. VI) is perhaps
unintentional, but see the Introduction for a discussion of
Leonard as an unreliable narrator deliberately minimizing his
responsibility.

143   *Flaminius . . . escape*: Flaminius was killed and his army destroyed by Hannibal's ambush at Lake Trasimene in 217 BC;
the quotation is from Livy 22. 5.

150   *place in another mill*: in ch. II and again in ch. VI Job's new
situation is said to be on a farm; the inconsistency is presumably an authorial oversight.

156   *meanfully*: perhaps a compositorial misreading of 'meanly' but
more probably a TH invention meaning with malevolent intent.

158   *Romans . . . Samnites*: described by Livy 9. 5–6; despite TH's
use of 'under', the Caudine Forks was the name of the defile in
which the Roman army was trapped and forced to surrender in
321 BC.

160   *Coleridge or an Emerson*: Samuel Taylor Coleridge, poet, critic,
and philosopher (1772–1834; *DNB*); Ralph Waldo Emerson,
American poet, essayist, and philosopher (1803–82).

161   *liever*: dialect for 'More willingly, rather' (Wright's *English Dialect Dictionary*; also listed in *OED*); TH used 'liefer' in his poem
'The Wedding Morning'. The *Household* text in fact reads
'never'; J. C. Maxwell was the first to suggest that the composi-
tor misread the dialect word ('Hardy's "Our Exploits at West
Poley": A Correction', *Notes and Queries*, NS 6 (1959), 113).

164   *The curate*: the 'original' of the unnamed curate was the Revd
Henry Moule, vicar of Fordington from 1829 until his death in
1880, and father of the seven Moule brothers, with all of whom
TH was on friendly terms. Like the story's protagonist, Henry
Moule as a young man was curate-in-charge of a small Dorset
parish (see n. to p. 166). He later became famous for his
invention of the earth-closet, his social activism, and—as cel-

ebrated by TH in his other Moule story, 'A Changed Man'—his courageous labours during the Dorchester cholera epidemic of 1854. His writings on subjects as diverse as the warming of churches and the extraction of gas from shale (see the list of works appended to his *Paupers, Criminals and Cholera at Dorchester in 1854* (St Peter Port, Guernsey: Toucan Press, 1968)) suggest that the installation of a sound-tube for a deaf parishioner would have been quite in keeping with his indefatigable desire to find solutions to practical difficulties.

164   *Corvsgate*: the 'Wessex' name for Corfe Castle (in south-east Dorset), derived from the Saxon name for the castle, Corfgetes.

165   *Enckworth*: the 'Wessex' name for Encombe, a large eighteenth-century house south of Corfe Castle.

Martinmas: see n. to p. 10.

166   *Anglebury*: the 'Wessex' name for the Dorset town of Wareham.

Kingscreech: presumably a merging of Creech—be it Barrow, Bottom, Heath, Hamlet, or Grange—with Kingston (Little Enckworth in TH's 'Wessex'), which may have been the approximate location TH had in mind. In other respects the village was presumably based on Gillingham (Leddenton in TH's 'Wessex'), in north Dorset, where Henry Moule was curate-in-charge of St Mary the Virgin from 1825–9. A sketch of the chancel of St Mary's by Moule's eldest son, Henry Joseph Moule, made during a visit to Gillingham between 1840 and 1844, is dominated by an octagonal wooden pulpit raised high above the floor, which accords with the description of the pulpit in the story. TH may have seen the water-colour and, in any case, he would have seen the pulpit itself on any visit to the church before 1883 (see A. F. H. V. Wagner, *The Church of St. Mary the Virgin Gillingham: An Historical Account* ([Gillingham]: 1956)). TH's placing Kingscreech in a different part of Dorset was evidently an attempt to prevent recognition of his 'original'.

she was scouring the fire-dogs: the insistence on Mrs Chundle's industry and cleanliness—and indeed on her good husbandry—may be to some extent a polemical statement, resembling TH's attempt in 'The Dorsetshire Labourer' to explode the caricature of 'Hodge' as 'a degraded being of uncouth manner and aspect, stolid understanding, and snail-like movement'.

167   *lumpering*: from the dialect verb 'to lumper'; in the 1912 edn. of *Wessex Poems* TH glossed 'lumpered' as 'stumbled'.

      plock: a dialect word meaning 'block'.

168   *jimcracks*: an alternative spelling of 'gimcracks'.

      Creech Barrow: the traditional name for a naturally formed conical hill, 634 ft. in height, just west of East Creech.

170   *en*: 'it'; a dialect word defined as 'it' or 'him' (according to context) in TH's glosses for *Select Poems of William Barnes*.

172   *as richer people's*: the paragraph initially ended at this point; the following sentence and paragraph (relating to Mrs Chundle's will and emphasizing her unjustified regard for the curate) were later MS additions.

      Peter at the cock-crow: 'And Peter remembered the word of Jesus, which said unto him, Before the cock crow, thou shalt deny me thrice. And he went out, and wept bitterly' (Matt. 26: 75; also described in the other gospels).

      walked on: in the MS followed by 'The end' and two notes in TH's hand: '(Written about 1888–1890. Probably intended to be included in the volume entitled "Life's Little Ironies", or "Wessex Tales.")' and '[Copied from the original rough draft]'. There is little reason to doubt TH's dating of the story, especially since between 1888 and 1890 he wrote more short fiction than at any other period.

173   *said the doctor*: the story's association with the *Group of Noble Dames* collection is suggested by its subject matter—TH having said of *Noble Dames* that its scenes were to be 'laid in the old mansions and castles hereabouts' and its characters 'exclusively persons of title of the last century (names disguised, but incidents approximating to fact)' (*Collected Letters*, vii. 113)— and also by its use of a story-telling frame and of a narrator identified only by his profession. The specific use of the doctor as narrator further suggests that the decision to exclude the story from the *Noble Dames* group had been made before 'Barbara (Daughter of Sir John Grebe)'—subsequently entitled 'Barbara of the House of Grebe'—was written, or at least before it was attributed to the Old Surgeon, since TH would probably not have used two medical men as narrators in the same collection. The two stories are also quite similar in their gruesomeness and sardonic tone, their emphasis on the response of a sensitive temperament to a horrifying object, and their inclusion of such details as the nobleman's dying without

issue and the family's becoming the subject of a sermon. 'Barbara' can in fact plausibly be seen as a replacement for 'The Doctor's Legend', the latter having perhaps been deemed unsuitable for publication in the *Noble Dames* collection because of its focus (neither of its noble dames is actually the central figure) and, more especially, because of its too close correspondence with the history of the Damer family (see following notes).

173 *mansion*: presumably Came House, Joseph Damer's residence before he purchased Milton Abbey; see next note.

a man of five-and-twenty: the 'original' of the unnamed protagonist was Joseph Damer (created Lord Milton in 1753 and Earl of Dorchester in 1792; d. 1798), who purchased Milton Abbey in 1752 and proceeded to rebuild the house and reshape the surrounding valley, eventually transplanting the entire village of Milton Abbas to a new site half a mile away. Because the bones of the dead were treated irreverently during the conversion of the old churchyard into lawns, he was said to have been cursed and to have died of a 'gruesome disease' (Herbert Pentin, 'The Old Town of Milton Abbey', *Proceedings of the Dorset Natural History and Antiquarian Field Club*, 25 (1904), 5; J. P. Traskey, *Milton Abbey: A Dorset Monastery in the Middle Ages* (Tisbury: Compton Press, 1978), 197). TH, well acquainted with the legend, wrote on 23 Feb. 1905 to the Revd Herbert Pentin, a local historian and the current vicar of Milton Abbas:

What a sinister figure arises from the past in the person of Ld Dorchester! "The evil that men do lives after them". You probably know the traditionary story about him & the Monks' bones, &c? It is extraordinary how firmly it was believed in by the old men who used to repeat it to me when I was young. (*Collected Letters*, iii. 156)

TH was also indebted to non-traditional sources, such as Horace Walpole's letters (see next note) and, especially, John Hutchins's *The History and Antiquities of the County of Dorset*, one of his favourite books. His personal copy of the third edition of Hutchins (now in the Dorset County Museum) is well worn and contains extensive markings and annotations, several of them in the Milton Abbas chapter.

one whom anything . . . soften: in his 20 Aug. 1776 letter to Horace Mann, Horace Walpole wrote: 'Lord Milton, whom anything can petrify and nothing soften' (*The Letters of Horace*

Walpole, Earl of Orford, ed. Peter Cunningham, 9 vols. (London: Richard Bentley, 1857–9), vi. 368).

173   *a poor woman with an only child*: the widow and her daughter—indeed the entire Death's Head plot—appear to be wholly imaginary; cf. TH's 1896 Preface to *A Group of Noble Dames*:

> The pedigrees of our county families, arranged in diagrams on the pages of county histories, mostly appear at first sight to be as barren of any touch of nature as a table of logarithms. But given a clue—the faintest tradition of what went on behind the scenes, and this dryness as of dust may be transformed into a palpitating drama. . . . [A]nybody practised in raising images from such genealogies finds himself unconsciously filling into the framework the motives, passions, and personal qualities which would appear to be the single explanation possible of some extraordinary conjunction in times, events, and personages that occasionally marks these reticent family records.

175   *Lady Cicely . . . county*: Joseph Damer married Lady Caroline, daughter of Lionel, Duke of Dorset.

176   *necrophobist*: not listed in *OED*; a 'necrophobe' is 'one who has a horror of death or of dead bodies'.

177   *a son and heir*: the 'original' of the unnamed son was John Damer, who was, however, neither an only child nor, apparently, 'exceedingly timid and impressionable' (Walpole described him as 'grave, cool, reasonable, and reserved' (20 Aug. 1776 letter to Horace Mann, *Letters of Horace Walpole*, vi. 368)).

An Uncle . . . husband: Joseph Damer's fortune descended to him from his great-uncle in Ireland who, like the fictitious squire's uncle, had been a money-lender; see also next note.

bethought himself of a pedigree . . . tree: cf. Walpole's 22 Oct. 1766 letter to George Montagu: 'You know my Lord Milton, from nephew of the old usurer Damer, of Dublin, has endeavoured to erect himself into the representative of the ancient Barons Damory' (*Letters of Horace Walpole*, v. 20).

an Abbey and its estates: Milton Abbas; see n. to p. 173.

178   *a beautiful woman . . . materials*: the 'original' of the unnamed daughter-in-law was Anne Seymour Conway Damer, described by Walpole in his 7 Sept. 1781 letter to Horace Mann:

> She has one of the most solid understandings I ever knew . . . [S]he writes Latin like Pliny, and is learning Greek. . . . She models like Bernini, has excelled the moderns

in the similitudes of her busts, and has lately begun one in marble. (*Letters of Horace Walpole*, viii. 76)

179   *As the natives . . . tears*: cf. John Hutchins's account of the removal of the Milton Abbey church-bells:

It being represented to his Lordship that bell-ringing tended to drunkenness, he sold all the bells in the abbey-tower, two only excepted, which were transferred to the new church . . . A tradition still lingers in the parish, that when the inhabitants saw the bells, after the sale, drawn through the village on their way to their respective destinations, they stood at their house-doors shedding tears for the loss of that peculiarly English music, endeared to them by so many hallowed associations. (*The History and Antiquities of the County of Dorset*, 3rd edn. (Westminster: John Bowyer Nichols and Sons, 1873), iv. 406)

182   *At four o'clock . . . deed*: cf. this passage and the references to the fictitious son's unpaid debts and unpresentable companions with Walpole's account of John Damer's suicide in his 20 Aug. 1776 letter to Horace Mann:

he and his two brothers most unexpectedly notified to their father that they owed above seventy thousand pounds. The proud lord, for once in the right, refused to pay the debt, or see them. . . . On Thursday, Mr. Damer supped at the Bedford Arms in Covent Garden, with four common women, a blind fiddler, and no other man. At three in the morning he dismissed his seraglio, bidding each receive her guinea at the bar, and ordering Orpheus to come up again in half-an-hour. When he returned, he found a dead silence, and smelt gunpowder. He called, the master of the house came up, and found Mr. Damer sitting in his chair, dead, with a pistol by him, and another in his pocket! . . .

What a catastrophe for a man at thirty two, heir to two and twenty thousand a year! We are persuaded lunacy, not distress, was the sole cause of his fate. (*Letters of Horace Walpole*, vi. 368)

John Damer's 'lunacy'—the verdict in fact brought in by the Coroner's jury (*The London Chronicle for the Year 1776*, 15–17 Aug., 167)—may have been one of those behind-the-scenes clues which led to TH's fabrication of the Death's Head narrative. TH presumably had in mind this Walpole letter (also quoted in the opening paragraph of the story) when in his copy of Hutchins he annotated the reference to John Damer's death 'suicide: see Walpole's letters'.

like Herod . . . remains: 'And immediately the angel of the Lord smote him, because he gave not God the glory: and he was eaten of worms, and gave up the ghost' (Acts 12: 23); the Herod in question is Herod Agrippa I (d. AD 44 at the age of 34), grandson of Herod the Great.

182 *title was extinct . . . name*: although Joseph Damer's title did become extinct within a few years of his death, the family name was revived by three of his sister's grandchildren.

182–3 *Isaiah XIV . . . saith the Lord*: the words are quoted accurately except that 'him' replaces 'them' in 'I will rise up against them'; the omitted verses indicated by the ellipsis are 13–21.

184 THE SPECTRE OF THE REAL: the story was originally entitled 'Desire', but after its ending was revised (see n. to p. 211) TH suggested 'The Spectre of the Real', offering as possible alternatives 'The Looming of the Real', 'A passion & after', 'To-day's kiss & yesterday's', 'Husband's corpse & husband's kiss', and 'A shattering of Ideals' (*Collected Letters*, ii. 38, 40).

waning age: Shakespeare, *The Taming of the Shrew*, Induction, ii. 63.

Ambrose Towers: the choice of setting was probably Henniker's: it seems unlikely that in 1893, when the concept of Wessex had become one of the dominant elements in his fiction, TH would have created a location so topographically undefined as Ambrose Towers, even in a story which as a collaboration would in some sense be distinct from his other work. With its sixteenth-century 'red tower', 'shrouded mullions', and 'old brick walls' surrounded by 'broad paths and garden-lands', Ambrose Towers could be any number of English country estates, and as such it is typical of Henniker's fiction.

Such a person . . . play: a TH addition, one of several revisions intended to emphasize the common Hardyan theme of post-marital disillusionment.

floor-stones of the Apocalyptic City: an allusion to the new Jerusalem, as described in Rev. 21: 19, 21: 'the foundations of the wall of the city were garnished with all manner of precious stones. . . . [T]he street of the city was pure gold'.

185 *at your Harmony*: i.e. at musical study or practice.

an officer in the Line: i.e. in one of the regular army regiments, as distinct from the more prestigious 'household' regiments (e.g. the Life Guards) responsible for guarding the person of the sovereign.

which is merely the older one . . . came: a TH revision of 'Further

back than my grandfather I am a little hazy as to my ancestors'.
A freeholder is an independent proprietor.

185 *Paladins*: the Twelve Peers or famous warriors of Charle-
magne's court.

187 *reaching deeps of sky*: a TH revision of 'velvet-like sky', one of
Henniker's characteristic descriptive phrases; in section IV TH
also changed her description of the colour of the sky from 'a
velvet-like blue' to 'a bottomless deep of blue'. The appearance of this and other characteristic Henniker formulae (pink
cheeks, shining eyes, white and tired faces, etc.)—as well as of
familiar narrative details and favourite romance and biblical
allusions (see nn. to pp. 190, 202)—helps to confirm that the
writing up of the first six sections of 'Spectre' was predominantly her work.

Prince's daughter . . . Beloved: in the Song of Solomon (7: 12)
the prince's daughter says to her beloved, 'let us see if the vine
flourish, whether the tender grape appear, and the pomegranates bud forth: there will I give thee my loves'.

Qualms of prudence . . . pelf: unidentified.

188 *land-agencies*: land-agents managed country estates and other
landed properties on behalf of their actual owners.

189 *great meat-market*: Smithfield.

189–90 *the fine old Norman porch*: although the location and the
subsequent description (see n. below) leave no doubt that the
church is the largely Norman St Bartholomew the Great, there
is no Norman porch, the original one having been destroyed
when Henry VIII dissolved the monasteries; the present
porches (West and North) were built in 1893, the year 'Spectre' was written. Perhaps Henniker was confused by the building work and assumed that in the late 1870s, the approximate
date of the story's opening chapters, the church entrance was
indeed still Norman.

190 *Two or three other couples . . . space*: cf. the Registrar's office
scene in *Jude the Obscure* (342; part V, ch. 4).

the beautiful building . . . sleep: the inclusion of architectural details in the story can be seen as a stage in the dialogue between
Henniker and TH, an attempt on her part to demonstrate that
she was as 'apt' an architectural student as he had predicted in
his June 1893 letter (*Collected Letters*, ii. 11). In the same letter
he had recommended St Bartholomew's as one of the London

churches containing 'excellent features for study'.

190   *From the crown . . . him*: the biblical passage describing Absalom in fact reads: 'from the sole of his foot even to the crown of his head there was no blemish in him' (2 Sam. 14: 25). That the passage is Henniker's is suggested by the fact that when the same biblical allusion appears in her novel *Our Fatal Shadows* the sequence is again reversed.

191   *a fashionable hotel on the Embankment*: the Savoy.

She had thoroughly abandoned . . . eagerness: a TH addition, one of several revisions intended to emphasize Rosalys's sexual attraction to Jim.

196   *after seven years . . . existence*: English common law at this period seems to have allowed for the possibility of a spouse's being presumed dead after an absence of seven years.

198   *the practical nullity . . . word*: cf. this summary of Jim's 'emancipated' views with the 'advanced' social principles articulated by Marcia in *The Pursuit of the Well-Beloved*: 'If I strictly confine myself to one hemisphere, and you . . . to the other, any new tie we may form can affect nobody but ourselves' (*Illustrated London News*, 15 Oct. 1892, 481). This serial version of *The Well-Beloved* was published October–December 1892, less than a year before work on 'Spectre' began, and the two works share several such familiar Hardyan plot devices as a clandestine marriage, the return of a long-estranged spouse in response to a newspaper paragraph, and the convenient disposal of a character through drowning or, in the case of *The Pursuit*, attempted drowning.

199   *late campaign in Egypt*: the reference is perhaps to the bombardment of Alexandria in July 1882.

His rigid notions of duty and honour: both TH and Henniker were fascinated by the notion of a figure possessing high and even idealistic standards of conduct. Parkhurst's Hardyan precursors were, of course, Henry Knight and Angel Clare, while of the several Henniker characters obsessed with uprightness and unblemished honour, the most notable is Janet Eames in 'Our Neighbour, Mr. Gibson'. Both Janet and Parkhurst naïvely see their loved ones as they would like them to be rather than as they are, Parkhurst assuming that Rosalys is 'good and perfect and innocent', while Janet says to Vernon, 'As if I didn't know that you have no faults! You are only too dear and kind to people who are not good like you!' (*Outlines*

(London: Hutchinson, 1894), 191). In Henniker's story Vernon, realizing that Janet would never be able to forgive his past, disappears on the eve of their wedding.

200 *during which, while recalling . . . house*: one of Henniker's descriptive passages which TH omitted and then, at her insistence, reinstated—though in revised form (see *Excluded and Collaborative Stories*, 267–9). Other reinstated Henniker passages include the descriptions of butterflies playing hide-and-seek, Rosalys whistling to a robin, and birds sleeping in the park.

202 *Home-Rule question*: the issue of Home Rule for Ireland dominated British politics throughout the last two decades of the nineteenth century.

       as if she were living . . . dream: one of Henniker's characteristic narrative details, at least thirteen of her characters experiencing a similar sensation; TH attempted to improve upon the trite idea by adding the reference to Rosalys's hearing Jim's voice 'as the phantom of a dead sound'. Henniker's characters also tend to answer questions with physical gestures (as do both Jim and Parkhurst), to smile with their eyes (as does Parkhurst), and to become oblivious of surroundings during times of intense emotion (as does Rosalys).

203 *bézique*: as a card-game for two, a curious choice for a social occasion.

205 *The sentence was broken . . . either!*: the most substantial passage omitted by Henniker when she collected 'Spectre' in *In Scarlet and Grey*; she also omitted the (not very) veiled allusions to Jim's renewed sexual relations with Rosalys (e.g. Rosalys's lament, 'O—O—what have I done! What a fool—what a weak fool!', and her sad survey of the 'state of her room' after his departure). Other *In Scarlet and Grey* revisions are also clearly bowdlerizations: after her clandestine marriage Rosalys feels 'so depressed, so dreadfully sad' instead of 'so dreadfully sad and sinful'; she and Jim meet 'at hotels or restaurants' instead of 'in the private rooms of hotels'; her desire wanes because 'the novelty of wifedom was past' not because 'the sensuous part of her character was satisfied'; their passion is 'resistless' instead of 'almost unholy'; and she has supposedly 'rejected all other men' rather than kept herself from them.

207 *Rosalys bowed herself . . . goes on*: cf. the scene in *Jude the Obscure* in which Arabella confesses her bigamy after spending the

night with Jude (222; part III, ch. 9).

208   *it is supposed he took . . . plank*: cf. the account of the drowning in 'The Waiting Supper':

It was supposed that . . . he had taken a short cut through the grounds . . . and coming to the fall under the trees had expected to find there the plank which, during his occupancy of the premises with Christine and her father, he had placed there for crossing into the meads on the other side . . . (*A Changed Man*, 81)

The two stories contain numerous other verbal parallels: e.g. Bellston defines his profession as 'Travel and exploration' (*A Changed Man*, 41), while Jim describes himself as a 'traveller and explorer', and Christine sends Nicholas away saying, 'I will tell you everything of my history then' (*A Changed Man*, 64), while Jim leaves Rosalys with the promise, 'and then I'll tell you all my history'. They are also fundamentally similar in their use of the familiar 'poor man and the lady' situation (complete with nocturnal meetings and the discussion of a secret marriage) and the unexpected return of the husband owing to the newspaper announcement of his wife's remarriage.

209   *There was the lake . . . drowned Jim*: cf. the description in 'A Tragedy of Two Ambitions' of the two brothers contemplating the meads where their father drowned: 'There were the hatches, there was the culvert; they could see the pebbly bed of the stream through the pellucid water' (*Life's Little Ironies*, 105). That there should be some resemblance between the two stories is not surprising, since it was the preparation of the *Life's Little Ironies* volume which delayed TH's work on the collaborative story (see *Collected Letters*, ii. 38).

she loved Lord Parkhurst: the earliest surviving version of this sentence—presumably written by TH (see n. to p. 211)—continues: 'and a title was a handy thing, a very handy thing, for a woman with a big house and park like hers'. The passage was deleted by Henniker and certainly a love of social position does seem out of character for Rosalys, who originally wished to marry an army officer in the customary way and 'get on as other people do'.

Rosalys allowed things to take their course: cf. 'A Mere Interlude', where Baptista similarly allows 'circumstances to pilot her along' (*A Changed Man*, 276) and remarries within hours of the drowning of her first husband.

210   *Ten minutes later . . . hand*: in the New York *Press*, one of the
      newspapers which purchased 'Spectre' through Irving
      Bachellor's syndicate (see *Excluded and Collaborative Stories*,
      282–4), the story ends at this point, hence 'happily ever after'.

211   *shot himself through the head with a revolver*: in 'An Imaginative
      Woman', a story written during the late summer of 1893 and
      clearly inspired by TH's feelings for Henniker (see Millgate,
      Biography, 342), Trewe chooses the same method of suicide,
      which is reported, like Parkhurst's, in a newspaper paragraph.

      . . . the rash act: textual evidence—and, indeed, surviving cor-
      respondence—suggests that virtually all of section VII was writ-
      ten by TH. There was evidently some discussion about the
      ending, as on 22 Oct. 1893 TH, working through Henniker's
      draft of the story (at that point still entitled 'Desire'), wrote: 'I
      have planned to carry out Ending II—since you like it so much
      better: I feel I ought not to force the other upon you—wh. is
      too uncompromising for one of the pretty sex to have a hand
      in. The question now is, what shall we call it?—"The
      ressurection [*sic*] of a Love"?' (*Collected Letters*, ii. 38). On 25
      Oct. he informed her that 'it may possibly be necessary to
      effect a compromise between the two endings: for on no ac-
      count must it end weakly', and by 28 Oct. he had come up with
      a new ending, one which, whether 'good or bad', he saw as
      having 'the merit of being in exact keeping with Lord P.'s
      character': 'It is, as you wished, very tragic; a modified form of
      Ending II—which I think better than any we have thought of
      before' (*Collected Letters*, ii. 39–40). Although the original ver-
      sion of Ending II preferred by Henniker cannot be recon-
      structed, what seems clear is that it, too, was 'very tragic'—her
      own fiction, although conventional, very rarely ends happily—
      but did not involve Parkhurst's suicide. More typical of
      Henniker would have been the accidental deaths of both Jim
      and Parkhurst, and perhaps of Rosalys as well. As for the
      'uncompromising' Ending I, it is tempting to think that it
      might have involved yet another reworking of the Elfride–
      Knight, Tess–Angel situation: confession followed by rejection.
      The conclusion as it stands is of course a variation on that
      theme, even though the 'real' may not on this occasion have
      been voluntarily revealed, and it is therefore not surprising
      that TH thought it the best.

212   *Blue Jimmy stole . . . flung*: TH, 'A Trampwoman's Tragedy', st.
      x; in the first line the correct reading is 'stole right many'. The

poem was included in *Time's Laughingstocks* (London: Macmillan, 1909), accompanied by several notes, including one on Blue Jimmy: '"Blue Jimmy" . . . was a notorious horse-stealer of Wessex in those days, who appropriated more than a hundred horses before he was caught. He was hanged at the now demolished Ivel-chester or Ilchester jail above mentioned—that building formerly of so many sinister associations in the minds of the local peasantry, and the continual haunt of fever, which at last led to its condemnation. Its site is now an innocent-looking green meadow.' TH gave Dugdale a copy of *Time's Laughingstocks* in December 1909, and his note is clearly echoed, with the kind of floral amplification so typical of Dugdale, in her description of Ilchester gaol at the conclusion of the story. G. Stevens Cox has pointed out ('A Tramp-woman's Tragedy, Blue Jimmy and Ilchester Jail', *Thomas Hardy Year Book* (1970), 82–5) that TH's description was not in fact accurate, some parts of the gaol having escaped destruction.

212 *"Blue Jimmy"*: the popular name of the notorious horse thief James Clace (d. 1827 at the age of 52). The story's named characters are based on actual people, all of whom figure in the newspaper paragraphs that, according to TH, Dugdale had 'been at some pains to hunt up . . . at the British Museum' (*Collected Letters*, iv. 114), specifically the reports of the 1825 and 1827 Somerset Lent Assizes in the *Taunton Courier* and *Dorset County Chronicle*, and the account of Jimmy's execution in the *Dorset County Chronicle*.

213 *each assize . . . a circuit*: assize courts were held periodically in each English county for the trial by a visiting senior judge (said to be 'on circuit') of civil and criminal cases falling outside the competence of the county courts.

On a December day . . . : the description of the events which led to Jimmy's being brought to the bar for the eighteenth time is heavily dependent on the 30 Mar. 1825 account of his trial in the *Taunton Courier*. Dugdale adopts not only the paragraph's details but also much of its wording; cf., e.g., Wilkins's insistence that he knows Jimmy and Wheller's attempt to recover his money and cart-horse with the following passage from the *Courier*:

Witness [Wheller] asked Wilkins if he knew Prisoner; he said he knew him well, that he was a . . . small farmer, and worth thousands. The ensuing day witness discovered that the mare

was startish, and went in search of prisoner, whom he found at
the Golden Heart, in Coombe St. Nicholas, and told him that
he suspected he did not come honestly by the mare, and
therefore requested to have back his money and his cart-horse.
Prisoner said he was quite willing so to do, and called to the
landlady for a pipe and some beer, and immediately brushed
out at the back door . . .

213   *Wheller, living near Chard, in Somerset*: according to the 30 Mar.
1825 *Taunton Courier*, Wheller lived at Coombe St Nicholas,
which is just north-west of Chard.

Stratton Fair: according to the 30 Mar. 1825 *Taunton Courier*,
Jimmy told Wheller he bought the mare 'near Tiverton';
Stratton is in Cornwall (near Bude) and Tiverton in Devon.

happening to pass just then: according to the 30 Mar. 1825
Taunton Courier, Wilkins was with Jimmy when the latter first
spoke to Wheller.

214   *startish*: i.e. nervous, skittish.

216   *he was ultimately found at Dorchester*: according to the 30 Mar.
1825 *Taunton Courier*, Jimmy was already in Dorchester Gaol
when Loveridge wrote to Sheppard. In TH's work Dorchester
is usually given the 'Wessex' name of Casterbridge.

Taunton: county town of Somerset, where the assize court
regularly sat; in TH's work Taunton is usually given the
'Wessex' name of Toneborough.

The learned Judge . . . examined: taken almost verbatim from the
30 Mar. 1825 *Taunton Courier*.

Fitzhead: Devon village north-west of Taunton.

217   *Mosterton*: Dorset village north-west of Beaminster.

217–18   *the last time he saw his mare . . . mitigation*: taken almost verbatim from the account of Jimmy's trial printed in the 11 Apr.
1827 *Taunton Courier* and possibly also in the *Dorset County
Chronicle* of the following day (unfortunately no copy of the
latter appears to have survived).

218   *chopped*: gave in exchange.

Alphington: Devon village, just south of Exeter.

twenty-five guineas: according to the 11 Apr. 1827 *Taunton
Courier*, the price asked was twenty-five sovereigns.

Bridport: Dorset seaport; in TH's work usually given the
'Wessex' name of Port Bredy.

218 *How Jimmy acquired ... historian*: a poorly integrated paragraph probably added by TH, who claimed to have supplied some of the story's traditional details (see *Collected Letters*, iv. 114).

  same old County Chronicle: evidently the *Dorset County Chronicle*, although the newspaper has not been previously mentioned.

219 *Ilchester*: Somerset town; in TH's work usually given the 'Wessex' name of Ivelchester. See n. to p. 212.

  Execution, Wednesday ... a very hard case: the quotations are presumably from the *Dorset County Chronicle* of 3 May 1827, the date recorded in TH's 'Facts' notebook (in the Dorset County Museum) after an entry summarizing Jimmy's final trial and execution. No copy of this issue of the *County Chronicle* appears to have survived, but a 2 May 1827 *Taunton Courier* paragraph sufficiently resembles both the 'Facts' entry and the 'Blue Jimmy' quotations as to suggest that the paragraph was essentially the same in the two papers. However, the concluding reference to the execution of the sheep-stealer William Hazlett (actually Hewlett) in 'Blue Jimmy' suggests that the two papers may at least have differed in their use of italics, since in the *Courier* it is not Hewlett's seeming to imagine that his 'was a very hard case' which is italicized but the explanation of that feeling: '*He said that he had never, previous to the commission of the above offence, stolen more than four and twenty sheep!*' One can only speculate as to whether the paragraph did actually appear in a different form in the *County Chronicle*, whether Dugdale's transcription was inaccurate, or whether she—or TH—merely exercised a little poetic licence in order to create a witty conclusion.

  postboy: postilion.

  Salisbury: Wiltshire cathedral-town; see n. to p. 104.

  A tradition ... stolen one: a TH addition.

  "flung his last fling": an allusion to the epigraph.

221 *an old Cathedral town*: Salisbury (see n. to p. 104) would meet the description here, but no specific identification seems to be intended.

227 *Wingate had been working ... alive*: a TH addition. In an earlier version of the addition the sentence continued: 'that which made another thought of union with Gertrude impossible. Thus Fadelle's own writing had opened a gulf between them,

if he continued the man of honour that he hoped [*illegible erasure*]'.

227 *to Town*: i.e. to London.

231 *they were uncanny now*: a TH addition. The first version of the addition included the clause: 'for by wooing Gertrude he would be failing his former friend'.

233 *that from the other side . . . won*: a TH revision.

JANE AUSTEN	**Emma**
	Mansfield Park
	Persuasion
	Pride and Prejudice
	Sense and Sensibility
MRS BEETON	**Book of Household Management**
LADY ELIZABETH BRADDON	**Lady Audley's Secret**
ANNE BRONTË	**The Tenant of Wildfell Hall**
CHARLOTTE BRONTË	**Jane Eyre**
	Shirley
	Villette
EMILY BRONTË	**Wuthering Heights**
SAMUEL TAYLOR COLERIDGE	**The Major Works**
WILKIE COLLINS	**The Moonstone**
	No Name
	The Woman in White
CHARLES DARWIN	**The Origin of Species**
CHARLES DICKENS	**The Adventures of Oliver Twist**
	Bleak House
	David Copperfield
	Great Expectations
	Nicholas Nickleby
	The Old Curiosity Shop
	Our Mutual Friend
	The Pickwick Papers
	A Tale of Two Cities
GEORGE DU MAURIER	**Trilby**
MARIA EDGEWORTH	**Castle Rackrent**

ANTHONY TROLLOPE   **An Autobiography**

The American Senator

Barchester Towers

Can You Forgive Her?

The Claverings

Cousin Henry

Doctor Thorne

The Duke's Children

The Eustace Diamonds

Framley Parsonage

He Knew He Was Right

Lady Anna

The Last Chronicle of Barset

Orley Farm

Phineas Finn

Phineas Redux

The Prime Minister

Rachel Ray

The Small House at Allington

The Warden

The Way We Live Now

The Oxford World's Classics Website

www.worldsclassics.co.uk

- Information about new titles
- Explore the full range of Oxford World's Classics
- Links to other literary sites and the main OUP webpage
- Imaginative competitions, with bookish prizes
- Peruse the Oxford World's Classics Magazine
- Articles by editors
- Extracts from Introductions
- A forum for discussion and feedback on the series
- Special information for teachers and lecturers

www.worldsclassics.co.uk

American Literature

British and Irish Literature

Children's Literature

Classics and Ancient Literature

Colonial Literature

Eastern Literature

European Literature

History

Medieval Literature

Oxford English Drama

Poetry

Philosophy

Politics

Religion

The Oxford Shakespeare